Warrior and Weaver

Book One of the Norse Family Saga

K.S. Barton

Dala Press

Copyright © 2021 K.S. Barton

Dala Press
Tucson Arizona

All rights reserved.

The characters and events portrayed in this book are fictitious. Any similarities to real persons, living or dead is coincidental and not intended by the author.

No part of this book may be reproduced, or stored in a retrieval system, or transmitted in any form or by any means, electronic, mechanical, photocopying, recording or otherwise, without express written permission by the publisher.

ISBN: 978-1-950667-02-4

Cover design by: More Visual Ltd | Graphic Design and Visualisation

Library of Congress Control Number: 2020921721

Printed in the United States of America

Contents

Dedication	1
Chapter One	2
Chapter Two	39
Chapter Three	52
Chapter Four	67
Chapter Five	75
Chapter Six	85
Chapter Seven	104
Chapter Eight	113
Chapter Nine	131
Chapter Ten	150
Chapter Eleven	170
Chapter Twelve	179
Chapter Thirteen	186

Chapter Fourteen	194
Chapter Fifteen	201
Chapter Sixteen	211
Chapter Seventeen	224
Chapter Eighteen	232
Chapter Nineteen	248
Chapter Twenty	257
Chapter Twenty-one	276
Chapter Twenty-two	290
Chapter Twenty-three	303
Chapter Twenty-four	314
Chapter Twenty-five	325
Chapter Twenty-six	340
Chapter Twenty-seven	361
Chapter Twenty-eight	372
Chapter Twenty-nine	381
Chapter Thirty	396
Chapter Thirty-one	402
Chapter Thirty-two	417

Chapter Thirty-three	427
Chapter Thirty-four	434
Chapter Thirty-five	451
Chapter Thirty-six	466
Also By	482
Author's Note	483
Acknowledgements	489
About the Author	491

Dedication

For Blake and Hunter

Chapter One
Sweden

The warning horn blew, the sound carrying across the air, long and ominous. Astrid's heart thudded. The horn could mean many things, her father's return, a friendly visit, or blood-thirsty raiders bent on the destruction of her village and family. She grasped her dress and waited, like a rabbit in the shadow of a bird of prey.

The horn sounded two more times, and Astrid rose to her knees. The next set of two bellows echoed over the entire area, sweeping all fear away.

Astrid jumped to her feet and shielded her eyes from the hot midsummer sun as she looked out onto the river, the high rocky embankment warm through the soles of her shoes. From her vantage point, she could see the ships, her father's longship out front, the black and red striped sail bulging with wind, the raven banner snapping from the mast.

"They are back," Astrid shouted to her older brother, Rikki. The racing of her heart subsided, and she swallowed down a lump in her throat that remained from the first call of warning.

"I can hear the horn too," Rikki said. He climbed up the rock face, his fingers and toes digging into the crevices in between the rocks. His face was red from exertion and his fingers white from the effort of pulling himself up.

"Hurry." Astrid left the edge to pick up her basket of white meadowsweet flowers. Their mother had sent Astrid and two of the household thralls out to gather the meadowsweet she used to flavor her mead and ale.

Rikki had joined her so he could practice climbing. "Father says to prepare for anything," he'd told her. Now that he was twelve, Rikki spent all the daylight hours, usually with his friends, strengthening himself and practicing with spear, sword, axe, and shield. Once the boys were old enough, they would go off to raid and fight with her father. It wouldn't be long. Her half-brother, Jori, was fighting for the first time this season.

After she'd gathered the flowers, Astrid had walked up the rocky embankment to watch the river flow by and to look at the islands that dotted the horizon. She loved the way the vivid blue water melted into the gray rocks on the shore, and then on up to the green grasses and trees. The colors made her want to go to her loom and create a new tapestry for her father's great hall.

She looked down at her hands; they gripped the basket so tight her knuckles were white. She pictured the ships as they had been when they'd sailed so many moons ago, all the men alive, healthy, and eager to be off. She held that image in her mind as she sent a prayer to all the gods that everyone would still be there, whole and unhurt.

"Let's go, *systir*." Rikki ran up to her, his breath still ragged from his climb. They signaled to the thralls to follow them, and Astrid and Rikki went to meet their mother and younger sister to go out to the docks to welcome her father. Jarl Tryggvi had returned home.

Other than the large feast hall, her father's longhouse was the biggest building in the village, and she and Rikki hurried to it.

Rikki peeled off at the path that led to the river and the docks. "I'm going to help bring them in." He smiled and disappeared, his light-blond hair shining in the sun.

The door to the longhouse was open on this warm summer day; Astrid hurried in and set the basket of flowers on the large oak table.

Her mother, Ingiborg, emerged from a small bedchamber, her dress a light linen, dyed as green as the grass in the meadow, a cream-colored apron fastened to it with bronze brooches. Her household keys jangled from her leather belt as she joined Astrid.

"Have you seen your sister?" Ingiborg patted her hair that was braided and wound at the back of her head, the color like a doe's fur.

"Gytha was at the barn looking after Baby," Astrid said. Her eight-winter old sister had taken in a lamb whose mother died in the spring. The head shepherd wanted to slaughter it, but Ingiborg let Gytha care for it. "Where else would she be?" Her sister loved animals, the more vulnerable the better.

Ingiborg gave a light laugh. "She will have heard the horn." She took in the house with a practiced look. She gave a few orders to the thralls who would prepare food, drink, and baths for the incoming men. Catching another thrall by the arm, Ingiborg told the woman to prepare the healing herbs and salves and to make sure things were ready for any wounded men.

Astrid went to the basin of water where she cleaned her hands and face, drying them on a soft cloth. She glimpsed the tapestry she had woven for her father; if there was to be a feast, she would present it to him then. She had woven it over the winter, starting at the end of Autumnmonth and continuing until the beginning of summer, sometimes working until her eyes watered and her hands ached. On the tapestry, she'd woven together red and black stripes to match the raven banner that flew on her father's longship, which was a black raven on a red background.

Done directing the thralls, Ingiborg took Astrid's arm and joined the villagers as they walked down to the docks.

"Mama. Asta." Gytha ran up, her lamb, Baby, following on a lead.

When they arrived at the crowded docks, everyone made way for Ingiborg and her daughters. Rikki, so excited he practically bounced, joined them, smelling of sweat and the dirt that still clung to him from his rock climbing. He was a little over one winter older than Astrid's eleven. They looked so much alike people often thought they were twins, both with golden-blond hair and wide, light-blue eyes.

The longships drew closer, and the men had furled the massive sail and rowed toward the pier. Even with forty men on a ship, their movements were in perfect time, Jarl Tryggvi's steersman calling out the rhythm. The jarl himself stood at the deck at the prow, his reddish-blond hair gleaming in the bright sun. He had a thick gold ring on his arm that caught the light, something new, and Astrid knew they'd had a successful start to the raiding season.

Ingiborg sighed and squeezed Astrid's hand. "Your father has made it home to us. We will make an offering to Freya for our good fortune." She touched a silver Freya amulet she wore, given to her by Tryggvi when she'd birthed their first child. Astrid loved the Freya amulet.

The massive ships drew closer, and as soon as they came within shouting distance, the men called out to those on shore, who waved and laughed in return. There was talk of the ships being so heavy they groaned with their cargo, and of weapons drinking so much blood it filled their handles. The laughing tone in the shouts going back and forth made the knot in Astrid's stomach loosen.

It did not take long for the men to maneuver the huge ship to the dock, the heavy ship thudding into the wooden pier. Men immediately tossed the sealskin mooring lines onto the pier and jumped out to secure the ship. Rikki was there in a flash to help the men and assail them with questions.

Jarl Tryggvi was the first one off, lightly landing on the boards and moving quickly to his wife. He did not break his stride, his fierce blue eyes on Ingiborg, and when he reached her, he swept an arm around her waist pulling her to him, the other cupping her cheek. They stared at each other for a long moment.

Astrid was old enough to recognize the love she saw in her father's eyes as he drank in his wife. A quick sweep of the boats told Astrid everything she needed to know. Her loved ones were safe and well. The knot in her stomach completely unraveled.

"Little bear," a booming voice called.

"Emund," Astrid cried, and she spied him over the heads of the other men. His long, shaggy, auburn hair and thick beard made him look ferocious. When she reached him, he scooped her into his arms as if she weighed no more than a rag doll. His thick arms held her tightly.

Emund swung her in a circle until she was laughing, her cheeks sore from smiling. When he was absent, it was like a great oak that shaded and protected her house had been cut down, and when he was home, she felt like the world had been set right. He was her father's best man, his brother by the blood ritual, and she loved him as much as she did her father. More, even.

As he set her down, Astrid wrinkled her nose with a grimace.

"Is it that bad?" Emund sniffed himself with a gleam in his eyes.

"My poor *systir* might never eat again." Astrid's half-brother Jori strode by and slapped Emund on the back.

"Watch it, lad. I can still thrash you." Emund gave Astrid a wink.

Her laughter died in her throat when she caught sight of Jori; the look in his eyes made her hesitate, and she leaned into Emund's comforting bulk.

At that moment Tryggvi jumped up to the deck on his ship, waving his two sons to join him by his side. It saved Astrid from having to talk to her brother. At sixteen, Jori had been on his first raid with their father, and it was like he'd shed a layer of skin, revealing a warrior underneath, something harder than what had been on top.

Tryggvi looped his arms over the shoulders of his sons, both young men beaming with pride. "My friends!" Tryggvi cried. His voice carried over his people, and Astrid wondered what he would sound like in a battle, calling to his men, directing them so they would not die.

Gytha's lamb bleated and people laughed as she tried to shush it. The men who had wives or women broke from embraces and kisses. They all faced Jarl Tryggvi.

Tryggvi pulled Rikki closer to him. As he did, he sent a smile to Ingiborg, one that spoke more than any words could. Ingiborg smiled back in a way that made her look young. It almost took Astrid's breath away, the great love her father and mother had for each other. It was like something out of a *skald's* story.

"My friends!" Tryggvi called out again. "The Allfather was with us, giving us victory and the spoils! The Danish dogs who have harried our coasts will lick their wounds until Ragnarok!"

The din as people shouted was loud enough for the gods to hear.

"Tomorrow we will feast our victory! Give our thanks to Odin!"

"Hail Odin!" The men raised their hands in the air as they answered their jarl.

With that, he released his sons and jumped down to the pier, rushing to Ingiborg's side. He looped an arm around her shoulders, and the two of them hurried back to their house.

"Go tell Old Stieg to have the pigs butchered," Emund told Astrid.

"And have the thralls start the fire for roasting," she added, her eyebrows raised. She knew what to do.

He laughed. "You are growing up, *bjarki*. I will trust you to help your mother." Something caught his eye, and he barked at one of the younger men as he went about unlashing the ropes that tied down their valuable cargo.

"Maybe I need *you* on the crew," he joked with Astrid.

She laughed and hugged him again, her arms barely reaching halfway around his bulk. She was happy to have her family together again.

"Astrid." Her father's wiry frame shadowed the threshold of the large pit-house where Astrid and her mother oversaw the preparations for that evening's feast. While the returning men slept and recovered, the women had worked all day to make sure everything was in order. The warm pit-house was where all the cooking for the family and Tryggvi's household guard happened.

Even though he had spoken to Astrid, Tryggvi's eyes were on his wife, and he took her hand, drawing her to him. He ran his hand over her hair and down her arm.

Astrid waited, used to them being like this when her father returned after being away for a long time. The constant touching and kissing, the sounds at night when the household was quiet, like what she'd heard the night before.

He finally turned his attention to her. "Astrid, go find Rikki. I want him with me when I talk to the shipwright to see about any repairs."

"Yes, Father." This would thrill her brother. He always loved doing anything with their father, especially if it was important. She was sure he'd brag about it to her tonight at the feast. When she got to the door, she turned around. "Did you bring me any gifts?"

He laughed, his normally hard blue eyes softening with his wife in his arms. "I might. Go find your brother. Have him meet me at the ships."

With that, she'd been dismissed. Tryggvi nuzzled Ingiborg's neck, whispering in her ear. Astrid could not hear it, but her mother's face broke into a lazy smile; whatever Tryggvi said had pleased her.

Astrid hurried to find Rikki, moving through the many people who were all outside on this summer day as they readied for the great feast, the feel of the village different now the men were back. A group of her father's household men, his *huskarls*, gathered at the door to the smithy, talking to him as he worked at his forge. Astrid could tell by the way they moved their arms, they were telling him about some fight they'd been in. One of the newer men shot her a look as she walked by, unnoticed by the others, and it sent a shiver of unease through her. Her mother had warned her that as she neared marrying age, men would notice her, and she needed to be on guard.

A clutch of hens ran in Astrid's path, squawking and fussing, and she had to skip to avoid them, and then she saw why they were running. Two young boys chased after them.

Astrid grabbed one boy's arm as he ran past. "Stop it. You'll scare the hens, and they won't lay eggs." She remembered chasing hens with her brother, and she was now grown up enough to tell the boys to behave. He nodded, but the little spark in his eyes told her he wouldn't listen for long.

As she neared her father's great hall on the edge of the village, Astrid saw the smoke and smelled the roasted pork they would eat at the feast that night, at least for her family and her father's personal guard. Those who did not get served the meat would get stew with fish and vegetables. Still, no one would go without in Jarl Tryggvi's hall.

She thought about the way her father touched and kissed her mother before in the pit-house. It was so gentle, like her mother was a precious jewel, silk, or fur that he had to handle with great care.

"When I marry, my husband will love me like that," Astrid whispered to herself. Not someone who ogled her like that man had done.

Astrid knew where her brother would be, where he always was now, with his friends Galm and Short Olaf at the practice field. It was another hot day and tendrils of hair stuck to the back of her neck. The looming great hall, taller than many trees, provided some shade. Thralls came and went, birch brooms and cleaning cloths in their hands, through the large red-painted door. Astrid could hear the scrape and thunk as others set up the trestle tables inside.

Rounding the corner of the hall, Astrid found the boys. Usually her father's men would be here sparring and practicing, but since they'd just returned the day before, they were asleep or doing other things.

"Rikki," Astrid called to her brother.

He ignored her.

Short Olaf saw Astrid and smiled at her, "*Hei*, Asta." The momentary lapse of concentration cost him, though, for Rikki leaped forward and stabbed Short Olaf in the belly. Short Olaf let out an '*oof*' and stumbled back.

"You're dead," Rikki gloated, and his eyes lit up with triumph.

"Watch out, Rikki," Short Olaf cried, and he pointed to Rikki's right. Their other friend, Galm, looked to take advantage of Rikki's distraction and made a sweep for the back of his friend's leg. Seeing the attack at the last moment, Rikki jumped in the air, his knees tucked high, and the wooden blade whizzed by under his feet. Galm lost his balance when he did not connect with Rikki's leg, and he toppled onto the ground, his sword flying out of his hand.

Short Olaf shouted. "Good one, Rikki."

Switching his sword to his left hand, Rikki grasped his friend by the forearm to get him to his feet. Galm dusted the dirt and grass off his trousers and went to retrieve his fallen sword.

"I thought I had you," Galm said to Rikki. "When have you been practicing to jump like that?" He was shorter than Rikki, with brown hair the color of mud and brown eyes that were sometimes light and sometimes dark, depending on how much trouble he was up to.

Rikki tucked his sword into his belt and straightened his tunic. "My father showed me. He says to always be ready for attacks to the leg. I have been working on it." He puffed up his chest. "He says that now I'm twelve, it is time to train for real."

Tired of them ignoring her, Astrid broke in, "Rikki jumps around the house all the time. He jumps over benches, chairs, shields. Like a rabbit."

"A rabbit!" Galm laughed, and Rikki's eyes narrowed.

"Asta," Rikki hissed.

Galm taunted, "Rikki the Hare, that's what we'll call you. Or..." Galm paused for a moment to think. "Rikki Hare Feet." As he said the last name, he jumped away. Rikki took off after him, and soon the two boys were wrestling on the ground.

Glancing at Short Olaf, who took no part in the brawl, Astrid said, "I am sorry I got you 'killed.'"

Short Olaf shrugged. "Next time I'll get him back."

He straightened up when her father's *huskarl* Gunnar walked up with her half-brother Jorund, who both laughed at the boys brawling on the ground. They still had the look that some younger warriors did when returning, of wild dogs, like they might bite at the slightest provocation. This was the first season Jori had gone out fighting, and Astrid was not sure how to approach him. Jori's eyes were different, like a curtain had been shut. The night before, instead of sleeping in the family's longhouse, he went with the other men to the building where the *huskarls* slept.

"*Hei*, Sissa," Jori said to Astrid. He gestured for her to come to him and when he did so, he gave her a bright smile. He had the same reddish-blond hair as their father, but instead of blue eyes, Jori had the green-flecked brown eyes of his mother, a woman Astrid had never met.

He squatted down to give her a tight hug, and all her misgivings about him melted away. Jori may be a warrior, but he was still her brother, and she was glad to have him home. Planting a kiss on her cheek, he asked. "What's going on?" He gestured to Rikki and Galm, who still pummeled each other while exchanging insults.

"They are fighting over a name Galm called Rikki." She gave an exaggerated sigh. "It doesn't matter. They will fight over nothing."

The men laughed and Jori gave her another squeeze. "I have a gift for you, Sissa."

She clapped her hands. "Where? I love gifts!"

"You don't even know what it is yet," Jori teased.

"I'll love it no matter what."

To her surprise, Gunnar laughed. "You are easy to please, Asta. It will make your future husband happy."

She stared at Gunnar, the mention of a husband stirring something inside her. Gunnar was the most handsome of her father's personal guard, his *hirð*; his wavy brown hair fell below his shoulders, and he had a nicely trimmed beard. He was twenty winters old, a full-grown man who had been in many battles and had killed many men. She looked into his eyes, the green so pale they looked like glass, and he gave her a wink and a smile.

"You'll be the prettiest girl in the region, that's for sure. *And* the jarl's daughter," Gunnar added. "There'll be no shortage of men wanting to be your husband."

"Enough talk about her marriage. She's just a girl," Jori said.

Astrid harrumphed. She was almost twelve, not a little girl.

Gunnar bent down to look Astrid in the eyes. "Don't worry. If any men come here wanting to marry you, they'll have to go through me first. Me and *Vaugnsnautr.*" He patted his side where he normally carried his sword, but he did not have it on him. Gunnar was proud of his sword. He'd taken it from the outlaw he'd killed after the man had tried to abduct Astrid. To counteract any bad luck associated with the sword of a dead man, Gunnar had made a sacrifice to Odin with the sword.

"Father is waiting for us," Jori reminded Gunnar.

"What about my gift?" Astrid asked.

"Don't be greedy! Later, Sissa, after the feast." He gathered her again in a hug and kissed her cheek. Then he clapped Gunnar on the shoulder.

Before he left, Gunnar put his hand on Astrid's head. "I will always look after you." He joined Jori, and they walked off toward Tryggvi's longhouse. Sometimes when she watched Jori, his gestures and movements reminded her of their father.

Astrid stared after them, the feel of Gunnar's hand still on her head. Ever since he'd saved her from the outlaw when he was only sixteen, they had formed a special bond, but this was the first time she'd ever felt anything for him other than what she'd feel for a brother. He was handsome and kind, strong, and capable. Her mind was ablaze with images of Gunnar as her husband.

Next to her Short Olaf said, "I wish I could go out when they leave again." He leaned on the fence and gripped his padded wooden practice sword by its hilt. He stared after the men. Smaller than Rikki and Galm, Short Olaf had light brown hair that he liked to keep trimmed close to his head.

"Why do you like to fight so much?" Astrid asked, shaking off thoughts of Gunnar.

"What?" he said, taken aback.

She pointed to Galm and Rikki, their brawl ending. "You fight all the time. Why?"

Short Olaf looked at his friends, then at the receding backs of Gunnar and Jori. "That's what we do."

"I know that. But *why*?"

He shrugged. "It's what men do. Why do women have babies? It's what women do."

"That's different."

Rikki and Galm, grass and dirt clinging to their tunics, made their way back to Astrid and Short Olaf.

"What's different?" Rikki coughed when he brushed dust off his tunic. He had a cut on his chin and a new bruise on his cheek, and his hair was all tangled. Galm had a trickle of blood coming from his nose and an abrasion on his cheek.

"Asta wants to know why men fight," Short Olaf told Rikki, incredulous.

Galm burst out laughing, "What a dumb question." He snorted and wiped the blood from his nose with some grass he picked. "Girls don't know anything."

Rikki held up a fist. "Don't insult my *systir*."

"You do." Galm inched forward, ready for another fight.

"*I* can, she's my *systir*. No one else can."

"Oh, for Frigg's sake!" Astrid cried, repeating something she'd heard her mother say when dealing with the boys.

Rikki and Galm turned to her. A spark popped into Rikki's eyes, remembering. "What did you want, anyway?"

Astrid had forgotten she had been sent to get Rikki. "Father wants you."

"Why didn't you say so?" Rikki looked stricken.

"You shouldn't ignore me then."

At her side, Short Olaf snickered. Rikki sent him a scathing look before straightening his tunic and tightening his belt.

"Where?" Rikki asked.

"At the ships. He wants—" She didn't even have time to finish before Rikki tore off in the direction of the river.

Galm continued to annoy Astrid. "Learning to fight is more important than having babies." He said the word *babies* like he'd eaten rotten meat.

"That's not true." Astrid felt like spitting at him.

"You will marry some old man, have a bunch of ugly babies and work in a house all day. I'd rather die."

"Take that back," Astrid said, lowering her voice. She drew up closer to him, her hands balled into fists. Even though she was younger, she was as tall as him, and she was the jarl's daughter, something she would not let him forget. She opened her mouth to speak when a new voice boomed out.

"Hey, now. What's going on here?"

Emund the Red approached them, his normally laughing green eyes narrowed as he looked at Galm.

As soon as he saw Emund, Galm took a step away from Astrid.

"Emund." Astrid was glad of his presence. She didn't know what would have happened with Galm.

Emund bent and wrapped a big arm around her, giving her a squeeze. Strands of his long hair blew into Astrid's face, and she brushed it aside. He'd bathed after their return, and he still smelled musty and sweaty from sleeping for so long. He was like a bear in hibernation after coming home, sleeping from the time they returned until late the next day, waking in time for the feast.

He asked again, "What is going on?"

Short Olaf dropped his arms by his sides and said nothing. Galm stared at Short Olaf to make sure he said nothing and then at Emund, arms crossed, defiant as usual.

"Asta?" Emund asked, one eyebrow cocked.

"Galm said women's work was not important. He said it was dumb."

Before she could continue, Emund said, in a threatening voice that should have had Galm trembling, "In Jarl Tryggvi's household, we do not talk to women like that. They are our helpmates."

He pointed a finger as big as a sausage at Galm. "Are you hungry for the feast, young warrior?"

"*Ja,*" Galm said, his voice still defiant, his eyes still burning at Astrid as if this were all her fault, but he puffed up at being called a 'young warrior.'

Emund smiled, and Galm relaxed a little. "Then you best thank a woman when your belly is full. It is she who prepared it." Rising to his considerable height, Emund continued, "Even the mighty Thor loved his wife."

Emund flicked his wrist to show they could leave, and the two boys took off at a run, disappearing past the great hall.

Leaning against the fence, Emund looked up at the sky and took in a breath. The area surrounding the practice field was covered with undergrowth of ivy, cloudberry bushes, and ferns, making it look like it was floating in a sea of green. Pine and spruce trees, their dappled leaves glittering in the sun, grew all around, like the ancestors standing guard.

"That boy is Loki-touched," he said.

"More than touched," Astrid added. "Loki forged."

Emund chuckled. "Aye. Your father was not much better when he was that age. Look at him now."

Emund had fostered with Tryggvi's father when he was a boy and knew her father better than anyone. He had been training the men in her father's household guard for as long as Astrid could remember. It was strange to hear him training her brother's friends, boys not much older than her. She was used to her father and Emund going off in the summer raiding season to fight, and they always came back; she wasn't sure she'd get used to her brothers leaving to be in so much danger.

She clambered up onto the top railing of the fence so she could be closer to his level and leaned against his broad frame. Having Emund home made her feel as steady as if he were one of the pillars that held up the great hall.

"I am glad you are back," Astrid said.

"Me, too, *bjarki*. Me, too." Emund sighed.

"I wish you didn't go away. I don't like it when you are gone."

"If I didn't, I couldn't bring you home any of the pretty things you like so much." He reached into the bag he carried on his belt and pulled out a piece of cloth.

Astrid straightened up and looked at him, down at his hand, then back at his face.

He unfolded the cloth in his big hand and when she saw what was in it, Astrid inhaled sharply. He held a beautiful glass bead as big around as his finger. It was a rich, glowing purple. Inside the bead were flecks of white, which made it glitter and throw off sparks of light when it moved.

"Oh," Astrid breathed, and her hand hovered over his, very much wanting to touch the amethyst bead. Her eyes flicked up to his for permission.

Smiling, his green eyes shining, he said, "It is for you. Found it at a market in Hedeby. As soon as I saw it, I knew it was yours. It practically jumped into my hand. Even your father agreed." He laughed.

But Astrid barely heard what he said, she was so engrossed with the bead. She gently picked it up and rolled it in her hand; it was perfectly round and smooth, not like some glass beads that had irregularities in them. As she rolled it, the white flecks sparkled in the light. It felt magical, as if the dwarfs themselves had created it down in Svartalfheim for one of the goddesses.

"Do you like it?" Emund asked.

Astrid started, jolted as if out of a dream, a dream spun by the purple depths of the glass bead. She gulped. "I love it. It is beautiful. Like something Freya would wear."

A gray and white blur of fur dashed out from under the trees and stopped in front of Emund's feet. Far enough away to be safe. Its tail rose and swished, its hair on edge.

"That cat hates me," he said.

"She hates everyone."

"Except you."

Kis-Kis skirted around Emund's legs and jumped up next to Astrid, balancing on the railing. Ignoring them both, the cat cleaned herself, tail first. Astrid closed her hand on the bead and petted Kis-Kis's head, the cat bumping her head into Astrid's hand. Kis-Kis smelled of pine, as if she'd been lying in the woods, and underneath her fur held the permanent smell of smoke.

Astrid thought of the glass bead and how beautiful it would look on the necklace she was making. One day she'd have enough pretty beads to make a whole necklace, one she could string from her brooches like her mother did. Her mother had three beaded necklaces that she strung between her apron brooches, and Astrid never tired of looking at them. On long winter nights, her mother would let her hold them, and tell Astrid stories of who had given her the beads and where they came from. Each bead told a story, as if they were the stepping stones of Ingiborg's life.

"Red," a voice called out and her father's steersman appeared. "We need you to settle a dispute."

"Aye," Emund said, and he pushed himself away from the fence.

Once the men left, Astrid opened her hand to look at the bead. It took her breath away how it glowed in the sun, like there were worlds inside of it that she could explore.

Kis-Kis meowed and bumped Astrid's arm.

"It is the most precious gift I've ever received." She showed it to the cat, who yawned and looked away, bored. Astrid laughed. "I will treasure it forever."

Loud talk and laughter filled the great hall as everyone waited for the feast to begin.

The central hearth fire burned brightly and oil lamps hung on the walls and from chains on the ceiling, their light flickering and dancing over the revelers. The pillars of the hall were painted black and red and carved with images of Odin and Thor, Frigg and Freya. Tapestries and furs hung on the walls to provide warmth. Shields of every color also decorated the hall, alongside swords, spears and axes. Thralls kept them polished, so the weapons gleamed in the firelight.

From her place on the bench next to her brothers and sister, Astrid watched as her mother circled the feast hall, presenting everyone with a large bowl of honeyed mead. Rounds of '*skål*' accompanied the drinking, everyone full of laughter. Many of the warriors had bruises and cuts and one man had a sling on his arm, but that was normal, and they all smiled and joked with each other. Each person took a drink until Ingiborg made her way around the large hall and took up her place next to Tryggvi in his high-seat.

The guests grew quiet as Ingiborg filled an elaborately decorated blue-green glass goblet with the mead. Ingiborg looked just as rich and beautiful as the glass. Her light-brown hair was braided in complicated twists that piled on top and at the back of her head. Over the top of her head she wore a delicate silk netting laced with pearls, a gift from Tryggvi, something he'd gotten from a trader who had been to the Great City, Miklagard. A gold circlet graced her brow, an emerald glittering at the center of her forehead. Her glass-beaded necklaces winked in the firelight, and her silver brooches were so bright it was like the sun shone on them. Her dress was a bright crimson, trimmed with silk, the collar lined with marten fur.

When she spoke it was as if the goddess spoke through her.

"My lord and loving husband."

Ingiborg held up the blue-green glass goblet so everyone could see as she offered it to Tryggvi.

"Bold warrior
Giver of gifts.
As this cup is full
So may be your ships, your friends, and your allies.
A drink to your health
Drekka heil!"

Tryggvi took the cup with a lingering look at his wife. He drank long and deep until he had finished the mead. When finished, he kissed Ingiborg on the lips, raised his empty glass and called out, "*Drekka heil*!"

"*Drekka heil*!" The guests drank from their own cups. The talk grew loud as friends and families toasted one another.

The merriment and toasting ended abruptly when the door to the hall flew open, banging on the wall behind it with a resounding thud. All eyes followed the progress of the man who had been on guard as he strode up to the high-seat. As he passed by Astrid, he brought a burst of cold air with him. He leaned over to speak quietly to the jarl.

A shiver that had nothing to do with the chilly air snaked up Astrid's back. "What is going on?" She asked Rikki, her gaze finding Emund, but he was no reassurance; he listened to the guard and paid her no attention.

"I don't know." Rikki gripped his knife.

As the guard spoke, Tryggvi nodded. The guard hurried out the door to stares from the guests in the hall, and he returned quickly, bringing with him a man Astrid did not know.

Her father's men muttered among themselves as Tryggvi spoke to the man.

The mead she'd just drunk sat heavy in Astrid's stomach as she watched her father's face turn stony and his blue eyes flash like a whip. The messenger recoiled as if he'd been struck. Ignoring the messenger, Tryggvi spoke in low tones to Emund. At their words, Ingiborg paled slightly.

When the messenger and guard left, Tryggvi rose to a clamor of questions. He lifted his hands to quiet the guests. "I have been informed that my brother Harald's ships were spotted near our waters." He told the men where Harald had been seen.

"That's close to your salmon run, Jarl Tryggvi," one man said.

"Father," Jori said, rising to his feet. "Who has alerted us to Harald?"

"Ketil."

"Ketil," Emund said, his deep voice like thunder. "Cannot be trusted."

Tryggvi's steersman spoke up. "It could be a trick. Lure us out to sea and attack by land."

After that the men all spoke at once, those in favor of heading back out to find Harald mixed with those who wanted to stay, convinced it was a trap set by Ketil. Harald's name flew through the great hall until Astrid felt like someone had thrown a wet cloak over her shoulders. Mention of her father's brother always brought with it the vague memory of the last time he had come. Astrid had been a little girl, too young to remember anything except for vague, dreamlike feelings of being afraid, of her mother holding her and Rikki as they hid in a dark place—of scared whispered voices, whimpering children, and the bleating of frightened animals. Her father-brother's name brought fear, death, and destruction.

Finally, Tryggvi held up his arms again. "Enough." When the men quieted, he turned to the one known for his tracking skills.

"Go at first light to find out if what the messenger says is true." The man nodded.

"Make sure the ships are ready. Use as many thralls and men as you need." Tryggvi ordered the shipwright.

Pointing to a group with lesser standing, he told them to join the guard. They rose to leave, their agitated voices heard from the anteroom as they donned their cloaks and gathered their weapons.

"Now." Tryggvi held his arms wide, encompassing the gathered guests in his massive hall. "If what the messenger said is true, Harald is two days away. Tonight we feast!"

Ingiborg gestured for the thralls to bring in the food, specially made for the feast. The guests set aside their worries of a prowling Harald and enjoyed themselves again. Everyone in the hall knew to appreciate a good meal and good company when offered. No one knew what would come the next day.

The smell of the food followed the thralls into the building. Spit-roasted hens and duck. Roasted pork made from the animal that Tryggvi had sacrificed to Odin in thanks for the men's success. Turnips baked in the ashes of the roasting meat, the heat cooking the insides so they were soft and perfect when covered in dill-flavored butter. A stew of turnips, kale, leeks, and mustard seeds, the broth cooked with fat from the pork to make it salty and rich. Thralls placed hard cheese on the tables, along with rounds of wheat bread, the yeasty aroma heady in the already warm hall. Astrid heard the cries of pleasure and awe from people further down the tables when they saw the wheat bread; it was a sign of her father's wealth that he could provide them with the exotic floured bread. Their trenchers, though, to hold the stew, were made from local barley bread. She and Rikki shared a trencher while Gytha shared one with Jori.

Rikki waved a knife in the air, his blue eyes shining as brightly as the blade as it glinted in the light from the fire and oil lamps. He turned it over and made a jabbing motion. The handle was made from walrus ivory and carved with runes that said, 'Rikolf, son of Tryggvi,' and on the edge of the handle right where it joins the blade was a silver band.

"I'll use this to cut out Harald's heart. Or Ketil's tongue if this is a trick," Rikki said.

His words burst in on her like an unwanted guest. With a sidelong glance at him, she could see he was getting worked up. "Can I see the knife?"

He hesitated, staring at it for a moment before giving it to her. She wanted to roll her eyes. Men were so possessive of their weapons, like if someone else touched them the blade would be contaminated. And this knife was not even a weapon.

The handle felt good in her hand, and it was warm; it had not been out of Rikki's hands since their father had given it to him earlier. With a quick movement, Astrid sliced off a small hunk of the roast pork she and Rikki shared. It went in easily. She popped the meat into her mouth, laughing as her brother's eyes narrowed.

"This is what you do with an eating knife, isn't it?" She smiled.

Rikki grabbed it back, grumbling while he wiped off the blade on the cloth that covered the oak table. "*Ja*, but not yet." He gestured to another knife on the table, this one much more plain. "Use your own knife."

His tone had changed, and she let out a long breath. Her distraction had worked. "Where is your hat?" He looked at her head as he swept his hair off his own face.

"It is too hot to wear in the summer." Her father had given her a gift so rich it had taken her breath away. A thick woolen cap, dyed a deep blue, and edged with the fur of an artic fox. "I wanted to wear it, though." She touched her head where the fur would be if she'd worn the hat.

"A rich gift. I've never seen fur so white. I wonder what Father will give the men." Rikki's voice was thick with longing for them to include him.

"I don't—"

The entrance of her father's skald interrupted their conversation. He approached and stood in the middle of the feast hall, his lyre in his arms. "Jarl Tryggvi, son of Olaf!" the skald sang in a voice that he'd developed to carry over a crowd of people.

Everyone hailed Tryggvi. Some called out his praises. Tryggvi simply smiled and rose his glass goblet, which now contained Frankish wine instead of mead, something he reserved only for feasts. He, Ingiborg, Emund, and Jori drank the wine.

"A generous ring-giver!"

"Free with his food!"

"Bold in battle!"

After each exhortation, the men and women cheered, some banging on the tables with their cups, knives, or hands. The tables vibrated under the onslaught.

"In the words of the Allfather," the skald went on.

"A great man shall be silent and wise,
And bold in battle;
Brave and glad, a man shall walk,
Until the day of his death has come."

Once the skald sang praises of Tryggvi, the jarl stood, flanked by his family and men on all sides. Behind him sat the trunks that held the gifts.

He turned to Jori, who rose at his father's beckon. Astrid's heart swelled with pride at her brother. His eyes were wide with anticipation, and his fingers drummed the sides of his legs as he waited to see what his father would present him with.

She gasped, along with everyone else, when Tryggvi held up a mail *brynja*, the metal links still stained with the blood of the warrior who had worn it.

"For my first-born son who acted with bravery when one of his Brothers was down. Who looked into the eye of the Corpse-Stealer and never wavered."

Tryggvi jangled the mail *brynja* and the household guard praised Jori. Once again the hall shook with the thunder of cups and hands banging on tables. Astrid clapped loudly and called out her brother's name. By her side, Rikki frowned, his teeth clenched, envy etched onto his face as he stared at the mail. She nudged him, but he remained silent.

"To Jorund!" Tryggvi called out, his pride making him glow like the fire that burned in the hearth.

"To Jorund!" Everyone replied, and they drank.

Jori went to Tryggvi and accepted the *brynja*, running his hands over the metal links, his eyes drinking it in like a starving man looks at food. He beamed at his father.

When he returned to his seat near Astrid, he caught her eye, giving her a wink.

After Jori, her father gave gifts to his other men, and they praised how generous a gift-giver Jarl Tryggvi was, and they hailed him to Odin. After a while, Astrid grew tired of the ceremony, eager to give her father her gift, her stomach flitting. Would he like it? With a sinking feeling, she wondered if she should give it to him here and now. If he didn't like it, if he didn't want to put it in his hall, it would humiliate her before everyone. A lump formed in her throat and she took a drink, but it didn't help.

Once Tryggvi finished, he was about to sit in his high-seat when Ingiborg nodded to Astrid that it was time for her to present her gift.

With a deep breath, she rose and said, "Father."

He looked at her, his eyebrows raised.

Astrid gestured to one of the household thralls to bring her the tapestry. It was heavy and folded carefully. She held it out in her arms as she approached the high-seat. Astrid cast a quick glance at her mother, who gave her an encouraging smile.

She ran one hand over the thick woolen tapestry with the vivid black and red stripes. "Father. I would give this to you."

He cocked his head. "What is it?"

Astrid gestured to the thrall who helped her unfold the tapestry to its full length. They held it up so Tryggvi could see it. "For your hall, Father. Your colors."

"And you wove this?" His voice had softened as he addressed her.

"*Ja.*"

"Bring it closer."

The hall had grown quiet as they watched the jarl's daughter present him with her gift. As it unfolded, the women remarked on it, as many of them had been there as Astrid created it.

Tryggvi ran his scarred hand over the tapestry, tracing first the black stripe and then the red. He became engrossed for a moment, and then his head jerked up. He stared at her.

"I will treasure it, my daughter." Then he raised his voice so everyone could hear. "I will hang it in my hall with pride."

Astrid's heart raced, and she could feel the blood flowing through her body like it was the river that ran by their village, swift and full. Her gift pleased her father. She anchored herself by catching her mother's eyes and then Emund's.

Emund mouthed, 'well done,' and gave her a broad smile, his emerald eyes sparkling, the lines around them crinkling.

As she returned to her bench, Astrid felt like the goddess Frigg had visited her with her gift of weaving, giving her something in which she could make her family proud. She settled onto the bench with Rikki by her side, Gytha and Jori next to them. Her mother and father sat together in the high-seat, Emund in a broad chair by her father's side. Throughout hall, men and women talked and laughed, the doors thrown open, a breeze from the river blowing in to cool things off. The only part of the night that troubled her was the thought of Harald Olafsson nearby. The ale and mead was not drunk in the quantities as was usual for a feast; the men remained wary and ready should Harald be spotted. He was like a stain on the fabric of their feast.

Gytha sidled up to her when Rikki left to join his friends in a game of dice. They watched as thralls lifted the tapestry to where it would hang on the wall.

"It is pretty, Asta." She snuggled up against Astrid.

At that moment Tryggvi said something that made Emund laugh so loud it could have shaken down the rafters. Ingiborg's lighter laugh joined him.

Astrid wrapped her arm around her sister. She would think no more of Harald, would give him no power to disturb her contentment. Right now, all was as it should be.

Bjorn's back and arms burned with fatigue, but he kept up the rhythm of pulling his oar. He would not be the one to falter as they fought the rough sea in his foster-father Harald's longship, *Sea Wolf*. Another wave loomed in front of them, and he thought he saw the face of the goddess Ran, laughing, but the moment passed. He held tight to his oar, and the ship crested up and over the wave, falling down the other side. A spray of sea water hit him, soaking him once again. He spit and flicked his wet hair out of his face. The boat filled with water, and the men not on the oars worked with a practiced rhythm to bail it out. Harald's voice shouted out orders, but Bjorn could barely hear him. They had just raided a village under Tryggvi Olafsson's protection, one that Harald said was on land that belonged to him, an area rich in salmon. The fighting had been harder than they had expected. During it all, a young man had escaped on a horse to warn Tryggvi, and even though Bjorn and his friend Galinn had chased after him, they could not catch a horse. The boy got away and Harald raged and ordered his warriors to make haste to take the battle to Tryggvi himself. They had been sailing and rowing for one day, their longships hugging the coast, when a squall rose out of nowhere, driving them off course and separating *Sea Wolf* from Harald's other two ships. Now they fought to keep from being engulfed, and Bjorn did not know how much longer he could hang on.

"Pull!" Harald shouted, his voice hoarse.

Bjorn pulled his oar, but his fingers, cramped from fatigue, could no longer hold on and the oar slipped from his hand. He careened off his sea chest and fell onto the hull of the boat.

"Bjorn," Galinn cried out, and he moved to help Bjorn.

"Hold your oar, Galinn," shouted one of the older men.

Bjorn, disoriented, shook his head and tried to stand up, but the water on the bottom made the boards slick and he could not gain purchase. He made it to his knees. The boat heaved and rolled, and he stumbled, crashing into the side.

"Hang on, Bjorn!"

His eyes widened as he saw the wave that threatened to swamp them. He grabbed the side with one hand and a thick walrus-hide rope with another and braced himself. The tremendous wave hit the boat with a force Bjorn was sure would break it in two. He was only aware of the rope in his hand and the frigid, salty water that rushed around him. Something hard and wooden hit him in the hip with a painful blow, and he was thrown over the side. Submerged in the frigid water, Bjorn fought to hang on to the hide rope, knowing it was the only thing that tethered him to life. He kicked to get his head above water, but white-hot pain shot through his left leg as the boat knocked into him. His head underwater, he heard a shout, and he pulled himself up on the rope until he broke the surface. With a gasp, he caught his breath and saw Harald looming, his burly hand outstretched. Bjorn grabbed hold of his foster-father, whose powerful arms helped him clamber over the side and fall into the boat.

Harald kicked Bjorn's sea chest back into its place. He picked up Bjorn and tossed him onto it, the movement making Bjorn hiss with pain, and handed him his oar. Shaking from cold, fear, and pain, and still clinging to the rope, Bjorn could not let go. Harald pried his fingers off the rope and put them around the oar.

Harald stared at Bjorn, his large hand squeezing Bjorn's. With his wet hair streaming down his face, his sodden clothes, his face and body tense, Harald looked like a watery demon out of one of Bjorn's nightmares where he drowns at sea, and which had nearly come true. He shivered. But he held on and watched as Harald slogged to the bow of the ship and grabbed onto the dragon head.

"Ran!" Harald shouted at the angry, churning sea. He pushed up his sleeve and pulled an arm ring off his forearm, every muscle tense. Another wave hit them, and Harald laughed as it passed, tossing his hair and spitting into the sea. He held up the heavy silver ring. "Ran. Water goddess. My men are not for you. I offer you this arm ring. It is soaked in blood. Take it to your underwater abode and when you wear it think of Harald, son of Olaf!"

With those words, he tossed the arm ring into the waves.

Bjorn gasped as he watched the valuable ring disappear into the raging sea. When Harald turned away from the bow, he had a crazed look in his eyes, but he gave the men a grin and shouted encouraging words as he pitched back to his steersman.

The storm continued and Bjorn took his turn at bailing, relieved that he no longer had to row. He worked next to Galinn, who was shivering, soaked, his face white and pinched with cold and exhaustion. Galinn's hands slipped when scooping up water, and Bjorn snatched the bucket before it washed away, surprised that he could do so, his hands so numb he could barely feel his fingers. The rain pounded on his head and back, and the waves continued to smash into the ship, spraying them with icy water. The older men never flagged, never seemed to tire. They'd been at it so long, Bjorn was beginning to wonder if they had perished and were now doomed to sail in Ran's realm, forever battered in a stormy sea.

As he handed the bucket to Galinn, they locked eyes, and he read in his friend's eyes the same fear. Would they ever get out of this?

"Do you think Ran accepted Harald's offering?" Galinn shouted at him over the din of the storm, his voice stuttering.

Bjorn shrugged, and he dumped his bucket of water over the side. As he turned back, he saw something he never thought he'd see again. The sun peeked out from behind a cloud, its rays shining down on the churning water. A shout went up, and the pilot steered the ship toward the calm pocket ahead of them. The ship lurched as the men pulled harder, eager to get out of the storm, so hard that Galinn toppled over. Bjorn grabbed his friend and helped him up. Galinn's tunic felt like ice, and Bjorn heard his teeth chattering.

It seemed like it took ages before the rain abated, and the sea calmed.

Bjorn took a deep breath. "Look." He pointed behind them. The sky was heavy with clouds as black as night, and the sea heaved and churned. "I can't believe we made it through that."

Galinn nodded, still shivering.

"Keep bailing!"

As soon as they reached calm seas and had left the storm far behind them, the men shipped their oars and collapsed or hung onto the side, breathing hard.

Harald and his steersman searched the sea to determine where they had ended up. With the last of the bailing done, Bjorn dropped the bucket, his arms and legs trembling with exhaustion from the effort. He studied the horizon but could see no sign of land. The storm had driven them off course, but how far? Not knowing what to do, he flung himself down and let out an exhausted sigh. At fifteen, this was only Bjorn's second time out raiding, and the first time fighting a sea this violent.

A blast of cold and wet hit him as Galinn slumped down next to him.

"Do you think the water barrels are intact? I'm thirsty," Bjorn told him. "I thought for sure we were doomed."

"Me, too." Galinn's voice was tired and strained.

As if he had heard them, Ingvar walked up and tossed Bjorn a water skin filled with clean rainwater.

"Thank the gods, water." Bjorn gulped some down and handed it to Galinn, who did the same, his hands clumsy as he put the skin to his trembling lips.

"Ingvar," Bjorn said before the man could leave. "What now?" All he wanted was dry clothes, a warm fire, and land. He'd had enough of the sea for now.

"We rest. Find land. If it's close, we row." He looked up at the sky.

Bjorn groaned and looked at his hands. He had a blister on one and the other had a tear on the soft part under his thumb. Calluses already covered his hands, but that had not prepared him for the effort of rowing through this storm. He wondered how long it would take to be as hardened as the older men.

"Wrap some cloth around it." Ingvar laughed. As he walked off, he said over his shoulder. "Rest while you can."

Bjorn settled back against the side of the boat and stretched his legs out in front of him, wincing when he moved. The boards were damp and cold, but he closed his eyes and tried to rest despite the discomfort. The rocking motion lulled him. His hip throbbed where his sea chest had hit him. The afternoon sun did not provide much warmth or heat. Galinn had pulled his knees up to his chest and wrapped his arms around himself, shivering.

"Think of a warm fire," Bjorn told his friend. "And a hot girl."

Galinn nodded and hugged himself. "Do you remember those two girls we met in Denmark?" His teeth chattered.

"Mm, Dora and..." Bjorn looked at his friend. "What was the other's name?"

"Etta. I think she wanted to go with you too. They always want you."

Bjorn grunted. "Not all of them. Not Hilda." He tried to make it sound like it didn't matter, but he felt the rejection again like a kick in the stomach.

"She refused you?"

"*Ja*. She reminded me I'm only fifteen and have nothing. She's marrying Stori."

Galinn sniffed and bumped Bjorn's shoulder as a sign of solidarity. "Sorry, Brother. Did you really think she would have you? She's Harald's daughter."

He *had* believed Hilda would take him, even if she was the daughter of a powerful chieftain and he, Bjorn, was nothing.

"At least you won't have Sigrun as a mother-by-law." Galinn's mouth twitched in a slight smile.

"Thank the gods for that," Bjorn said with a laugh. Harald's wife hated him, and would no doubt have made his life miserable. He was glad to have Galinn by his side. Earlier that summer they'd done the blood-brother ritual and bound themselves until one of them died.

"What about Maude?"

"I don't want to marry her," Bjorn said. "Harald would never allow it, anyway. She's a thrall."

"Is the child she carries yours?"

"I think so." The thought of a child warmed Bjorn. He liked children and wanted many of his own, especially a son to carry on his name. "I hope it's a son."

A thought came to him, and he turned to Galinn and gripped his arm. "When we return, I'll ask Harald to free Maude. I can't marry her, but I can make sure the mother of my child is not a thrall."

Galinn gave him a tired smile and sneezed. "There is good under the Pretty Bjorn face."

Bjorn grimaced at the nickname.

"Now let me rest before we have to row again." Galinn groaned.

Despite his discomfort, Bjorn closed his eyes, thoughts of being in a fire-warmed room, in a bed with furs covering him and his beautiful Hilda in his arms, warming him. A pressure in his bladder woke him. He had not expected to sleep, and he was stiff and frozen, his chilly friend asleep at his side. The sound of men's voices and a dice game rose above the lapping of water against their beleaguered boat that creaked as it moved. With a swift glance around, Bjorn saw Harald deep in conversation with his steersman and Ingvar, while the other men checked the food supplies and gear, slept wrapped in sodden clothes, or played dice to pass the time.

Bjorn got up with a groan, his left hip aching from the blow to it earlier, and took a piss off the side of the boat. Relieved, he wove his way through sleeping men to his chest to see if he had a dry tunic. A wave swelled underneath the boat and Bjorn, his leg sore and unstable, lost his footing and stumbled into a dice game. The antler bone dice spilled.

Styrr, one man playing, jumped up quickly and grabbed Bjorn by the front of his tunic. "Watch yourself, boy," he said, smiling, but his voice was full of menace. Years of fighting had taken their toll on Styrr, and he had a scar running along his jaw and at his hairline, but for all that he remained plain looking. He was only three or four seasons older than Bjorn, had light brown hair, like the color of beach sand, and unremarkable brown eyes. His smile could mean treachery or friendship. Right now it meant treachery.

"Clean up this mess and do it quick. Clumsy little *shyt*." He sniffed. "So weak you can't even hold on to an oar. We should drown you like a mewling kitten." Quick as lightning, he pushed Bjorn over a chest.

Burning with rage, Bjorn straightened up and looked around. They had drawn the attention of the men who watched in anticipation of a fight.

Rising to his full height, Bjorn sized up his opponent. Small, but wiry, Styrr was quick as a striking snake. Bjorn was taller, broader, and more muscular. He fixed his tunic deliberately and stared at Styrr. The other man stared back.

"I said to clean up the mess, boy," Styrr taunted.

"Do not call me boy." Bjorn spit out that last word.

Styrr barked out a laugh, but it turned into a grimace as Bjorn lashed out, punching him in the stomach. Taken off guard, Styrr hunched over, and Bjorn hit him in the jaw. Styrr's head flew back and he stumbled. He put a hand to his jaw, his eyes gleaming with fury.

A laugh sounded in Bjorn's ear. "You asked for it now. You've made him mad. It will take more than that to take down Styrr." Ingvar slapped Bjorn on the shoulder and moved out of the way, joining the other men to watch.

Styrr flew at Bjorn with a coldness that took him by surprise. Knocked back by the ferocity of the smaller man's attack, Bjorn wildly threw a punch to Styrr's face, but Styrr blocked it and retaliated with a perfect shot to Bjorn's left cheek. Pain exploded in his head, as if he'd been hit in the face with Thor's hammer. Before he could regain his balance, the hammer landed again, this time in his gut. He doubled over. Styrr did not relent, but this time Bjorn saw the next punch coming out of the corner of his eye. He jerked his head to the side enough that Styrr's fist glanced his jaw rather than connecting with it. Bjorn bit his tongue and tasted blood.

With a growl, Bjorn rounded on Styrr and tried to grab him by the waist to take him down. If he could get on top of Styrr, his superior weight would give him an advantage. Styrr had been expecting it and did not go down, moving easily out of the way. Bjorn yelled in frustration as he went sprawling, smashing into the side of the boat. One man helped him up and tossed him back into the fray. Bjorn stepped forward and lashed out. Styrr easily dodged the punch and hit Bjorn in the gut again. He gulped, trying to get enough air to breathe.

"Had enough, pretty boy?" Styrr grinned.

A quick glance and Bjorn saw that the men expected him to relent, but then he saw Harald's impassive face, and it reminded him of the night Harald gave him the boar necklace. It still rested on his chest, and the thought of it gave Bjorn renewed energy. He remembered how the cornered boar had not given up, not even when pierced through by a spear. He had fought until the end.

"Maybe you should be back at home with the women weaving," Styrr taunted again. Some of the men laughed, one called him a *fljod*, a woman, and made womanish squealing sounds while making obscene gestures.

Bjorn met Harald's eyes and held them while the men laughed and taunted. To show his foster-father that he would not back down, Bjorn rushed in and grabbed Styrr in a bear hug, squeezing his arms at his sides so tight he could not get away. Styrr struggled. Bjorn threw him down, the impact of their bodies thudding on the wooden boards. Pain from Bjorn's injured hip seared into him, but he gritted his teeth and rode it out. Close to Styrr now, he could smell the other man's pungent odor of sweat and dirt. Styrr struggled face-down underneath him, but he could not escape. With a laugh, Bjorn grabbed his hair and slammed his head against the bottom of the boat. It made a satisfying smack.

"*You* are in the woman's position now," Bjorn said. He let out a laugh that turned into a yelp of shock as Styrr head-butted him.

Pain shot through Bjorn's head, and he released his grip on Styrr, who struggled to his hands and knees. Despite the throbbing in his leg, Bjorn got up to kick Styrr in the side.

"Enough," Harald shouted.

Strong hands grabbed Bjorn's arms and pulled him away from Styrr. Both of the fighters panted for breath as they stared at each other.

"You fought well," Ingvar told Bjorn. It was his hands that had dragged Bjorn from the fight. Bjorn shrugged his arms to make Ingvar release his hold.

"Get away from me," Bjorn hissed. The other man dropped his hands and stepped back. His entire body racing with battle lust, Bjorn did not know if he could trust himself to not lash out at Ingvar. He curled his hands into tight fists, every muscle in his body tense.

Pacing to the opposite end of the boat from Styrr, Bjorn took deep breaths to calm himself. Although aware that Galinn had shadowed him, Bjorn did not turn to talk to him. Instead, he looked out over the sea, the gentle swells rising and falling, the water sparkling in the lowering sun. Bjorn took stock of his injuries. His cheek throbbed, his jaw ached, but he explored his mouth with his tongue and found no loose teeth. Good. He was proud of his straight, white teeth and did not want to mar that with a missing tooth. The pain in his hip was another matter. It ached so badly, it hurt to even stand, and every step sent a sharp pain down his leg.

He was about to check for bruising, when he felt Harald's presence. He did not turn around, but waited for him, arms crossed, legs splayed to absorb the boat's sway. He'd come to foster in Harald's household six summers before, had been one of his men since he was thirteen, and he still felt that little trickle of fear as Harald approached. He had learned long ago about his foster-father's unpredictable moods.

As soon as Harald stood next to him, Bjorn said, still looking out at the water, "You did not need to stop the fight. I can handle myself."

"You think I did that for you? I need you both if I'm to prevail against my brother. You will need your strength when we land."

Bjorn nodded. "Do you know where we are?"

"Thorvald thinks so. We are not that far off course. That squall cost us the element of surprise with Tryggvi. The boy who got away will reach him soon, if he hasn't already." His voice had taken on the edgy quality it always had when he talked of his brother, Tryggvi. "You should have killed that boy when you had a chance."

Bjorn didn't answer. He could not have caught a horse, but Harald would hear no arguments.

"Do not let anyone take what is yours, Bjorn. And if they do, never rest until you get it back or you get revenge."

"Like Tryggvi took everything from you?"

"*Ja*. My land, my woman, my jarldom. I should have been the jarl, not my brother. Instead, I had to fight for what I have. I earned these ships, these men, by my own wits. Not by marrying a jarl's daughter." Harald spit into the sea.

"It makes him weak," Bjorn said, surprising himself. "He has more to lose."

Harald barked a laugh and gave him an appraising look. "You're right. Now, let's go take everything Tryggvi holds dear."

"Look!" Bjorn pointed to the distance, spotting a patch of brown moving parallel to their boat.

"Sea lions," Harald said, seeing the same thing. Before he could move away, the steersman yelled to man the oars. Sea lions meant land was not far away.

Men scrambled to their chests and oars. They would follow the sea lions to land. Bjorn moved to take his place when Harald stopped him, a meaty hand on his shoulder. No longer the giant he had been in Bjorn's youth, he could still be imposing.

Blue eyes surrounded by crow's feet wrinkles from season upon season of sailing and staring into the sun held Bjorn to the spot. "I was right about you. You are a valuable member of my guard."

"I am your man."

"Serve me loyally and I will richly reward you."

In his mind's eye, Bjorn saw an image of Hilda, the only treasure of Harald's he'd ever wanted. But then, a thrill rushed through Bjorn. This was what he trained for. The old warrior valued him. Bjorn touched the boar tooth necklace, then took his seat at the oars, all his pains fading away.

Chapter Two
Tryggvi's village, Storelva

In the *kvenna hus*, the women's house, Astrid spoke to one of the thralls who dyed the wool that would be spun into the thread they used for clothing. She picked up a piece of test wool to check the color.

"This is—" The sound of barking dogs and men's footsteps running by outside the open door interrupted her.

A shout went up. "Rider!"

A cacophony filled Astrid's ears as she hurried out of the *kvenna hus*, and fear sent shivers throughout her body. The way her father's men gathered arms told her it was no trader or visit from a friend.

She searched for Emund, her father, or Jori.

"Asta," Emund called to her, and she spotted him coming up the path from the river's edge and the ships. When he caught up to her, he took her hand.

"What is it?" She searched for the cause of the disruption. "Is it Harald?"

"Don't know." They made their way through the villagers who had gathered to see what was going on.

A young man who looked to be about fourteen winters bent over as he tried to catch his breath, his dirty and ripped clothes and the blood on his face a testament to fighting and hard riding. He leaned against his horse. The poor beast heaved, lathered in sweat.

Tryggvi stood by the young man's side, waiting.

Astrid tightened her grasp on Emund's hand, sidled up closer to him, and looked around. Her father's men crowded around, their hands on their weapons as they watched the rider and her father expectantly. The women gathered with children on their

hips or held close to their sides. Male thralls had frozen mid-work, buckets and tools hanging from their hands, while the female thralls waited in doorways to hear the news. The only person Astrid wanted to see was her mother, but Ingiborg was nowhere around. Astrid looked toward their family longhouse, the pit-house, the brew house where they brewed and stored the ale and mead. Where could her mother be?

"Tell me," Tryggvi said to the rider.

The young man straightened and took a breath. "Our village..." he wavered on his feet. Tryggvi grabbed him by the arm to steady him. "Attacked. My father...my father told me to take his horse...ride to you. Right before...an axe cut him down." He looked Tryggvi in the eyes, his own eyes filled with pain, and hurried through that last part as if saying it quickly would make it not true. "I barely got away. Two raiders chased me. One caught hold of my stirrup. I kicked him away."

"Who attacked your village?" Tryggvi asked, his voice frosty.

"Harald Olafsson." He paused and wiped his mouth with the back of a dirt-caked hand.

Tryggvi's jaw clenched, but he said nothing, only nodded.

The *huskarls* shouted that the messenger from Ketil had been right, Harald was on the prowl, and a hiss of anger slithered through them. Tryggvi's men instinctively reached for their weapons. Talk turned to whether they should venture out in the ships to engage Harald that way or stay here knowing he was coming. If the men waited for him to come to the village, the women and children, the livestock, and their homes would be at risk.

Astrid searched again for her mother, and a shiver of panic made her blood run cold. If Harald Olafsson was this close, her mother was in danger.

Tryggvi held up his hands to quiet the men. He stepped closer to the young man, who looked as if he had more to say.

"Do you know that name?" the young rider asked as he studied Tryggvi's reaction.

Tryggvi gave a brittle, angry nod. "I know him." He ran a hand through his hair. "When was this raid?"

The young man looked up at the sun. "The sun has risen three times since the raid on my village."

The *huskarls* let out shouts of dismay.

Buri, Tryggvi's steersman, spoke up. "With favorable winds, they might be coming up the river now."

"I rode as fast as I could," the young man said in a pleading voice.

Emund let go of Astrid's hand and stepped forward. "Brother," he said to Tryggvi. "The boy's village was a stop along the way, a blow to gain control of the salmon. But you and I both know what Harald wants. He will be here soon."

The young rider's eyes went wide as Emund said these words, and the young man caught Astrid watching him. She saw panic in his face, and she could see he did not want to be in the middle of another fight with Harald Olafsson.

She wanted to tell him all would be well, that her father was a powerful jarl, that he and Emund and the men would protect them all. They were fierce warriors, all of them. She did not get the chance to say anything.

Four short blasts from a horn rang out, followed by an unnatural stillness.

The sound of a warning horn echoed across the water, but Harald's warriors did not stop rowing. They had met up with one of his other ships, the third still lost or gone, and the two vessels sped up the river toward Tryggvi Olafsson's village.

"They know we are coming, men," Harald shouted over the sound of sloshing water as it hit the sides of the boat. "No matter. We are sea-wolves!"

As if in answer, his wolf-head banner snapped in the wind. The men yelled back, some throwing back their heads and howling.

"Jarl Tryggvi is a rich man. Silver! Gold! Jewels!" Roars from the men punctuated each word. "Women!" At this they all let out lusty roars.

Bjorn felt his blood lust rising, and it took all his effort to slow down and row to the rhythm of the other men. He fidgeted on his sea chest, his eagerness to jump over the side and start the fight making his legs shake with anticipation.

Harald had donned his wolf-skin pelt, the wolf-head on top of Harald's head, its dead eyes staring out at them all, its teeth bared, threatening. He loped back and forth as he shouted at them, his own eager eyes shifting from his men to the village up ahead. A fence mostly enclosed Jarl Tryggvi's village, Storelva, and a wooden walkway led from the harbor to the center of the village. The jarl's great hall roof rose above all the other buildings, and Bjorn stared at the raven image at the tips of the gabled roof. He saw himself and Harald's other men sitting in that hall, and he pulled his oar harder, the boat gliding smoothly underneath him. In the village, smoke rose from the smoke holes in the roofs of the houses as if nothing was wrong and this was an ordinary day. But Bjorn knew its people would scramble to flee to safety, taking their children and animals and whatever valuables they could carry into the woods. Tryggvi's household men would gather their weapons and shields, readying themselves for the onslaught.

Hot energy raced through Bjorn's limbs as he thought of the shield wall that no doubt awaited them on shore. He licked his salt-dry lips and tightened his hands on the pine oar.

For a moment, everyone froze as they listened to the dying echoes of the warning horn.

Tryggvi spun to Emund and hissed, "Harald," his ice-blue eyes hard with fury. Those eyes caught sight of Astrid, who had continued to stand as close to Emund as she could. "Get her to her mother." With that, he turned to bark orders at his men.

Where was her mother? Astrid searched, desperation welling up inside her. Before Emund and Astrid had time to move, a breaking voice called over the din.

"Father!"

It was Rikki.

Tryggvi stopped. People swarmed around him as they hurried to either get weapons and armor or to flee into the surrounding woods. Astrid felt the fear in the air, heard it in every shout of dismay. It froze her body, and she wanted to never leave Emund's side, feeling she would be safe only if she was with him. The thought of having to move away from his protection was too frightening to contemplate. She tightened her grip on him.

"I want to come with you. I want to fight." Rikki pleaded with his father.

Before Tryggvi could answer, Gunnar ran up to him with the news the incoming ships were definitely Harald's. They sported Harald's red sails, and the ship in the lead flew a wolf-head banner.

"We will meet them on the riverfront with a shield wall," Tryggvi said. "We have prepared for this."

Gunnar nodded and ran off toward the beach, collecting the other *huskarls* to him. A man ran by and Tryggvi called out to him. When the man stopped, a bow in his right hand and a leather container full of arrows hanging on his back, Tryggvi told him to gather all the archers and have them take their places behind the shield wall.

"And have the fire arrows ready," he added, and he looked out toward the river. The raiding ships were now visible. Two longships approached quickly, their dragonheads menacing, promising death and bloodshed.

"Father," Rikki repeated. "I want to fight too."

"No. I need you to look after your sisters and mother." His eyes darted to the woods, and he grabbed Rikki by the arm. "Keep them safe. Do that for me."

Rikki gulped and nodded. "I will."

Without another word, Tryggvi gave his son a slap on the shoulder and headed to the river. Buri ran up to his side and brought him his sword, shield, and spear. Tryggvi hooked his sword onto his belt, grabbed his shield with his left hand, and hefted his spear in his right. Astrid wondered if this was the last image of her father she'd ever have, of him striding off to battle fully armed and bristling for a fight.

She did not have time to burn that image into her mind because Emund was moving, releasing her hand and shoving her gently toward her brother.

"No," she cried out, and even though she knew Emund needed to arm himself and join her father, she tugged at his arm. "Don't go."

"My place is by your father's side." He squatted in front of her, and she could feel his anxiousness. His voice remained calm as he talked to her. He threw a glance at her father as he armed himself.

A thrall pulled two crying calves by them, his face a mask of fear. "Go with Rikki and find your mother. You need to get to safety."

Astrid scrunched up her face to keep back the tears.

"I will see you soon. Be brave, my little bear." He laid his big hand on her head, and in one quick movement he leaped up and rushed off. She felt the imprint of his hand after he left, like he had given her some of his courage.

"Come on, Asta," Rikki said, as he took her arm and pulled her away.

"Where is Mother?" Astrid's voice squeaked with panic. "Gytha! Where is Gytha?"

"I don't know. We must stay together."

When they reached the edge of the village, the shouts of the men and the clanging of metal weapons subsided, and Astrid felt the eerie stillness of the calm before a battle. The animals and birds had all taken flight, and even the wind itself had stopped blowing. The only sounds, the panicked farm animals, the bleating sheep let loose from their shearing, the bellowing dairy cows wandering around, freed from their barns, and the braying goats. They had been freed, hoping they'd escape into the woods to be fetched later. If Harald and his men got hold of them, they'd be killed, and the villagers, if any lived through the raid, would starve over the winter.

A clutch of villagers huddled around, and there she was, Mother. Astrid let out a gasp of relief. Ingiborg, the other women, children, and old men waited at a designated spot on the outskirts of the village, the farthest point from the shore where raiders would attack. All the other men of the village, even those who were not her father's guard, had joined in the fight to protect it from Harald, even if they only had a scythe, pitchfork, hoe, or hammer. Ingiborg moved through the crowd, searching for her own children while trying to ease the fears of those who relied on her. Even amid the worried people, Ingiborg looked as if she were presiding over a feast, her face showing no fear, her movements smooth and calm.

But as soon as Ingiborg saw her children, she pulled Astrid to her body and then grabbed for Rikki. "Thank the goddess," she sighed. Then she looked around. "Where is your sister?

"I saw her playing with Sefa's baby," Astrid said, remembering.

Ingiborg caught sight of Sefa and ran to her, pulling Astrid with her. Rikki followed close behind.

Reaching the woman, they did not see Gytha.

"Where is Gytha?" Ingiborg asked. Panic seeped into her voice.

"I thought she was with you."

"No," Ingiborg breathed. She turned to Rikki. "Stay here with Asta. I'm going to find Gytha."

"No!" Rikki and Astrid both cried out together.

"I'm coming with you," Rikki told her, his hand gripping his dagger. "Father said I have to keep you and the girls safe."

Astrid grabbed onto her mother's waist. The world spun, and she had a hard time breathing. She would not leave her mother's side, not for anything.

Before Ingiborg could move, Old Stieg walked up to them. He leaned heavily on a stick for support, one of his ears missing and a scar on his face showing he had seen his share of battles. Now he helped her father and mother take care of the village business, making sure everything ran smoothly. He shot a glance toward the waterfront. They couldn't see it from where they were, on the edge of the woods, but they could all imagine what they'd see. He gestured his head behind him. "Ingiborg. We must get to the woods. Now."

Her own need to find Gytha made her jittery, and Astrid could feel her mother's body tense.

"Go," Ingiborg said to the old man. She straightened up, her hand grasping Astrid tightly. "Everyone! Get to safety."

Taking Astrid's hand and signaling for Rikki to follow, Ingiborg hiked up her dress with her free hand and ran back to their longhouse.

The sound of the battle horn echoed, followed by the *thump, thump, thump* of men banging on their shields with their weapons. Harald's men were so close Astrid could feel the menace in the air. She could hardly breathe. She stumbled, and if not for the steely grasp of her mother's hand in hers, she would have fallen. They rushed by naked sheep, their eyes wide with fright at the noise, and she saw a dog cowering under a bench, his tail wrapped tightly around his legs. Astrid wanted to take it with them to safety, but Gytha was more important. The dog watched them run by with his big, sad, brown eyes.

They ran to their longhouse and Ingiborg threw open the door. It banged against the wall and they heard a squeak come from Ingiborg and Tryggvi's small sleeping chamber. Other than that it was empty, the quiet eerie and foreboding. Their longhouse was always bustling with activity and people. A low fire still burned in the hearth, and the light spilling in from the sun threw off strange shadows. The dark-blue pillars at the back of the longhouse were deep in shadow and looked like men waiting to attack.

"Gytha," Ingiborg called. "Come out. Hurry."

Without waiting for a reply, Rikki dashed into the room and found Gytha hiding underneath the bed. He pulled her by her arms, one of her hands clinging to her favorite rag doll. She screamed. Astrid imagined her little sister being dragged out like this by one of Harald's warriors, and her mouth went dry. They had to hurry. They had to get to safety.

"It's me, Gytha," Rikki soothed. "Come on." She went limp when she saw her brother. Her little body dragged on the floor as Rikki hauled her out from under the bed. By the time her body cleared the bed, Ingiborg was by her side and drew her daughter into her arms.

She ran her hand over Gytha's face. "We must hurry, Gytha."

"I was hiding from the bad men," she said, her lips quivering. She hugged her doll close.

"We have a safe place. Come with us." She let go of Astrid's hand and grabbed Gytha's.

Rikki took hold of Astrid's hand and they ran out the door.

The thumping of shields had grown louder and more intense during the time they had been in the house. It felt like the heartbeat of a terrible beast. Astrid trembled and Rikki squeezed her hand. Between two of the barns, she caught sight of one of the dragon ships, and it filled her with such dread that all the blood left her body.

Astrid stopped in her tracks, eyes wide as she took in the fearsome spectacle. Dozens of men stood in the longship, huge and armed, one standing at the prow wearing a wolf-skin. A harsh yank on her hand lifted her out of her frozen trance. Shaking her head to clear it, she ran, barely able to feel her legs, with Rikki and her mother toward safety.

As soon as they turned from the village and plunged into the trees, Astrid heard her father roar, "To me!" and the answering call of "Tryggvi!" rising from her father's men.

"Pull up," Harald shouted and the men, as one, shipped their oars. Momentum carried the huge ship toward land with the steersman expertly guiding them in.

As soon as he stowed his oar, Bjorn grabbed his shield from the slot on the side. The round shield with its large iron boss protected him from knee to shoulder. He did not have mail, just leather chest armor over a stuffed woolen pad, but it would protect him against glancing blows. A helm of iron with a nose guard protected his head, a gift from Harald when he became one of his household guard. Bjorn picked up his spear and jiggled it in his hand until he found the right spot. His battle axe rested lightly in his belt, ready to take out in a moment.

Harald prowled by, shirtless, the muscles in his chest and arms flexed and pumped. He had two blue wolf-heads marked into his skin, one on each side of his chest. They moved when he moved.

Without a sound, a volley of arrows rained down from the sky.

"Shields up!" Harald cried out.

Bjorn crouched down and covered himself with his blue and yellow painted shield. An arrow thwacked into it and the *thunk* of arrows hitting shields and boards sounded up and down the boat. One man, still putting up his oar, took an arrow in his side. Other arrows fell harmlessly to the bottom of the boat or skidded on the water. Another volley followed close behind the first, filling the sky with the dark missiles. Another man went down.

Risking a peek, Bjorn saw they had nearly landed. Tryggvi and his men waited for them in a shield wall on the shore of the river, a solid wall of colored shields behind which stood men bristling with weapons. Spears stuck out from between and over the shields. Men thumped their shields with their weapons, and the loud rhythmic *thump, thump, thump* made Bjorn's stomach flip. He searched for archers in the tree line or on top of the houses but did not see any; that did not mean they were not there.

The boat slid onto the river sand as easily as a knife slicing into butter. Before it even came to a stop, Bjorn and the other warriors leaped over the sides, shields up, screaming battle cries. Another volley of arrows, but this time spears and other projectiles came with them. Several of Harald's men fell in the barrage, their blood spilling onto the muddy ground. A spear landed much too close to Bjorn, so close he felt it disturb the air.

"Shield wall!" Harald shouted over the screams, his deep growling voice designed for this purpose.

Amid splashes as they ran from the boat to shore, the men gathered to Harald and each other. An anguished cry flew from the mouth of the man running next to Bjorn as an arrow caught in the chest. With no mail or armor of any kind, he went down, his blood staining the water red.

Bjorn held his shield up, watchful for arrows, and ducked as one came at him.

"To me," Harald shouted. "Shield wall!"

They were too close for the archers now, who would join the other men behind the shield wall, and Bjorn raced to Harald and joined him at his left side. Ingvar was on Harald's right, his best man, protecting their leader's vulnerable spot. The men all gathered in close, shield overlapping shield, weapons out. Up close, Bjorn could hear and feel the heavy breathing of his comrades, feel their hearts racing in anticipation. Behind him, Galinn took up his place, his shield held over Bjorn's head to protect it. Men gathered, the heavy wooden shields *clunking* together to form a cocoon of protection. Galinn lifted his spear over Bjorn's shoulder and poked it through the shields in the front of the wall. It shook slightly and Bjorn frowned.

"Galinn. Hold your spear steady."

He heard Galinn suck in a breath, and his hand tightened on the spear. It steadied.

A body muscled in next to Bjorn. With a quick glance, Bjorn saw it was Styrr. The other man flashed him a quick grin, and he let out a laugh.

"This time we fight on the same side, boy," Styrr said, his face bruised where Bjorn had hit him.

Bjorn nodded, thinking of his own bruised face, but he forgot about it and his other hurts when he looked over the edge of his shield and took in the enemy. He gasped. The man opposite him, the one at Tryggvi Olafsson's right hand, was enormous, like a red-haired giant, and he held a long battle axe. It looked like it could reach for leagues in his long arms. Bjorn's insides turned to liquid and his breath came in quick gasps.

"Steady. We take him together," Styrr said. "He bleeds the same as us."

Bjorn felt Harald move. "Tryggvi is for me," he shouted to his men.

They held for what felt like ages, as Harald and Tryggvi stared at each other across the sand that divided them. Behind Harald and his men, the river; behind Tryggvi, the village he protected. Tryggvi and his men had much more to lose. If he fell, his village and all his women and children would be lost, raped, killed, or sold into slavery. All Bjorn and the rest of Harald's men had to lose was their lives. A small price to pay and they'd join the Allfather in Valhalla. If Bjorn died here fighting, he would go to his ancestors and would feast in Odin's great hall. All nervousness left him, and his spear felt light in his hand, his shield felt as if it were a part of his body, not heavy at all. He was ready.

Chapter Three

Bjorn stared at the huge man across from him, the one at Tryggvi's right hand. He couldn't see the man's eyes through his helm, but his mouth turned up in a slow grin as he saw Bjorn. Bile rose in his throat, fear of what the giant man could do to him. With a withering look and a slight snicker, the red-bearded man turned away from Bjorn and focused his gaze on Ingvar in his place next to Harald.

Harald and Ingvar exchanged words, but Bjorn couldn't hear them.

With a shout of 'attack' Harald's men moved, Bjorn keeping in step with Styrr by his side and Galinn at his back. He saw a shiver of movement course through Tryggvi's warriors, their spears, swords, and axes twitching in their hands.

Tryggvi shouted his own, "Hold!" The movement ceased, his men waiting in anticipation.

Tryggvi broke from the wall quickly, hefted his spear to his shoulder, and let out a cry of "For Odin!" as he threw it high and over the heads of Harald's army. Someone screamed behind Bjorn. Odin, the Corpse-Stealer, had claimed a man.

A barrage of flaming arrows flew over their heads toward Harald's longships. A scream from one of Harald's men who had stayed behind to defend the ships sounded through the air. Flames leaped from *Sea Wolf*, and the men left behind had to work to snuff out the fire. If not, they would be stuck with no way home.

Bjorn could give the ships no more thought. Then it happened.

"Attack!" Tryggvi shouted, and his warriors surged forward as one.

The air filled with war whoops and battle cries as both sides advanced toward each other, but both leaders held their men

together. A spear flew over Bjorn's head, right toward the red-bearded giant, and he caught it on his shield as if it weighed nothing. Arrows flew, but either flew too far or thwacked into upraised shields.

Harald snarled and howled. Bjorn followed, and his wolf howl tore at the air with his Brothers. The two shield walls continued to lumber toward one another, like great armored beasts.

The day had grown warm and some of the untrained men twitched and adjusted their weapons in their hands. A jittery farmer on the end of Tryggvi's line broke out with a battle cry and, armed only with a sharp hoe blade, raced toward Harald's shield wall. A throwing axe hit him in the chest. He fell, and both sides halted amid shouts and taunts. One more of Tryggvi's men gone.

The two shield walls stopped.

"Tryggvi," Harald shouted above the din. "My *brother*. This village. The land you stand on. Your women. They belong to me now. They have always belonged to me."

"I see your mouth move, Harald, but all I hear is the squealing of a sow. You will get no farther than where we stand now. No women will be yours today. No riches."

"There is only one woman I want. That is Ingiborg. She was meant for me. I will take her right in front of your eyes. Would you like that, brother?" Harald shouted loud enough for his men to hear. They laughed.

The men surrounding Emund shouted out insults to Harald.

Tryggvi waved his sword in front of him, dismissing Harald's words. With a laugh, he shouted. "You call yourself a wolf and wear the wolf's skin as your own. But you are nothing more than an *argr*."

This time it was Tryggvi's men's turn to laugh while Harald's men grew agitated and their hands twitched on their weapons, the entire shield wall vibrating with their movement, like an animal. To be called an *argr* was to diminish your opponent's manhood.

Harald pointed his sword at Tryggvi. "I will cut off your balls for that. I will make you watch while I cut your sons to pieces and have my men rape your daughters. If they survive, I will sell them into slavery."

"You threaten my children because you are too much of a *mare* to father sons of your own. Where are your sons, Harald?"

"Enough of this talk, brother. Come and meet me." Harald adjusted his shield into place and raised his sword.

Tryggvi did the same, and the two leaders stepped into the breach. They circled one another. Their men waited for the first strike. It came from Tryggvi. He jabbed his spear at Harald, who deftly caught it on his shield.

At the first strike, the other men took up their weapons and attacked.

Yelling, "Harald!" Bjorn rushed into the men opposite him, the fear gone as soon as his feet moved.

The giant barreled right toward him and Styrr, crashing into them with his shield. The breath left Bjorn's body at the glancing blow, and he fell back onto his heels. He and Styrr righted themselves quickly, and Styrr swung at the red-giant with his axe. The other man absorbed the blow easily on his shield.

Seeing a chance, Bjorn approached at his right, his spear thrusting for red's unprotected leg. The other man jumped back to avoid it.

The fighting raged, the sounds of men screaming and dying, the clang of swords, axes, and spears as they met in combat, and the smell of blood and bodily fluids as the frightened and dying men lost control of themselves. The heat roasted them and sweat ran down Bjorn's back. But he was not tired. His body felt like he walked on air, his spear and shield light in his arms. By his side, Styrr showed no signs of relenting either, and they kept besieging the giant red-beard.

When Bjorn came in high with his spear to the other man's throat, he deflected it and kicked Bjorn in the chest, sending him sprawling backward. He felt something crack, the air knocked out of him, a searing pain like someone had stabbed him. Spots danced before his eyes.

Red roared and swung his axe at Styrr's head. Styrr deflected it with his shield, but the red-beard's strength was too much, knocking Styrr to his knees. He swung again, the force so great Styrr screamed out in pain.

With a great effort, his ribs shrieking in pain, Bjorn lunged at him with his spear. The big man jumped aside, but not before Bjorn's spear pierced through skin. It was not deep, and Red leaped forward and smashed his shield into Bjorn's, sending him careening into Galinn.

The red-giant loomed over Bjorn and Galinn, his face red with effort, sweat running down into his beard. His green eyes glittered with menace, and Bjorn knew this was the last thing he'd ever see.

"Red!" Ingvar shouted, and the red-beard turned to face him. Ingvar had blood spatter on his face, his brown eyes burning out brightly from the gore.

"'Bout time. I was getting tired of playing with the children." He adjusted the shield in his hand and lifted his battle axe in readiness.

At the moment Red's attention turned to Ingvar, Galinn gathered Bjorn and hustled him away to the edge of the fighting to regroup. Bjorn's body felt like he'd been mauled by a troll, the spot where the red giant kicked him ached so bad it hurt to breathe.

Bent over, hands on knees, Bjorn tried to catch his breath. It came out in difficult, short breaths, every movement painful. "Where is Styrr? Did the giant kill him?"

"I don't know."

The timbre of Galinn's voice alerted Bjorn. He cocked his head toward his friend. Galinn looked like the undead, pale and sickly, and he swayed on his feet.

Remembering how Galinn's spear had wavered in the shield wall, Bjorn said, "You are ill. Get back to the boat."

"No."

"You can't fight like this."

"I have to. I—" The battle cry of one of Tryggvi's warriors cut him off. The man screamed and rushed at Bjorn and Galinn with his spear out.

Bjorn scrambled to right himself, the pain in his hip and the new one in his chest making him stumble. When he met the eyes of this new threat, he couldn't believe his luck. He looked like Tryggvi Olafsson, only younger. A son. Bjorn's heart did a flip; Harald would reward him richly for killing Tryggvi's son.

"You think you will take this land from my father. Instead, *your* blood will spill," the young Tryggvi shouted.

Eyes gleaming, Bjorn grasped onto his axe. But before he could move, Galinn stepped in between him and the young Tryggvason.

"No," Bjorn shouted at his friend.

Tryggvi's son thrust his spear at Galinn, who deflected it with his shield. But in Galinn's weakened state, the movement of the heavy shield made him stumble and it sagged at his side. Tryggvi's son did not hesitate. As soon as he saw the opening, he jabbed his spear into Galinn's exposed belly. Galinn's eyes widened at the shock and he dropped to his knees.

Tryggvi's son let out a howl of victory.

"Galinn," Bjorn cried as his friend crumpled to the sand before him, his axe dropping out of his hand as he grasped onto the wound in his stomach.

Bjorn turned to Tryggvi's son, and his eyes misted over in a cloud of fury. He attacked with no understanding of what he did or where he struck. He struck blindly, savagely, the rage for his friend fueling him. But Tryggvi's son met each strike with his own fury-filled blows. If Bjorn had a body, he could not feel it. He was his weapon and his shield, striking and deflecting, nothing more. He felt no pain. He had no mind. He was a wolf, tearing into his prey without a thought. His only instinct—to kill the man before him.

And then the man vanished.

Panting from the fight, sweat trickling down his back, Bjorn blinked and watched as Tryggvi's son ran back to the main fray. It was only then he heard the cry of 'to me' rise from both camps.

He ignored it and rushed to Galinn's side, propping his shield next to them for protection. Galinn lay curled on the sand, but his eyes were open, and his chest rose and fell. His blood stained the ground.

"Galinn." Bjorn moved Galinn's hands away from the wound and sucked in a breath. The wound was deep, and the putrid smell of insides leaked out.

"I know I'm going to die," Galinn whispered.

A knot formed in Bjorn's throat and he could barely breathe, but he gave Galinn a bright smile. "It's not that bad."

Galinn chuckled, then grimaced. "You're a liar, Brother."

A flash of the day they'd become blood-brothers raced through Bjorn's mind. The smell of their combined blood as it dripped and soaked into the ground, the smell of the turf as they put it back into place over the blood.

"We are bound by blood, Brother," Bjorn said. "No matter what happens, we will see each other again."

The shout of 'to me' rose again over the din. Bjorn cocked his head to listen to the sounds of battle. His body churned with confusion. He needed to take up the fight but did not want to leave his friend.

"You have to go," Galinn wheezed.

Bjorn found what he needed. Galinn's axe lay nearby. He took one of Galinn's hands and slipped his axe into it, wrapping his friend's fingers around the handle. "I'll be back."

Fed by rage, Bjorn hefted his shield again and rushed back to the main battle.

As he ran, he spotted an archer taking aim at him, and he quickly dropped to his knee and held up his shield. The arrow hit the wood harmlessly. He thought of Galinn, lying helpless in the sand, easy to pick off. His only hope, that Galinn looked too dead for an archer to waste an arrow on. He limped from the pain, his breath coming out in ragged bursts, pain from his chest on each breath making his head spin.

The ground grew slick with blood and gore the closer he got to where Harald and Tryggvi fought. The bodies of men lay sprawled on the ground, their eyes lifeless, their faces permanently frozen in their death throes. Bile rose in Bjorn's throat, but he swallowed it down. His head burned with heat inside the iron helm.

A scream tore the air near to him, and he saw Ingvar brought to his knees by the red-giant. Blood poured from Ingvar's side and the red-giant loomed over him, his axe raised, his face covered in blood, the whites of his eyes blazing through the gore. Bjorn froze in place as he watched the big man cleave Ingvar's head in two with his battle axe. Ingvar's body slumped to the ground.

Without a thought, Bjorn rushed at the big man to avenge Ingvar, but he had turned toward the fight between Harald and Tryggvi. Bjorn staggered to join his comrades who formed behind Harald. Styrr's was still alive, bloodied and bruised. His shield was gone, and he held his swollen and bruised left arm close to his body.

Coming to a stop, Bjorn gaped at the spectacle of Harald and Tryggvi fighting. By now, the two warlords had been fighting hard for a long time. Harald's shield lay in two pieces on the blood-soaked ground, but he had taken off his wolf-pelt and held it in his left hand, flinging it out every time Tryggvi struck at him. Circling one another to find an opening, both men staggered with each step, their hatred the only thing holding them up. Both bled from many wounds on their arms and legs. Tryggvi struck at Harald who wrapped up Tryggvi's sword in his wolf-pelt and tried to pull it out of his hand.

Without warning, the young man who had escaped the village they'd attacked, rushed out of nowhere, a spear in his hand, and screamed, "For my father!" Aiming for Harald's chest, the boy missed and hit him in the arm instead. It pierced deep and Harald bellowed in pain. As he fell backward, he yanked on the wolf pelt and Tryggvi's sword dropped from his hand with a crack and a howl of pain. One of Harald's men charged at the young man, but the red-giant leaped in front of him and deflected the blow.

The distraction was all Tryggvi needed. With the last of his energy, he smashed Harald in the head with his shield, the crack echoing over the men. Harald crumpled to the ground. Tryggvi reeled back, the effort of that last strike too much for him. He dropped his shield, his weakened arm no longer able to hold it up. One of Tryggvi's men grabbed hold of him and pulled him back behind a line of shielded men. Another grabbed Tryggvi's dropped sword and quickly retreated.

Bjorn watched his foster-father fall in disbelief. And then the hot fury overtook him, and he turned to Tryggvi's men and snarled. One wolf might be down, but they had another wolf to contend with.

Tryggvi's men shouted and rushed at Harald's men.

"Bjorn," Styrr shouted, and a firm hand gripped Bjorn's arm before he could run to meet Tryggvi's men. "Help me with Harald."

Bjorn turned on Styrr and growled at him, but Styrr did not let go. "Help me get him to the boat. He is not dead."

The clash of steel and the shouts of men rang out, and Bjorn saw the red-giant fight his way to Harald's prone body. With a battle cry that nearly tore his aching ribs in two, Bjorn ran to protect his foster-father, Styrr by his side. Their fury and the onslaught of their weapons kept the big man at bay...barely. More of Harald's men joined them and held off the red-giant while Bjorn grabbed Harald under the arms and tried to drag him toward the river and safety. Harald's body was wet with blood and sweat and Bjorn couldn't move him. Sharp pain shot through his chest, and he crumpled to his knees. More men jumped in to protect their leader, and Styrr grabbed one of Harald's arms with his one uninjured hand.

"Bjorn," Styrr said.

A last jolt of energy sped through Bjorn's body and with Styrr's help, they pulled Harald with excruciating slowness toward *Sea Wolf*.

The smell of water and earth alerted Bjorn that they were almost there. He could hear the soft lapping of the water against the boat. The softness of the sound was at odds with the violent clashes. Frigid water rushed around his ankles, water that had turned red in the fighting. The men who had stayed behind to safeguard the boats leaped over the side and took Harald's body from Bjorn and Styrr and hauled it to safety. A horn sounded their retreat and Harald's men fought their way back to the boats.

"Galinn," Bjorn said. He could not leave. Before anyone could stop him, Bjorn ran back to the spot where Galinn still lay. No one noticed him as they were all fighting near the boats.

Skidding to a stop at Galinn's side, Bjorn dropped to his knee. Galinn's blood had stained the sand under him, and his face looked waxy and pale.

"Galinn," Bjorn said, although he knew his friend would not answer. He gave a relieved sigh when he saw Galinn still gripped his battle axe. He removed it along with Galinn's small silver arm ring and the copper Tyr amulet he wore around his neck. Tryggvi's men would get no booty from him.

He laid a bruised hand on Galinn's quiet chest. "We will meet again in Valhalla, my Brother. Save me a seat and the prettiest Valkyrie. You know I always get the prettiest ones."

A horn sounded twice. Harald's men were leaving. If Bjorn did not move quickly, they would leave him behind.

Reluctantly leaving Galinn's side, Bjorn hefted his shield, which felt as heavy as stone, and ran back to *Sea Wolf*, limping from the pain in his hip and gasping for every breath.

Astrid's hands slowly worked through one side of Gytha's hair, braiding it to the tip and then undoing it and starting again. She wiped sweat off her forehead and did the same for Gytha. The dark cave scared Gytha, and Astrid had soothed her by braiding her hair until her sister fell asleep. Doing something with her hands calmed Astrid, and she wished she could sleep, but every time she closed her eyes, all she could see was her father and Emund as they ran off to battle. Burning tears threatened to leak from her eyes again, and she squeezed them shut.

A baby cried in the dark, followed by the soothing coo of a mother's voice and the sound of suckling as she put it to her breast.

The voices were all hushed and soft. Astrid could hear her mother as she talked to Old Stieg and the other women, but she could not make out what they said. Fear filled the cave, smothering them all as if they lay under a heavy blanket. Even the goats, sheep, and cattle they saved from the village remained quiet. The smell of animals and droppings mixed with sweaty human bodies made the enclosed space of the cave unbearable. But Astrid knew it was the safest place to be.

When she opened her eyes, she saw a brief flash of Rikki's dagger in the dim candlelight as he twirled it in his hand. He still held it in case the stone at the cave's entrance moved. He had taken his father's last words to protect the women seriously and sat alert, watching and waiting. But what a boy twelve winters old could do against a full-grown warrior, Astrid did not want to think about. Unwanted, she recalled the feeling of the strong hands of the outlaw who had kidnapped her four summers before. If her father and Emund fell in their attempt to protect the village from Harald Olafsson, Astrid knew this would be her fate, dragged off by her father's enemy. Only this time there would be no one to save her.

"Rikki," she whispered.

"*Ja?*"

"How long has it been?"

Astrid felt him move next to her, and she could smell the day's sweat and dirt on him. His shoes scraped on the dirt floor. She thought of him practicing sword fighting earlier in the day, how important that practice was. And how futile. The image of her father and his men fully armed brought home to her how young and small Rikki was, and how poorly equipped he'd be to protect her and her sister

"It must be well after midday. The oil lamp has nearly burnt out." He ran his hand along his knife. "I wish I was fighting with *fadir*." His arm grew tight as he gripped his knife.

"Wouldn't you be scared?"

"Were you scared when that outlaw took you?" Rikki asked. They had not spoken of that in a long time, and it surprised her when he brought it up.

"Yes." She could barely breathe with the thought of that day. She didn't want to talk about it or even think about it here while they were hiding from raiders.

"But you fought him, Gunnar told me you did. He said you were trying to get away when he found you. You were scared, but you fought anyway."

"Fighting didn't help. If Gunnar hadn't come, the outlaw would have..." She took a breath, her entire body quivering with the past fear. "Taken me and sold me."

"It did help. If you hadn't fought, Gunnar never would have found you. Harald is like that outlaw, trying to take something from us. I want to fight him. Can't you understand that?"

Astrid sighed. "I understand. But you are just a boy. Do you really think you could fight someone like Father? Or Emund?" Emund towered over most grown men, and a young man like Rikki would not stand a chance against someone like him. "They would surely kill you. I don't want you to die!" The heat and darkness felt stifling. The thought of her brother dying made it worse, like she would suffocate.

"Thank you for your confidence in me, *systir*," Rikki said through gritted teeth. He got to his feet and made his way along the wall away from her, among quiet complaints as he accidently tripped over legs and small children sprawled on the ground.

She heard him whisper, "Galm," and then the equally quiet reply. No doubt they would complain about Astrid's lack of belief in their fighting skills, telling each other they were not children and could hold their own.

The jostling made Gytha move in her sleep. Astrid stroked her sister's sweaty hair and lay down next to her, closed her eyes, and tried to sleep.

The indistinct murmur of voices, the slow breathing of her sister, and the warmth of the cave all lulled Astrid into sleep. Like before, as soon as she drifted off she saw an image of her father fully armed running away from her, Emund at his side. Their backs morphed and turned into the outlaw who had abducted her, with his leering smile and talk of selling her for silver. In her half-sleep she heard and felt every movement and sound in the cave. Her breath quickened, and she held onto Gytha as if holding a lifeline. She thought of her cat, Kis-Kis and hoped that she would be safe, that she knew to keep herself away from the fighting. Her imagination ran away with her, and she saw her father and Emund fall in their fight with Harald, Harald's men racing into the woods to find the treasure and the women and children.

With a cry, Astrid sat up, blinking to see in the dark cave. The movement disturbed Gytha and she, too, awoke with a start.

"I am right here, girls." Strong, but gentle arms wrapped around the two girls and their mother's scent enveloped them. She always smelled of the herbs she used in her healing salves, a scent both sweet and bitter. Her mother's whisper betrayed no emotion.

"I don't like it in here," Gytha whined. "When will Father come for us?"

Ingiborg's body grew rigid at the mention of Tryggvi. "I do not know. We must be patient."

In the firelight, Astrid watched as Gytha set her rag doll on their mother's lap and made her dance around. The image reflected a shadow on the cave wall that grew to a grotesque and menacing height. To Astrid it looked like an undead *draugr* dancing over the bodies he'd killed; she averted her gaze and reminded herself it was a harmless doll.

"It is so hard," Astrid said.

"It is." Ingiborg rubbed Astrid's back. "Waiting here is the hardest, the not knowing what happens out there. Not knowing what we will find when we emerge." Astrid felt her mother take in a deep breath, but it was shaky, before she continued, "I trust your father and his men. He has never failed to protect us."

"I wish I could do something." Astrid worried her bottom lip. "Why do Father and Harald fight? They are brothers."

"They have hated each other for as long as I have known them. As the older brother, Harald thought he should have been the jarl, should have married..." Her voice hesitated as if she were holding something back. "Now they fight because they have been fighting for so long they don't know what else to do."

"Ingiborg," Old Stieg said. "It has been too long. The battle should have been decided by now."

"We cannot know that."

"We should gather all the weapons we have. Be ready," he said in his scratchy voice.

"For what? Will *you* fight them? Our young boys? You will prepare them for their slaughter."

"Better for them to die with a weapon in their hands than to die cowering in the dark," he quipped.

Gytha put her hands to her ears and cried. Astrid wanted to do the same. Instead of crying, she shushed her sister.

"He is right, *modir*." Rikki. They had not heard him approach over Gytha's crying.

"We will fight," Short Olaf said.

"*Ja*," echoed Galm.

Astrid saw that the boys stood with her brother, all three of them holding their daggers in one hand and spears in the other, their eyes burning with the desire to prove themselves.

Ingiborg looked at her son and his two young friends, future warriors if they got the chance. Astrid watched as her mother's expression changed from refusal to acceptance.

Ingiborg rubbed her eyes and nodded. "Yes." She turned to the old man and told him to gather anyone who could wield a weapon.

The women and children gathered together as far from the entrance to the cave as possible and the remaining men, boys, and a few women sat in readiness at the entrance, forming a barrier.

Chapter Four

A large swollen bruise had formed on Harald's head where Tryggvi's shield had hit him, and though he was unconscious, he still breathed. They had settled him in the bottom of *Sea Wolf* with little ceremony, as they had to fight to keep Tryggvi's men from overtaking the boat. After some initial fierce fighting, their enemies had to give up as Harald's men rowed away from the riverbank. One of Tryggvi's men tried to climb over the side to get at Harald, but several of Harald's guard swarmed and hacked at him before throwing him overboard.

Bjorn left one farmer bleeding in the river from a blow to his shoulder. It had not killed him or even taken off his arm, but it was enough to send him reeling backward away from the boat. As soon as he had dispatched the man, Bjorn rushed to his spot and took up his oar. He let out a yelp, the pain in his chest so bad with each pull it felt like something was stabbing him. The men on Harald's other longship did the same, and Bjorn watched the water churn under the impact of dozens of feet. Bloody men with their blood-soaked weapons scurried up onto the boat, some hacking at enemies as they did so.

A heavy thud behind him made Bjorn turn around, expecting to see Galinn at his place. A lump formed in his throat when he saw it was not Galinn.

An image of Galinn's dead body lying on the sand formed in Bjorn's head, and he desperately wanted his friend to come leaping over the side of the boat when he heard the steersman shout. Through excruciating pain in his chest, Bjorn pulled his oar and the dragon ship moved away from the shore. A sickening taste rose in his mouth when he saw Tryggvi's men lift their weapons in the air and shout curses at them. Someone threw a spear that landed harmlessly in the water short of the

boat. He hated fleeing like this, but their leader was down, and they could not sustain any more losses. The weight of Galinn's Tyr amulet necklace and his arm ring lay heavy against Bjorn's skin.

A fire arrow struck near Bjorn's feet, but there was too much water in the bottom of the boat and the fire extinguished itself before it even started. More arrows landed around them, one hitting a warrior, making his oar stutter, and the boat lurched. He was only hit in the arm and continued to row, blood turning the water in the boat's bottom pink.

They rowed until they emerged where the river let out into the sea. The sound of waves crashing against the shore was a welcome one, and once they reached a safe place, they dropped anchor. Bjorn shipped his oar before collapsing against the side of the boat. After taking a few painful breaths, he slowly got up and limped back to where they had laid Harald. Two of the men pulled a tarp up to form a shelter to protect Harald from the elements. Another of the guard sprawled next to him with a long, deep gash in his leg, the bandage soaked through with blood and dirt. Fresh blood dripped from the wound, and the man looked in danger of bleeding to death. Bjorn shivered, for if the man died on the boat, they might throw him over as an offering to Ran. Bjorn hoped for his sake that he held out until they got closer to home.

Bjorn joined Styrr at Harald's side. Styrr had attached a cloth that looped around his neck to hold his arm close to his body. Out of habit, Bjorn looked for Ingvar by Harald's side, but he remembered seeing Ingvar's head being cleaved in two. He staggered to the side of the boat and grasped onto the wood so hard it turned his knuckles white while breathing in the salty air to steady himself.

"Bjorn," Styrr called after a while.

He turned back to Harald and winced at the movement, every little ache and pain in his body asserting itself now the fighting was over.

Harald's blue eyes were partly open and looking at Bjorn. That ice-blue stare had so often disconcerted him, but now he found it reassuring. Harald could not die.

"Bjorn," Harald said in a pained whisper.

Trying not to show his own pain, Bjorn knelt by Harald's side, the damp boards cold against his knee.

"*Tak*," Harald said.

Bjorn raised his eyebrows in question.

"Styrr..." Harald squeezed his eyes shut and took a breath. He opened them again. "Styrr said you pulled me to safety."

Bjorn nodded.

"I will not forget that." Harald raised his hand and touched the sore spot. It was swollen and an angry deep purple bruise covered his temple and traveled down to his eye. He winced when his hand touched the tender spot.

"Help me up."

Taking a firm grasp of Harald's arm and with Styrr on the other side, they helped Harald to a sitting position. When he sat up, his eyes fluttered as if they could not focus. The black parts of his eyes were enormous, like a black moon covered up the blue. Harald moaned and weakly pushed Bjorn to the side before throwing up.

"You should lie down," Bjorn told him.

"No." He looked down at the spear wound on his arm and gingerly moved it up and down. He winced, but then flexed his hand. "It will heal. So will my head."

"Where was your helm?" Styrr asked.

"Knocked off..." he took a slow breath when a wave of pain hit him, "when Tryggvi and I got close. I almost got my sword into his belly, but he moved away too quickly. I have forgotten how quick my brother is."

"Let me get you some ale," Bjorn said, and he got to his feet. As soon as he put weight on his leg, he stumbled. He sucked in a breath, but that sent a stab of pain into his chest. The pain made him hunch over, hands wrapped around himself. He waited for the pain to subside and then staggered to the ale barrel, stepping over several men on the way. Several moaned with pain. Others tended to their wounds.

Bjorn passed Galinn's sea chest, and he stopped short. His friend should be sitting on it or rummaging through it looking for his favorite *tafl* set. Bjorn knelt by the chest and opened it. There on the top was Galinn's tafl set, the square board and wooden pieces where he had placed it after their last game. Bjorn could beat Galinn at all the athletic and fighting competitions, and always got the best girls, but Galinn won at tafl. Bjorn picked up the little wooden pieces and put one of his light pieces in the middle and surrounded it with the dark ones.

"You win, my friend," he whispered. He thought of his friend already feasting and fighting in Valhalla, and he smiled. "We always said we'd go out fighting, and you did. I will miss you."

Leaving the pieces on the board, he closed the lid and went to get a cup of ale for Harald. They had to regroup and recover. They would meet Tryggvi again. When they did, he would find the son of Tryggvi who killed Galinn.

And he would kill him.

Astrid and the others sat for what felt like the entire day, fear of who might find them choking them into silence. Even the babies were quiet. Ingiborg waited with the rest of the women, her arms around both Astrid and Gytha, her body tense.

When the stone that barred the entrance finally moved, a sense of relief flooded the cave. What they waited for was coming to pass. Good or bad.

After being in the dark for so long, the sunlight nearly blinded the men waiting with their weapons. They stumbled back and threw their hands up over their eyes. Astrid had forgotten there was light anywhere.

"A fine lot you are," a familiar voice bellowed, but the joking banter sounded forced.

"Emund!" Astrid shouted, but her cries disappeared in the general tumult. She jumped up and worked her way through the crowd of expectant wives and mothers. A wail of despair rose from one woman, and she fell to the ground. Astrid hesitated, not wanting to move forward for fear of what she'd find out. That woman's husband or son was dead. A lump formed in Astrid's throat. What if her father had been killed? What if Jori had been killed?

Her mother touched her shoulder. "Come, Asta. We have to meet whatever waits for us."

Propelled by her mother's strength, Astrid continued on. When she neared the front of the cave, Astrid stopped short again. Emund was covered in gore, his usually pale face so dark that his bright green eyes shined out of the murk like candles in the darkness. One side of his lip puffed up, and he had a cut on his forehead. Blood soaked a leg of his trousers at the knee, and he moved carefully. His red hair was black with sweat and blood and hung limply on his head. The sharp smell of blood wafted off him and all the men. Someone gagged at the smell. A woman with a baby in her arms, tears rolling down her face, rushed by Astrid and threw her arm around her farmer husband. He did not respond to her, but stood inert and accepted the embrace, his hand still holding onto the bloody scythe he had used as a weapon.

Emund saw Astrid's hesitance and knelt. She stepped back, and her eyes took in all the blood spatter and dirt. When the men came home from raiding, they were dirty and grubby, but they had cleaned off the gore that came from hard fighting.

"It's not my blood, Asta." He touched his face and looked at the blood on his fingers. "Well, at least not all of it." He smiled and then grimaced as it pulled at his swollen lip. He reached out a hand to her, but she recoiled from him and backed into her mother. The softness of her mother comforted her, and Ingiborg rested her hand on Astrid's shoulder.

"Were you brave, little bear?" Emund asked as he brought his bruised and cut hand back to rest on his knee.

"She was very brave," Ingiborg answered for her.

Astrid stared at Emund. No matter how scary he looked, he was still her Red-Beard. "I was scared for you," she whispered.

"For me? It will take more than Harald and his band of puny men to kill your Red-Beard," Emund boasted. He lifted his gaze to Ingiborg.

"Tryggvi?" Ingiborg asked, her voice trembling, and her hand tensed on Astrid's shoulder.

"He is alive…"

"Thank the goddess," Ingiborg breathed out.

"But he is hurt. He and Harald fought hard for a long time. Gunnar—"

He did not finish before Ingiborg jumped in, "Where is he?"

At that moment Rikki ran up. "Red. Where is Father?" He was breathless and red-faced from searching for their father. "Buri said he is bad hurt."

"Come with me," Emund answered.

They did not have to go far, for as soon as they emerged from the cave, Tryggvi staggered toward them, aided by Jori and Gunnar. Tryggvi looked worse than Emund, unable even to walk on his own. A huge purple and black bruise bloomed on his face and one eye was mostly closed shut. Someone had wrapped his right hand up in cloth, holding the fingers together. Above that, his arm swelled. Like Emund, he was covered in blood and dirt, his normally reddish-blond hair dark with sweat.

"Father." Rikki dashed to him.

Tryggvi managed a smile for Rikki. "Son." He looked up at Ingiborg, Astrid, and Gytha. "I see you kept our women safe."

Astrid frowned. Rikki hadn't kept them safe. Her father, Emund, Jori, Gunnar and all the other men had done that. She heard one of the women sobbing softly and turned to see Thorkell the Steersman's wife cry into her son's arms. The men had kept the women and children safe, but at a cost. Tears burned Astrid's eyes with the thought she would never again see Thorkell at their house talking to her father about the weather to determine when it was best to sail out. She liked the way Thorkell joked with her and Rikki, and now he was gone. She heard Thorkell's son tell his mother that his father died fighting. Looking back at her father, Astrid thought that to die fighting was a comfort to the men, but not to the women they left behind. While Thorkell the Steersman feasted in Valhalla, Thorkell's wife had to continue to live. Their daughter, Ragnhild, a girl two winters older than Astrid, and her friend, joined her mother and brothers as they comforted each other.

But it was not that way with all the women. One farmer's wife, whose husband had picked up his scythe to help Jarl Tryggvi protect the village, did not shed a tear when she heard her husband had been killed. Astrid remembered how the husband always barked orders to his wife and grabbed her roughly. The first time Astrid had seen it, she'd asked her mother why the farmer was so mean. Her father always handled Ingiborg gently, and Emund was always been tender with the children, so she did not understand the farmer's rough ways. Her mother had told her that some men and women were angry and their lives harsh, so they did not treat each other well.

Tryggvi indicated for Jori and Gunnar to help him up onto a rock. With their help, he stood before his men and their women and addressed Thorkell's wife. His voice was weak but still carried authority. "Do not cry for your husband. Thorkell fought bravely. With his axe, he took out many of the enemy before the Allfather took him home. He will feast with the gods and the ancestors tonight."

"We must thank the Allfather," Tryggvi continued. "We owe our victory to him. We sent the cowards running! We need not fear Harald Olafsson for a long time." Although he looked near to collapse, Tryggvi kept himself standing before his people.

Tryggvi took in a raggedy breath and, with the last of his energy, made one more announcement. "Tomorrow we will feast to honor our dead."

Astrid watched her father as he talked to his people, and she saw that they trusted him and knew he would take care of them. They would follow him anywhere. Even injured to near collapse, dirty and blood-spattered, he exuded confidence and authority.

He nodded to Jori and Gunnar to help him down from the rock, and Ingiborg rushed to his side. When her mother took her place by Tryggvi's side, Astrid made a vow to herself that she would settle for no less than a man as strong and brave as her father.

Chapter Five

Four years later. Harald's village, Ulfdalr.

It was late in the season, the barley recently harvested and stacked and drying in the outlying buildings, when Bjorn stopped outside Harald's longhouse to enjoy the last of the colors, the russet, orange, and saffron of the dying leaves. He took in a breath, the earthy smell of the barley mixing with the clean breeze from the sea. The air was brisk, the sky a brilliant blue, and no sign of snow. Good weather for sailing.

As he stood outside Harald's longhouse, he heard a little boy's excited squeal. Bjorn smiled.

When he stepped inside, he caught sight of the cause of the squealing. A boy with shaggy blond hair sped through the house, avoiding benches, chairs, and the thralls who prepared the evening meal. Harald's wife Sigrun's sharp voice carried through the house as she chastised the thrall who ground the grain. The night before Harald had bitten into his bread and caught a tooth on a barley seed that had not been ground well.

"If we so much as chip a tooth on your grain, I will have your own teeth removed," Sigrun threatened.

The thrall's face paled as he nodded.

The little boy jumped onto a sleeping pallet and then off again, almost crashing into Sigrun. She tried to grab his arm, but the boy got away and, spying Bjorn at the door, ran, a gleeful smile on his face, right into the arms of his father.

Bjorn knelt on a gray knotted wool rug, his knees sinking into the soft pile, and caught him. The momentum made them both spill over onto the rug, Bjorn hugging the boy to his body. His son Tanni shrieked with laughter. "Again, Papa!"

Bjorn released him and Tanni ran another circuit of the large house, his shouts making Sigrun wrinkle her nose with distaste. This time Bjorn caught him in his arms and threw Tanni into the air. The boy squealed with glee, his hazel eyes wide and bright. Bjorn tucked Tanni into his arm and gave him a hug.

Tanni struggled to get down, and with a sigh, Bjorn set him on his little feet. He liked holding the boy, and enjoyed the feeling of trust that his son, who had been born nearly four winters before, had in him. No matter what, Tanni always believed his father would be there to catch him.

Sigrun approached them. "Bjorn." She looked at him like she always did, like she'd eaten some spoiled meat. He'd been a part of Harald's household for ten winters, and she still hated him as much as the day he arrived. "I don't want him under foot all the time while you are away. Tell your thrall woman to care for him. He is her son, isn't he?" Her voice was cutting, like always.

Tanni spent most of his time in Harald's household, where there were more people and much more activity than in his own house. Like his father, Tanni enjoyed all physical activities and there was usually something going on with the men in Harald's longhouse.

"Yes." Bjorn straightened up. "Maude is his mother, but she is not a thrall. Not anymore."

Sigrun waved that away as if it did not matter. It mattered to Bjorn. Not being a thrall meant he could protect Maude, that the men in Harald's household could not abuse or rape her without impunity.

Ignoring the tension, Tanni tugged at Bjorn's hand. "See what I did."

Glad for the interruption, Bjorn shot Sigrun a look saying she would not rule him. He knew she had convinced her daughter to not marry him four summers ago, and his beloved Hilda was married to an old man and constantly with child. Her shining green eyes that had once looked at him with so much love, were now dull, and when she looked at him, it was with pain and longing of what could have been.

Allowing himself to be pulled along, Bjorn followed his son. They left the house and stepped out into the yard as a brisk breeze blew in from the sea. Bjorn could taste the tang of salt in the air.

The boy was intent on what he wanted to show his father. "Come see."

They rounded the corner of the house and there, tethered to a bench by a lead, was Bjorn's favorite hound, Floki. When the dog spied his master he whined, thumped his tail, and tried to go to him, but his lead held him back. Bjorn laughed at the sight of the dog. Little Tanni had wrapped him in one of Bjorn's old leather armor vests. The vest kept slipping and the dog bit at it in annoyance.

"Floki is a warrior dog!" Tanni said with pride.

"I see that." Bjorn bit his lip. He did not know what to say. The dog was clearly miserable tied up and encumbered by the leather, but Tanni was so proud of it, Bjorn did not want to make him take it off.

"How did you catch Floki?" The dog usually steered clear of the boy.

"Vefinn helped me."

"Ah..."

Bjorn knelt in front of Floki, who nudged and licked his hand. He was petting the dog when Tanni leaned up against him. The contact made Bjorn's heart flip over.

Changing the subject, Tanni commented, "Mama will have a baby."

"*Ja.*" Maude was large with child again, her time near due. They would have another child by Yule.

Bjorn pulled his son up onto his knee and the dog licked him, making the boy giggle. "She will have a brother or sister for you."

"Brother."

"It might be a sister."

Tanni crinkled up his nose. "Brother."

Bjorn thought of his own brother, taken or killed in a raid when Bjorn was a young boy, before he came to foster with Harald. His memory of the boy was like wisps of smoke. Now when he thought of brothers, he thought of the conflict between Harald and his brother Tryggvi. He vowed to never let that happen to his sons. If he had another son.

With a shiver, Tanni said, "Cold."

Bjorn wrapped his arms around the boy and squeezed him. "Better?"

Tanni nodded, but he still fidgeted.

"We need to release Floki. He does not like to be tied up." Before Tanni could argue, Bjorn added, "You can help me."

They untied the lead together, Bjorn helping Tanni's little fingers work the knot, and then they removed the leather armor from the dog's back. As soon as he felt the leather slip from his back, Floki yipped a triumphant bark and shot away from them as quickly as his old legs would go, kicking up dust as he went. He had to skirt two big human legs to get away.

"Papa Harald," Tanni yelled.

Harald approached the longhouse, his worn looking mistress by his side. He had been with her since the spring, and she still hadn't quickened with child. He ignored her like he tired of her. When he shooed her away, she hurried off.

With a snort of derision, Harald said. "She bleeds again. She's no use to me. I'll give her to one of the men."

Bjorn was glad Harald had freed Maude when she grew heavy with his child. She was pretty, desirable, and Bjorn did not want her ruined by Harald's interest. He said nothing to his foster-father about the bleeding woman, feeling pity for her.

"Are you ready? We leave at first light." Harald eyed Tanni, ruffling the boys' hair as he talked.

"I am." Bjorn gritted his teeth.

Harald inclined his head toward the boy. "I thought you might want to stay home with the women and children." He said it as a joke, but Bjorn heard the displeasure in his voice.

"What you plan is important. If we can gain King Ingjald's favor, then we can destroy Tryggvi and his sons." Bjorn thought back to the son of Tryggvi who had killed his Galinn, and all the old anger rushed through him.

Harald clapped him on the back. "Good." He looked at the house. "When you marry, make sure it is a woman who can manage the household while you are away. But not so much that she thinks she can control you. My first wife thought she could rule me." His voice dropped dangerously low. "She was wrong."

With that he swooped into his longhouse, calling out, "Wife." When the door closed Bjorn was glad he was not summoned inside.

A small hand tugged at his tunic. Kneeling, Bjorn took his son's hand and turned sideways to offer his back. "Climb on."

With light feet that barely dug into Bjorn's thigh, Tanni climbed onto his father's back and wrapped his hands around his neck. Bjorn took hold of Tanni's small legs, which were losing their baby fat. "Hold on tight." He felt his son's hands tighten on his neck. He ran.

"Faster!" Tanni cried out, his joyful child-voice ringing in Bjorn's ear. He kicked Bjorn's stomach like he was spurring a horse.

A smile lit up Bjorn's face. If faster was what his son wanted, he'd get faster. The boy weighed less than a shield, and he could run with him on his strong back for a long time. With a spurt of energy, Bjorn sprinted off through the village, making a thrall jump out of his way, and then he side-stepped two women who were walking with pails of buttermilk in their hands. He leaped over an overturned barrel and thought his heart would burst with pride when he heard his son shriek with excitement.

Bjorn had never imagined how he could love anyone as much as he loved his son. His own father had been attentive and loving, but he had been dead for nine winters. Harald was the only father Bjorn had known since then. And Harald did not become overly attached to anyone, not even his sons. When his last son had died, he'd grieved for a short time before saying that he could 'make another one just as easily.' Unfortunately for Harald and Sigrun, and the many mistresses Harald had been with, no child had been born.

Not wanting to think of dead sons with his very alive son on his back, Bjorn sped off into the fields, the sound of Tanni's voice spurring him on.

Hovgarden, King Ingjald's stronghold.

Bjorn swayed with the movement of the longship as the steersman navigated *Sea Wolf* past Birka Island and its rich trading town toward Hovgarden, where King Ingjald had his home and hall. The late afternoon sun shone on the smattering of snow that rested on the trees and the wharf that normally held dozens of ships, growing quiet as winter descended; a few ships were there, its men checking the rigging to make sure all was well to sail again. Bjorn could see smoke as it wove into the sky from the many houses and shops on the island. A giant rock rose from one end of the island, gray and imposing, a great place for a lookout.

They had to slow to make it through the logs put in the Malaren Sea on the approach to Hovgarden; there was no way raiders could make it to the island undetected. The logs and the network of beacons at the islands along the route made it impossible for someone to surprise the king. The king's island of Hovgarden was surrounded by an earthen rampart with a tall wooden fence with wooden towers strategically placed along the perimeter.

"King Ingjald takes no chances," Bjorn said to his friend Rekja, as they pulled on the walrus-hide rope to bring in the sail. The heavy wool sail swung his way, and he had to dodge to avoid it, stopping any more conversation while they focused on lowering the huge mast and storing it along the length of the keel.

"There is the king," Vefinn said, his eyes squinting against the glare of sun on water. He was another friend, made in the years after Galinn had died, although no one could replace Bjorn's blood-brother.

They cruised in, their steersman guiding them to the dock where a party of men awaited them. King Ingjald watched them. He wore a dark blue tunic embroidered with gold braiding around the edges, a belt with gold buckles hung at his waist, a Frankish sword sheathed at his side, emeralds and rubies sparkling in its hilt. Over his shoulders was draped a deep crimson cloak attached with a large gold clasp, two dragon heads with eyes of pearl holding the rich woolen material in place. His arms and neck glittered with silver, gold, and precious gems. The king's household men had arranged themselves at his back, watchful, with their hands on their spears. While not dressed as elaborately as the king, his men still wore their wealth and status, their own arms heavy with rings.

Bjorn followed Harald as he disembarked. Before arriving at King Ingjald's compound, Harald and his men had donned their own finest clothes and wealth, the clothes kept safe and dry, wrapped in oiled sealskin bags kept in their sea chests. His men surrounded Harald as he walked down the pier to meet King Ingjald. The two leaders stepped forward from their men and faced each other.

"*Heil og sael*, King Ingjald Anundsson," Harald greeted Ingjald with a fisted hand to his chest. He had purposely worn his most valuable arm ring on his right arm so everyone would see it.

"*Velkomin*, Harald, son of Olaf." Ingjald inclined his head slightly to Harald and lifted his own hand to his chest. "And to your men." Ingjald's piercing gaze swept over Harald's men to include them all in the welcome.

"Come," he added. Turning with a sweep of his cloak, he walked toward his great hall. Two of his men fell in behind him while Bjorn and Styrr took up their places at Harald's back. The men exchanged glances, but all of them kept their faces blank. The rest of Harald's guard stayed behind with the ship until they knew that all was well.

Ingjald's great hall rose as tall as two pines standing on top of one another, shaved wooden posts standing sentinel as they held up a wooden shingle-covered roof that overhung the outside of the hall. At the front, two crimson planks met each other in an elaborate swirl that rose like the horns of a bull. Bjorn had never seen a mead hall so large, and he tried not to gape. When they reached the thick oak door with heavy iron hinges, a woman waited for them. She looked like she had stepped out of the pastoral scene carved and painted on the framework of the door. On each side of the door two carved deer stood on their hind legs; twisting vines grew out of their front legs and wove their way around the door.

When the party of men reached her, she stepped forward, her arms out in welcome.

"Husband," she said to Ingjald. She kept her distance from him. She turned to the men. "*Velkomin*," she said in welcome, although it sounded forced. "Come in and refresh yourselves. We have food and drink."

The two leaders entered and seated themselves at a table while a thrall set a plate of hard cheese and wheat bread.

Another thrall brought out mead in silver cups.

Bjorn and the other *huskarls* remained standing behind their leaders while they talked of the reason for Harald's visit. Ever since the raid on Tryggvi Olafsson's village four seasons earlier, Harald had nursed an even greater grudge against his brother than before. But the defeat at Tryggvi's hands made Harald more wary of attacking his brother directly, so he took out his anger in lands far to the south, accumulating wealth and men. Now, more powerful than before and worthy of notice, he sought an alliance with King Ingjald. With Ingjald's men and ships, Harald knew he could destroy his brother. Harald and his household guard were there to winter with Ingjald and prove that he should ally with them.

After the attack on Tryggvi's village, Harald had suffered for nearly three moon-cycles from the head injury he had sustained from Tryggvi's shield. He could not leave the house, for any light gave him a searing headache, so he closed himself off in dark places where he nursed his injury and his grudge with ale and bitterness. When he could finally walk in the light, he had developed a hatred for Tryggvi so great it consumed him. With the loss of Ingvar, Styrr had become Harald's man, catering to his needs and agreeing with his every whim.

Not wishing to get caught up in Harald's enmity, Bjorn had distanced himself from Harald and Styrr. His friend Galinn was dead, and then he had had to watch while Hilda married Stori Salvesson. As soon as she rode off with old Stori, Bjorn had gone off on a drunk that lasted nearly the entire winter. If it hadn't been for Rekja and Vefinn joining Harald's men, and their friendship, Bjorn was not sure what he would have done. When Bjorn's mistress Maude gave birth to a boy who looked like him, he had delighted in being a father.

A small smile came to his face as he thought of his son, but then he frowned. He would not see the boy again until the spring, at least. Tanni might not even remember him when he returned. A lump formed in Bjorn's throat, and he wiped thoughts of his son out of his mind.

Chairs scraped on the wooden floor as Harald and Ingjald rose from their repast.

"One of my women will show your men where they will stay," Ingjald told Harald. "We will feast tonight."

The two men embraced and clapped each other on the back. A young, dark-haired female thrall appeared to show them to the small building where Harald and his men would stay. She was pretty and Bjorn eyed her, but then he saw Ingjald's gaze linger on the young woman. He would not encroach on Ingjald's property. Not yet.

Chapter Six
Jarl Tryggvi's village, Storelva

Astrid gave her friend Ragnhild a hug and smiled. "You are a beautiful bride, Ragna. Now I have to go find Gytha and leave you with the married women."

Eyes wide with excitement, Ragnhild returned Astrid's smile. "I am so happy to marry Dyri."

"I'm happy for you. You are lucky."

"Shoo, Asta, we have to finish getting Ragnhild ready," Amma said. Along with Ingiborg, she was the woman who performed the female rituals.

With a wave, Astrid left the married women and looked for her sister on her way to where the marriage would take place. Ragnhild and Dyri were not rich, so it was not a big wedding, mainly people from her father's village and the surrounding farms.

She took in a breath when she came to the sacred grove. One of her favorite places, the grove was under a canopy of pine and birch, and a weak early winter sun filtered in through low clouds. In pride of place, a heap of stones created as an altar rose from the ground. Thor's sacred oath ring rested on top of it. A slight breeze brought with it the smell of roasted meat, food for the after-wedding feast. The river flowed alongside the grove, its steady rhythm soothing.

Astrid took hold of the Freya amulet that hung on her beaded necklace. Today was Freya's Day, the day for weddings. When she closed her eyes, she could feel the damp earth beneath her feet, the sun warming her head, could smell the tang of the river and the savory roasted meat, and knew the goddess would be pleased. She rubbed the necklace between her fingers. Her mother had given her the Freya amulet when she had become a woman. The

amulet, a silver circle in which the fertility goddess stood with legs splayed and arms at her belly, had belonged to Ingiborg, and since she no longer wanted to bear children, she had given it to Astrid. To make it even more special, she'd had a silversmith attach Astrid's cherished purple bead to the bottom of the amulet, and it looked as if the goddess were standing on it. The bead, given to her by Emund, glimmered in the light and the white flecks looked like clouds moving across a purple sky.

The conflicting smells of horse and soap assaulted her and made Astrid open her eyes.

"That's a sly smile on your face, *systir*," Rikki said as he sidled up next to her. He looked handsome in cream-colored trousers and a blue tunic, his bright hair brushing his shoulders. A silver necklace graced his neck and a twisted silver arm ring wrapped around his upper arm.

She ignored his comment. "It is a good day for a wedding. The goddess will be pleased."

"If you say so. I want to get this wedding over with so we can get to the feast." He rubbed his belly and sniffed the air. "The smell is making me hungry, and there is good mead waiting for me."

"You are always hungry." She laughed. "You can wait. The marriage ceremony is important." She nudged him in the arm. His solidity surprised her. At nearly seventeen, he was a warrior with her father and had the muscular body to show for it.

He shrugged and tensed. Their half-brother Jori approached them, Gytha's hand in his. He smiled at Astrid. "You look pretty today, Sissa."

Jori met Rikki's gaze. "Rikki."

"Jori."

The half-brothers stared at each other for a too-long moment before Jori turned back to Astrid and winked. "It won't be long before *your* wedding."

"What?" she replied, her voice coming out squeaky. "Do you know something?"

"No. Don't fret." He grinned when he saw her startled face. "You are old enough to marry, and it's time to think about it." He sounded like their father.

She looked at the guests, the altar stones, and knew Jori was right. It was time for her to marry. Astrid pulled Gytha to her and put her hands around her sister's shoulders. "I hope he's someone like Dyri...or Gunnar," she mumbled into the top of Gytha's head, a flush rising to her cheeks.

"Look, Asta, look at *fadir*," Gytha breathed, awed.

Turning to the altar, Astrid took in her father. In his capacity as *godi*, the spiritual leader, he looked magnificent—a crimson tunic embroidered at the neck, hem, and sleeves with gold braiding, blue trousers tight at the knees, with gold colored leg-wrappings, soft calfskin shoes on his feet. At his neck he wore a thick silver braid chain with a Thor amulet, and on his brow a gold circlet inlaid with a garnet over his forehead. The gold gleamed in the sunlight, proclaiming to all that Tryggvi Olafsson was a powerful, and very rich, man. His red-gold hair hung loose to his shoulders, and he had twisted his beard into two points, and at the end of each hung a green glass bead. He would preside over the wedding ceremony and make the ritual sacrifice.

"He looks frightening," Gytha said, her voice quiet.

Rikki and Jori chuckled, Rikki leaning in and whispering to her, "You should see him at the prow of *Wave Stallion*."

Shooting her brother a warning look, Astrid told her sister, "He's the link between us and the gods."

"Do you think the gods talk to him? Will they talk to him now?"

Astrid studied her father. She could imagine the Allfather whispering in his ear, telling him secrets or warning him of impending danger.

"Perhaps."

"What about Freya? It is a wedding. Will she be here?" At this Gytha's head turned, as if searching for the goddess.

"She is here, but not in a body. Listen to the wind in the trees, the sound of the river water rushing by, the earth under our feet. That is her."

With a look of exaggerated dismay, Rikki picked up his feet like he didn't want to be standing on the goddess. Gytha giggled.

Astrid's gaze went from her father to the groom, handsome Dyri, with the ceremonial sword in his hand, as he stood beside the altar, accompanied by the other married men of the village, waiting for his bride to arrive. His father or uncle should have been there, but they were dead, so Tryggvi had brokered the arrangements and the bride-price between Dyri and Ragnhild's brothers, since her father was dead too. Dyri, the young messenger who had warned them of Harald's attack four summers before, was now one of her father's *huskarls*. After the fight between Tryggvi and Harald, Dyri had gone home only to find his family dead. He returned to Tryggvi, who took him in. Tryggvi held him in high esteem as he had become an exceptional steersman; he had taken Thorkell's place at the steering oar of Tryggvi's longship, *Wave Stallion*.

The married men who stood with Dyri had been talking, but turned their heads all at once to a point behind Astrid.

She turned with them and saw the bridal procession.

The bride, Ragnhild, walked toward them escorted by the married women of the village, her face alight with happiness when she saw Dyri standing at the altar. Astrid looked back to Dyri in time to see him return her smile. It was not often two people married for love.

"She is beautiful," Gytha said.

"She is."

Ragnhild wore her bridal wreath, the crown of a woven vine garlanded with flowers, sitting atop her head, her honey-brown hair long and loose and flowing over her shoulders. When she passed, she smelled as fresh as a meadow in spring, the herbs and flowers that scented her body and hair a prayer to the goddess of fertility. Ragnhild shot Astrid a quick smile, which Astrid returned easily; she and Ragnhild had been playmates when they were girls. Now Ragnhild would be given the keys of a wife and leave behind her childhood ways. The thought gave Astrid pause, as she realized that she was being left behind. She was fifteen winters old. Jorund's words echoed in her mind. Would she be standing here next year, a husband waiting for her at the altar? Her own hair adorned with the bridal wreath? Her eyes searched for Gunnar, and when she found him her heart skipped a beat. He looked so handsome, and she traced the curve of his strong shoulders, arms, and chest with her gaze. When he shifted and looked her way, she turned her gaze back to the ceremony.

At the altar, Dyri and Ragnhild stood facing each other, the ceremonial sword between them, their hands on the hilt as they said their wedding vows.

Next to Astrid, Rikki fidgeted, and she put her arm through his to settle him down. He squeezed her arm in return. Her focus was on the ceremony, smiling as she watched the couple say their vows and pledge themselves and their families to each other.

The sound of dozens of voices mixed and rose to the high rafters of Jarl Tryggvi's feast hall. The laughter of Ragnhild and Dyri filled the great hall as everyone waited for the wedding feast to begin.

Light from the hearth fire and oil lamps on the wall illuminated the happy faces. Astrid loved a wedding feast. As she leaned in to talk to Rikki, the tapestry she had presented to her father four summers ago drew her eye. The bright red was diminished from smoke, but next to it hung a new tapestry she had given her father during the previous Yule feast. She had the wool dyed a dark crimson and mustard-yellow to do the knotwork pattern. She'd woven four spirals into each corner, and her father's black raven emerged out of each spiral.

The smell of food permeated the hall. Thralls had been preparing the feast for days and everything smelled of roasted meats, roasted and baked vegetables, and breads.

Rikki groaned.

"What is it?" Astrid asked.

"I'm so hungry."

"You know you have to wait for Mother and Father to start the feast."

He groaned again, leaned forward and banged his forehead on the hard-oak table. Astrid laughed. "You are acting like a child."

"A man needs to eat! I can't survive on pretty dresses and pretty words like you." His voice was muffled as he spoke into the table.

She patted him on the back until she saw her mother rise from her seat. Rikki sat up, hope lighting up his eyes.

From her place on the bench next to her brothers and sister, Astrid watched as her mother offered the large ceremonial bowl of honeyed mead to each person, and then taking up her place next to Tryggvi in the high-seat. When Astrid and Rikki were young, they would sometimes squeeze in with them, the seat large enough for all four of them. It hadn't been that long since Gytha had left the high-seat and joined her brothers and sister as bench companions.

Once done, Astrid and Gytha rose to pour drinks for the more prominent men in attendance. Astrid walked around the high-table to serve Ketil and his son Sigmund. When she got close to these men from Scania, her hand shook a little, even though she had served many important men before. Sigmund gave her a hungry look that had nothing to do with the feast, and she hurried away from them as quickly as she could while still being polite. She then filled the cups for Ragnhild and Dyri, their happiness at the marriage filling them like the sun and water fed the crops.

Astrid imagined herself in her mother's place, the wife of a rich and powerful man, her wealth displayed for all to see. With a quick glance at her father, she felt her heart give a tug. Her father looked at his wife with such open love and admiration it took Astrid's breath away. She cast another quick glance at Dyri and Ragnhild; they had their heads together, and he whispered something in her ear. Ragnhild smiled, her cheeks turning a pretty pink, and he kissed her. Astrid had to look away. She knew that kind of affection was rare, but she hoped to have it in her own marriage. If she had to marry, then why couldn't she love the man? Her eyes then sought Gunnar. He was not far down the table as one of Tryggvi's personal guard. His wavy brown hair looked silky in the glow from the oil lamp behind him. He caught her stare and smiled at her.

"My friends!" Tryggvi called out and everyone grew quiet.

"My friends from near." He turned to salute Emund. Emund raised a silver goblet to Tryggvi, the cup nearly disappearing in his big hand. "And far." He raised his cup to Ketil and his son Sigmund.

Everyone cheered again. "To friends! *Skål!*"

With that, the feast and festivities began.

"Finally," Rikki said. "It's time for the food."

Thralls brought in the food, specially made for the feast. The sacrificial pig killed in honor of Frey had been roasted over a slow fire, its skin crispy, the meat tender and juicy. Fish stews laden with turnips, white carrots, kale, wild onions, and hunks of perch, pike, or herring. Different kinds of bread, barley, rye, even oat and wheat, the rare grains a treat only enjoyed during feasts. They topped little cakes made of ground hazelnuts with tart cherries. Barrels of blackberry ale and meadowsweet mead were rolled in and flowed freely.

Astrid laughed and watched as her brother tore into his roasted pork, stabbing it with his eating knife and dipping it into a plum sauce. He groaned after taking a bite.

"No wonder they have roasted pork in Valhalla. It is food fit for the gods." He gave Astrid a smile. "I wish we could eat it every meal. It's better than boiled meat."

"Then it wouldn't be a treat," Astrid reminded him. She picked up the cool jar that held butter. Dipping her knife in it, she slathered it on her baked turnips, the flesh from the vegetable soft and flavored from the juice that had dripped from the pig.

Rikki didn't respond, too busy eating. He tore off a piece of the wheat bread and smoothed butter onto it. He put a piece of the pork on the bread and popped it into his mouth all at once.

A loud, high-pitched laugh came from the men who sat across the table from her father, a place of honor reserved for guests. The laugh was much too high for a man, and it made Astrid cringe.

"Do you know why Ketil Egilsson and Sigmund are here?" Astrid asked Rikki, although she was fairly certain why they would be there; she'd seen the looks they'd both given her as if she were a horse they wanted to buy. Sigmund's gaze made her skin pimple up like goose flesh.

"I heard them talking about making it safer to travel the Oresund."

"And what will Ketil and Sigmund be getting?"

Rikki gave her a sideways look.

Their father's skald walked into the middle of the tables, his lyre tucked into his arm.

"Let us hear your words, skald," Tryggvi said, leaning back in his seat, his hand resting lightly on Ingiborg's thigh.

The skald sang Jarl Tryggvi's praises and once done with that, he turned to the newly married couple. The first song told of their virtues, Ragnhild's beauty and skill with a needle, and Dyri's prowess in battle and skill steering the ships. He sang of a king from long ago, how he married a woman so beautiful it was like the sun's rays had created her. The king loved his wife and their marriage lasted a long time and produced many children. When the wife died, the king mourned her bitterly. His counselors advised him to take another wife, but the king would not do it. He told them he would remain loyal to his beloved wife until his death. When the king fell on the field of battle, the One-Eyed god personally taking him, the king found himself in Valhalla. A serving woman approached him, her hair like gold, her skin as smooth as ivory. The king knew those hands. He grasped onto her hand, drawing her down so he could look in her eyes. It was his beloved wife. It was a joyous reunion.

As the skald sang, Astrid watched Gunnar. What would it be like to have a man love her like the king loved his wife? Love her so much he would wait for her and they could be together in the land of the gods. It made her shiver.

When the skald finished his song, he wished Ragnhild and Dyri as much happiness as the king and his wife. They kissed, beaming at one another. Then he sang a song about Tryggvi and Ingiborg, of their love and how Jarl Tryggvi boasted to the world what a good woman he had married.

With the skald's words, the great feast hall seemed to fill with a warm, honeyed air, like a gift from Frey or Freya, and men and women all down the tables kissed their wives and husbands, their lovers, their children.

"Your words are powerful magic, skald," one man called out. He had his arm around his wife. "Many children will be born in late summer!" He pulled his wife closer. Others cried out their agreement.

Now that they had broken the spell, the skald's songs became raunchier until everyone was red-faced with laughter.

After the songs, the skald took a break and thralls removed the food and dishes from the tables. As two female thralls gathered the cloths that lined the trestle tables, male thralls broke the tables down, taking the top boards and the frames outside to one of the storage barns. They left only the drinking table behind, a large barrel of ale on it, a dipper left in it so guests could fill their own cups. With the tables gone, there was room for dancing and games. The high-seat was moved to the end of the hall so Tryggvi and Ingiborg could see everything. Filled with excellent food and drink, the wedding couple and guests began the festivities.

Astrid joined her mother at a bench that lined the wall to make room for dancing. It was late into the night, and she needed a rest.

The wedding guests sang a festive song and danced in a circle while holding hands. Dyri danced next to Ragnhild, and holding her other hand was Emund, his flaming red hair loose and flying around his ruddy face as he danced. Although a fearsome warrior, he was a terrible dancer, and being deep in his cups did not help matters. One edge of his tunic had come loose from his belt and hung low, the neckline exposing a pale, freckled shoulder. He paid no mind to the state of his clothes.

Astrid laughed. "He looks like he's trying to get away from a snake. I might start calling him Emund the Snake Dancer."

"He would not like that. Emund thinks he can dance. Always has. The trick is to not have to dance next to him. That is what I do," Ingiborg said, a twinkle in her eyes. She shifted the small child she held on her lap. Leif was only three and had grown tired after the long day of activity. His mother, Amma, was among the dancers, so he had gone to Ingiborg for a soft place to land, falling asleep immediately. The shifting had disturbed him, and he muttered in his sleep. Ingiborg ran a hand over his head to calm him, and he quieted once again. Astrid noticed that her mother looked at him with a mixture of love and sadness.

"I'll remember that and steer clear," Astrid said. She took a drink of mead from her silver cup. The sweet honeyed liquid slid down her throat and warmed her entire body, making her feel soft and relaxed.

At another table Rikki and his friends Short Olaf and Galm played a drinking game with visiting young men, and they all looked to be fully drunk. A girl walked by, the daughter of a rich sheep farmer who lived outside the village, and she gave Rikki an appreciative look as she passed. Guests came from all over to enjoy a splendid wedding feast. Rikki downed his drink, gave his friends a quick goodbye salute, caught up with the girl, and they walked outside together.

In another corner Astrid's father played a dice game with some other men, among them the visiting Skanian jarl Ketil Egilsson and his son Sigmund the Left-Handed. Astrid still had not been told why Ketil Egilsson, who ruled a stronghold on the coast opposite Denmark, was here at all. This was a small family wedding and feast, something for friends, not an occasion for a visiting jarl and his men. When their longship docked at the pier, her father had welcomed him and his son, but he did not seem happy to see them and the visit was unexpected. Ketil Egilsson was an old man, his hair gray-streaked, and he had the scars to prove that he'd seen many battles. Astrid did not like him. He talked too loudly and smelled bad. His frequent looks at Astrid made her feel sick, knowing what they meant. She was more than old enough for her father to be getting requests from fathers for their sons to marry her.

Sigmund Ketilsson looked to be over twenty winters with long hair and a thick beard dyed the same saffron yellow color as his hair. Astrid stared at him in the flickering firelight from the hearth fire, for she had never seen a man with dyed hair before. She knew men did it, but the men in her father's household were not among them. In the days before the wedding, Astrid had been too busy with the preparations to notice him much. When she finally saw him, he strutted like he was the son of a king, wearing tunics and trousers of the brightest blue and red, a sword at his right hip with a gleaming silver hilt decorated with jewels. She'd also seen a thrall leaving his large, brightly colored tent with a terrified look on her face. Astrid could not tell if the girl had been frightened by what had happened with Sigmund or if it was something else.

Sigmund picked up the dice in his left hand and tossed them onto the table and groaned dramatically when the throw did not go his way. Tryggvi, his gold torc gleaming in the firelight, his wealth displayed as if that itself were a competition, then grabbed the dice and threw a winning toss.

"The luck of the gods is with you, Tryggvi Olafsson!" Sigmund shouted in dismay. He drained his glass of wine and then flourished it for a thrall to fill it again. It was the same girl Astrid had seen leaving his tent before, and he looked up at her, his eyes glassy with drink, and rubbed his crotch. "Come to my tent later," he said to her. The girl nodded, resigned, and filled his cup while he continued to stare at her hungrily.

"This is my house," Tryggvi said, his voice a little slurred. "The gods are always with me here." Tryggvi held his cup to the girl as well, a shining silver cup embossed with runes and encrusted with jewels. He did not give her even the slightest notice. Instead, Tryggvi caught Ingiborg's eye and winked at her, his blue eyes soft with drink. Astrid saw Ingiborg smile back at him and thought the playfulness mixed with the child in her lap, the soft firelight and hazy smoke of the hall, made her mother look like a young girl.

"The gods are fickle, Tryggvi Olafsson. Their favor can turn as fast as a north wind," Sigmund said.

Tryggvi narrowed his eyes.

One song had died down, and the revelers took up another dance. Before Astrid could say something to her mother about Sigmund, Gunnar appeared at their table, his hand out.

"Join me, Asta? I need a partner."

Astrid looked at Gunnar's outstretched arm, two rings of twisted silver on his forearm, then up at his face. He was flushed from dancing, and it made him even more handsome than ever. He smiled at her, his green eyes shining down at her, his wavy brown hair loose on the shoulders of his green tunic edged with yellow braiding. A twisted silver torc graced his neck. She placed her hand in his and he closed his fingers around hers, his hand strong but gentle, as he lifted her to her feet.

They joined the other dancers. A lyre played a lovely tune and one of the men played a reed pipe while the dancers moved in a circle, kicking their feet to the rhythm of a drum. At a sound from the piper, everyone in the circle surged inward and raised their clasped hands in the air. Dyri let go of the partner next to him and ducked under Ragnhild's arm, and then everyone followed, looping and ducking under each other's arms in the circle. Even as Dyri and Ragnhild broke away and moved through the dancers, their eyes remained locked on each other.

As she watched her friend Ragnhild beam at her new husband, Astrid was keenly aware of the feel of her hand in Gunnar's, of his presence next to her. He danced with grace and ease, and he did not stumble like some other men who were drunk. She glanced up at him and flushed when she saw he was staring back at her, his gaze soft and admiring. Her body flooded with a pleasant warmth.

Gunnar inclined his head toward the end of the room, away from the central fire, where other dancers had lined up, men on one side, women on the other. Astrid lined up facing Gunnar and soon the dance called for them to join hands and dance together closely. She trembled at his closeness. He smelled of sweat and smoke, a man's smell, but when he turned she caught the slight smell of scented soap in his hair. She smiled; Gunnar had always been vain about his hair.

He caught her smiling and moved closer to her as they circled one another, the heat from his body making her legs go weak. He held her closer, his hand tight on her waist.

"You look lovely," he said in a throaty voice.

Astrid's stomach flipped at the tone. "*Tak.*" She glanced down at her dress, the dark blue apron pinned with silver brooches to a rich, cream-colored dress. The blue apron was trimmed with gold tablet weaving at the hem and at the chest. "Gytha said I should wear it because it's blue like my eyes." With a gasp, she put her hand to her mouth. She wished she could take that back. It sounded silly.

He gave her an indulgent smile. "Well..." He leaned down and whispered into her ear, his breath tickling her neck. "Your sister is right." Her skin tingled where his breath touched her neck. His finger traced the edges of her dress. "Your work?"

"*Ja.*"

"You have a great skill. Your husband will appreciate you."

All the breath left her body.

Gunnar pulled his head back to look in her eyes, his own eyes flashing something she did not understand. Then it passed. He smiled. "Did you enjoy the wedding?" He placed his palms against hers in the dance. They were calloused and hard from wielding a sword and shield.

"*Ja.*" She looked over to Ragnhild and Dyri. "They are very happy." But her mind was not on the newly married couple; she imagined Gunnar's hands, the same hands that could fight also running down her body. She trembled, confused at her own thoughts and feelings.

"It's warm in here. Join me outside for some air?"

She nodded and followed Gunnar out of the feast hall. As soon as they got outside, the clear, cool air hit Astrid, and she took a deep breath.

Gunnar chuckled. "Better?"

"Yes."

Children played hide-and-find out among the buildings, and it reminded Astrid of when she, Rikki, Jori, Ragnhild, Short Olaf, and Galm used to play together outside while the adults danced and played games in the hall.

"Let's walk," Gunnar said.

Astrid glanced back at the hall, the sounds of the music and laughter carrying out over the entire village. She imagined the noise of the revelry flying on the wind like a bird, spreading all the way to the halls of the gods, who loved a good feast. She felt content and happy, and she walked next to Gunnar to nowhere in particular, talking about everything. She enjoyed talking to Gunnar. It was easy. With him by her side, the village looked different, prettier. The plain wooden buildings, the thatched roofs, the fences that surrounded homes and enclosed gardens, all seemed washed clean and peaceful. Laughter and singing came from the hall, and the village lay quiet as if it were watching the two of them.

They reached her father's barn, where he kept his best horses. The noises inside were not coming from the animals, though. The deep timbre of a man's voice that sounded like her brother was followed by a woman's giggles. Astrid held back a cry of worry, wondering if this was what Gunnar had in mind for them, but he turned them away from the barn and back toward the feast hall. It did not keep her mind from thinking about what it would be like if Gunnar touched her in a way to make her sound like the woman in the barn.

"Do you remember that time you wove all those flowers into my hair when you were a little girl?"

"Oh, yes." She was relieved to have a safe conversation. "The others called you Gunnar Flower Hair. I'm sorry I did that to you."

Gunnar laughed. "That name stuck for far too long. But how was I to resist you?"

"I think Emund made sure you couldn't. I was a silly girl."

"You are not a silly girl any longer." Gunnar took her hand and gently pulled her toward him.

She did not resist, but allowed him to draw her in until she was so close she could feel the heat radiating from his body.

He put his hand on her cheek, and she leaned into it. "You are a beautiful woman now, Asta." The way he breathed out the word *Asta* made her body tingle all the way to her toes. She looked up at him, into his green eyes, and did not move when he bent down and placed a kiss on her lips.

His lips were soft and gentle. He broke the kiss, but his eyes never left hers.

Astrid could not move. She had felt nothing like this before, this explosion of heat running through her body, the desire for him to kiss her again, and she tentatively touched his lips with her fingers.

He inhaled sharply as soon as she touched him. He laced his fingers through hers and kissed her again, this time deeper and with more intensity. His tongue flicked across her lips and she opened for him, tasting him. A flush of heat and fluidity rushed through her body.

She pushed at him and backed away, breathless, her body shaking. What was happening to her body? Why did it feel like this? She brought her hands up to her cheeks to cool them off.

With a thud, Gunnar fell back against the side of a house and ran a hand over his face. They stood like that for a long moment before he said, "I'm sorry. I should not have kissed you."

A flood of emotions surged through Astrid. He was right, he should not have kissed her like that. He was not her husband, nor were they promised to each other. But it had felt so good, she wanted him to do it again. Her body longed to have him kiss her again. She touched her hand to her lips as if to keep the kiss safe in case there was never another.

"I...I wanted you to," her voice came out all fluttery.

"Are you sure?"

"Yes." She had loved Gunnar ever since the day he'd rescued her from the outlaw. Then it was a little girl looking up to the young man who'd saved her. She'd developed an attachment to him. But as she'd grown, she'd discovered Gunnar was not only strong and brave, but kind and generous too. With her. With her brothers. With her sister. She could not imagine her life without him in it.

She'd learned early on that the world was a hard place that ripped people away too soon, and if you found someone you loved, you did it with all your heart. If you didn't, you might lose that person.

"Yes," she said again.

Gunnar wrapped a strong arm around her waist and pulled her to him. He kissed her again, and this time there was no hesitation.

The thump of the door from the feast hall jarred Astrid, and she jumped away from Gunnar lest they be caught. Emund's burly voice rang out into the air, calling back to someone in the hall, "Gotta take a piss! Hold on to your silver so I can take it from you." He chuckled as he stepped over the threshold.

Astrid went rigid with fear. She did not want anyone to find her alone with Gunnar. But Emund went the other direction, and as soon as he was out of sight, Gunnar grabbed her hand. Exhilarated with desire and the fear of being caught, Astrid laughed. With one last squeeze of her hand, Gunnar let go. He gave her a quick kiss on the cheek, his close-cut beard tickling her face, before moving away from her.

Astrid slipped through the door, the feel of Gunnar's lips remaining on her cheek. She flushed at the thought of their stolen kisses, glad it was hot and stuffy in the hall, so that no one would notice. All the warm feeling vanished when she nearly ran into Sigmund the Left-Handed as he led the thrall toward the door.

"Oh!" she squeaked and regretted it. It made her sound guilty. "I did not notice you there."

"Astrid Tryggvisdottir," Sigmund said in a startlingly high voice, giving her a nod. He shoved the thrall aside and straightened his tunic dramatically. "In all the bustle of activity, I have not had the chance to introduce myself. I am Sigmund Ketilsson."

Now he was so close to her, she saw he wasn't that tall, not much taller than her, and he had a thick, muscular chest and arms. As he spoke, his eyes, brown with flecks of green, traveled over her hair, her face, and her body. He gave her a nod and a slight smile of appreciation. It made her squirm, but she tried not to show it.

"I know who you are," she said, a little too abruptly. His eyebrows raised at the retort, and she had to recover quickly. "We are pleased you are here to share in the joyous occasion with us. Your father and my father are..." She faltered. What were her father and Ketil? Not friends. Not even allies. They used each other when the need arose. Ketil had come by his jarldom by force and violence, and she had heard her father tell Emund that any dealings with the man had to be done carefully.

Smiling at her lack of words, Sigmund said, "Yes, your father and my father are...something. Soon, they will be something closer." He chuckled and leaned in closer to her.

"When I have my way."

She took a step back from him. Sigmund made her feel like running away. She wished she could be like Kis-Kis who would scratch people she didn't like and then dart out the door.

"It will be good for them to be friends," she stuttered.

He chuckled again, his voice higher than his muscular build would suggest. "Friends, yes. And more. I am eager for things to...develop."

At the word, his gaze slid over her body again. Her arms rose with gooseflesh at his implication. She searched the feast hall to see if someone would rescue her, but there was too much activity with dancing, drinking, and gaming for anyone to notice this tiny exchange of words. A quick glance in her mother's direction and she saw that Ingiborg dozed with young Leif still in her lap, his little head resting on her chest.

A waft of cool air lifted the hem of Astrid's dress as the door opened and Gunnar walked in. He paused when he saw her talking to Sigmund, and then he moved toward them. Sigmund misunderstood Gunnar's intention and grabbed the thrall girl who was standing not far away.

"You'll have to get your own, Gunnar. This one is mine."

A fleeting look of disdain passed over Gunnar's face.

"You're welcome to her, Sigmund." The sound of Jori and a few of the *huskarls* laughing carried over the feast hall. "I'm going to join them." Turning to Astrid, he said, "You should find your mother."

"It was a pleasure talking to you, Astrid," Sigmund said in his slippery voice. "We will see each other again. Of that you can be sure." He pushed the thrall out the door.

She cast Gunnar a look, but he was already making his way across the floor to Jori's table. An image flitted across her mind. By this time next season, she might dance at her own marriage feast. Her head spun with thoughts of happiness when she imagined it being Gunnar, but then she looked toward the door where Sigmund Ketilsson had gone, and she shivered. It was more likely to be someone like him.

Chapter Seven

The next morning, her head still fuzzy from drink and Gunnar's kisses, Astrid and Gytha accompanied the family's thralls tasked to clean the great hall after the night's festivities. With a headache from the night before, Astrid had grumbled about having to oversee the thralls, but received no sympathy from her mother. It was a woman's duty to make sure everyone was well cared for, provided with food, drink, a place to sleep, and Ingiborg needed Astrid to learn her duties.

In the late morning light, the great hall looked less magical than the night before, the red of the door and pillars muted, unlike the vibrant crimson they'd been after the wedding. They approached the hall just as Jori stepped out. He appeared pleased and grim at the same time. Behind him followed Rikki, his posture tense as he studied his half-brother's back. It was odd to see them together, especially without being flanked by either Gunnar or Galm and Short Olaf, but none of them were around. Astrid glimpsed Emund's red beard in the doorway.

As the two half-brothers walked out the door, Jori paused and Astrid heard him say.

"I would have you at my back, brother."

Rikki stopped, as if stunned, and stared at his brother for a beat before grasping his forearm. He nodded. "We are the sons of Tryggvi."

Emund's full form appeared behind them, and when they caught sight of him, they pulled apart, Jori heading right toward the women.

He stopped when he saw Astrid. She waved Gytha and the thralls ahead to tend to their duties, telling them she would join them later.

"What was that about?" she asked Jori, her eyes on Rikki's retreating figure.

"Come with me. I need to find someone," he said, and he headed toward the field where the men held their competitions. Something must have been going on since people walked past them, talking and laughing as they went in the same direction.

"I have work to do. Mother—"

"I will tell Ingiborg I needed you for something," Jori said.

Astrid let Jori lead her and they went toward the building where the *huskarls* lived. It was close to Tryggvi's longhouse, and they passed village houses, the sounds of women and children coming from inside, hens pecking in the dirt and grass. A streak of white and gray flashed past, followed by a group of dogs, all of them barking as they chased their prey.

"Kis-Kis," Astrid said, watching her cat fly by. She tried to stop the dog in the lead, but he was too fast. So quick she was a blur, Kis-Kis jumped onto a fence, ran along the top railing, before leaping onto the roof of the closest house. The dogs barked and paced by the fence. Astrid laughed as the cat's tail twitched in the air, and she looked down at the dogs. "That's my girl."

Jori chuckled and led Astrid on. He glanced down at her as they walked. "I am leaving as soon as I can get my men and supplies together."

"Where?" Then she realized he'd said, 'my men.' "What do you mean, my men? Is Father not going too?"

"No. I'm going to Hovgarden to see King Ingjald. Harald..." He stopped when she gripped tightly onto his arm. "Harald is there—"

"No," she breathed. "You can't go there. Not without Father or Emund. Harald will kill you." It came out in a rush before she'd given it any thought. She felt Jori tense at her side, felt the insult she'd given him.

"You think I need Father and Emund to protect me?"

"That's not what I meant. You can't go alone, Jori."

"I won't be alone. I'm taking men with me. Gunnar..."

She heard none of the other names he listed. The only one she cared about was Gunnar. He'd just kissed her the night before. He couldn't leave her now, not to walk into certain danger.

"...Harald is there trying to convince King Ingjald to give him father's lands, claiming that their father gave it all to him."

"But that was so long ago," she said. "Why does he keep fighting with Father? Why can't he leave us in peace?"

Jori barked out a laugh. "There are two things Harald wants, and he won't stop until he gets them, or he dies. Father dead and In—" He stopped himself.

They had reached the edge of the competition field, where men and women talked and children all ran around, their talk and laughter flying through the air like birds. Two men had taken up the middle of the field and her heart leaped at the sight of Gunnar's wavy brown hair that he was tying back with a leather cord. Another man walked in front of him, and she recoiled when she saw Sigmund the Left-Handed, his yellow-dyed hair unmistakable. Her stomach clenched remembering the way he'd touched her, the way he'd tried to claim her, as if she would ever want someone like him.

"It is an honor for me." Jori had continued to talk. "This is important, and Father trusts me."

An honor. To walk into a wolf's den.

"It will be dangerous."

She looked into his face, his eyes sparkling with excitement as if he had no heed of his own safety. They never did. They left it to the women to fear for them.

"Do you think me a coward?"

"Of course not," she said with emphasis. It was true. She thought him no coward. "I would be afraid to be near Harald. I hope I never have to see him."

Then she remembered why she'd wanted to talk to him in the first place, the exchange she'd seen between him and Rikki, so unlike them to share a moment like that.

Her heart raced. "Is Rikki going with you?"

"No."

She sagged with relief. One brother near Harald was almost more than she could bear, especially since he was taking Gunnar with him. If Rikki had gone too, it would have torn her heart to shreds with worry.

She touched her Freya amulet. "Thank the goddess."

"He wanted to."

"I'm sure he did." She would have laughed and could see clearly Rikki asking their father for his chance to prove himself.

"Father said he would not allow both of his son's within Harald's grasp."

She wanted to hug her father for that. She thought of the look on their faces when Jori said he and Rikki were both the sons of Tryggvi. Ever since Jori had come to live with them when he was a young boy, he and Rikki had not gotten along, each one trying to be first in their father's favor. But things changed.

"And you and Rikki have joined together, blood against a common enemy."

"*Ja*. Father wants me to talk to King Ingjald, to make him see that the land and the jarldom," he swept his hand around, "belong to Tryggvi. Harald has no claim to any of it."

"I don't know what King Ingjald can do," Astrid said. He didn't have that much power.

"I don't either," Jori answered, surveying the crowd, looking for the men he would take with him. "I'll find a way."

He spotted someone and called out to him.

Turning back to Astrid, he took her shoulders in his strong hands. "Don't worry, Sissa."

She smiled at the pet name. When Jori came to live with them, he'd been at the age when his two top front teeth had been missing and when he'd tried to say '*systir*,' it came out more like 'sissa.' That became his name for her.

"Harald won't touch me. We are the sons and *dottirs* of Tryggvi Olafsson. We will defeat Harald. Now, you'd better go back or Ingiborg will be displeased."

He kissed her cheek and strode away to gather men to him. As she watched him walk away, she was torn between her feelings of pride for her brother, so strong and brave, and her fear for him.

Hovgarden

The ceiling of King Ingjald's great hall soared above the guests' heads, the support pillars painted a deep red, like the color of dried blood, carved to look like the branches and roots of the World Tree, Yggdrasil, its roots planted in the underworld, its branches reaching out to all the Nine Worlds. On the walls hung shields, spears, and furs; along each of the long walls, tables and benches had been set up and were crowded with men and women, all drinking and talking after the feast. Firelight danced from the central hearth and from beeswax candles placed in iron fixtures that hung from the ceiling. Bjorn had never seen so many beeswax candles before and burning them was a great luxury that only a king could afford. Seal-oil lamps burned on the tables.

In a recess set back from the main hall, King Ingjald had his high-seat, and behind it hung tapestries depicting the king's lineage from Odin himself.

Bjorn was studying one of the tapestries when a dark-haired thrall, whose job it was to refill the drinking cups of the feasting men, caught his eye, as she poured wine into Harald's glass goblet. The glass was as red as a ruby and gleamed in the firelight.

Harald paid her no attention as he was deep in conversation with King Ingjald. Bjorn wasn't much interested in politics and had deliberately seated himself away from the high-table, even though, as Harald's foster-son, he should be in on the talks. He liked to fight and have a woman warming his bed, but did not care about the gift-giving and maneuvering involved in making alliances. The thralls' dark eyes widened in appreciation when they alighted on him, a look he never tired of seeing from women, and he waved her to his side by lifting his empty cup. As she approached him, his eyes grazed down her form. Even in her drab, brown, coarse woolen thrall dress and with her dark brown hair cut short, she was pretty and shapely in all the right places.

She poured his drink with a steady hand, and up close, Bjorn saw she was older than he had first thought, nineteen or twenty winters old, he guessed. Pleased to see that she did not back away as soon as she finished, Bjorn leaned back, straightened his blue tunic, and flashed her a smile with his straight white teeth.

"What is your name?"

"Selime."

"Seh-lee-mae." He let the name linger on his tongue. "Lovely."

One of his crewmates asked Bjorn a question, but he waved the man away and turned back to Selime.

"How long have you been serving King Ingjald?" Bjorn asked. He let the word 'serving' linger to see the girls' reaction. He had no doubt that Ingjald would have enjoyed such a lovely woman.

Selime did not react and looked toward the head table. "I have been here a long time. The winter has come and gone four times."

"Does he treat you well, Selime?" Bjorn asked with such sincerity that she started and looked him full in the face for the first time. Her dark eyes were big and wide and at his question she arched her eyebrow slightly, just enough that he could see and no one else.

"I am a thrall..." She inclined her head toward him and a wisp of hair escaped from her head covering and touched her cheek.

"I am Bjorn Alfarsson," he said, his voice low. He reached up and brushed the stray hair back from her face. She did not flinch or pull away. "And you did not answer my question."

Selime dropped her head and her voice grew hard. "Ingjald treats me better than most."

"Indeed. But some..." He took a drink, but his eyes held on to hers. "Would treat you much better."

He could feel her soften toward him, the warmth of her body increasing.

"Girl!" a voice shouted from behind her and a hand grabbed her ass roughly. Selime jumped and then lowered her head and turned to him. "More ale!" He raised his cup so she could refill it.

Bjorn sighed and resisted the urge to punch the interloper in the teeth. He got to his feet. "Atli," he said, "Don't be such a brute."

With a surprised look on his face, Atli said, "She's a thrall. I'll do what I want with her."

"You should try pleasing a woman sometime. Then maybe your wife wouldn't always have a scowl on her face."

"Atli's wife could shrivel the nuts off a giant," Bjorn's friend, Vefinn, quipped.

"Mine are intact," Atli said as he grabbed his crotch. He sized up Bjorn. "My wife would eat you alive, pretty boy."

Bjorn laughed.

Vefinn clapped him on the back. "Most men hide their women when Pretty Bjorn is around, Atli. Not throw her in his direction."

"My wife wants a real man," Atli scoffed. "Not a man as pretty as a woman."

"That's not what your wife said," Bjorn added quickly, "When she was under me squealing."

Atli choked on his drink and nearly spit it out. "If my wife was under you boy, you'd be the one squealing for mercy." He waved his drink at Bjorn and some of its contents sloshed over the top and spilled on the ground at Bjorn's feet. It just missed splattering on his leather shoes. He took a step back slowly and bumped into Selime.

Selime watched the two men, her hands clutching the ale pitcher, her eyes flitting from man to man as they bantered. She inched toward Bjorn and out of Atli's reach.

Giving Selime a conspiratorial smile, Bjorn took the pitcher from her hands with one hand, his rings clinking against the clay, and set it on the table, and with the other hand he moved her behind his body and away from Atli. Once behind him, Selime put her hand on Bjorn's waist, and he took it as a sign of trust.

The feel of her warm hand through his tunic brought his desire back up.

"As much as this talk of your wife excites me, Atli, I have better things to do." Bjorn turned his back to Atli and in one fluid motion, slipped his arm around Selime's waist. The wool dress was coarse, but underneath, her body was warm and pliable. She went with him without hesitancy.

Bjorn gave a quick glance over his shoulder at his foster-father at the high-table before leaving the feast hall. Harald noticed him and gave him a slight frown, the scar on his right cheek just above his mouth pulling his face down into a scowl. It was a look Bjorn had seen before, and he shrugged it off. For all he knew, Harald was talking with King Ingjald about finding Bjorn a suitable wife. He tightened his grip on Selime's waist. Bjorn enjoyed a woman whenever he wanted. He had a fertile woman at home who had already given him one son and was about to give him another child. Unless it was Hilda, he had no need of a wife. With a grin and a tip of his head to his foster-father, Bjorn led Selime out of the feast hall and to his living quarters.

Chapter Eight
Storelva

A large crowd had gathered to watch Gunnar wrestle Sigmund Ketilsson. Astrid did not want to go back to the great hall to help clean; Gytha and the thralls could do it. At the sight of Gunnar, her heart had sped up, and she wanted to watch him defeat Sigmund.

The shipwright and a shepherd from an outlying area busied themselves roping off the wrestling ring with a thick hemp rope. Men, women, and children, especially young boys, gathered to watch and encourage their favorite, most of them for Gunnar since he was a local. The blacksmith wove through the men, taking their bets.

Galm, Short Olaf, and Dyri were deep in conversation with Gunnar, no doubt giving him advice on what to do, and they often stole glances over at Sigmund, sizing him up, as he prepared with his own companions. As Gunnar conferred with his mates, he stripped off his tunic and hung it on a post at the edge of the ring. He removed his arm ring and pulled off his necklace, dropping them into Short Olaf's outstretched hand. A *glima* match, although done for sport, was a fierce competition with few rules. The men wanted as few encumbrances as possible. He couldn't risk having the cord from a necklace be used to choke him.

Astrid could not take her eyes off Gunnar as he circled his bare arms, ran in place, and stretched his neck from side to side, readying himself for the match. The muscles in his arms and chest rippled with the movement. She thought of their kiss the night before, how those powerful arms had held her around the waist, the way his lips felt on hers, and she felt the heat rising to her face. He caught her staring at him, and he smiled. The look made her entire body tingle, and she turned away to stare at the ground, as if she had dropped something. When she peeked in his direction, he had gone back to talking to the others.

An older man from a neighboring farm who had no man in the match, walked out to the center of the ring to judge, and then the two men wrestled.

Astrid searched the crowd for Emund or Rikki. Frowning, she wondered where they could be. They always attended the competitions, especially Emund, who liked to gamble, and Rikki, who would compete against anyone in anything. He would wrestle, run, or swim with the slightest suggestion. The news about Jori must be keeping them away.

She shrugged and went back to watching the match, yelling encouragement to Gunnar, wanting him to thrash Sigmund. The two men struggled, grappling with each other, sometimes on their feet, sometimes on the ground. At first Sigmund's left-handedness threw Gunnar off guard, and he took a few hard hits and throws before adjusting to the different angle of Sigmund's reach and attack. They soon grew sweaty and dirty, and their movements grew slower and more deliberate. In a flash, Sigmund lunged at Gunnar's legs, lifted him up, and slammed him onto the ground.

Astrid shouted in dismay. The force of the impact was great enough that she could hear the thump through the noise of the crowd. She gulped. So intent was she on the match, that she did not hear the footsteps as someone approached.

"Ah, well done!" A thick, boozy voice said near her ear.

Startled, Astrid jumped.

Ketil Egilsson laughed, the smell of ale on his breath. His eyes ran over her body, and Astrid had to resist the urge to cover herself with her hands. She knew she was fully dressed, but his gaze made her feel naked. Recoiling, she took a small step back.

He gestured toward the two wrestlers with the hand holding his drink. A little ale sloshed out of the top of his cup. "That's my son. I bet a silver arm ring on him. He'd better win," he growled.

He took in Astrid again, and once again his bleary eyes grazed over her body.

Every time he did that, it made her squirm.

"I've been watching you, Astrid Tryggvisdottir. My son needs a new wife. You will do. The look of you pleases him. It pleases me, too."

She had to bite down on the nausea. It was as she feared. Her thoughts went to the last time she'd seen a rabbit in a snare. The rabbit had not been killed but struggled and bit at the snare to escape. She felt like that rabbit, caught in a trap and unable to get free.

A shout went up from the crowd watching the wrestling match. The shout took Ketil's attention away from Astrid and he cursed. She looked over and her heart leaped with pride. Gunnar had somehow turned the match around, and he was the one in control. He had Sigmund pinned in a headlock. The muscles in Gunnar's back were red from abrasions and shone with sweat as he strained with the effort to keep Sigmund down. After a while, Sigmund went limp and Gunnar staggered to his feet, leaving the other man on the ground. As the only man standing, Gunnar was the winner. Galm, Short Olaf, Dyri, and many of Tryggvi's men swarmed to congratulate him. Astrid laughed and cheered. Good. Gunnar won, and Sigmund and Ketil defeated.

Ketil threw up his hands, spilling his drink on his arm. "*Shyt*! He said it would be an easy win." He glowered toward his son, who had rolled over onto his back while he caught his breath, his yellow hair dark with sweat fanned out around his head.

Cursing herself for not slipping away when she'd had the chance, Astrid hoped Ketil would forget about her. She started to leave, but he turned his attention back to her with a renewed intensity.

He leaned down and put his face close to hers. Up close, his skin was loose, and she could see a small scar on his chin. His breath overpowered her with the smell of ale. "Why do you smile, girl?" His glance went to Gunnar and then returned to her. "You want him? He is nothing compared to my son. My son has already fathered many children. He would put a baby in your belly easily enough." His eyes took on that acquisitive look again, and he put a callused hand on her chin.

The touch sent a jolt of panic that rooted her to the ground. She did not know what to do. Every part of her wanted to push his hand away and run as fast and as far as she could. But she could not move.

"Ketil, you best take your hand off her before I remove it for you with my knife," a deep voice growled, a voice that sounded to Astrid like it had been sent by the gods.

Ketil did not remove his hand. He turned toward the voice. "Red."

Emund's hand went for the dagger he carried on his belt, but he never took his eyes off Ketil. "Your hand."

Ketil dropped his hand.

Astrid took a step away from him and toward Emund, who still had his hand near his dagger and at the ready.

"What is going on?" Tryggvi came upon the stand-off.

"Tryggvi," Ketil called, his voice filled with comradeship. "I was just talking to your daughter."

Astrid thought she heard Emund growl like a dog with his hackles up. She wished Emund would bite Ketil's offending hand off.

Her father scowled. "You do not talk to her, you talk to me."

Relief flooded through Astrid with Emund and her father there. They would let no harm come to her.

"Let us talk, Ketil. But not here," Tryggvi said, and he cast a glance at Astrid.

"Excellent," Ketil answered as if they'd already made the deal.

The two men made their way back to Tryggvi's longhouse, Ketil clapping Tryggvi on the back like an old friend. He walked with a limp, but she knew it did not impair him at all. Ketil was a fierce warrior, rich, and he had dozens of men who followed him. His son was rich himself, with his own men and ships. It would be a suitable match for her father to make. They were also from Scania, which would provide her Swedish father with a Danish ally.

Astrid's mind raced, and she looked to Emund. His face gave her no clue what her father intended, but he gave her a kind smile. She went to him and he gave her a quick hug, and kissed the top of her head.

"He won't touch you again like that, I promise you, my little bear. Go find your friend Ragnhild. It's a wedding feast. You should enjoy yourself." Emund gave her one last squeeze before following Tryggvi and Ketil.

Astrid made it look like she headed off to find Ragnhild, but instead she escaped to the back of one of the storehouses where she could be alone. She leaned against the wooden wall of the building, the feel of it strong and reassuring, and she rubbed her hand over her face where Ketil had touched her. The feel of his hand had seeped into her skin and she rubbed so hard her face burned.

She heard the shouts and cries of fun as the festivities carried on. Astrid leaned her head back against the storehouse and looked up at the trees, tears streaming down her face. Sigmund Ketilsson was the type of man she'd have to marry. Not a man like Gunnar. No, not someone handsome and good, someone she knew and trusted. Gunnar was simply a *huskarl* and had nothing her father wanted. Not like Sigmund. The thought of him, his dyed blond hair and his yellow clothes, made her skin crawl.

Laughter and footsteps intruded on her solitude. Rikki and the girl he'd left the feast hall with the night before, approached, their heads together in an intimate conversation. He had his arm around her waist, and she leaned into him as they walked.

They stopped short when they saw Astrid standing there; Rikki's eyebrows shot up. When he noticed she'd been crying, he asked, "What's wrong?" His eyes traveled over her and her clothes, looking to see if she had any bruises or a torn dress.

Astrid shook her head and Rikki slipped his arm away from the girl. "I'll find you later," he told her as he pulled her to him and kissed her. She gave him a smile and ran her hand over his chest before leaving.

"Come with me to our spot?" Astrid asked her brother.

He nodded, and they strolled into the forest behind their village, following a barely recognizable path littered with gold and russet leaves. Birds sang overhead and small forest animals scurried away as the siblings made their way to their secret place.

"Why are you damp?" Astrid reached up and took a strand of his hair in her fingers. Her gaze traveled down to his tunic.

He snorted. "Emund dunked me in a rain barrel."

"Why?" She laughed.

"To sober me."

"But why did he need to do that?"

"Father heard news about Harald and wanted to talk to me and Jori. Emund found me in the barn with Tola." He gestured to the girl who had just left. "I was still drunk..."

"So Emund dunked your head in a rain barrel?"

"*Ja*. Much to Galm's amusement."

Astrid laughed. "I hope that didn't give Galm any ideas. He'll start dunking everyone."

As they walked, he told Astrid about what their father had said and that Jori would leave soon to spend the winter with King Ingjald. She remained quiet, listening to her brother's voice, letting him tell her what she already knew, the concerns he had, and she felt her chest tighten. The ground felt uncertain under her feet, like they were all walking in the middle of a frozen lake.

Pine and birch trees soared over them, and Rikki would occasionally touch a marked tree. The mark looked like something natural, and only Astrid and Rikki could tell that he had carved it. They heard the falling water before they saw it, a gentle waterfall cascading over sloping rocks surrounded by foliage and birch. They had discovered this place the spring after their little brother Olaf had died. A large boulder smoothed by ages of water marked the entry to their private hideaway. Rikki had tried to carve a runestone on the boulder for little Olaf.

It read, *Rikolf and Astrid carved this in memory of their brother Olaf. He was a good brother.*

Without the right tools, it was a crude carving. Still, they had this stone for their brother.

Astrid touched it as she passed, and Rikki did the same.

"Do you ever wonder what it would be like if he and the baby had both lived?" Astrid asked. Not long after Olaf died, their mother had given birth to a still-born baby.

"Crowded." Rikki grinned.

"I'm serious."

"No. I don't. They are dead, and there is nothing we can do about it. We made this runestone..." At the word he gave a little snort. It was a childish attempt at a runestone. "To remember Olaf. That is all I need."

He flopped down on the soft grass near the edge of the pool where the small waterfall fell, his elbows resting on his knees as he watched the water tumble down the rocks. It was soothing and one of the reasons they sought it out when they were troubled.

Astrid sat down next to him as he picked up a pebble and tossed it into the pool. The water rippled out. "Ketil Egilsson is here to ask father to marry me to his son Sigmund." Astrid swallowed hard after saying the words. It made her feel sick.

She had expected surprise, outrage, something from Rikki, but she received nothing. "I thought that was the reason."

"I don't want to marry him."

He turned to look at her. "Good. He's a *bacraut*. He's been strutting like a cock in the henhouse." Rikki gave her a crooked grin. "Galm wanted to get him so drunk he'd pass out. Then we'd shave off his ridiculous dyed hair and beard."

"That's terrible, Rikki! Sigmund would be as mad as a wet hen." Astrid giggled at the thought of the preening Sigmund with a bald head and no beard. "I would like that."

"He deserves it."

"Father and Mother would not be happy either. Sigmund is a guest."

Rikki shrugged and got to his feet, looking for a stick. When he found one, he got out his knife, sat back down, and began to shave off the old bark.

"Do you think Father will agree to it? The marriage?" She wanted him to soothe her by saying no, that their father would never do it.

"I don't know." Rikki didn't take his eyes off his work when he talked, something Astrid was used to. Her brother always thought better when he worked with his hands. His hands moved with such dexterity that she never tired of watching him whittle and carve. "Father and Ketil need each other. But Ketil keeps berserkers among his men, and Father doesn't trust them."

"Berserkers?" Astrid cried. "Does Sigmund keep them too?"

The warriors who turned themselves into crazed animals when fighting scared her. Tryggvi didn't trust them among his men, and certainly not near his family. He said they were as likely to turn on the leader as the enemy.

"*Ja.* That alone might make Father say no to the proposal. But..."

Astrid groaned. She did not want to hear what came next.

"A marriage between you and Sigmund would help ensure there was peace between Father and Ketil. Sigmund is rich, too, and controls part of the waters between here and the east, where we need to pass every raiding season."

"That's not what I wanted to hear." She jumped to her feet. "I can't marry him. He's awful. His father told me he's already fathered many children. Have you seen the look on the face of that thrall he's taken with? I don't know what he does with her or to her...and I don't want to know...but it must be bad. What would happen to me?" She paced and wrung her hands in her apron-dress, feeling the panic rising in her chest.

Rikki set his knife and woodwork aside and rose. He stood in front of Astrid and took her by the arms, his hands strong and firm. "Asta. Calm down."

His deep voice got through her panic, and she blinked at him. She took a breath.

"That's better," Rikki said. "I don't know what I can do. Father does not listen to me."

A hint of bitterness crept into his voice, and Astrid remembered that he had been with their father earlier.

"Talk to Emund," she said.

"*Ja,*" he said. "I will. You talk to Mother. Don't forget you have the right to refuse the marriage."

"What would Father do if I refused?"

"It would not be good."

They were quiet, both thinking of their father's anger. They had both been at the wrong end of it, especially Rikki, and it was frightening.

There was a flurry of birds in the treetops and the sound of brush being disturbed. Rikki picked up his dagger and looked around.

After a while, with nothing or no one intruding, he sheathed the knife.

"We should get back."

They headed back out of the clearing, both of them touching the runestone as they left. Halfway back to the village, they heard another disturbance in the foliage. Rikki pushed Astrid behind him.

"I wish I'd brought my axe," he muttered. "Or even my seax."

A shot of alarm ran up Astrid's spine. She was taken back to the day when the outlaws had ambushed her and Emund. That day the men had come out of the woods and circled them; she had come close to being taken away and sold as a slave. She tamped down the fear and vowed that no one would ever take her like that again. She'd die fighting.

Astrid heard a hiccup and what sounded like a woman crying. She grabbed onto Rikki's arm, which tensed at her touch. He must have heard it too, because he nodded, and they walked toward the sound.

As they pushed aside some undergrowth, they found a woman kneeling on the ground, clutching herself. When she heard them, she shook her head and shouted, "Don't take me back to him! I can't do it!" She whipped a knife out of her sleeve, and so quickly that not even Rikki could react, she sliced it up her arm in a deep cut and then did the same on the other arm. Blood spilled onto the ground, turning the yellow-gold leaves crimson.

"No," Astrid cried. She rushed to the young woman, looking for something to bind the wound. The metal tang of so much blood made Astrid gag. She unfastened her apron, and approached the thrall so she could bind the wound with it, but the woman fought her, thrashing, hitting at her, and screaming. A blow hit Astrid on the side of her face, stinging her momentarily, and making her eyes water. Blood still streamed from the woman's arms, and some had flicked onto Astrid when she struck out. Rikki had come up behind the thrashing woman and captured her in a bear hug. By this time, the blood loss had made her movements slow. Astrid grabbed one of her arms, wrapped it with one end of the apron, and then wrapped the other end around the other arm. Blood immediately seeped through the fabric, so Astrid put pressure on the wounds, holding them with her hands as the woman trembled with rage or fear or pain. The blood flow eased, and the woman calmed down, her eyes rolling up in her head. She lolled against Rikki.

Astrid gave her brother a look that he returned; his jaw clenched. This was the work of Sigmund Ketilsson, she was sure of it.

Low, angry voices came from the Tryggvi and Ingiborg's sleeping chamber. It was a sign of his wealth that they even had a separate room to sleep in. This was one time Astrid wished they did not have a room where they could close the door. She wanted to hear what they said. The thrall she and Rikki had found in the woods was alive and being cared for by one of the older female thralls. The young woman had bled so much she nearly died, and only Astrid and Rikki finding her had saved her.

Astrid eased over to the door, hoping no one would catch her trying to listen in to her mother and father's conversation. Most people were over at the feast hall or outside, still celebrating the marriage of Ragnhild and Dyri, the last night of feasting and dancing.

"...Rikki and Astrid..." Astrid heard her mother say, but the thump of the outside door to the longhouse made her jump away, her heart leaping into her throat like a fish as it jumps out of the lake.

It was only Rikki. He raised his eyebrow at her in question and joined her, his footsteps in his leather shoes as quiet as a cat. They leaned into the door to hear.

"...is a guest, Inga," Tryggvi's voice, frustrated. "Guests are welcome to the thralls."

Astrid suppressed a shiver. Female thralls were used by the men and offered to guests, and when the thrall was a young woman, no older than she was herself, it made her give thanks to the gods she was not one of them. She still had nightmares where she would dream of Skalli the outlaw dragging her away from her family and safety, except in her dreams no one rescued her.

"Guests are not welcome to *abuse* our thralls, Tryggvi. Or terrorize them. That might be the way in other households, but not this one."

"We don't know that Sigmund terrorized the girl. We only have what she said. The girl tried to slice open her arms. She is not right in her head," Tryggvi said, his voice taking on that tone when he was losing patience. "I need Sigmund and Ketil. I will not push the issue with them," Tryggvi added. "No. Leave it be, wife."

Rikki gave Astrid a look. She could tell he was thinking the same thing as her. In her mind, Astrid could see her father holding up his hands to quiet Ingiborg's objection. She'd seen him do it many times privately and in his role as jarl. As far as Astrid could remember, the only people her father could not silence with a raised hand were her mother and Emund. Her mother did not disappoint this time.

"What about Astrid?" Ingiborg demanded.

A thump sounded, like her father had taken off something heavy and laid it on their pine chest. "What about her?"

Astrid straightened at her name and looked at her brother again. He mouthed 'Sigmund.'

"You must not agree to a marriage between Sigmund and our daughter. He is a brute."

"We don't know that."

"Yes, we do. Tryggvi. Please." Her mother pleaded, something Astrid had not heard often.

Tryggvi sighed. "I have not decided. But, it is my decision."

Astrid's eyes widened. Rikki looked ready to burst into the sleeping room; his jaw clenched and his hands curled into fists.

"There are other options. Other husbands. Other men to ally with." Her mother's voice was far from the door.

A knot formed in Astrid's stomach. This is what she was now. A piece to play in a game. Someone to move around the board to best advantage her father and his interests. She had always known it, but hearing it so boldly like this was too much.

She moved away from the door. When she walked off, Rikki grabbed hold of her arm. "I can't hear any more," she whispered. He nodded and let her go.

She needed her friend Ragnhild, but she was so involved in the wedding celebration Astrid did not want to bother her. Then Gunnar's face appeared in her mind. She would find him and...what? Tell him all about a man who wanted to marry her? She could throw herself at him, let him do what she knew he wanted. Even that wouldn't matter, wouldn't ruin her; men preferred a virgin bride, but it wasn't necessary. She doubted a man like Sigmund would care.

Walking outside, the twilight sky burning with orange streaks, Astrid heard her sister's laugh. What she saw made her breath catch in her throat. Sigmund Ketilsson knelt next to Gytha as she showed him the baby goat she had adopted as her own. He stroked the kid's head and let it nudge his hand, giving Gytha a smile as he listened to her tell him about the kid's mother and how she died.

"What are you doing?" Astrid barked at them. They both looked up.

"Asta! Sigmund helped me find baby Tangri when he got away from me. He helped me."

Sigmund unfolded himself so he stood facing Astrid. "I was on my way to talk to your father when I saw your sister in distress that she'd lost her baby goat. We wouldn't want a wolf to get it, now, would we?" He smiled, and it made Astrid feel sick. An image of the stricken thrall screaming at her and Rikki to not take her back to 'him' arose in her mind. She could still smell all the blood.

Astrid moved next to Gytha and put her arm around her sister protectively, not that she could do anything if this man decided to hurt them. Looking him up and down, Astrid knew he would not do anything as obvious as hurt Gytha in public.

"Thank you, Sigmund," Gytha said, holding the baby in her arms and nuzzling it with her face.

"You're welcome," he said with a dramatic bow to Gytha.

His face showed no sign that he had been the reason behind the thrall hurting herself. Maybe Astrid had imagined it all? Imagined that the girl was frightened of him? Could the girl have been mad, and Astrid assumed it was Sigmund that had done something to her? That still did not explain why she, herself, recoiled every time he was near.

"I am on my way to inform Tryggvi that my father and I intend to leave in two days' time. The tides are with us and some of our men need to get home to tend the last of the harvest."

Astrid could not wait for him to leave. She was her mother's daughter, though, so she would be polite. "May the winds be at your back and your harvests plentiful."

He smiled and leaned toward her. "*My* harvests are always plentiful. We will see each other again soon, Astrid Tryggvisdottir. Count on it." He headed toward her father's longhouse. Gripping onto her sister's shoulder, Astrid watched him walk away. She hoped it was the last time she ever saw him.

"Asta, that hurts," Gytha said, squirming out from Astrid's grip.

"Sorry." Taking a breath, she let go of her sister, and tried to wash Sigmund from her mind.

She knew one thing for sure. No matter her father's wrath, she would not marry that man.

Two mornings later, the sky dawned with the sun leaking out from behind the clouds, when Jori, Gunnar, and a small band of Tryggvi's men, gathered in the yard to say goodbye. It had sprinkled in the night, and the ground was muddy. Tryggvi, Emund, and Buri huddled in talks with Jori and Gunnar for the last time before they left, while their horses shuffled and stamped, impatient to leave. Her father kept Rikki close, and he stood right behind him, taking in every word.

Astrid hated that they would spend the winter in the presence of Harald Olafsson. Her hatred of him was as bright as the sun on a hot summer day. She picked at a callus on her finger from weaving.

Gytha came up next to her and grabbed hold of her arm.

"I am scared for them," Gytha said in a thick voice. She had never been the same since the attack on their village by Harald. Already an affectionate and gentle girl, the attack, hiding in the cave in fear, and the aftermath of injury and death had made her even more timid and afraid than before. Seeing a decapitated man and an eviscerated man had sent her over the edge for a long time, never to return completely.

Astrid looked down at her sister. Tears streamed down the younger girl's hazel eyes, leaving sparkling streaks on her cheeks.

"We must be brave for them," Astrid said.

"I don't want to be brave." Fresh tears ran down her face. "What if they never come back?" Gytha's voice sounded panicked, and Astrid had to take a breath to not let her sister's fear crash into her.

But it was a fear she shared. What if this was it? The last word, the last goodbye. She loved her half-brother, and as she watched him talk with their father and Emund, she wanted to shout at them that this journey to meet with King Ingjald and Harald Olafsson was not worth it. Tryggvi embraced his son, saying something into his ear that only they could hear. He then gave Gunnar a hearty hug, but when he pulled away, he held Gunnar by the arms and said something while nodding toward Jori. Whatever words he said were serious, for Gunnar nodded gravely and put his hand on his sword hilt.

Her stomach lurched, and she stared at Gunnar to burn an image of him into her mind. She had grown up with him in her life and now that she wanted him, he was leaving.

A sobbing hiccup from Gytha brought Astrid back from her thoughts. She looked at her sister and her tear-filled eyes. "Gytha. Stop crying." Her voice sounded harsh, but it was the only way. It had the intended effect, and Gytha gulped down a sob. "Your tears do not help. Do you see *modir* crying?"

Ingiborg stood removed from the small group of people, watching, but not a part of the leave-taking.

"She does not love Jori," Gytha said.

Astrid started. Sometimes Gytha behaved so young Astrid forgot that she was nearly eleven. Old enough to notice that there was no love between Ingiborg and Jori.

Deciding to be honest, Astrid answered, "Maybe not, but she cares about him for Father's sake, and does not want him to come to harm. And she loves Gunnar like one of her own." She bent down to be at Gytha's level. "You can cry later, sweet one. For now, try to be strong. Yes?"

Gytha nodded and wiped her hand across her eyes. She let go of Astrid's hand and made her way over to their mother.

"*Hei*, Asta," Short Olaf said, as he walked up to her, a smile on his face when she turned to him.

"Hi, Olli." She sighed, relieved to see him. "Where is Galm?"

"Sleeping off a drunk somewhere. I'd bet Rikki would give a few pieces of silver to be in bed with that pretty Tola and not here."

"And you?"

"Ugh." He scrunched his face and stuck out his tongue. "I couldn't keep up with them. They drank me under the table."

"I saw you. You looked very sweet drooling on the floor while Rikki and Galm played dice." Astrid smiled.

Horrified, Short Olaf's freckled face grew red. "Oh, no!"

"Yes." She put her hand on his arm. "Don't worry. It wasn't the first time I've seen you like that."

He groaned. "By Thor, I will never drink with them again. No more ale for me." He gestured with his chin toward Jori. "It looks like they are ready to leave."

Jori strode over to them. "Sissa." He pulled her into a tight hug.

She hugged him back, not wanting to let go. "Stay safe," Astrid implored as he broke the hug.

"Don't worry about me," Jori said, lightly. "When I return in the spring, I'll bring you a gift. More beads for your necklace?" He held up her beaded necklace with a finger.

She smiled. "I'd like that."

He kissed her on the cheek, said goodbye to Short Olaf, and strode back to his horse. Gunnar was already mounted and ready to go, his pack draped across the animal's back. On an impulse, Astrid approached Gunnar. He watched her, his green eyes taking her in.

"Asta," he said with a smile.

Hearing her pet name on his lips lightened her step until she stood at his foot in the stirrup.

"Gunnar." She checked that no one was watching them, and she touched his leg. The muscle twitched under her touch, and he arched an eyebrow. "Take care of yourself."

"Always."

The way he said that simple word sent a shiver down her back.

He leaned down to her, the leather of his saddle creaking under his weight, and said with a whisper and a wink. "I will tell you all of my adventures."

His horse stamped and moved, and he tightened his hands on the reins.

A powerful impulse rushed over Astrid, and she used the distraction of Gunnar's horse to remove her Freya necklace. Once in her hand, she slipped it into his saddle bag. Then she stepped back from the horse, her heart racing in her chest as if she'd just run a long way.

Gunnar brought the horse around to face her again. "He's ready to go." He smiled and gave the horse a pat on the neck.

"Let us go," Jorund cried out to his men.

"I will see you when the world turns green again, Asta," Gunnar said with a smile. Then he followed Jori out of the village.

"When the world is green, Gunnar," Astrid whispered, although he could not hear her. She put her hand up to touch her Freya pendant, but it was gone. Her throat felt naked without it, and she hoped the goddess would look after Gunnar and keep him safe.

Chapter Nine
Hovgarden. Winter.

Bjorn and King Ingjald raced, their skis *shushing* underneath them, past the merchant square on the king's island, the square noisy and vibrant—the clang of the smith's hammer, the rasp of the woodcarver's saw, the clack of the women's looms. Even in the winter, the tradespeople had to work. As they skied by the sturdy buildings, Bjorn's arms burned from the effort of propelling himself, his face stinging from cold. They hit a small hill that led toward the king's compound, set a distance from the lake, and at the bottom, Ingjald turned sharply, snow flying from his skis. Bjorn let out a shout and had to swerve to avoid the snowy projectile. They had been racing for a long time, and Bjorn enjoyed the blood rushing through his legs and the way the icy air bit his face. Two members of the king's *hird* skied with them, keeping their distance, but watchful for any dangers.

The king's compound loomed before them, the great hall towering over all the other buildings; Ingjald slowed up with a laugh, his cheeks and nose red with cold, but his blue eyes were clear as the sky. "Do you not have snow where you come from?" He joked as Bjorn caught up to him. The king had on a thick gray woolen cap that fit down over his ears, marten fur lining the brim along his forehead.

"Not nearly so deep. Even your snow is rich, King Ingjald," Bjorn said, a hand on his chest.

They continued on side-by-side, the movement of their pine poles and skis in sync.

"You have not joined your foster-father during the last two meetings with me. Do you not agree with this alliance he seeks?"

"Harald has Styrr with him."

Ingjald waited for Bjorn to give him more. "That does not answer my question. You are his foster-son and should be with him."

Not knowing how much to reveal, Bjorn skied on in silence. He knew the alliance would break Tryggvi Olafsson and end the feud, and he would fight to the death to make sure they destroyed Tryggvi. After all, it was Tryggvi's son who had killed Galinn. Once the son was dead, Bjorn wanted a simple life as one of Harald's guard with no more worries than which woman he could get into his bed.

His breath coming out in white puffs, he said. "I am loyal to Harald and will do what he orders."

Bjorn could feel Ingjald watching him as they skied on, waiting once again for Bjorn to reveal more, but he did not turn to face him.

They approached Ingjald's compound, the high wooden fence that surrounded the king's buildings and the horned tip of his feast hall roof that towered over everything. People made their way on wooden walkways clear of snow and ice. It would have been an idyllic scene if not for the clutch of armed men who crowded the gate, their angry voices promising bloodshed soon.

Bjorn recognized Harald's growl as one of the men who barred the way through the gate. He noticed several of Ingjald's household men in the fray, trying to get between the two groups.

"I am here to see King Ingjald Anundsson," a man's voice shouted, and Bjorn halted. That voice sounded familiar, but as if in a memory.

"You should not have shown your face here, boy," Harald snapped. "Take your men and leave before we kill you all."

A new voice jumped in, Ingjald's man. His voice was as cold as the ice that hung from the trees. "Harald Olafsson, you do not speak for King Ingjald. We will wait for the king to return."

As they neared the gate, Ingjald stopped and signaled for the closest thrall to come unbind their feet from their skis. Once free, he strode over to the angry mob, Bjorn close behind.

The two groups parted as King Ingjald walked up. When they did, Bjorn glimpsed the man whose voice he had heard. It took him back to the battle at Storelva. Hot rage bubbled up inside Bjorn, and his fingers twitched at his side near his dagger. He could easily slip up to Tryggvi's son and slide that blade right into his heart, watch him bleed as Galinn had bled into the sand that day. With a gulp, he stopped his hand from pulling the blade from its sheath, but he let his fingers hover above it, just in case. He had waited four seasons. He could wait until a better time.

Tryggvi's son turned to Ingjald, pleased to see the king approach. He was not much older than Bjorn. "I am Jorund, son of Tryggvi. We seek your hospitality, King Ingjald. I wish to speak with you on my father's behalf."

Harald exploded. "King Ingjald. You cannot give this man your hospitality. He is the son of my enemy, so he is my enemy."

One of Jorund's men stood at his back and closed in when Harald spoke, his own hand near a sword hooked to his belt. Bjorn saw in his eyes he'd like nothing more than to kill Harald here and now. Moving quietly, Bjorn maneuvered himself so he stood with Harald and Styrr, and he watched this other man. If he should make a move toward Harald, Bjorn would be there. The conflict between Tryggvi's son, Ingjald, and Harald absorbed everyone else. A quiet presence made himself known at Bjorn's back, and he recognized Rekja. Without looking, Bjorn knew his friend had a hand on his own weapon.

The movements alerted Tryggvi's man. He glanced at Bjorn, at Rekja, then at Bjorn's hand that still rested on the hilt of his dagger. The short blade would be deadly in these close quarters, and Tryggvi's man knew it.

Bjorn sized up this man; he was a warrior, no doubt one of Tryggvi's most trusted. He wore leather armor and a leather arm guard on his right forearm. These men came prepared for a fight. The man noticed Bjorn's appraisal and inclined his head toward him, the corner of his mouth tipped up in the slightest hint of a smile.

This all happened in the space of a few moments. Ingjald's voice broke over bickering men, clear and decisive. "I would hear what you have to say, Jorund Tryggvason. You are welcome to my home." He clasped his fist to his chest. Jorund returned the gesture.

Ingjald turned to Harald, his eyes hard. "I expect all who winter here to keep the peace."

With a curt nod to Ingjald, Harald turned to Jorund and looked him up and down. Stepping in close, he said, "You look like my brother." With a deliberate pause, he stared at Jorund. "I hate my brother. Keep out of my way." His gaze swept over Jorund's men before he spun on his heels and walked off toward the building where he and his men were staying, Styrr alongside him.

Bjorn lingered to see the reaction of the son of Tryggvi. To his credit, he did not recoil or waver at Harald's words, but his hands clenched at his sides. Without warning, a vision of Jorund racing toward him on the riverfront at Storelva rose in Bjorn's mind, Galinn dying, Ingvar's head cleaved in two, his body slumping to the ground. Bjorn could hear the crunch of bone as the red-giant's axe cut through Ingvar's head, and he smelt the blood as it drained from Galinn's body. His hand was on his dagger before he knew what he was doing. A firm hand landed on Bjorn's right arm, locking it into place, and Ingjald's voice sounded in his ear.

"Bjorn." None too gently, Ingjald whipped Bjorn around to face him. Ingjald's blue eyes swam behind a red haze, and Bjorn heard him as if from underwater. "Bjorn. Do not break my peace."

The pressure of Ingjald's hand tightened until Bjorn had to let go of his blade. "Go." He let go of Bjorn's arm.

Eyes clearing, Bjorn nodded.

Without another glance at Jorund and his men, Bjorn spun and walked to the guest quarters, passing Ingjald's wife Gyrid on his way, Selime a few steps behind her. Gyrid stopped him.

"I hear we have more visitors."

"*Ja*," he grunted.

She did not press him. She turned to Selime. "It will be crowded. You must find room for them all." The household keys jangled at her waist as she walked on to meet Ingjald at the gate.

Selime lingered for a moment, and he stepped in between her and the king's wife. He laid his hand on Selime's soft waist.

"You look troubled, Bjorn."

He shook his head.

Her eyes showed that she understood not to ask anything more. With a quick glance toward Gyrid over Bjorn's shoulder, Selime saw that no one watched them. She touched two of her fingers to his lips in an intimate gesture. "Ingjald will be busy with Gyrid tonight. It is her breeding time." She lifted her eyebrows and tilted her head, questioning.

"Come to me," he said.

"Yes. I will take that troubled look off your face."

Grunting his assent, Bjorn moved away from Selime and hurried to meet up with Harald and Styrr in their quarters. He did not look back.

Bjorn kept the peace by keeping to himself as much as he could without raising any suspicion. On most days, he left as soon as it was light, strapped on his skis, grabbed his poles, and disappeared until the evening meal. Rekja was the only man Bjorn allowed to join him. Today was not a day to ski or skate. A fierce snowstorm had blown in and kept everyone indoors. Harald's and Jorund's men occupied opposite sides of the feast hall.

Sprawled on a fur-lined bench, Bjorn drained his ale cup and dropped it on the floor rushes. One of Ingjald's dogs rushed over to lick up any spilled liquid, and Bjorn rubbed the dog's back. He watched smoke from the central hearth spiral up through the smoke hole in the roof high above and thought about his birth father, Alfar Bjornsson, so different from Harald. His thoughts went back to a day much like this one, stuck indoors, the hearth fire burning brightly, oil lamps throwing dancing light on the walls, stomachs full from a good meal of beef stew. The hungry months were still far away and Bjorn, six winters old, was content. His little brother Alfvadr slept next to his mother, curled up on the furs. His father pulled Bjorn onto his lap and spoke in his storytelling voice. Bjorn settled in, leaning his head against his father's chest, and played with an arm ring his father wore on his left wrist. It was made of small beads as black as night, each one separated by a smaller bead of silver. When Bjorn looked at it, it made him think he was standing outside in the woods in the deepest part of the night, looking up at a sky that glittered with stars. He traced the smooth beads with his little fingers.

His father turned his wrist so Bjorn could see the arm ring better. It caught the light of the fire and the black beads flickered as if alive. "Many generations ago our ancestor Asbjorn the Fair," his father said and gave him a little squeeze, "was out hunting during early winter. He was an expert hunter, good with a bow...but not this time. The new moon grew while he was out until it became full and bright, and still he caught nothing. Asbjorn grew weary and knew he had to turn back to his home. The air changed, and he could feel and smell that the first snow would fall soon. As he turned toward home, he spotted a doe drinking at a pond. Asbjorn crept up on the doe, keeping himself hidden in the bushes. It was what made him an expert hunter; he could walk without making much sound."

Shifting in his chair, Bjorn's father said in his ear, "I have watched you as you sneak up on the dogs. You move as silently as your ancestor, my son. You will make a good hunter."

Bjorn beamed at the praise.

His father continued, "Our ancestor Asbjorn took aim at that doe and his arrow flew straight. It pierced the doe in the heart. She dropped where she stood. As he knelt by the body of the doe, Asbjorn felt the ground tremor as if many people walked nearby, but when he looked around, he saw no one."

With an intake of breath, Bjorn asked his father, "Was it the elves?"

"You will find out. Asbjorn cut the heart out of the doe's body and held it, still-warm, in his hand. He thanked the doe for its life and then took a bite out of her heart. In that moment, he felt the tremor again, but again, he saw nothing. He knew he needed to take that deer back to his village. They needed the meat for the winter, the bones for their broth. They needed the hide for their clothes and shoes. They needed the bones for their cups, combs, and needles. But instead of dragging it home, Asbjorn created an altar in the woods right next to that pond. On a flat rock, he cut open the deer and bled it into another rock, one shaped like a bowl. He marked himself with the blood and offered the animal to the *alfar*. Then he left the deer and the bowl of blood in the clearing. He headed home with empty hands."

"The storm Asbjorn had sensed blew in before he got home. Before long, he lost his way."

His father paused. Their own storm buffeted the walls of their house, but it was cozy and warm before the fire and in his father's lap. Bjorn thought of being lost in the snow and shivered.

"It was freezing. Asbjorn knew how to make a snow cave, but the dark had come on as suddenly as the storm, and he could not see. He understood he would die in the storm, so he leaned up against a tree and closed his eyes, knowing he would never open them again."

Young Bjorn sat up. "He died?"

With a chuckle, his father answered, "No. He woke up." He leaned over to whisper in Bjorn's ear, and his breath tickled Bjorn's neck, making him giggle. "Surrounded by beautiful people who glowed in the darkness."

"The *alfar*!" Bjorn cried out.

"The *alfar*. They saved him because he had sacrificed that deer to them."

Young Bjorn clapped his hands.

"Asbjorn stayed with the *alfar* all winter. When the next Autumnmonth came, he visited them again because..." He paused and laughed when Bjorn wiggled impatiently.

"Why?" Bjorn asked.

"Our ancestor Asbjorn had a son. A half-elf son. This son married and had children. And on down until you. These are your ancestors."

Young Bjorn shifted so he could look at his father, his little face scrunched up in thought.

His father nodded, his dark eyes gleaming like the beads on his arm ring. "You have *alfar* blood in you, son. The light beings..." He held up his thick arm to show the ring. "Gave this to Asbjorn, and he gave it to his son, and on until I came to wear it. You will wear it when you are a man."

Bjorn traced the black beads again with his small fingers. He thought about being a grown man and wearing the arm ring. He jumped off his father's lap. "I will find our *alfar* ancestors when I am grown," he told his father. Bjorn looked at his own hands, turning them over and over as if he could detect the light-beings in him. When he finished with his hands, he looked up at his father. Leaning on his father's legs, Bjorn put his little hand up to his father's weathered, but still-young face and poked at him.

Alfar laughed, catching Bjorn's hands in his own rough ones. "You would not be the first of our men to try. No one has found them yet, but it may be your *wyrd*." He leaned his face closer to Bjorn's and squeezed his hands. "Remember the stories, Bjorn, for you may need them one day."

"Bjorn!"

The shout brought him out of his drunken memory, and he caught himself rubbing his wrist where his father's arm ring should have been. He scowled at the nakedness of his wrist. He had not been with his father when he died, and his father's wife, in her greediness, had taken the arm ring for herself. It was lost forever. The bitterness of the loss made Bjorn's stomach churn.

"Bjorn is our man!" The shout came again from Vefinn.

With a grunt, Bjorn pushed himself to a sitting position. Looking around, he saw that several men from both camps were pushing tables and benches up against the walls to clear a spot on the floor. One of Ingjald's men came in the door with a thick, walrus-hide rope loop, a flurry of snow and cold blowing in with him when the door opened. A thrall rushed over to close the door behind him, and the heavy wood slammed with a thud.

With Vefinn's laughing eyes on him, Bjorn rose and strode over to where the men had assembled. Ingjald's man dropped the rope in the center of the floor in front of Ingjald, who stood in between the two groups.

Bjorn sidled up next to Rekja and Vefinn and eyed the loop of rope. "*Toga honk*?"

"*Ja*," Vefinn answered. "Jorund Tryggvason boasted that any one of his men could out-tug the best of our men, that his are the superior oarsmen. Couldn't let them best us, could we?" He cocked his head and lifted his brow.

"Which one of them will it be?" He eyed Jorund's men opposite them, but he had an idea which one he would compete against. His theory was right, and the man he had sized up on their first meeting stepped forward to one end of the rope loop. Gunnar Sigvaldsson.

Styrr started the betting. He knelt and threw a small piece of hacksilver on the floor. Hands reached into belts and men tossed more hacksilver onto the ground.

A shout rose to start, and Styrr slapped Bjorn on the back and pushed him toward the rope. "I'd better get that silver back," he told Bjorn.

Bjorn walked to the rope. He cracked his neck and flexed his hands. Ever since the time when he had washed overboard, Bjorn had determined that he'd never lose his grip on an oar again. Whenever he could, he found a tree with a low-hanging branch and would jump up and hang from it. He hung there for as long as he could stand it, until his hands and forearms trembled from the effort, and his shoulders screamed from being pulled down. He never lost his grip again, no matter how rough the seas.

Confident that he could beat Gunnar, he turned up the sleeves of his tunic and removed his two finger rings. He sat down on the floor and took hold of the rope. Gunnar did the same. They put the soles of their feet together and waited, staring at each other.

Ingjald's man squatted down, a cup of ale in one hand, and held the rope in the other, so they wouldn't start until he said to. He looked from one to another, his eyes glazed with drink. "You win when you pull the other man over."

Bjorn never took his eyes off Gunnar. He watched the other man's hands and arms for the slightest movement. They would each try to get the first jump and gain the advantage. Bjorn would be ready. He tightened his grip.

Ingjald's man pulled his hand away with a flourish, and Bjorn pushed his feet against Gunnar's and tugged on the rope as hard as he could. As soon as they started, the men all shouted encouragement to their man and threw insults at the other. Gunnar did not move as much as Bjorn had anticipated, and the lack of movement jarred him. With a tug of his own, Gunnar pulled Bjorn forward, and Bjorn knew this would not be as easy as he had thought. He looked over at Gunnar, who stared him down as they both pulled back and forth in a rowing motion. After the initial test, they stayed even, neither one giving much. Bjorn allowed his body to sway with the movement, trying to feel out Gunnar's weakness. Would his legs give out first or his hands? They moved back and forth, pulling harder at times and lightening up at others. The muscles in their forearms and thighs bulged like cords of rope, and sweat trickled down their faces. Bjorn's hands burned, but he knew he could hang on for a lot longer. He glanced at Gunnar and saw that he had to keep tightening his hands on the rope, a sign that his grip grew tired. Through his feet, Bjorn could feel that Gunnar's legs trembled with fatigue. The corner of Bjorn's mouth went up in a slight smile.

"Come on, Bjorn," Styrr shouted near him. "Finish him. My sister could row better than that!"

"I've seen your sister. She's as big as a troll," Bjorn retorted through gritted teeth.

He relaxed the pressure of his legs against Gunnar's as a distraction. The loss of pressure tricked Gunnar into thinking Bjorn tired. Gunnar pulled hard, and Bjorn let himself fall forward until his hands were nearly touching his feet. When Gunnar leaned too far back, Bjorn tightened the muscles in his legs, braced his feet and gave a mighty heave at the rope.

Gunnar's arms jerked forward, and his legs buckled. He toppled over onto Bjorn's legs, the rope slipped out of his hands, and a roar rose from Harald's men at Bjorn's victory. Bjorn leaned back and gulped in deep breaths while Gunnar moved back and knelt on the floor.

"I underestimated you, Pretty Bjorn," Gunnar said in between breaths. He brought his arms up and leaned on his knees.

Bjorn caught the joking tone in Gunnar's voice and grinned. "You are not the first," he said as he got to his feet. His legs still pumped with blood from the exertion, and he held out his hand to help Gunnar up. Gunnar clasped his forearm, and Bjorn pulled him to standing.

"I will not be the last, I am sure."

"No. It can serve me well."

"Does it serve you well in other areas? Men underestimate you. Women want you?"

Bjorn smiled. It was true.

"The smile that makes women fall to their knees," Vefinn said as he walked up to the two men. He plied Bjorn with a cup of victory ale. Already drunk, he splashed some on Bjorn's tunic. "If I had that power…" he trailed off as his gaze landed on one of the serving thralls.

Gunnar ignored Vefinn and leaned into Bjorn. "Another time, Pretty Bjorn. And next time I will not underestimate you."

"It will not help."

Gunnar laughed. He looked about to say something, but Jorund approached his fallen champion and pulled him away. Once on the other side of the hall, Jorund stared at Bjorn as he talked to Gunnar, a deep hatred in his eyes that was not born of his friend's loss at this harmless competition. Bjorn recognized the look, for he returned it. A hard pat on his back made him turn.

"Sent that *shyt-karl* sprawling like a woman at your feet," Harald boomed loud enough for everyone to hear.

Styrr laughed and held up his hand. Several pieces of hacksilver shone in the firelight. "I nearly pissed myself when you fell forward. I thought you'd lost."

"Bjorn is my son. He will not lose to Tryggvi's mare," Harald boasted.

Harald's men laughed, Styrr loudest among them. The implication, that Gunnar was the mare to Tryggvi's stallion, could turn this harmless game into a real fight, one Bjorn did not want tonight.

A round of lewd comments followed a young thrall who approached Bjorn with a pitcher of ale, her head down but her eyes on him. She could not have been more than fifteen, and she was pretty, with red hair and green eyes, likely one of the English or Irish. With an appreciative glance, Bjorn thought that Ingjald knew how to entertain his guests; he had good food and desirable thralls. He watched Ingjald as he sat at his high-seat, and when Ingjald caught his glance, he nodded and gave Bjorn a smile. The girl was a gift. Bjorn smiled back and lifted his cup to Ingjald. But he did not want this girl. The woman he wanted sat next to Ingjald's, and his hand stroked her leg. Selime nuzzled Ingjald's neck and whispered something to him. He raised his eyebrows, and his hand trailed even higher up her leg.

Bjorn turned away. The red-haired girl waited for him.

"What are you waiting for, Bjorn," Harald said.

He led the girl to the door where he threw on his cloak, red fox-fur wrap, and hat. The girl tucked herself in next to him and they plunged out into the storm.

Storelva

"Here, Asta, let me carry that for you," Short Olaf offered, hurrying up to Astrid's side as she left Ragnhild's house.

When he caught up, Short Olaf took the bentwood basket in which she carried her spindle, whorl, wool thread, her deer-bone needles, and the linen loose-fit trousers she'd been sewing for Jori. The wood of the basket had been dyed alternating red and green stripes, and it made her think of the evergreen trees and holly berries of Yule.

"*Tak*, Olli. But it is not heavy."

"I know. I just want to help." He cocked a shy smile at her. His face was shaded under a hat made of straw. He wore it whenever he went fishing.

Astrid laughed lightly as she gave him an appraising look. Although not that handsome, he had kind eyes, a light-brown beard starting to grow on his cheeks in patches, a smattering of freckles, and thick hair that he kept short. He had also grown tall.

"What?" he asked. "Why are you looking at me like that?"

"We might have to give you a new name...*Short* Olaf."

He laughed. "*Ja*. I don't know if I would answer to any other name. I've been Short Olaf for as long as I can remember." He took her arm to steer her away from a patch of ice. Leaning in close to Astrid's ear, he said, "I like it that you call me Olli."

Astrid flushed, his breath tickling her neck. She swatted his head playfully and took a step away from him, unsure of how she felt with him so close. They had been playmates since she was a little girl, but things had been different this winter. He had been different.

"I remember the first time I called you Olli. We were playing hide-and-find. I couldn't find any of you, so I started to cry. Rikki came out first and then I yelled, 'Olli!' I was afraid a troll or *vargr* or something had snatched you."

He grinned at her. "I must not have heard you or I would have come out. I never liked to see you cry. Still wouldn't. I would never make you cry on purpose." Short Olaf's voice had taken on that earnestness Astrid had been hearing from him lately. He had always been the kindest of Rikki's companions, but now his tenderness took on a different tone, like he was trying to prove something to her, that he could take care of her.

"I know. You always protected me from Galm. Remember the time he had that dead rat on a stick and kept poking it at me, even though he knows I hate rats? Well...*because* I hate rats."

"You were so upset!" He laughed.

"I was young," Astrid retorted, embarrassed that she had made such a scene.

"Not *that* young."

Her eyebrows went up. "You keep talking like that and I'll stop thinking of you so fondly."

"Wait," he continued. "Did you ever find Galm?"

"No. But I wasn't as worried about Galm as I was about you."

"Even trolls would have brought him back, saying he was too much trouble."

Astrid laughed again. "*Ja*, surely."

Short Olaf turned serious. "Galm is a good friend, despite his tricks. He would give his life for me or Rikki...or you, Asta," he said, bumping her gently on the arm. "He's fierce. Fierce in his tricks, but also in battle and with his loyalty."

"Then you are all lucky to have each other."

"We are. And your father, Red, everyone. When we are fighting, it is like we are all brothers. We take care of each other." He removed his hat and ran his forearm across his forehead.

They had reached the pit-house where she could hear her mother talking to the thralls about the brewing. The earthy smell of fermenting grains wafted out of the door; Ingiborg must be checking the vat of ale. The pit-house was a building just off the longhouse, with a hearth for cooking, and an oven next to the entrance where the thralls baked bread. Further in the house stood side benches where meat was laid out for drying. Above that were shelves to hold pots and pans and jars for storing food. Herbs hung from the rafters to dry. Astrid loved the pit-house, the smell of drying herbs, the baking bread, and bubbling stews, although not as much in the summer as in winter when it was warm from the fire and oven. When one of the local chieftains had wintered with them, his wife had marveled at the house dedicated to cooking. The brew-house was an adjacent building to the pit-house, dedicated to the brewing of ale and mead.

Short Olaf handed the basket back to Astrid, presenting it as if it were a great gift. "We will protect you too. Even Gal—" Short Olaf started, but then two arms wrapped around his neck and pulled him back. Short Olaf twisted in the arms and turned inward toward his assailant. He threw a punch, hitting him in the gut.

"Oof..." Galm let out. He stood, a wicked smile on his face. "Nice one, *Olli*." He released Short Olaf's neck with one arm and let the other remain on his friend's shoulders, while he gave Astrid a once over.

"Asta, you look very pretty today," Galm told her, waggling his eyebrows.

She sighed. "Galm. Is that how you always say hello?"

He nodded. "Just keeping our Shortie sharp. Don't want him to become soft over the winter." Galm turned to Short Olaf, who was picking his straw hat off the ground where it had fallen. "I saw you carrying a lovely little basket, *Olli*. Maybe you should stay home next season and help with the womanly chores." He tightened his arm on Olaf's neck, but Short Olaf ducked out from under it, grabbed Galm's hand and gave it a twist. Galm yelped.

"What were you saying about being womanly?"

"I hear you, Brother."

"Let's go."

Short Olaf looked at Astrid with longing, as if he wanted to continue their conversation, but Galm pulled on his sleeve.

"Bye, Asta," Short Olaf said.

"Thanks for walking with me."

He smiled and gave her a wave as they walked off. Astrid watched them go, thinking about this new solicitousness of Short Olaf. Then she heard Galm say, "Did you tell her you want to *marry* her?"

"Sh, no."

"What do you think Jarl Tryggvi would say?"

But the two young men had walked out of earshot, and Astrid did not hear what Short Olaf said. Shocked at Short Olaf's words and intention, she watched as two of her father's men walked by, and she wished one of them was Gunnar.

She went into the pit-house and through that to the brew-house in search of her mother. She was at the top of a loft, two female thralls beside her as they dipped a ladle into the mead to taste it. The vat of mead was so large it rose to the top of the house.

"More meadowsweet," Ingiborg told the older thrall, indicating the dried flowers stored in a nearby jar. The thrall nodded. Ingiborg handed the ladle to the younger girl and turned to Astrid, the household keys on her waist jingling.

"What is it, Astrid?" Ingiborg asked as soon as she saw Astrid's face.

When Astrid didn't answer right away, Ingiborg gestured that they should climb down the ladder to the ground floor. Ingiborg moved to the shelves where she checked the stores, Astrid taking stock of the dried herbs and greens.

Astrid paused. "Would *fadir* marry me to someone like Short Olaf?"

A clay jar of pickled herring in her hand, Ingiborg turned to Astrid. "Why do you ask? Has Olaf said something to you?"

"No." Astrid shook her head. "He's acting like that's what he might want."

Ingiborg sighed. "I was afraid of that. To answer your question, no. Your father would not marry you to Olaf. We love Olaf as if he were one of our own, but he is not the type of man your father wants for your husband. You will marry a man much more important."

Astrid looked away, at the woman tending the cauldron of stew for the evening meal. How could she tell her mother the thought of marrying someone like Sigmund Ketilsson frightened her more than anything? She knew she had to be brave. Her mother had married a man she barely knew and had done it for political reasons. She would understand.

"Do you want to marry Short Olaf?" Ingiborg asked, alarm in her voice.

They stood in silence for a moment, Astrid thinking. "No," she said. "Although..."

"He would be safe?"

Astrid picked at her belt. "Yes, he'd be safe. He's always been so nice to me. I think he loves me."

"Yes, he does. He has loved you for a while now. Have you not noticed?"

Astrid nodded. "I think I wanted not to notice."

Ingiborg set aside the jar she was holding. "Olaf will make a good husband, but not for you."

The thought of Short Olaf with another woman, giving him children, made Astrid feel very jealous. He had always been hers.

"You're right. He will be a good husband for...someone." She picked up a dried stalk of thyme and smelled it. Tossing it back into the bowl, she turned to leave.

"Astrid." Her mother's voice stopped her. "You are stronger than you know. When the time comes, you will be able to handle whatever marriage your father arranges for you. Do you understand?"

"I need to tend to my duties." She wished she could believe her mother.

Chapter Ten
Hovgarden

His stiff fingers fumbled as Bjorn tied the ski to his foot. The morning sky was the bluish black of a fading bruise, and a fresh layer of powder lay over the world, soft as a pile of white furs. His breath plumed out, and the crisp air bit at his face, but he wanted to be out.

The night before, he had taken the very willing Keena, the gift from Ingjald, to his bed, but he had no interest in her. Instead of bedding her, he told her to take a rest, and he lay down next to her small body, keeping her warm with the promise he would not tell Ingjald they had done nothing. Lying on his bed with his arms pillowed behind his head, the memory of his father came back to him again. He thought of his home village, Raudvatn, of the people there like Eydis and Vaesten that he cared for. They were not his father, or even his long-lost mother and brother, but the old couple were as close to a family as he had. Reminding himself that he needed to make a trip to Raudvatn and take Tanni, he'd drifted off to sleep only to be awoken by his drunken bunkmates and their inquiries about the girl. He made up some lurid details that satisfied their curiosity before they stumbled off to their own spots.

He tied the second ski to his shoe and moved his foot back and forth to make sure it was secure and adjusted the quiver of arrows on his back. The storm had kept him cooped up indoors for too long and he longed to get out, to stretch his legs, to feel a weapon in his hands, even if it was a bow. Harald had once used an archer who used his right hand to hold his bow, and he loosed his arrows with his left hand. Strange. But he could get a slightly different angle on the enemy than the right-handed archers, and it came in handy from time to time. He was long

dead now. Bjorn heard the crunch of shoes on snow. Looking up into the weak morning sun, he saw Styrr approach.

Bjorn adjusted his fur wrap, picked up his bow, and rose to his feet. "Styrr." He sighed as he stuffed his hands into heavy woolen mittens.

"Harald wants you in a meeting. King Ingjald has news for us. Jorund will be there too." Styrr blew into his hands and studied the frigid sky, the pine trees heavy with snow. "It's colder than a frost giant's teat out here."

"It *is* winter," Bjorn quipped, irritated.

Styrr snorted. "And those of us who have sense stay indoors before the fire with ale and food warming our bellies. A good rut with a woman helps too. How was that little red-haired thrall? I might get her to warm my cock. Or the other one, the one with the dark hair that you like so much. She must be good to keep your interest."

"Good depends on how you treat them," Bjorn answered as he bent to unclasp his skis. He pointed the tip of his ski into Styrr's belly. "They are all good if you treat them well. Touch them in the right way in the right place and they respond. It's simple."

He walked off, and Styrr joined him.

"It's simple for you, *Pretty* Bjorn," Styrr said, his voice betraying his envy.

Bjorn wished he knew some magic, some *seid*, to rid himself of the Pretty Bjorn name. It was no fitting name for a man. "What is King Ingjald's news? Do you have any idea?" Bjorn asked to change the subject as they returned to Ingjald's compound.

"No."

They entered King Ingjald's feast hall, Bjorn once again admiring the intricate knotwork carvings on the oak door of Odin and his eight-legged horse Sleipnir. As the son of a silversmith, he appreciated beautiful artwork.

King Ingjald, Harald, Jorund, and Gunnar were already at the large table, while Selime placed trays of dried cod with heaps of butter to spread on it, hunks of cheese, and wheat bread. The red-haired thrall, Keena, poured what looked like wine into silver cups for the men and a glass goblet for King Ingjald.

Ingjald gestured for Bjorn and Styrr to have a seat at the table. Bjorn took a sip of his drink and had to hold back an urge to spit it out. Wine. He didn't understand why these kings and jarls drank the Frankish swill. He wasn't sure if he'd drink wine even if Ragnarok was upon them. Give him ale or mead. He dripped some honey on a piece of the wheat bread, loving the lightness of the grain and the sweetness of the honey.

The king talked of the threats that faced him from Denmark and the Jomsvikings, among others. It became clear where he headed with the talk.

Ingjald swirled the ruby liquid in his glass cup before taking a drink. "I will not involve myself, my men, or my ships in this feud between you. You must cease the feuding."

Both Harald and Jorund spoke at the same time. "No."

Jorund opened his mouth to speak, but Ingjald held up his hands. "I have heard it all. You know my mind. I will not help either of you, and I do not want to hear complaints from my people about you raiding each other's land."

"If it continues, both you," he said to Harald, "and your father," he gestured his cup toward Jori, "risk banishment from these lands."

With those last words, he finished his wine and rose from his chair, his men moving back to make room for him, their hands on their spears.

Scowls on their faces, Harald and Styrr stalked out of the hall. Bjorn started to follow them when he spotted Selime standing toward the back of the feast hall. Raising his eyebrows, Bjorn indicated to Harald and Styrr that he'd catch up to them later.

As he approached Selime, her eyes lit up with anticipation, but she also looked over Bjorn's shoulder toward Ingjald. She was his and would have to go to him if he called to her. When Bjorn reached her, he put his hand on her waist. "Come to me tonight. Or are you with him?"

She ran her hand over his arm, down to his stomach, before lingering just above his crotch. He sucked in a breath. With a slight smile, she said, "I will come to you. I will come *with* you."

Ingjald's voice jolted Bjorn, and he grabbed her hand to keep her from doing anything else. He listened, but Ingjald was not talking to him. "Jorund, you have a sister, do you not?"

Bjorn dropped Selime's hand as he turned to see what was going on.

"Two," Jorund answered slowly, like he did not want to tell Ingjald about his sisters. Bjorn didn't blame him. If he had sisters, he wouldn't want any man to know about them.

"Is one of marriageable age?"

"My sister Astrid is old enough to marry."

Gunnar's entire body went rigid, like he was ready to fight.

"Is she promised to anyone?" Ingjald rubbed his beard.

A long moment stretched out before Jorund answered. "No. Although it will not be long before she is."

Gunnar's hands tightened into fists. Bjorn studied Gunnar, trying to understand the other man's unease at this questioning. It was reasonable to question whether Tryggvi had a daughter.

"Good," Ingjald said. He turned from them and caught sight of Bjorn with Selime. He gave Bjorn a calculating look. "She might come in useful."

Gesturing to Bjorn, Jorund, and Gunnar, Ingjald said. "Some of my men are arranging a skating race. They are competitive, although it has been a while since they spilled any blood. Maybe our luck will change today!" He laughed and swept his cloak around him. "Join us at the lake at midday."

Bjorn stared after Ingjald, his mouth open in question. The look he'd given him meant something, and Bjorn did not like it. If Ingjald thought to marry Tryggvi's daughter to someone, he did not want it to be him.

Yule had come and gone. Bjorn broke the barrier between the two factions that had separated on either side of the central hearth fire, when he took his drink and approached Gunnar as he sat in a corner whittling a piece of wood. Brightly colored shields hung on the wall behind him, along with a wool tapestry depicting the story of Odin with his spear Gungnir.

Bjorn inhaled the scent of fresh wood and thought he should make something for little Tanni. An image of Tanni's laughing face surfaced, and it made Bjorn's heart hurt from missing his son; he turned his thoughts to something else.

Gunnar did not look up when Bjorn stepped over the bench and sat next to him.

"I hear you leave soon," Bjorn said.

"We did what we came for. Jori wants to return home. Jarl Tryggvi needs to know what the king decided."

Bjorn looked over at Jori, who had joined in *flyting* with some of Ingjald's men. The man who spoke flailed his arms in an imitation of a battle, no doubt describing his own battle prowess. *Flyting* was about besting the other men with exploits of what you've done in battle. They were all drunk and the man talking nearly fell off his bench when he got excited and Jori laughed at him. His laughter ceased when he caught Bjorn staring at him. They glared at each other. An urge to cross the crowded, smoky room and take Jori's head off overcame Bjorn. Someone said something to Jori, and he turned his attention away from Bjorn.

Taking a breath, Bjorn swirled the ale in his cup, watching it spin and spin. He thought about what Ingjald had said, that the feuding was to stop, but how could he do that when Jori was still alive? He'd promised himself he'd kill Jori Tryggvason.

"I will be glad to leave," Gunnar added, as he leaned over to pick up another piece of birch.

A bright purple flash caught the corner of Bjorn's eye. He turned to Gunnar and caught sight of a necklace; a purple bead was attached to a pendant, round, with a woman's figure and outstretched arms filling a circle.

He leaned closer. "Is that...Freya?"

Gunnar jerked back as if he'd been hit. He grasped the necklace and started to tuck it back under his outer tunic.

"Not so fast." Bjorn laughed.

Gunnar sighed, still holding on to the necklace. He studied it and ran his finger over the bead. "*Ja*, it is Freya. A woman gave it to me."

"Ah..." Bjorn's eyebrows lifted in understanding. "A special woman, I take it." He was glad for a topic he knew.

"Yes."

Bjorn stretched out his legs, the fire warming his feet in their leather shoes. "Tell me about her. Is she pretty?"

"Yes." Gunnar stopped whittling and held up the wood to inspect it. It still had no apparent form, but Gunnar looked pleased as he blew off the wood dust.

"She's special and pretty. Does she have a name?"

"Yes." There was a long pause. The fire crackled and the sounds of men and women talking and laughing floated through the large hall.

"You're not going to tell me."

Gunnar's lip twitched as if to laugh, but he held it back. "No."

Bjorn ran his hand through his hair. "Understood. She's either married, and you can't have her. Or she's too far above you."

Although he did not get an answer, Bjorn watched Gunnar's reaction to determine which question hit the mark. He saw Gunnar's jaw tighten at the last bit. So, the girl was above him.

"Either way, it's not impossible to have her. Be creative. Discretion helps too, if the husband or father is protective."

Bjorn brought his legs up, rested his arms on his knees, and continued, "I remember one young wife of a Norwegian jarl..." He smiled in remembrance. "She was lovely, unblemished skin, clear green eyes, hair like a burnt orange sunset. I wanted to touch her, run my fingers along that perfect skin, and bury my face in her hair. She had yet to give birth, so her body was still fresh and..." He cleared his throat. "...tight. She was much younger than her husband. He did not treat her badly, but he was old and had a wound on his leg that sometimes oozed and smelled. I was young, healthy. The girl took to me like a flower starved for water."

"Did her husband find you out?" Gunnar had stopped whittling.

Bjorn shook his head and smiled. He twisted his father's ruby ring on his finger. "No. That is my point. Husbands. Fathers." He waved his hand in a dismissive gesture. "If the woman is willing, you can work around them."

"I owe her father everything," Gunnar said, his voice gruff.

"That complicates things."

"Yes, it does."

"Can I see the necklace given to you by this beautiful young woman?"

Gunnar untied the necklace and handed it to Bjorn, who held it up to the firelight, the marbling in the purple creating shadows and light that made the bead look as if it were fathomless.

"She put it in my saddlebag. I discovered it later," Gunnar said.

"Hm." Bjorn flicked his eyes to Gunnar, then to the pendant. "She is giving you a promise with this pendant."

"A promise." Gunnar stared at the necklace as if seeing it for the first time. "*Ja.*"

This was not the kind of pendant a young woman would give up lightly. "She is promising to wait for you. Sending this Freya pendant is her way of doing that. Is this something she values?"

"Yes. Very much."

Bjorn could see by the look in Gunnar's eyes that he was thinking of this young woman. Bjorn moved the pendant back and forth. The weight of the silver felt good in his hand, balanced, well made. Whoever made it, or had it made, did so lovingly. He handed it back to Gunnar, who tied it onto his neck again, possessively.

"The woman is yours, Gunnar."

"I think so too. But..." he hesitated. "She cannot give herself to me."

"Her father?"

"Yes."

Then it dawned on Bjorn who this young woman was. Tryggvi's daughter. That explained why Gunnar had looked so stricken when Ingjald asked Jori about her age and if she was promised to anyone. Gunnar wanted her. He studied Gunnar, who stared into the fire as if the low-burning flames could solve his problem. It made Bjorn think of Hilda, Harald's daughter. How he wanted to marry her but couldn't. He could still remember the softness of her lips when he kissed her, the silkiness of her hair when he ran his hands through it, her joyful laugh when she was with him. With a pang, he thought of her now, worn down from being continuously with child, her eyes dull from the grief of losing several children.

Her soft lips drew tight from bitterness, and her silky gold hair hung lifeless and dull. He would not wish that fate upon any woman. Not even the daughter of Tryggvi Olafsson.

"Good luck with this woman, Gunnar." He would need it.

Storelva

Astrid and Ragnhild had their heads together, Astrid working on her tablet-weaving, Ragnhild nalbinding, and talked quietly. They did not need to be quiet; the longhouse buzzed with evening activities, dice rattling in cups and thrown onto the ground in the middle of a group of men, their shouts of victory and disappointment, children laughing and squealing while they played with their toys, and women talking while they spun, sewed, or knit.

With an exaggerated shake, Dyri tossed the bone dice and shouted in dismay when he saw what turned up. "Luck is not with me tonight." A greedy Buri held out his hand for the silver he'd won.

"*I* am lucky," Ragnhild told Astrid. She looked to Dyri, the streaks of blond in his brown hair shining in the firelight. "Dyri is a loving husband."

"You are lucky."

"Not like Hildegard, poor thing, the way her husband hits her and yells at her."

"Like when the last of their sheep died?"

"It wasn't her fault."

"He blamed her anyway. He is a hard, cruel man. If he wasn't such a talented shipwright, I don't think Father would have him around."

They fell silent, Ragnhild watching Dyri with a gleam in her eyes.

He must have sensed her glance, for he looked up at that moment and gave her a long stare. With a smile, he gave her a wink and went back to his game.

The look and wink were so intimate Astrid blushed watching them. She thought of Gunnar and how he should be at that table with the men playing games and laughing, if her father had not sent him away with Jori. She imagined him, his green eyes winking at her with that look, and she felt the heat rising to her cheeks.

"I want to have that," she told Ragnhild.

"Who knows? Maybe your father will marry you to someone young and handsome." Her voice was chipper. "And rich."

Astrid laughed when Ragnhild added the rich part. She stopped her weaving and turned to her friend. "If we're doing that, let's make up the perfect husband for me."

"Yes, let's." Ragnhild shifted on the bench. "What's first? Rich or handsome?"

"Handsome. I wouldn't want to marry a rich man if he looks like a troll."

"But what if he were sweet like Short Olaf?"

"Olli doesn't look like a troll!" She hadn't meant to say it so loud, and quickly made sure no one had heard her, especially Short Olaf. He and Galm played tafl in one corner of the house while Rikki watched. Rikki whispered something in Galm's ear, but he shooed Rikki away and made his move. With a triumphant flourish, Short Olaf moved one of his pieces and Galm threw up his hands in defeat. Rikki snickered and said, 'I warned you.'

Astrid turned her attention back to Ragnhild. "Let's start over. This is the perfect husband, right? He will treat me well."

"We have a handsome man who treats you well. Rich?"

"Yes." "How rich? A warrior with booty or as rich as your father?"

Astrid had to ponder that one. She looked at her father who sat in his chair at the end of the house talking to Emund, his face lined with concern. Ingiborg walked up and handed him a drink in a silver cup, a gentle hand on his shoulder, and when he took it he looked up at her with gratitude and affection. Seeing her mother and father together reminded Astrid of the day that Harald had raided their village. Her father standing on the rock, talking to them all. Her mother going to his side.

"Like my father."

"So you want your husband rich *and* powerful," Ragnhild said. "You don't want much," Ragnhild laughed. "Back to handsome. That's the fun part. What does he look like? Brown hair or yellow?"

"Brown." All Astrid could see was Gunnar.

"Blue eyes?"

"Green."

"Beard?"

"Yes."

"Close-shaved or shaggy?"

Astrid giggled at the thought of a shaggy-bearded man kissing her. "Close."

"Tall?"

"Yes, but not too tall. A little taller than me. I want to be able to kiss him without standing on my toes."

Ragnhild snickered. "He's tall, brown hair, green eyes, close-shaved beard." She paused as if a thought had occurred to her. She narrowed her eyes at Astrid and asked, "Does he carry a sword or an axe?"

"A sword. He's a rich man, remember?"

A long pause followed that, and Astrid watched Ragnhild as she searched the room crowded with men. She leaned in close and whispered, "Except for the rich part, this perfect man sounds like Gunnar."

Astrid's eyes widened at being caught.

"Gunnar, Asta?"

At first Astrid thought to deny it, to shy away from her friends' conclusion, but she crossed her arms and said, "Yes. Gunnar."

A smiled flitted across Ragnhild's face. "I remember you dancing together at the wedding feast."

"Mm, yes." Astrid said. Her body tingled at the memory.

Ragnhild took Astrid's hand. "I should have seen it. Has anything happened?"

Astrid looked down at her hands. "Uh...he kissed me."

"And?"

"That's it. He left soon after." That had been in the early winter, and now it was past Yule. The moon had gone through three cycles, and they still had not heard from Jori or Gunnar, but she supposed not hearing from them was a good thing. If things had gone badly, Jori would have sent a messenger to alert her father.

"You cannot risk being with Gunnar."

Astrid pulled her hand away. "What you just said about Dyri? How you want him near you all the time? That is how I feel about Gunnar. It hurts me he is not here now. I want to see him, talk to him, hear his voice."

"Oh, Asta." She put her arm around Astrid's shoulder.

A heavy thump jarred the bench, and the smell of an unwashed man assaulted Astrid's nose.

"You two look like you're conspiring. Should we worry?" Galm asked, his face too close to Astrid's.

She scooched over on the bench. "Yes," Astrid said as she cocked her head to the side. "I know your secrets, Galm."

For a moment he looked genuinely worried, but then shrugged. "Tell away, Asta." He gestured toward Short Olaf. "It's Shortie who has the secret. Should I tell them?" With a mischievous glint in his eyes, he leaned into Astrid and Ragnhild to tell the secret, but stopped at the last minute and said with a laugh at Short Olaf's stricken face. "Don't look so worried. I will never tell."

Short Olaf rolled his eyes at Galm, and Astrid told him with a smile. "Don't worry, Olli. I would never believe anything Galm told me."

"He has a Loki tongue," Rikki added.

The other men had quit their dice game, and Dyri made his way over to Ragnhild. When he reached their bench, he lifted her up, sat down, and pulled her back down onto his lap. He rested his hands lightly, but possessively, on her belly.

Emund took up his place by the fire, and others gathered around him to hear a story. A pang of jealousy hit Astrid when Emund pulled little Asleif into his lap for the storytelling; that had always been her place as a little girl. But she was no longer a child. Rikki had shoved Galm out of his spot next to Astrid, and leaned back up against the wall to listen to the story, a piece of pine, a knife and a file in his hands so he could do his wood carving. Rikki could only sit still for a story if he occupied his hands, and he had a talent for creating spoons and boxes. Many of the spoons they used in their household had been carved by Rikki in his idle moments.

"What are you making?" Astrid asked her brother as everyone settled. Short Olaf and Galm sprawled on some furs thrown on the floor in front of them. She gave Galm a little shove with her foot, but he grunted and ignored her.

"A comb." He held up the wood for her to see. With his guidance, she could visualize the hair comb that he would create out of the raw wood. It took life before her eyes.

She smiled. "It will be pretty."

He took his carving knife to the wood, the smell of fresh pine surrounding them, and Astrid laid her head on Rikki's shoulder, the movements of his arms comforting as he carved.

Emund's deep voice quieted everyone; the only noise, the sound of the fire crackling in the hearth and the click-clicks of knitting needles and Rikki's knife.

Shifting young Asleif on his lap, Emund pointed to the soapstone cauldron that hung from the rafters over the central fire. "Do you think that cauldron is big enough to prepare all the ale the gods needed?" He asked the little boy.

"No." Asleif shook his head.

"That's right. The gods and goddesses have mighty appetites!"

"Something you would know about, Red," Tryggvi teased.

"*Some* of us work hard all day, but I'm sure it's tough to..." he raised an auburn eyebrow at his old friend. "*Jarl.*"

Tryggvi barked out a laugh while he scratched the ears of his hound.

"Where was I?" Emund said with an exaggerated sigh.

"The cauldron!" Asleif said.

"Aye. The gods wanted to have a feast, but Aegir, who brewed the best ale, told the other gods that he didn't have a cauldron big enough to suit their needs. Tyr knew of the very cauldron they wanted. It belonged to his father, the giant Hymir. It was a *sjomil* deep!"

Little Asleif's eyes widened.

"That's right. A sea mile deep. Surely a cauldron that big would be big enough for the gods and their feast. So, Thor, in disguise, went to see Hymir to get his cauldron. The giant received the thunder god and even invited him to dinner. At dinner, Hymir served three oxen and grew angry when Thor ate two entire oxen at the meal."

"Rude!" Ragnhild said.

"Aye." Emund's eyes sparkled at her.

"Sounds like someone we all know," Ingiborg said.

Emund put a hand to his chest, looking put out. "Humph. The next day Hymir told Thor that if they were to eat again, they had to go fishing for more food, and Thor had to find his own bait. What did Thor do? He pulled the head off Hymir's largest ox!"

At those last words, Emund made a loud popping sound, making Short Olaf, who had been dozing on the floor, jump.

"Hymir was not amused or pleased. But they went fishing together, anyway. Thor took the oars and rowed out to sea. Hymir caught two whales, but then Thor rowed them out even farther. Hymir, wisely, was afraid of Jormungand, the Midgard Serpent.

"Have you ever seen Jormungand?" Gytha asked.

Emund met her eyes and lowered his voice. "Once, we were far out at sea, so far we were days from land when I saw a giant black shadow pass underneath our boat. It was much bigger than a whale. The air grew cold, and the water stilled as if the sea itself knew a great menace were in its presence."

Gytha shivered and shrunk next to Ingiborg. "Were you scared?"

"So scared I couldn't move."

Next to Astrid, Dyri chuckled and whispered to Ragnhild, "Not true. Nothing scares Red."

Rikki snorted and said under his breath to Astrid, "Except ghosts."

"You see why even a giant like Hymir wouldn't want to anger the great Serpent. When they stopped, Thor placed his enormous bait on his fishing hook and cast off. Although Hymir did not know it Thor *wanted* to catch Jormungand. And he did."

He paused for effect. "Thor caught the giant serpent on his hook and as Thor brought him up, the serpent thrashed and spit poison. Thor, with his god strength, stretched out to brace his legs, and they went right through the bottom of the boat and onto the floor of the ocean. Jormungand struggled and fought, so Thor got out his mighty hammer, Mjolnir, and beat the serpent with it."

Emund made movements like he was Thor wrestling with the giant serpent, tipping Asleif off his knees and then back again, to the little boy's delight.

"Then, Hymir panicked and cut the line, allowing Jormungand to break free. Jormungand returned to the sea but held a lasting and fatal grudge against Thor. Angry with Hymir for cutting his line, Thor threw Hymir overboard."

"That's what you get when you get between a fisherman and his catch," Short Olaf murmured. Astrid laughed, and he grinned up at her.

"When they arrived at shore, Thor carried the boat and the two whales that Hymir had caught back to the hall."

The image reminded Astrid of when the men hauled her father's longships onto land to store them for the winter. Her father's ships, though, were so big the men had to place log rollers on the ground, and it took many men to move them.

"As they feasted, Hymir fumed and challenged Thor to break a glass goblet against a pillar. Thor threw the goblet, but instead of breaking the glass, it broke the pillar. Hymir's wife whispered to Thor and told him to try breaking the goblet against Hymir's head instead, which she said was harder than stone."

"Hm," Ingiborg mused. "That sounds familiar."

Everyone laughed at Tryggvi's expense, and he raised his drink to them with a smile. His hound let out a loud series of yips in his sleep, as if to stress the point.

"Thor smashed the goblet against Hymir's head. It broke. Hymir, feeling outwitted and undone, gave Thor his cauldron. But only if Thor could carry it. He put the giant cauldron on his shoulders and walked away with it. Thor brought the cauldron back to Asgard and gave it to Aegir. The cauldron was worth the effort. They could drink all they wanted, and the ale never ran out."

Little Asleif clapped his hands.

"Too bad Inga doesn't own a cauldron that big," Tryggvi said. "She could use it to feed you, Red."

Emund started to retort when a shock of cold air rushed into the house and Amma, Buri's wife, bustled in the door. She made her way straight to Ingiborg and with a simple nod from Amma, Ingiborg rose and quickly left the large central room and went to her sleeping chamber. Astrid, sleepy from the warmth in the room and the familiar story, lifted her head from Rikki's shoulder and leaned over to Ragnhild.

"I think Halldora's time has come."

"It looks that way."

Ragnhild gently removed Dyri's hand from her waist, and, with a kiss on his cheek, she rose to join the women. He looked at her with a question, and she whispered in his ear. With a kiss, he let her go.

"What's going on?" Rikki asked.

"Halldora is giving birth."

"Oh." He shuddered.

Astrid laughed. "You men are so afraid of childbirth. You can face an enemy horde in battle, but show you a woman in her birth pangs, and you go running the other way as quickly as if the giant serpent was chasing you!"

"I'd rather face Jormungand than a birthing woman." Rikki shivered. "Go with the goddess, *systir*. I'll keep the monsters at bay with a spear, an axe, and Tyr by my side."

Astrid waved goodbye to her brother.

When Ingiborg emerged from her chamber with her basket of herbs and midwifery tools, Astrid and Ragnhild joined her.

"The pains became close quickly and took Halldora by surprise," Amma told them. "Egil fetched me right away. The poor man thought he might have to deliver the baby himself."

Ingiborg gave a soft laugh. "Frigg forbid. Hurry over. We are not far behind." As Amma opened the door, the frigid night air blew in.

Astrid shivered and rushed to get her cloak. As she walked, she twisted her unbound hair into a tight braid to keep it out of her face, as she always did when she worked.

"Don't braid your hair, Astrid," Ingiborg reminded her.

"I forgot." Astrid unwound it and ran her fingers through her hair to get all the knots out. Ragnhild unwound hers as well. There could be no knots of any kind in the birthing woman's house or near her, or else her baby could be tied up in her womb. Putting on their cloaks and hoods, the two young women followed Ingiborg out the door.

When they reached Halldora's, her husband, Egil, rushed over to them. He was not old, but his face was haggard with worry. Halldora had lost children before. It was a rare woman who had not.

"The pangs came so quick," his voice sounded higher than normal in his panic. "Is that bad?"

Ingiborg laid a hand on his arm. "It is normal. It may even mean this birth will go easier than the others. Frigg willing."

By the time Halldora had delivered her baby, it was morning and Astrid was exhausted. She stayed with her mother as she made sure the baby took to Halldora's breast. When Halldora put him to her breast, he latched on with ease and suckled well.

The women all smiled. "Thank Frigg, he is a stout and healthy boy," Ingiborg said.

Halldora's face was radiant as she watched her new son take nourishment from her body. She ran a finger gently over his downy cheek. "He looks like Egil."

"Yes, he does," Ingiborg said. She smiled and touched his wispy brown hair.

Halldora looked to Ingiborg, Astrid, and Amma. "Thank you for guiding my son into the world. Blessed be."

"Blessed be," Ingiborg answered. "You have a son to be proud of. I will make up something for you to drink and then be back later to check on you. Amma is staying with you now." She spoke to Amma. "Make sure she drinks it. It will help with the after pains and bleeding."

"If anything happens, I will send for you," Amma said.

Ingiborg turned to Astrid, who tried to hide a yawn. "Help me make the tea, and then we can go home and rest a while."

Astrid stood at the side of the bed watching Halldora and her new baby. They both looked so peaceful in that moment, baby at the breast, mother watching him as if she had never seen anything so beautiful or precious. Astrid felt a stirring in her heart for the same. She saw herself with a beautiful child in her arms. But then her thoughts ran to some unknown husband, someone cruel like Sigmund, or old and horrible like Ketil, and she grew cold. What if her husband beat her children? Astrid swallowed hard, banished those thoughts, and reached over to touch the new baby's head.

"That was an easy birth," Ingiborg said when Astrid joined her, as she stood at the fire dropping herbs into boiling water and stirring them.

"It didn't look easy," Astrid said, thinking she'd have bruises on her arms where Halldora gripped her during the birth pains.

To Astrid's surprise, her mother laughed. "No birth is easy. But some are better than others. One day you will see a difficult birth and you will know what I mean." She touched the Frigg pendant at her neck. "Frigg willing, it will not be one of your own." Ingiborg looked as if she were thinking of her own personal difficulties.

The thought of going through that travail gave Astrid a start. As the earthy aroma from the herbs rose in the steam, Astrid remembered the awful scene of her mother's last childbirth. A terrible storm, the inability to get the midwife, she and Rikki, too young to help and huddling in fear in the bed closet while they listened to their mother's screams of pain, their father's desperation, the still-born baby swaddled and lifeless, waiting for burial at the first thaw. Since then her mother had been drinking a tea to ensure she never became with child again.

"I'm afraid, *modir*," she choked out.

"We are all afraid." She stirred the tea, then leaned in to smell it, wafting the steam with her hand. "But we have to endure it if we want the rewards of children." She nodded her head toward Halldora. "Look how much joy she feels for that child. That makes it worth it." Putting her hands, the same capable hands that had just delivered a living child, on Astrid's cheeks, she said, "You make it worth it."

"You will be strong when the time comes, my daughter."

Chapter Eleven
Hovgarden

A sheen of sweat glistened on Selime's tawny skin, and Bjorn licked her neck. It was hot in the building where Harald's men were quartered. He pushed up onto his elbow and trailed his fingers over her stomach. She turned to him, her eyes smiling, and she ran her hands through his hair and traced the lines of his cheeks and nose.

"You are very handsome," she said.

"I know."

Selime laughed as he leaned in and kissed her neck softly. "Again? It has not been that long." She murmured and ran her hands down his body.

"No, not yet." Bjorn stopped her hand and laid it on his chest. She rested her head on his shoulder and curled up next to him.

Bjorn pulled the furs up over them, closed his eyes, and enjoyed feeling warm and satisfied. He was nodding off when Selime spoke, hesitant. "Bjorn."

He liked the way she said his name with a soft richness, her accent extending it so it sounded like 'Bee-oooorn.'

"Mmm." He really wanted to sleep. The building was empty except for the two of them, and he wanted to take advantage of the quiet while he had the chance.

"Bjorn," she said again. "I was with Ingjald last night."

"And?" His eyes popped open, and he stiffened. Sharing a woman was not usually a problem for him, but every time Ingjald's name crossed her lips, it made him want to lash out.

He felt her body contract into itself as if preparing for a blow. "He..." she trailed off.

"He what?" Bjorn sat up, dislodging Selime from his body.

He immediately regretted it, for she scuttled across the bed from him, her eyes wide with fright.

He sighed and reached out to bring her back. She recoiled. "I will not hit you," he soothed.

With a nod, she scooted back, and they resettled themselves. She put her head on his chest, and he stroked her hair. He wished it were not cut short, for it was beautiful, soft and thick, and he wanted it to drape over his face when she was on top of him. The thought made him grow hard, but then he remembered she wanted to talk about Ingjald, and that killed his desire.

"What about Ingjald," he said with a weary sigh.

She kept her face turned from him and trailed her fingers back and forth through his chest hair. "He said you leave soon," she whispered.

"We are."

"Oh." A sigh escaped her lips, and it tickled his skin. "I hoped it was not true."

"Why would he lie?"

"No reason..." Selime hesitated. "He also said you offered to buy me from him."

"Ingjald says a lot," Bjorn said, not sure how to address the offer with her. He had offered Ingjald one of his valuable arm rings for the girl, a ring he had seen Ingjald admiring. Although Ingjald considered the ring was generous, he did not want to give Selime up. At least not now. He had told Bjorn to ask again at the summer Thing, the meeting where all the jarls and chieftains assembled, if he was still interested.

"I would have liked to go with you," Selime said as she continued to stroke his body.

Bjorn thought of telling her about the Thing but decided against it. No point in planning for a future.

With his finger, he lifted her chin to him and kissed her. She ran her hand up and down his chest, his belly, and then traced the line of hair that ran from his belly down to his cock. She bent her head and kissed him, her lips following the same trail.

The door opened and Selime startled, but Bjorn ignored the interruption, figuring it was one of the guard. He ran his hands through her hair to get her to continue and groaned at the feel of her lips on his stomach.

A man cleared his throat, and Bjorn opened his eyes in irritation. Styrr stood in the door, waiting.

"I don't want an audience."

Instead of his usual quip or taunt, Styrr said, "There is a messenger here with news for you."

Bjorn rolled Selime off him and sat up. "From home?"

"*Ja*. He's waiting in the great hall."

A hand touched his forearm. "I hope it is good news," Selime told him.

"What did the messenger say?" Bjorn asked Styrr.

The question made Styrr pull his attention away from leering at Selime's naked breasts. "He wouldn't tell us. He said he'd only talk to you."

"How did he look?" Bjorn pulled his trousers on, and Selime handed him his tunic.

"Like you don't want to hear his news."

"The baby. Maude." Bjorn breathed out, and his hands froze in the middle of pulling on one of his shoes. Maude had looked healthy when he'd left. When he asked her about it, she had told him all was well, but he knew that anything could happen in childbirth. Women and babies died all the time.

He and Styrr walked to the hall, Bjorn's feet feeling like they were anchors weighing him down.

Someone handed Bjorn a drink, but he did not notice who, although he caught the slightest whiff of sage. He ran his thumb over the cold glass goblet, noticing that it had no imperfections. The messenger had given him glad tidings. He had a healthy new daughter. But Maude was dead, succumbing to childbirth sickness not long after the baby had been born.

"Who cares for the child now?" Bjorn said into his cup. His thoughts went to Tanni. How was the boy handling the death of his mother? Bjorn wanted to return home, wanted to hold his young son and his new baby daughter.

The young messenger looked down at his feet and shifted uncomfortably at the talk of children. "The blacksmith's wife recently gave birth and she...ah...suckles your child as well as her own."

"And Tanni?"

"Last I saw him, Harald's mistress Katrin had taken the boy in."

At least Sigrun wasn't taking care of Tanni. Bjorn didn't want her hatred of him to bleed over to his son.

Someone sat down next to Bjorn. "The community looks after your children. They will care for the body of your woman too, until you reach home," Ingjald's wife Gyrid said. She meant it kindly, even if her voice was hard. "This is not the first time a child is born without its mother, nor will it be the last."

She was right. Straightening up, Bjorn looked at Gyrid. "A toast for my new child and for Maude."

She summoned her thralls to fill a drinking bowl for a toast.

Once full, Gyrid offered the bowl to Bjorn, and he held it up. "To Maude, who like all women, bravely went into the danger of giving birth. She now lives with Freya in her Hall. *Skål!*" He held the bowl in both his hands and took a drink of the earthy ale.

"*Skål!*" Everyone repeated and Gyrid carried the bowl to Harald, Styrr, Rekja, and then took a drink herself before handing it lastly to Ingjald.

When the bowl returned to him, Bjorn lifted it one more time and gave a toast to his new daughter, although she would not receive her name until she sat upon his knee and he recognized her. Each person drank to the new child.

Storelva

Astrid held up the dress tunic she'd finished embroidering for Rikki and smiled. She had sewn a light green twisting vine that ran along the edge of the darker green tunic. She fluffed it and turned it to examine the back.

"It's beautiful, Asta," Ingiborg told her as she entered the women's house. She sat down next to her daughter, after checking on the progress the thralls made with their spinning. The wool they spun would become the thread that they used to sew their clothes. The thrall's talked among themselves as they spun, their hands automatically pulling out pieces of raw wool and spinning them onto their whorls. It was a never-ending job Astrid was glad she didn't have to do often.

"*Tak*. Do you think Rikki will like it?"

"He will not even notice it." Ingiborg gave a gentle laugh. "Your brother does not care for such things. You do lovely work, *dottir*. The man you marry will be the best-dressed man around."

With a deep breath, Astrid asked in as calm of a voice as she could manage, "What does Father plan to do? Will he marry me to Sigmund Ketilsson?" The thought of that man made it hard to breathe.

"I do not know. He has mentioned other choices." Ingiborg sat down on the bench next to Astrid in a jingle of keys, scissors, and other small household implements she wore around her waist.

"Who?" Astrid choked out.

"He will not tell me."

"I want you to know I voiced my concern about Sigmund Ketilsson." She shook her head. "A marriage between the families would benefit your father a great deal, but Sigmund is a vile man."

"Did Father listen to you?"

"He heard me. Emund also told him he did not want you to marry Sigmund."

"Thank the goddess," Astrid breathed.

"I think your father will wait until the summer council. All the most important men will be there, and he can find out who would be advantageous to make a match with." She paused. "He needs to hear what happens with Jori and King Ingjald first. Tryggvi might have to handle Harald if things do not go well in Hovgarden."

Astrid sighed. "It is all so much."

"It is. Remember that when you marry, it will be for a greater good. It worked for me."

Although she knew her mother meant it to help, it did not. She didn't want to marry someone to make a trade alliance or make sure her father's access through certain waters was safe. She would have to sacrifice herself, and she wasn't sure if the greater good would be worth it.

Astrid nodded to assure her mother, even though she did not feel agreeable. A stray piece of hair escaped Astrid's braid, and Ingiborg tucked it behind her ear. Her eyes noticed Astrid's left cheek, and she touched it. "Your scar."

Astrid grimaced and tried to duck her head, but her mother's hand was too strong. "That horrible outlaw cut me when he hit me. I hate that the scar mars my face."

Ingiborg gently traced her finger along the small white line. "It is not a terrible scar."

"All scars are bad," she said, but then thought of the scars she'd seen on the men. Scars littered their hands, arms, and bodies. Gunnar had one on his chin and another on the back of his right hand. She did not think those were bad or ugly; just the opposite, she found them appealing, little reminders that he was a man, that he could fight. "Scars on a woman's face at least."

"Whether or not our scars show," Ingiborg said, and her voice sounded far away as if thinking of her own. She instinctively touched her abdomen. "They are the markers of our lives. You have seen the scar on your father's back?"

Astrid nodded. She recalled seeing her mother and father days earlier, sitting before the fire, her mother stroking that scar.

"Your father was stabbed there by a spear during a boar hunt. A man he had been hunting with went to jab his spear at the boar, but at the same moment your father moved, and the spear hit him in the back."

Astrid gasped. She knew how dangerous boar hunting could be.

Ingiborg continued, "Your father was young, and we had not yet married. I was already showing some skill at healing, so his father sent for me. I was young and afraid I would hurt him, or worse, that he'd die under my watch. His father and mine had a fragile friendship, and I did not want to make a mistake. When I saw Tryggvi, he was in great pain. I knelt so I could look him in the eyes and tell him what I needed to do. Through his haze of pain, I saw trust."

She looked into the distance, as if seeing again Tryggvi's pain-filled eyes. "Your father has trusted me to care for him ever since. That scar on his back is a link between us. As much as the ring on my finger, it is a reminder of the bond we share."

She touched Astrid's cheek again. "Perhaps this scar will be a reminder for you, *dottir*. A reminder of strength and the will to fight." She kissed Astrid on the forehead. It felt like a blessing.

"Was that why you and Father married?"

Ingiborg did not answer for so long Astrid wondered if she would.

"It was not so simple. You might as well know. One reason your father and his brother fight is because Harald believes he should have married me and become the jarl."

"Why have you never told me this?"

"It is enough that Tryggvi and Harald are at odds over their land. We did not want to frighten you and your brother and sister that if he could, Harald would take me for his own."

Astrid shivered. She knew what her mother was saying. It also explained to her why her father hated Harald so much. It was more than land. It was personal. Harald threatened his wife.

"But your father and Harald hated each other long before that."

"Why?" Astrid asked.

"I think it is a curse from Odin."

Astrid wanted to ask more, but two of her father's dogs broke the moment when they spotted Astrid's fluffy gray and white cat, Kis-Kis, who had taken possession of a pile of warm furs next to her. One dog yipped and nipped at Kis-Kis, who leaped up and hissed at the offending dog, while taking a swipe at him with her claws.

"Harri! Stop it!" Astrid yelled at the dog, but he had gotten the worst of it; he yelped and ran off in search of easier prey. Kis-Kis preened, stretched, and curled back up as if nothing had happened.

The conversation with her mother pushed out of her mind, Astrid put the tunic aside and pulled a heavy Kis-Kis into her lap. The cat was cushy and pliable, like warm dough, and her head was soft as Astrid petted her. "I will be like Kis-Kis. If a man does not please me, I will show him my claws."

Astrid and her mother laughed. "Yes. You do that."

Chapter Twelve
Hovgarden

Bjorn slammed his empty cup down to the shouts of the other men at the table. His head swam with that last drink, but he held it steady and pointed at the man who had challenged him. "At the Thing this summer. Running the oars."

"Summer, then." Ingjald's man downed his own drink, and they stared at each other for a long moment. "Gotta piss." He rose from the table and left the feast hall.

Bjorn studied the man as he walked out, looking for a weakness. He was average height and build, strong. Nothing to indicate he couldn't meet the challenge. As he walked out, an icy wind blew in, a flurry of snow with it. Men cursed him, but they quieted as soon as the door shut behind him. Bjorn studied the door, the vivid cinnabar color in which it was painted, and wondered if he could afford the dye to paint his own door with it.

"Can you run the oars?" Gunnar asked him, his voice surprisingly clear and focused. He had been nursing that first drink for much too long.

"Can Pretty Bjorn run the oars?" Vefinn had come up to them, and he put his arm on Bjorn's shoulder, stumbling a little. He smelled of ale. "He's never lost a challenge. Balance like a cat."

"Unlike you," Bjorn said with a snort and he pushed a drunk Vefinn away from him.

Styrr, who had been listening in, stumbled his way over to sit at the spot where the other man had just left. "What about you,

Gunnar Tryggvi's Man? Can you run the oars? Or are all of Tryggvi's men like him? Weak." He took a drink and stared at Gunnar over the lip of the cup.

Bjorn felt Gunnar's body tense as he shifted on the bench next to him, saw the knuckles of his hand grow white as they clutched at his cup. But he did not rise to Styrr's taunts.

"And cowardly," Styrr said, and he slammed his cup on the oak table, the sound like a blow to the head.

Gunnar jumped to his feet, his own cup knocked to the side as he reached for his sword, a sword that was not hanging at his side. They had left all weapons in the anteroom to the feast hall.

At the same time a new voice shouted from another table, and a bench scraped on the floor. "What did you say?"

Arms circled Styrr's chest, lifted him backward and slammed him to the floor, making one of the dogs snap at him. Gunnar flew over the table and joined Jorund, who had taken Styrr down. Styrr twisted, and with a knee to Jorund's side, kicked his body out from underneath Jorund, and received a punch in the jaw from Gunnar as soon as he rose to his knee. He buckled and fell back.

Gunnar put his face in Styrr's. "Tryggvi is not weak or a coward."

Rising again, Jorund grabbed Styrr's neck in a choke and pulled him to his feet. With teeth bared, he snarled, "*We* defeated *you*." He tightened the choke, making Styrr splutter and grasp at Jorund's hands to release their hold.

The sound of Jorund's voice, the mention of the battle between Tryggvi's men and Harald's made Bjorn's breath quicken, and his vision grow dim. Fiery anger flooded his body, and a ringing sounded in his ears. He dashed around the toppled bench as quick as a cat. Bjorn knocked Gunnar out of the way with an elbow to the face, then spun and struck Jorund on the back of the head with his forearm before the other man could react. There was a loud crack as bone hit bone. It was enough to make Jorund loosen his grip on Styrr, who then thrust his elbow into Jorund's gut.

"He's mine," Bjorn said, quickly jumping in before Styrr could do anything more. Blood rushed in his ears, making the world sound like he was underwater.

At hearing those words, Jorund spun and swung a fist at Bjorn's head. Bjorn ducked, but not quickly enough, and the blow glanced off his cheek. Another swing came in, but Bjorn saw this one and ducked under it, throwing a punch to Jorund's stomach. It landed and the other man reeled back from the impact. He hit a table which kept him upright, and when Bjorn came in for another punch, Jorund kicked him. Images of his friend Galinn raced through Bjorn's mind, of their days fighting with Harald, always side-by-side, watching out for each other.

One's back is vulnerable unless one has a Brother.

Galinn had been Bjorn's Blood-brother; they had blended their blood together and had always watched each other's back. He was gone. The final image, of Galinn falling on Jorund's spear, sent heat racing all throughout Bjorn's body.

He spun and rushed to the door to retrieve his sword from the alcove outside the hall. He did not want to fight with fists and feet. He wanted Jorund's blood wetting his blade.

The voices of men shouting and cursing sounded throughout the feast hall. They welcomed a good fight.

Footsteps pounded behind him. With a bitter smile, knowing it was Jorund, Bjorn hurried to grab his sword. He spotted it leaning against the wall of the alcove, its hilt beckoning him. Bjorn wrenched open the door to be met by frigid air and snow falling beyond the balcony. He did not register the cold as Jorund burst out the door. The two men ran to the open ground beyond the hall.

Bjorn pivoted and delivered his first strike to Jorund's unprotected left side. Without a shield, Jorund had to leap out of the way of the strike. He was quick on his feet, battle-trained and ready. Bjorn heard another man shout and appear next to Jorund. Gunnar had a sword in his own hand, ready to back up his friend. A bruise was forming on his chin from where Bjorn had elbowed him.

"My fight is not with you, Gunnar," Bjorn shouted over the noise of people as they spilled out into the yard, shouting, eager to watch a fight. He spared Gunnar a quick glance, but his focus was on Jorund.

"Go," Jorund told Gunnar, nodding, but never taking his eyes off Bjorn.

Gunnar stepped back into the circle of men, and Bjorn saw from the corner of his eye he did not sheathe his sword.

With a shout, Jorund leaped at Bjorn, his sword aimed at Bjorn's neck. He jumped to the side and swept Jorund's strike aside. The clang of their weapons rang out in the dark night. Someone brought out torches, and the flickering light on the snow gave the scene an eerie look. Bjorn had the feeling that he was in a dream.

Jorund's sword flashed in the torchlight as he gave another attack that Bjorn met easily. The shock of the weapons meeting sent a jolt of energy up Bjorn's arm. He had not fought for a long time. Hot anger spread through his arms and legs, and he grinned as he launched himself at Jorund. Like the first time they'd met, Bjorn lost all sense of time and place; he was the sword that struck at his enemy. No thoughts. Just strike after strike. Parry the blows that were too easy, like Jorund was a child and Bjorn was playing with him.

At one point he heard the distinctive growl of Harald, 'finish him.'

He swung for Jorund's neck. Jorund made one last effort to protect himself; his sword came up, and he ducked. It was a weak attempt, and Bjorn's sword slid off the blade and sliced into the side of Jorund's face. A horrible shriek pierced the air, and before

Jorund could fall to the ground, Bjorn sunk his sword into his enemy's heart. When he pulled his sword out of Jorund's body, it slumped to the ground, blood flowing onto the snow. It glowed in the flickering torchlight, like spilled rubies.

Seeing Jorund's weapon on the ground, Bjorn snatched it up. As he held it, he whispered to himself, "You are avenged, my Brother." He saw Galinn's face smiling as he sat at a table in Valhalla, saw Galinn raise a horn of mead to him.

The fragile peace broken, Harald's and Jorund's men swarmed and fought with one another. Gunnar rushed in straight toward where Bjorn stood over Jorund's broken and bloody body, and Harald stepped in front of his foster-son, battle axe raised, but Bjorn stayed his arm. Instead of attacking Bjorn, Gunnar ignored the fighting and knelt next to his friend's body. Without thinking, he looked for Jorund's weapon, but it was in Bjorn's left hand. When Gunnar met his eyes and then flitted down to the sword, Bjorn shook his head.

Before he could decide anything, Harald came up beside him. "What will you do with the sword?"

Bjorn wanted to fling it away before it tainted him. "It did not serve Jorund well. It is bad luck."

"I do not fear the bad luck of Tryggvi's son," Harald said with a cruel laugh.

"It is yours then," Bjorn told him, and he handed his foster-father the sword.

As Bjorn handed it to Harald, Gunnar gave him a look of dismay. Bjorn turned his back on the man.

Ingjald's men, fully armed, broke up the fights, but not before several men had been downed by injuries; there were no more deaths.

Flanked by two of his men, Ingjald strode over to where Jorund lay, his blood still darkening the snow. He looked down at Gunnar, who knelt by his friend's side. "Is he dead?"

"He is dead," Gunnar said, his voice thick with anger and grief.

Ingjald turned on Bjorn, his blue eyes as icy and bare as a winter lake. "You have broken my peace. Why did you kill him?"

Blood still racing through his body from the fight and from finally getting revenge, Bjorn stared at Ingjald. "Jorund Tryggvason killed my blood brother. I avenged him. It is done."

Ingjald took a few moments to study Bjorn. Everyone had grown quiet waiting for Ingjald to speak. "It is good to avenge a Brother. It is not murder, but you must pay a wergild to Jorund's family."

When Ingjald told him the amount, Gunnar shot to his feet. "Jorund is the son of a jarl. He is worth more than that."

"Bjorn did it in front of witnesses, and Jorund is Bjorn's equal. You are lucky to get anything," King Ingjald told Gunnar, folding his arms over his chest. He turned back to Bjorn. "You will pay it to Gunnar who will take it back to Jorund's family."

With a nod, Bjorn acknowledged Ingjald's demand.

Ingjald ordered thralls to clean up the mess, and then, done with his duties as king, gestured for his men to follow him. He turned away from Harald and Bjorn without another word, knowing that they would obey this command, and disappeared into the feast hall.

Bjorn caught sight of Selime watching him, her dark eyes wide with fear and what looked to him like excitement. His blood was still singing, and he wanted to take her back to his bed. No, he wanted her right now. To his dismay, one of Ingjald's men came out and took her back into the hall, no doubt back to Ingjald. Bjorn ground his teeth in frustration. He needed a woman.

A heavy hand clapped Bjorn's shoulder. "My balls are freezing. Let's go inside," Harald said.

He handed his axe and Jori's sword to one of his guard and stalked off to the housing where his men slept, Bjorn by his side. Snow flurried around them, collecting on Harald's hair and shoulders, making him look like a huge white wolf as he stalked back to his den. Crunching footsteps sounded behind Bjorn and Rekja caught up to him, Styrr flanking him.

Once inside the building, Harald turned to Bjorn. "I will pay the wergild. You killed my brother's bastard son." He clapped his hand on Bjorn's shoulder.

It was a generous offer. Bjorn found a cloth and sat down on his sea chest to clean his sword before the blood dried on it. "That was for Galinn," he said.

"You should avenge a friend," Harald said.

"Now we have one less son of Tryggvi," Styrr said.

"My brother loves his sons. Too much. It will be like he lost one of his balls!" He stood by the hearth, the snow melting off his cloak and dripping to the floor.

"He will come back at us with everything he has," Rekja reminded them. "We need to be ready."

With a wave of his hand, Harald swatted that idea away. "I know Tryggvi. He will wait until after the spring planting when he has all of his men. He is cautious, my brother, and no fool. But then neither am I. We have time. When Tryggvi comes for us, we will be ready."

"It will be a bloody season," Bjorn said.

"*Ja*," Harald growled. He clapped his hands together. "I can't wait."

Chapter Thirteen
Storelva

Astrid admired the new tunic she'd finished for Rikki before folding it and putting it into her sewing chest. She looked over at a large table where her father, Emund, and Buri consulted, Emund's deep rumbly voice carrying through the house. Her mother spoke with her most trusted household thralls. One of the male thralls opened the door to bring in firewood, and the gleaming white of the snow beckoned to Astrid. She wanted some air, so she fetched her cloak, pulled up her marten fur-lined hood, and went out. Once outside she took in a deep breath, the cold hurting her lungs, and blew it out slowly, a white plume escaping from her mouth. It was quiet outside, especially compared to the house, and she took a moment to appreciate the way the snow glistened on the roofs of the buildings and weighed down the branches of the trees.

Astrid heard boisterous male laughter, the barking of a dog, and then a shout of alarm. She turned toward the shout when Short Olaf came tearing around the corner of the barn, snow flying from his shoes. He crashed into a farmer, nearly knocking the poor man over and, escaping that, he leaped over little Asleif who was galloping by on his stick-horse, followed by the older Hak, who chased him. Short Olaf stumbled forward but righted himself and made his way toward Astrid's house.

Alarmed, Astrid turned to the ruckus.

"Asta!" Short Olaf cried upon seeing her.

"What happened?" she asked, her breath coming quickly, her heart racing.

"Rikki," was all Short Olaf got out, before grabbing her hand and pulling her after him.

They ran to a clearing behind one of the barns, and she stopped short when she got there.

Rikki lay on the ground, one leg up on a bench, blood darkening the side of his tunic and dripping onto the snow, turning it pink. When the warm blood hit the cold air, it steamed. One of Short Olaf's dogs, Dag, stood over him barking, while Galm paced next to him, a bloody spear in his hand, muttering, "*shyt, shyt, shyt.*"

Without a thought, Astrid rushed to her brother's side. She knelt next to him, her knees hitting the wet snow, and breathed out a sigh of relief when she saw his blue eyes looking back at her.

He gave her a crooked grin and pointed at the barking hound. "Dag tried to kill me."

Frowning, Astrid looked from Rikki to the dog to Galm. She shushed the dog and pushed him away. "Go," she commanded him. He gave one last bark and slunk off.

Astrid examined the tear in Rikki's tunic and the cut underneath. It did not look as bad from up close as it had from above. She untucked his tunic from his belt and lifted it gingerly to expose the wound. It was red and raw and bleeding, but the cut was not deep enough to cause serious damage.

"It's fine," Rikki said.

Galm knelt and grasped Rikki by the arm to help him to a sitting position. "We thought you were dying."

"*Ja*. You weren't breathing," Short Olaf said.

"Got the breath knocked out of me. I landed crooked. That's all." Rikki shook his head like a dog, and the snow flew from his hair. He pushed Astrid's hands away and lowered his tunic. "Leave it."

"We should stop the bleeding at least."

Galm laughed. "Shortie lost his mind when he saw you'd taken a hit. When you weren't breathing after the fall, he took off to get your mother."

Rikki rolled his eyes and turned to Short Olaf. "You worry like a woman."

"You looked dead."

Rikki got to his knees and then stood, holding onto his side as he did so. If he was in pain, he tried not to show it.

Astrid looked to Rikki and Galm, then to the bloody spear head, her eyes narrowed. "What happened?"

The commotion had drawn an audience, including the younger boys who looked up to Rikki, Galm, and Short Olaf. Asleif and Hak watched with bright eyes. Galm threw up his arms and growled at the boys, "Go away." The two younger boys jumped and scattered like squirrels. Galm laughed meanly at their departure.

Rikki staggered over to the barn and leaned against it, his face pale, and pulled his tunic back up so he could look at the wound. Besides the cut, he had a nasty bruise forming. The bleeding had stopped, but Astrid could smell the blood as it had soaked into the fabric of his tunic. She wanted to clean the wound, but she had nothing on her.

"Let me get mother's healing bag."

"No." Rikki let his dirty tunic fall back down and Astrid suppressed a shudder; she needed to clean that wound. She'd find him later and do it when the others were not around. Men and their pride.

Astrid picked up the spear Galm had dropped. He snatched it away from her and cleaned off the spear head. "Are you going to tell me what you were doing?" Astrid asked and turned to Galm. "Why did you stab my brother?"

"It was an accident," Rikki told her. "I wanted to practice against a spear unarmed and without my shield. Galm went for my thigh, so I jumped on the bench to avoid it."

"That's when Shortie and Dag showed up," Galm said. "And Shortie's idiot dog thought—"

"He's not an idiot," Short Olaf said.

"Your dog is useless, like an old man's cock."

She heaved a sigh. Sometimes they still acted like they were ten, and not seventeen, like men.

"Dag thought Rikki was playing a game, so he hopped onto the bench right as Galm parried. Rikki stepped back and tripped over him," Short Olaf explained.

They laughed again at how ridiculous it all was. Astrid joined in until she realized what could have happened.

"You're lucky you weren't hurt worse. Why did you practice with a sharp blade? Why not the blunted practice spear?"

Rikki and Galm gave each other a look, like she had asked a question that had an obvious answer, then snorted in amusement.

"We have to keep ourselves sharp, for when we are in battle," Galm explained. "There is no risk with the blunted blades."

"I wanted it to be real," Rikki added.

"He could have killed you." She shook her head.

"I have more control than that," Galm said. "It's nothing. Go home."

"Don't tell me what to do, Galm," she spat. "It is not nothing to me." The way they talked frustrated her. "Do you not care if you live or die?"

Rikki sat down on the bench and circled his right arm to test the wound. "I care *how* I live. I care *how* I die. I do not want to die the straw-death of an old man."

"Getting speared by your friend won't get you into Valhalla." She sat down next to her brother.

"What would you know about it?" Galm said. "You are a woman. If we don't go down fighting, or even trying something crazy, then what is the point?"

"What is the point? Marriage, children, farming, caring for peo—" Astrid started.

Galm snorted.

Then Rikki spoke up. "Those are important to you, *systir*. But you don't know what it's like to sail on the whale-road, to ride the waves, to fight in a shield wall, to stand on the edge of your life, knowing that one little misstep..."

"I don't want to hear any more," Astrid told him.

"Come on, Rikki. Let's go," Galm said, as if he were weary of talking to her. He helped Rikki up from the bench.

Rikki sucked in his breath in pain as he moved. Earlier, she had been embroidering the hem of Rikki's tunic and the thought of him not being there to wear it made her heart hurt, especially since one brother was in the hands of the wolf, Harald.

Her expression must have moved something in Rikki. "I do not want a quiet life. If I die fighting, or even practicing, it's better than growing old and dying in my bed from old age or disease."

He looked at her so earnestly she nodded. "You are my brother. I don't want you to die in any way."

"I know." He, Galm, and Short Olaf walked toward the house where her father's personal guard lived. Before he got out of sight, he turned and said to Astrid with a flourish, "Let's have fun while we are still alive, *systir*!"

She couldn't help herself. His face, so like hers, looked so open, amused, and free of care that she laughed with him.

He flashed a grin at her when she waved. Astrid went back to the house and met her mother at the door.

"Is everything all right?"

"Yes," Astrid said.

"Get used to it. One day you will have sons of your own."

"Frigg help me."

Ulfdalr

Bjorn glanced down at the baby in his lap. Swaddled in a blanket, she pursed her tiny pink lips in and out as if nursing in her sleep. She let out a delicate coo, and he smiled at her, touching his callused and rough finger to her perfect cheek. It was as soft as goose down. He was at the house of Naestr the Smith and surrounded by a few friends to celebrate the naming of his daughter with what food and drink they could manage. The Marrow Sucker months were upon them, and they had to conserve their stores until summer when the pigs, cattle, and sheep gave birth and produced milk. And autumn when the barley harvest came in.

It had been a hard journey when they left King Ingjald's stronghold. There was a reason they traveled overland and not by sea during the winter months. The rough sea and freezing storms made it dangerous, and Bjorn had never been so happy to touch land as after that trip.

Bjorn knew Harald had no interest in girl children, so he was not in attendance. He'd sent a small gift with one of his thralls. Most of the other household guard thought Bjorn's love of his children unseemly, and he kept them away too.

"Would you like me to take her now?" Thora, the blacksmith's wife, asked him, her arms out. Her own baby was swaddled in a wrap on her chest.

"No." He shook his head. "She sleeps peacefully. Let's not wake her." He lightly touched her eyes and nose. So tiny. So vulnerable.

Thora leaned over him and looked down at the baby. "Aud. A good name, Bjorn. She is certainly a treasure."

"*Ja.*"

"Papa. Me." Tanni came up to him and tried to push Bjorn's arm away from the baby. He couldn't budge it, so Bjorn opened the arm not holding the baby to welcome the boy. Tanni climbed onto his lap. Bjorn hoisted him up to sit on his other knee from baby Aud.

"Do you like your new sister?" Bjorn asked as he gave the boy a squeeze.

Tanni wrinkled his nose. "No. She is boring!"

Bjorn met Thora's eyes, and they laughed.

"Come find me when she is hungry," Thora said, and with a smile, she caressed Aud's swaddled head before joining her husband. Thora was feeding Bjorn's babe with her own milk.

Bjorn adjusted the baby in his arm, and she opened her eyes. They were hazel and stared at him. Tanni put his hand on the blankets and patted his sister too hard. Bjorn grabbed his hand.

"Easy. She is delicate." Holding his son's hand in his, he gently patted the baby. "Like this."

Tanni did not let Bjorn move his hand for long before he wrenched it out. He pulled the blanket down so he could see this new interloper's face better and leaned his own face close to hers. The boy made such a strange face, Bjorn was afraid he'd lick the baby. Aud's hazel eyes widened at her brother, but she did not cry. Done with his sister, Tanni tried to climb on his father's back, his feet digging into Bjorn's thigh. His son was bigger than he had been when Bjorn left at the beginning of the winter.

"Horsey ride, Papa."

One of his small feet kicked Bjorn in the side.

"Tanni, don't...let me...hang on..." Bjorn bent over to allow the boy to climb onto him, while adjusting the baby who still nestled in the crook of his other arm. He swung one arm over Tanni's back to keep him from falling, and Aud fussed at the commotion. A ripple of anxiety flooded his body at her fussing, as he worried he'd crush her in his strong arms.

Naestr the Smith let out a belly laugh, joined by a few others, as they watched Bjorn fumble with his two children. His anxiety flew away, and he laughed with them, aware of how he must look, a tiny baby in his arm, a little boy climbing on his back. He plopped back down onto the seat, Tanni hanging on to his neck so tightly it was hard to breathe, Aud crying at being jostled so much. He jiggled her like he'd seen the women do, trying to calm the baby. To his surprise, it worked, and she settled into his arm. His heart flipped in his chest. She was so trusting, knowing only that strong, warm arms held her safely.

He leaned down and shrugged Tanni up higher on his back to relieve the pressure on his throat. Tanni scooched up and rested his face next to Bjorn's. His breath tickled Bjorn's cheek. With his son on his back and his daughter in his arm, Bjorn felt fuller than he'd ever felt in his life. He made a silent vow to protect them. Always.

Tanni broke the silent moment by touching the silver torc at Bjorn's neck. "When do I wear..." he stopped to think. "Toke?"

"Torc." Bjorn laughed, and he touched Tanni's hand on the silver ring at his neck. "When you are grown, you can wear my torc."

"Yay!" He squealed in Bjorn's ear. "I want to be grown *now*."

Bjorn tried to imagine Tanni as a grown man, but stopped himself, not wanting to tempt the gods. He thought of Jorund Tryggvason's sword hanging in the Harald's hall, of Bjorn's pride when he'd told the story of how he'd killed his enemy. It was a harsh reminder that a son's life was easily cut down. His hands shook slightly as he held his baby daughter. He had these children now, and that had to be enough. He held up baby Aud so he could smell her baby scent and kissed her forehead.

Chapter Fourteen
Storelva

The door to the women's house slammed open and startled Astrid so much she fumbled on her tablet-weaving.

"What is it?" Ingiborg asked, her voice calm despite the sudden way young Hak had appeared at the door.

"They've returned!" Young Hak said.

"Who?" Astrid pulled out the thread so she could start over.

"Jori's traveling party. I saw Gunnar—"

"Gunnar! Jori!" Astrid abandoned her weaving and hurried out the door. Her mother, Ragnhild, and the other women, minus the thralls, followed close behind.

The air outside was cool and brisk, the sun high overhead, and Astrid ran like an excited child. Her brother and Gunnar had come back! A smile lit up her face when she arrived at the horse corral as the men came into sight. A few young men from the village walked beside the horses, which was strange since they normally ran with them, laughing and joking. Astrid's smile faded at the sight of the serious men and boys.

Gunnar led the group, and his shoulders slumped as if he carried a heavy burden.

Astrid searched the group. "Where is Jori?" she whispered to her mother.

"I do not know."

They exchanged worried glances as Tryggvi and Emund walked up, Rikki by their father's side. Astrid watched her father take in the men just as she had done, searching for his oldest son.

He approached Gunnar as the younger man slid off his horse. Wet and dry mud covered his shoes and *winingas*, a testament to long riding through rough roads and paths wet with
snow melt.

They did not exchange pleasantries.

"Where is my son?" Tryggvi asked. He kept looking down the path as if expecting Jori to be lagging. Jori was not the type of man to do that. When he met the eyes of the other riders, they looked away or at the ground.

Gunnar pulled a small bag out of his saddlebag and poured the contents into his hand—a silver necklace with a Thor amulet and an arm ring of twisted silver with two ravens on the ends.

"No," Astrid said, holding her hand to her mouth. She felt sick.

Her father's face blanched as he took the items from Gunnar and held it up. The silver gleamed in the sun, and the rubies in the raven's eyes glinted like fresh blood.

"Jori is dead," Gunnar said, although it was unnecessary.

Astrid let out a cry. This couldn't be true. Not her brother. Her breathing came in quick spurts, as if she'd run a long way. Ingiborg took her hand and squeezed it. Tears blurred Astrid's eyes as she looked at her father. His face was as hard as stone. Emund stepped up and put a large hand on Tryggvi's shoulder. He gave Gunnar a sympathetic look. "Who?"

"Harald." Tryggvi growled.

Gunnar shook his head, and Astrid noticed how unkempt he was. Her heart went to him. How hard it must have been to travel all the way from the king's island, only to come back home with such dire news.

"No, not Harald. It was…" Gunnar swallowed hard. "Harald's foster-son. Bjorn Alfarsson."

Bjorn Alfarsson. In an instant, the name branded itself on Astrid's heart. The man who killed her brother. She imagined the name leaving Gunnar's mouth and floating up to the gods in Asgard like a ribbon to Vidarr, the god of vengeance.

"How did it happen?" Emund asked.

The pained expression on Gunnar's face said he did not wish to tell the story.

Rikki spoke up for the first time. "Tell us." His voice was full of a smoldering rage. Rikki and Jori may not have gotten along, but they were brothers, both of Tryggvi's blood. It was always the way in their family and among Tryggvi's men. If one of them died, the others felt it sharply.

Closing his eyes and taking a breath, Gunnar said. "It started as a drunken brawl. Nothing more. One of Harald's men insulted you, Tryggvi, and Jori jumped in to fight. One moment Bjorn was watching and the next he threw himself at Jori like..."

"Berserk?" Rikki asked, and his eyes flashed.

"No." Gunnar looked down. "Not berserk. It was personal. Revenge. Jori killed Bjorn's blood-brother." Tryggvi and Emund exchanged a look.

Gunnar continued. "He and Jori went outside, took up their weapons and fought. Jori fought well, but Bjorn showed no weakness. Bjorn killed Jori. Stabbed him in the heart."

Everything grew quiet, except for the occasional snort and stamp of the horses, the clink of one of the rider's weapons, and the sniffles of crying women.

The palm of Tryggvi's hand closed around Jori's necklace and arm ring so tight that the knuckles turned white. Everyone was silent as they watched Tryggvi. A line of blood trickled from his hand where he clenched his dead son's things.

Gunnar took another bag out of the saddlebag, this one heavy and clinking. He held it out to Tryggvi, who only stared at it.

"*Wergild* for Jori's life," Gunnar said. "King Ingjald made Bjorn pay it."

Astrid stared at the bag too, her tears blurring everything. Her brother was dead and in exchange, treasure. As if the silver could replace her brother. She knew that was how the world worked, and had watched her father work as jarl, making judgments for his people about who would pay in a dispute over land, livestock, or even thralls. It was different when it happened within her own family.

Unable to hold her tongue, Astrid spat out, "Silver. He should pay in more than silver. Bjorn Alfarsson should pay with his blood."

Rikki moved to stand next to Tryggvi. "Asta's right, Father. They will pay for this." Tryggvi's brow furrowed as he looked at his son, as if he did not know who he was in that moment. When his eyes cleared, he grabbed onto Rikki and pulled him close.

"They will pay in blood," Rikki said.

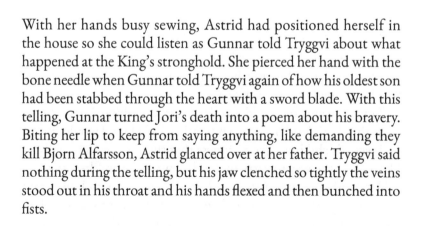

With her hands busy sewing, Astrid had positioned herself in the house so she could listen as Gunnar told Tryggvi about what happened at the King's stronghold. She pierced her hand with the bone needle when Gunnar told Tryggvi again of how his oldest son had been stabbed through the heart with a sword blade. With this telling, Gunnar turned Jori's death into a poem about his bravery. Biting her lip to keep from saying anything, like demanding they kill Bjorn Alfarsson, Astrid glanced over at her father. Tryggvi said nothing during the telling, but his jaw clenched so tightly the veins stood out in his throat and his hands flexed and then bunched into fists.

It was Rikki who spoke first, his voice laced with fury. "This Bjorn must die. I will make him pay for what he has done. I will kill him."

"We will hit Harald after the spring planting when I have all my men and my ships are ready. We do not run off in anger. We will bide our time." Her father's voice was level.

Rikki looked as if he wanted to say more, but something in their father's face made him hold back. He nodded. "Let me have Bjorn Alfarsson. He will feel the blade of another son of Tryggvi."

Tryggvi grasped hold of Rikki's shoulder. "He is yours."

Astrid gripped the fabric of the tunic. First Jori had thrown himself into danger, and now Rikki. Why couldn't her brothers have been farmers, content to stay at home and tend to their fields?

Tryggvi spoke up. "What say you, Brother? We take our revenge on Harald and his son in the spring."

"Aye," Emund said. "I look forward to it. I will make sure the men are ready."

She saw Rikki start to say something and then stop, his eyes on Galm, who had given Rikki a quick shake of his head. Astrid frowned. What was that about?

"Astrid," her mother's soft voice broke into her thoughts. "You need to go to bed. You don't need to hear this."

"Yes, I do. I am not a child, and Jori was my brother."

The smell of herbs wafted over her, soothing, as Ingiborg sat down next to her. She put her hand on Astrid's back, the gentle touch making her bite back tears.

"Since you are not a child, I will tell you something. I have always been afraid this feud between your father and Harald would spread to Tryggvi's children, like an illness that sweeps through a village. I know it is the way to carry on feuds. I want my children alive."

Her mother afraid? Astrid had never seen Ingiborg look afraid of anything. She remembered the past harvesting season when a farmer had nearly cut off his leg with his scythe. The wound sickness had set in, and Ingiborg had shown no fear when she'd had to cut it off. She had sent Astrid and Gytha away, but they had heard the man's screams.

"Jori is not my son, so I have no claim on him."

"You raised him."

"Your father and Emund raised him."

"But—"

Ingiborg shook her head. "Rikki wants to avenge his brother, and there is nothing I can do to stop it. It is his right. I don't want the feud to consume you, too."

She touched Astrid's cheek, her finger grazing over the scar. Nodding, she rose and left Astrid alone again. She didn't know what her mother meant. How could the feud between her father and Harald not consume her? It had taken her brother. She wanted revenge as much as Rikki did.

The scraping of benches brought her back, as Rikki and Gunnar rose to leave, Galm and Short Olaf close behind. They blew out of the longhouse like thunderstorms.

With them gone, Emund brought a drink for her father. They nursed their ale, neither of them talking for a long time. The silence, only broken by the scuffle of thralls tending the fire and doing their work, grew too big, and Astrid wanted to leave, and yet she did not want to move, for fear that they would notice she remained in the house awake.

"Jori died fighting, Brother," Emund said quietly. "He is feasting with your ancestors in Valhalla now."

Tryggvi put down his cup and stared at Emund.

"The Raven-God," Tryggvi said, "is not pleased with me." He rubbed the hilt of his dagger with his left thumb, thinking. "I will make a sacrifice to him."

"The Lord of Valhalla wanted Jorund, son of Tryggvi, for himself, to fight alongside him when the time comes," Emund said, putting on his storytelling voice. "You know he wants only the best warriors with him come Ragnarok."

Tryggvi's eyes shone with gratitude at his old friend. He drained the last of his ale and stood. Emund rose along with her father. "I will join you."

"No. I need to do this alone."

Chapter Fifteen
Storelva. Spring.

Astrid and Gytha ate their morning meal of stew with salted pork and turnips left over from the previous night's meal, along with some early spring greens they'd thrown in to freshen it. Astrid allowed Gytha to tell her about the piglets she had been given to raise and breed. Anything to keep her from thinking about Jori or Gunnar. Since he had returned from Hovgarden, they had found moments to be alone, and as soon as that happened, she'd fall into his arms. The grief and anger they both felt for Jori propelled them toward each other. Some moments they stole were so fleeting, the kiss had to be a quick brush of lips, or a touch of fingers, but that only made it even sweeter when the times were longer. Then the kisses raged as hot as a fire left out of control. Afterward, it took her a long time to gather her wits and tend to her duties. One time her mother noticed that her hands were shaking when she knitted a pair of socks, and Astrid did not know what to say.

"Asta?" Gytha's voice cut into her thoughts of Gunnar. Talk of the piglets had not distracted her.

"Hm?"

"I asked…do you think Father and Emund will kill the wolf? I don't want it to kill my babies."

"Of course they will, my sweet. Father and Emund will keep the wolves away." She thought not of the animals, but of Harald and his crew of men, including Bjorn Alfarsson.

A few weeks after Gunnar had returned, when the winter snows and ice had begun to melt, a pack of wolves preyed near the village, taking chickens and several lambs. The farmers and shepherds in the district were fearful for their animals, and the mothers kept their young children close to home. Tryggvi had
organized a party to hunt the wolf pack.

"*Vargr*," Tryggvi said when he'd been told of the wolf attacks. "It's an omen. The gods have sent it to test me. I must kill the wolf if I am to take on Harald and his wolf pack."

Now her father and Emund, some of his *huskarls,* and men from the village and nearby farms, were out hunting the wolf pack. Gunnar and Rikki had stayed behind to be in charge and to be on hand in case the wolves showed themselves in the village.

"I'm going to check on the piglets." Gytha put a few greens in the satchel she liked to carry around.

"Don't be too long. Mother will be waiting for us." Astrid normally liked to sew, weave, and embroider, as it soothed her. Ever since Jori's death, all she could think of during the long days of work was how much she missed him and how much she wanted revenge.

As Astrid finished the last of her morning meal, Gunnar and Rikki entered the longhouse, hungry for their food after patrolling the village for the prowling wolves. A thrall rushed over to them with stew. On the table she put some smoked pork and dried beef.

"Any sight of the wolves?" Astrid asked. Thrilled to see Gunnar, she shared a long look with him, and he rewarded her with a gaze that raked over her body. It made her feel warm and tingly from head to toe.

Mouth full of warm stew, he shook his head.

"I wish it would come around," Rikki added. "I'd like to kill something…or someone." His face was set in a grim mask, making him look much older than seventeen, and his blue eyes, normally bright with excitement, burned with a simmering rage.

Gunnar gave him a wary look.

Rikki scooped up his stew and ate with urgency. The door to the longhouse opened and Galm and Short Olaf came in. Galm took a seat next to Rikki on the bench and helped himself to a large piece of Rikki's smoked pork.

"No wolves?" He said around a mouthful of food, grabbing Rikki's buttermilk and taking a drink.

"No."

"That's good milk. Better than my mother's."

"I'm sure she'd be happy to hear that, Galm," Astrid quipped.

He shrugged. Rikki ate with even more urgency, and Astrid wondered what had them in such a hurry. She looked to Short Olaf. Like Emund, he had a hard time keeping a secret, and she caught on his face signs that something was going on with them.

"What are you doing?" she asked.

With a scrape of his spoon along the bottom of the wooden bowl, Rikki finished his meal and rose to his feet.

"No concern of yours, *systir*," he said, his voice full of fake airiness.

She narrowed her eyes and turned to Short Olaf. "Really?"

"Leave it, Asta," Galm snapped, pushing Short Olaf out of the house before he could say anything.

Ragnhild came in as they were leaving, pausing at the door, a frown on her face as she watched them. Her husband Dyri had gone on the wolf hunt. As soon as the three young men left, she said, "*God morgan*, Asta. Gunnar."

She sat down on the bench and looped her arm through Astrid's. "It is a glorious day. The dark months are behind us and spring will be here soon. I can't bear to spend the day inside working." She stretched her fingers out in front of her, wiggling them. "Let's walk along the river."

"You'll get her in trouble with Ingiborg," Gunnar said with a grin.

Ragnhild waved his concerns away with a flick of her wrist.

"*Ja*, let's go for a walk." Astrid rose to leave.

The two young women said goodbye to Gunnar, who seemed content to linger over his meal a little longer. Astrid kept her gaze on him as she gathered her cloak from a hook by the door.

As soon as she stepped outside, she knew she'd made the right decision to walk with Ragnhild. It was a beautiful day. The sun was warm, fluffy clouds drifted through the sky, and birds everywhere sang their song of a new beginning. If Gunnar had been with them, it would have been perfect.

"Do not get too attached to him," Ragnhild said, as they walked the path that led to the river.

"Who?"

Ragnhild gave her a sideways glance. "You know who. I can see the way you look at Gunnar. You need to be careful. If I see it, others can too. Like your mother. Or, Freya help you, your father."

"Oh." Had she been so obvious?

"Has anything more happened?"

"No. Yes. We meet sometimes..."

Ragnhild raised an eyebrow.

"No, not that," Astrid assured her. "Still just kisses."

Astrid felt Ragnhild relax next to her.

"Ragna? Gunnar is one of my father's best men. Do you think he would allow us to marry?"

"Has Gunnar said anything about marrying you?" Ragnhild asked.

"N-no." She ducked her head, feeling foolish.

"Asta, my friend. I know you are afraid, not knowing who you might have to marry—"

"You know what Sigmund did to that thrall. I would die before I married a man like him."

Taking a breath, Ragnhild continued, "Don't let this get too far." Her voice grew angry. "He should not be doing this. Gunnar knows better."

"I want it too."

"That may be, but he is a man and you are still young, just sixteen...."

"Past time to marry. Old enough to have children. Old enough to know what I want."

At those words Ragnhild rubbed her belly, still flat with no child. It had been a concern that she had not quickened with child yet.

"You're right. But be careful. When your father finds you a husband, what will happen then? To you and to Gunnar. You could put him in danger."

That was something Astrid had not considered. She was ready to face her father and mother if she and Gunnar were found out, but she didn't think anything terrible would happen to her. Gunnar was like a son to Tryggvi. Would he feel betrayed? What would he do to Gunnar?

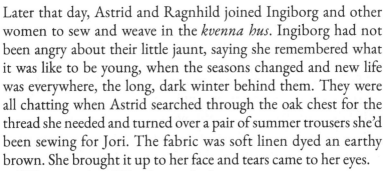

Later that day, Astrid and Ragnhild joined Ingiborg and other women to sew and weave in the *kvenna hus*. Ingiborg had not been angry about their little jaunt, saying she remembered what it was like to be young, when the seasons changed and new life was everywhere, the long, dark winter behind them. They were all chatting when Astrid searched through the oak chest for the thread she needed and turned over a pair of summer trousers she'd been sewing for Jori. The fabric was soft linen dyed an earthy brown. She brought it up to her face and tears came to her eyes.

"What is it, Asta?" Ingiborg asked.

She held up the half-made trousers. "I was making these for Jori. He told me he liked the way I cut and stitched trousers best, that they fit perfectly."

Thinking of her brother far away, a feast interrupted and gone wrong, a fight with the son of an old enemy, a stab right through the heart, and it was too much. She threw the trousers on the floor. The thralls who were spinning wool gave starts of surprise. Ingiborg shooed them out, and they took their spindles and whorls and left the house, Ragnhild leaving with them, knowing that mother and daughter needed privacy.

"I wish I was a man," Astrid said through clenched teeth. "Then I could kill this Bjorn Alfarsson myself."

Ingiborg came over to Astrid and took her by the shoulders, her hazel eyes, deep with wisdom, studying her daughter. "That is not our role, *dottir*. We are healers and weavers. Me. You. My mother. Her mother before her. We create life. We do not take it unless forced. I have watched this feud between your father and Harald tear at us all. Do you remember Emund's wife, Sitha?"

She blew out a breath to dispel her anger. "A little."

"Harald's men killed her."

"What?"

"The first time Harald raided our village, you were very young. Gytha was not born yet. Harald nearly destroyed us."

Searching her memory, Astrid remembered vague pieces of that time. Hiding in the dark. Smoke rising from burnt houses. Dead farm animals slaughtered and left to rot. Crops ruined. A hungry time.

"Sitha was out, traveling from her brother's village back home, when two of Harald's men caught her and her companions. They killed the others and…" she swallowed.

"No," Astrid breathed out. She understood what happened to women caught in a raid and did not want to think about it.

"Emund and your father found her and saved her, but it was too late. Sitha was a gentle woman, and what they did damaged her beyond repair. Both her body and her mind."

Feeling weak in the knees, Astrid sat down heavily on the sewing chest. "That poor woman." Then she thought of Emund and how much he needed to protect those he loved. "Poor Emund."

"Yes. After she died, he left without telling anyone, not even your father, where he was going. He took his revenge and killed so many of Harald's men that Harald and your father called a truce."

Astrid picked up the sleeve of her dress and ran the braided edge through her hands. "Good. I'm glad he killed them." She flung the fabric away from her again. "Emund has never talked about that."

"No. He does not, and he never would with you."

"She was your friend, wasn't she?" Astrid asked. If the same thing had happened to Ragnhild, Astrid knew she would be so angry, she'd be as fearsome as one of the Valkyries, picking out men to die.

"Yes." Ingiborg fell silent for a moment, staring off into the distance, lost in memories. "I mourned her deeply. That is why I do not want to hear you talk about killing Bjorn Alfarsson, for what he did to Jori. We can keep killing each other in revenge until we are all dead. I am a healer and peacemaker. I want to stop this killing before it consumes my children, like a fire left untended. Do you understand?"

Astrid nodded. "I understand. But I don't know if I can stop feeling this need for revenge."

Ingiborg took hold of Astrid's hands and held them up. The look she gave Astrid pierced right through her. "These are not the hands of a woman who kills. These are the hands of a woman who creates beautiful things. You are a weaver, my *dottir*, not a destroyer. We do not yet know the fate the Norns have woven for you. I do know that you still have a part to play, one that does not involve killing."

The next day, on her way to check the stores of mead, Astrid spotted Rikki, Galm, and Short Olaf, cloaks on, armed, making their way to the horse barn from behind the houses.

"Strange," she muttered, frowning. She hesitated for only a moment before following them. When Astrid entered the barn, she saw them securing packs onto their horse's backs. "Where are you going?"

"Go away, Astrid," Galm told her.

Glaring at Galm, she walked over to her brother and put her hand on his pack, "Rikki?"

He shoved some dried meat into the pack, closed it, and gave her a look that made her freeze. His eyes looked determined, like their father's, like ice. "I told you. You don't need to know." His voice was cold, but she could detect the faintest hint that he wanted to tell her.

"Does Father know?"

"No." He exchanged a look with Galm, and in that moment, Astrid understood.

"You mean to go after him. The man who killed Jori." She shot a glance at Short Olaf. He never could keep a secret from her, and the look on his face confirmed that she was right.

"Bjorn Alfarsson. That's his name." Rikki said his name like a curse.

Not sure whether to be happy someone wanted to avenge Jori or terrified that it was Rikki, Astrid opened her mouth to speak, but was at a loss for words.

Galm broke the silence. "Your father wants to wait until after the spring planting to go after Harald." He gave a derisive snort. "We don't want to wait that long. Who knows what will happen before then? Bjorn could die falling off a horse. Or from sickness. We want to avenge Jori."

Finding her voice again, Astrid said to Rikki, "You didn't even like Jori that much." It sounded weak and childish, and she knew immediately what he'd answer.

"He was my brother. We are both sons of Tryggvi. I will not let an attack on that name go unanswered." He brushed her hand off his saddlebag and finished securing it.

Astrid felt a dread so heavy it threatened to pull her down. "Please tell me you aren't going to sneak up on him and murder him." She wanted Jori avenged, but not if Rikki would be considered a murderer and outlawed.

"It won't be murder, but we intend to kill him," Rikki said. Without warning, Rikki took hold of her arms. "He was our brother. We have to avenge him. It is our duty to our family."

"If your father won't do it, we will." Galm added. He looked forward to this.

"Harald and Bjorn will expect an attack from Father. They will not expect the three of us." Rikki paused and then said quietly. "I have to do this." He bent and held her eyes in his. She knew her brother so well, she could see in the depths of his stare, his anger, his need to do something, anything, and more than that, his desperation to prove himself to their father.

Despite her fear of losing another brother, she discovered she wanted him to go, to do this. This was her family. Jori must be avenged. Bjorn Alfarsson must pay for what he had done to her brother, someone she loved dearly. No one hurt her family and got away with it. She remembered the anger she had felt when she had heard what happened, her determination that Bjorn Alfarsson should die. Anger that had been smothered by her mother's soft words burned again.

"Do it. May Tyr be on your side, brother."

She stepped back and Rikki grabbed the reins of his horse, Galm and Short Olaf following his lead. Not wanting to watch them leave, Astrid waited in the warm horse barn, the musky smell of the animals still strong in their absence. She heard Rikki tell the stable master that he and his friends were going to catch up with the wolf hunters.

The sound of the horse's hooves cracking in the remains of the last snow grew faint, and Astrid ran outside in time to see Short Olaf, riding in the rear, look back in her direction. He lifted his hand in farewell. Then they disappeared.

Chapter Sixteen
Ulfdalr. Spring.

The practice area rang with the clang of weapons, the grunts of men exerting themselves, and the laughter and taunts of those watching. Even in the mud and slush, Harald's household men had to practice and hone their fighting skills. Just like the farmers who were out cultivating the fields for planting, Harald's guard readied themselves for battle. They knew they would need these skills soon.

Bjorn rested on a bench, his long legs stretched out before him, his sword sheathed and propped up by his side, as he watched Styrr and Vefinn trade blows. Vefinn had a height and reach advantage, but Styrr was fast and agile, dancing away from the sweep of Vefinn's axe until he found an opening and flittered in to give what would have been a killing blow on the battlefield.

"You are like a mosquito, Styrr, zipping in to bite before your opponent even knows you are there. When we go to swat you away, you are already gone," Bjorn called out to him.

"Annoying as a mosquito, too." Vefinn chuckled. He was a hard man to discourage.

Styrr smirked and sheathed his short sword, his preferred weapon when fighting in close. As they approached the bench, Bjorn tossed Vefinn a water skin, ignoring Styrr.

"Papa!" Tanni ran up, and Bjorn shook his head with a smile. Tanni never walked when he could run and always left behind a wake of chaos and adults shaking their heads in dismay. This time the adult in his wake was Katrin, Harald's concubine, who had been helping Bjorn take care of his children. She was a young woman with the dark hair and eyes of the Franks.

"I wouldn't mind trying her out in the straw," Vefinn mumbled as he took a drink of water.

Bjorn eyed him. "She is Harald's woman. Best keep your hands and cock to yourself if you want to keep them."

Before Vefinn could respond, Tanni threw himself at his father and Bjorn caught him easily.

When Katrin caught up to the boy, Bjorn saw the baby she carried wrapped to her chest was Aud. Katrin lifted the baby from the wrap and held her so Bjorn could see her. She slept and Bjorn rubbed his finger across her soft cheek, and his heart swelled. He never tired of looking at his beautiful daughter.

"Ready, Papa?" Tanni asked.

Surprised, Bjorn looked into Tanni's big eyes. "Ready for what?"

"Elves!"

This did not help. Bjorn tried to figure out what his son was talking about.

"You promised him you'd go looking for elves the next time the sun was out. He's been pestering me to find you, until I couldn't bear it anymore," Katrin told him, fatigue in her voice. Bjorn knew Harald kept her busy at night. She cocked her head to the side and laid a hand on his shoulder. "Do you not remember?"

He shook his head. "I did...what?"

"Want to see elves!"

This time Katrin laughed, making Bjorn wonder what she would be like, if not cowed by Harald. He gave a pointed look at her hand, and she removed it. "You'd had a few cups of ale when you made this promise."

Bjorn grunted and called up the memory, and vaguely remembered the day, the freezing sleet beating down on Harald's longhouse, Tanni frustrating everyone with his constant peeks outside to see if the sleet had stopped. Every time the boy had seen the steel gray clouds hanging low and thick in the sky and felt the rain on his face, he'd whine and then slam the door shut. After each check outside, Tanni would blow through the house like his own bad storm on his wooden stick-horse, shouting, banging into things, knocking into people. Tempers had run short and Bjorn had eventually wrestled Tanni onto his lap to tell him a story.

He supposed this was when he'd promised the boy to take him to see the elves. With a sigh, he set Tanni on his feet, and he knelt in front of the boy.

"We have to walk to find the *alfar*. You sure you want to go?" Bjorn regretted the question as soon as he said it. He knew what Tanni would say.

"*Ja*! I want to see elves!" He marched his feet in place and wiggled his body.

Just watching the boy made Bjorn tired. He had spent the early morning sparring and fighting with the men and was taking a well-deserved break when Tanni had run up. What he wanted was to sit before a warm fire with a hot bowl of stew. A woman would not be unwelcome either.

He could do that later. "Let's go get our mud boots."

Tanni ran ahead, and Bjorn watched the boy as he zig-zagged down the path to their house, his shaggy blond hair blowing behind him, his arms out at his side as if he were a bird. Bjorn smiled and grabbed his sword from the bench, strapping it onto his belt. The men had been watching, and a few laughed. Vefinn mouthed 'elves!' Bjorn pointed at him with a look that dared him to say something about how easily his son could get him to do his bidding.

"Where are the elves?" Tanni asked, after they'd been walking for a while, their boots making a sucking sound in the mud. Not knowing what else to do, Bjorn had taken his son to a clearing near a small creek that he liked to go to when he craved solitude. A copse of spruce trees clustered next to the creek, their white slender trunks soaring toward the afternoon sun.

The creek was mostly thawed now, pillows of snow still piled against the north side of trees and rocks, and it felt magical to Bjorn, and he hoped Tanni would notice it too. They stopped and listened.

"You have to be quiet," Bjorn whispered, and Tanni's eyes grew wide as he looked around. Bjorn knelt to look in the boy's eyes. "The *alfar* are light beings, so if you see one he will glow like the moon."

Tanni's eyes widened, and Bjorn smiled at him. They scoured the clearing together looking for any trace of elves, although Bjorn had to make up what that would be, because every stick or rock was an elf relic to Tanni. They laughed and made pitiful, dirty snowballs from the last of the snow to throw at each other. Looking up at the sky, Bjorn told his son it was time to go back home.

"I'm going to take a piss behind that tree. You stay right here." He pointed to a rock.

Tanni nodded, serious, and rubbed his hand across his nose, which was runny from the cold.

His trousers were down when Bjorn heard footsteps, too heavy to be his son's. As he hurried to stop the flow and pull himself together and reach for his sword that leaned on the tree, a voice, so full of hate that it hit him like an arrow, called out to him.

"Bjorn Alfarsson with his trousers down. My lucky day."

Storelva

Astrid poured a cup of ale and carried it over to Gunnar. He was sitting alone on a fur-lined platform in a corner of the longhouse, checking Tryggvi's *brynja* to make sure there were no broken links and to oil it where necessary. Being far too valuable, most men did not have a *brynja*. It was the mark of a successful warrior, and Tryggvi was proud of his. Gunnar often offered to care for it for him as a sign of respect.

He looked up from his work and took the cup. "*Tak*."

"I am worried about Rikki, Olli, and Galm." She settled next to him with a quick glance at her mother. Not that it was forbidden for Astrid to sit with Gunnar, or even unusual. They had grown up together, eating, talking, and playing games in her father's house. It was her own mind, and body, that made sitting close to him feel illicit.

Gunnar took a pull of the ale. "It is a long way for them to travel and difficult. It will take some time before they come back." He left unsaid the words both of them were thinking. *If they come back.*

Astrid heard the note of worry in his voice. "You know this Bjorn Alfarsson." It surprised her to hear his name came spitting out, much like the way her father said Harald Olafsson. Was this how it started? The anger at losing a loved one turning you into someone hard and callous? She thought of her mother's warning, about how she was a weaver and not a destroyer.

Gunnar cocked an eyebrow at her tone. "*Ja*, I know him."

"Can he fight well?"

"Yes, he can fight well." He spit out the words and tensed next to her. His hands gripped the ale cup tightly. "Harald Olafsson does not keep men who cannot handle a sword." He grimaced. "I should have stopped it. I should have taken Jori out of there before it went that far. It happened very fast. One moment we were drinking and the next they were fighting each other."

Astrid could tell he was reliving the night in his mind; she could see the faraway stare in his eyes. She understood the burden of a terrible memory, to have it flash through your mind over and over.

"And now Rikki is after Bjorn."

"Your father..." He took a deep breath. "He will blame me again."

Astrid hated to see Gunnar like this. Her father had been angry with Gunnar for what happened to Jori, telling him he should have had Jori's back and protected him.

"No one could have stopped Rikki." To change the subject, she gestured to her father's *brynja*. "Can I help you?"

He gave her a half-smile and slid the mail so part of it was in her lap. She picked up a cloth and dipped it in the seal oil. They worked like that for a while, speaking softly and exchanging heated glances. She took every opportunity to reach across him to get the oil or to adjust the *brynja*.

At one point, he reached up and untied something on his neck. Holding her breath, Astrid watched as Gunnar pulled her Freya pendant out from under his tunic and placed it in her hand. It was warm from his body, and she put it on right away to keep the feeling of him close to her.

"Why did you put that in my bag and send it with me?" He asked.

"To keep you safe. I wanted Freya to watch over you. It worked. You are here now."

"You know I was mocked for wearing a woman's necklace." He grinned.

"You didn't have to *wear* it."

"I wanted to." He hesitated, thinking. "Asta." Gunnar leaned in so close his breath tickled her neck. "I want to marry you."

She nearly fell off the bench, she was so shocked by his words. Her hands froze in midair.

"Asta? Do you want to marry me?"

He sounded so hopeful, so much younger than he was, that her heart gave a tug.

She gulped, but she couldn't look at him. This was what she had wanted, so why was she so afraid? "Yes."

When Astrid looked up at him, he smiled at her, his green eyes bright, and everything clicked into place, and she felt happier than she had ever felt. Smiling back at him and taking his hand in hers under the *brynja*, she thought she could survive on nothing more than him looking at her like that and his kisses.

"I will talk to your father soon. I have no father or father-brothers to petition him for me..."

Her giddiness crashed down. Her father. It always came down to her father. Her mind raced for ways to do this without his approval, without his even knowing. She opened her mouth to suggest this to Gunnar, but as soon as she looked in his eyes, she knew he would never do anything like that.

An idea popped into her head. "Talk to Emund first. He will do it for you." She was sure of it.

"Red would do anything for *you*...but..."

"Are you afraid of Emund?" She asked with a laugh.

"Of course I'm afraid of Emund the Red! Everyone is. Everyone except you." He leaned into her. "Red could tear me apart. He *would* tear me apart if he knew what we'd been doing. Like a bear tearing apart a fox."

She liked the image of Gunnar as a fox. "I will protect you from the bear, little fox." She squeezed his arm, and they laughed together. It was too loud, and Astrid glanced up to see her mother watching her, a frown on her face as she looked between the two of them.

Astrid scooted away from Gunnar and focused on her work. She smiled down at her hands, thinking of how nice a wedding band of his would look on her fourth finger. Gunnar wanted to marry her. If he went to Emund, Emund could convince her father this was the right thing to do. In her mind she heard her mother saying her father would not marry her to someone unimportant, and she heard Rikki telling her that Father would marry her to make an alliance. She silenced their voices.

Ulfdalr

As the man walked closer, all of Bjorn's thoughts flew to Tanni, who was on the other side of the trees. He did not know who this man was or how he knew his name, or what he intended, but it didn't matter. He was a threat. Bjorn eased over to his sword, silently throwing word to Tanni to stay quiet and not move.

"Don't worry," the other man said. "I'm not here to murder you while you take a piss. Get your sword. I want this to be a fair fight."

When he spoke again, Bjorn watched him and saw that he was young, and he had a familiar look to him. He tried to puzzle out who the young man was. Someone from a neighboring village? The brother or father of a woman Bjorn had been with? As he sized up his opponent, two other young men appeared out of the trees. One of them strutted forward to flank Bjorn, and his narrowed eyes told Bjorn that he was enjoying this; the other had less threatening eyes, and showed no enjoyment, but he took his place to protect his friends.

Bjorn picked up his sword and as he wrapped his hand around the hilt, he realized who this young man looked like. Jorund Tryggvason, only with blue eyes. Another son of Tryggvi? The brother here to avenge his kin? Bjorn tightened his grip on his sword; he'd brought this vengeance upon himself,

"You are a son of Tryggvi."

"That's right."

"I knew your brother," Bjorn taunted. The young man clenched his teeth and his blue eyes flashed in anger, but he did not approach any closer. "How do you know me?" Bjorn tried to stay calm; his son was not far away.

"I was told they call you Pretty Bjorn." The son of Tryggvi looked him over with a smirk. "Gunnar told me what you look like."

Gunnar. Bjorn had forgotten about him.

Tryggvi's son's two friends shifted but made no move toward Bjorn. They did not worry him. He could tell from their distance and their stances they had been told to leave Bjorn to Tryggvi's son, that he alone wanted vengeance. They would only get involved if their friend went down. He turned his focus to the young Tryggvason.

"Papa!" Tanni ran from the trees he'd been behind. "You talk to the elves?"

Fear shot through Bjorn at the sound of Tanni's voice, and he made a move toward his son. "Tanni, run!" He shouted, his voice betraying him. Tanni stopped short at his father's shout, his little eyes wide with fright. "Run home! Fast as you can. To Papa Harald."

Bjorn wanted Tanni with Harald if anything should happen. Thankfully, the boy did not question him. He sped off as quickly as he could run.

The man with the cold eyes made to go after him, but the other grabbed his arm. "No, Galm. He's a child."

"He will alert Harald's men." The one named Galm said as he wrenched his arm out of his companions' hand.

"I'll catch him." He shot Bjorn a quick, nasty look, and added as he ran off. "For motivation."

Bjorn started to run after him, every muscle in his body screaming to protect his son, but the other two young men moved to intercept him. "No." The young Tryggvi son said. "We are not done."

Anger bubbled up in Bjorn, so hot and thick at the thought of them threatening Tanni his vision became cloudy. He took a deep breath to calm himself. He needed to keep his wits about him.

"You should have killed me when you had the chance. I will show you no mercy." Bjorn was torn in two. He wanted to go after Tanni, but he needed to neutralize this threat. Bjorn brought his sword up. He wished he had a shield. His opponent carried one and without his, Bjorn was at a disadvantage. But he had practiced without his shield like this many times, and he knew he could handle himself.

The young Tryggvi son tossed his shield onto the ground, the black and red paint that decorated it bright on the snow. A raven with its wings unfurled. Tryggvi's raven.

"I want no advantage." Rikki had his battle axe up, and he studied Bjorn.

Enough talk. Bjorn needed to end this quickly so he could get back to Tanni. When he lifted his sword, it felt heavier than normal, like this was not his sword, the one he'd been fighting with for two seasons. He shook his head to get rid of the strange feeling. He swung at Rikki's left side, but he easily stepped out of the way. Rikki countered with a strike of his axe, and Bjorn barely got out of the way in time. Even though it was almost dry here, he felt like his feet were stuck in mud. What was happening? Where was the clarity and lightness he always felt when fighting?

His mind drifted to his son, and he uttered words to the thunder god to give the boy wings on his feet to fly home.

"Prayers to the gods will not help you, Bjorn Alfarsson," Rikki said, as he struck at Bjorn's leg. He jumped back to evade it and slipped, lucky to have not fallen to his knees.

"I've already sent one son of Tryggvi to Valhalla. You're next."

Rikki rushed in and swung at Bjorn's sword arm when he slipped. Bjorn blocked it and delivered a blow to Rikki's arm instead. Rikki grimaced and moved back as blood bloomed through his tunic. The sight and smell of blood returned Bjorn to his senses, but not fully. He still moved too slowly, and his sword still felt too heavy. They fought for a long time, the sky growing darker, until they were both injured, bleeding, and stumbling in the snow.

"Come on, Rikki," his friends said.

That spurred Rikki and he lunged for Bjorn's leg, slashing him on the thigh. Sharp pain sliced into Bjorn and his leg grew slick with blood.

With his leg bleeding, Bjorn had a hard time staying on his feet. He staggered as he moved out of the way of Rikki's axe, although his opponent also moved slowly, his axe missing Bjorn. The surrounding ground had turned a dark red with their blood, and steam rose from their bodies as the sweat from their exertion hit the cold air. Rikki exhaled heavily and stepped back.

Bjorn went down on his knee, and that was when he heard hurried footsteps. He glanced up to see Galm return, his face red with exertion. In the distance, he heard the clink of weapons.

"We have to go," he said to the others, as he took in the sight of Rikki, exhausted, catching his breath. He looked then to Bjorn, kneeling on the blood-spattered ground, his sword still in his hand, but weak. Galm unsheathed his short sword and took a step toward Bjorn. "Let me finish him."

"No," Rikki said. "He's mine." He straightened up and hefted his axe.

"We need to get out of here," the other said. "They are getting close."

Bjorn tightened his grip on his sword, expecting an attack, when he heard the shouts and the one voice he wanted to hear above all others. Harald. "Bjorn!" His foster-father's deep, booming voice broke like thunder through the sparse trees.

"Harald," he shouted back, but his voice sounded weak, and he hoped that it traveled far enough.

"Do it, Rikki." Galm hissed.

Bjorn struggled to his feet as Rikki closed in on him, axe swinging. He put up his sword to deflect Rikki's axe. Rikki stumbled at the last moment, and his strike was off and weak. Even so, Bjorn felt the blade as it bit into the side of his head. Hot blood flowed down his head to his neck, and his vision grew fuzzy.

He dropped to his hands and knees and watched as his blood dripped to the ground. He'd never seen so much of his own blood before. His head roared, like waves in a storm, and then he heard footsteps, so many footsteps he didn't know which ran away from him and which ran toward him. A gruff voice gave orders to follow the men who had attacked Bjorn, and powerful hands grabbed him under the arms and turned him over, until he lay on his back. It surprised him to see that it was already near dark, the sky a deep purple. Harald's grizzly face bent over Bjorn.

"Tanni?" Bjorn croaked out.

"Fine."

Relief flooded through Bjorn, warming him. Fingers prodded his head, making him wince with pain. He heard the rip of material and then pressure on his head where the axe had hit him.

"Your boy raised the alarm." Harald continued to exert pressure on the wound. "Who?"

"One of Tryggvi's sons." Bjorn squeezed his eyes shut. His head throbbed. It was so bad, he forgot the pain in his leg.

Bjorn drifted away from the pain and awoke to the tramp of shoes approaching. "It's too dark. We can no longer track them." Rekja's voice.

"We'll go out at first light," Harald said.

"They will...be long gone," Bjorn said with some effort. "I'm cold."

Harald called for men to pick Bjorn up and carry him back to his house. Pride broke through the pain and weakness, and Bjorn hit their hands away and struggled to sit up. His head spun, but he waited until it passed, then he eased himself to his knees and then to his feet. Blood dripped into his eyes, and he swiped it away. He swayed on his feet, the wound on his leg shooting pain through him, and Harald held him steady. With a nod from Harald, Rekja and Vefinn grabbed onto Bjorn, and the two of them helped him walk back to the village. He was silent, all his energy and will spent to remain upright and walking. A wave of pain washed over him, and he clenched his teeth to ride it out.

It was full dark when they made their way into the village, and the light from torches was a welcoming sight to Bjorn's weary eyes. Finally able to let his guard down, he stumbled.

"We'll get the Tryggvi spawn," Harald growled.

Bjorn caught sight of Tanni, his eyes wide in a dirty face, his blond hair tousled, staring at his father. Bjorn sunk to his knees. Tanni broke from Thora's grip and he ran up to his father.

"Papa. I did what you said. I ran!"

"Good boy." Bjorn wanted to hug his son and never let go, but he was covered in blood and kept himself back. Harald's words about getting back at Rikki Tryggvason echoed in Bjorn's mind as he took in his son's face. When would it stop? This blood feud was not what he wanted to leave his son. He was a son of Alfar, not Harald, and in that moment, his head hurting him to distraction, his leg aching, Bjorn wanted to take his children and return to the village where he'd lived with his family. His son glowing like a luminous elf was the last thing Bjorn saw before he collapsed to the ground.

Chapter Seventeen
Storelva

"They did what?" Tryggvi said with such venom that even Ingiborg stepped away from him. A stable thrall cowered near the doorway where he answered Tryggvi's questions. The poor man surely thought Tryggvi or Emund would thrash him.

Tryggvi turned on Astrid, his blue eyes flashing like a snake's skin in the sun. She swallowed hard.

"They..." She stumbled to find the words.

"Spit it out."

That didn't help. She looked over at Gunnar, who stood behind her father watching her. He held her gaze and gave her a nod of encouragement.

"Tryggvi," Emund stepped in. He turned Astrid to face him, and she relaxed. "Tell us what you know." Emund did not raise his voice, but Astrid could hear the hint of frustration in it.

She glanced at her father, whose eyes still snapped at her, and then looked away. Focusing on Emund, she told her father what Rikki had told her of his plans.

Summoning her courage, she straightened up. "They want to avenge Jori. They said Father would not do it, so they needed to."

Tryggvi's eyes flashed again, a clear warning he was angry, and Astrid had to keep herself from backing away from him. "Walking into Harald's camp—"

"They will not be walking right into Harald's camp," Emund answered, and he stood in between her and her father.

"Red," her father said, his voice measured with an undercurrent of frustration. "Rushing off in anger is not the way a man handles his enemies." He looked at Astrid. "He waits. Bides his time. Then he strikes."

"Brother," Emund answered. "We have trained them better than that. They will wait until Bjorn is cut off from the rest."

"Rikki's right," Astrid spoke up, and every head turned toward her. Emund shook his head slightly at her in warning. Astrid wished she had not spoken up. Women did not offer their opinions about these matters, at least not out in the open. They did it in private.

"Astrid," Ingiborg rebuked her. "Leave it be."

"No. Let her speak," Tryggvi said. He focused his attention on Astrid, and his eyes bore into her. Crossing his arms over his chest, Tryggvi waited.

Bracing herself, Astrid faced her father. "Rikki is right." She did not want to show weakness to her father, so she took a breath before continuing. "What kind of man would he be if he did not avenge Jori? I am proud of Rikki. If he should die, he would die well."

Her words of Rikki dying made her father turn his back to her, and he rested his hands on the table. "I will not lose another son." It came out quietly, and the pain in the words made Astrid's own throat constrict. Losing Jori was like sitting on an unfinished chair and unable to get comfortable, pricking at her, reminding her of it.

Ingiborg moved over to her husband, but he shook his head at her.

"Brother," Emund spoke up. "Rikki is beyond your help. We will continue to gather the men, prepare the ships, and wait for him to return."

Tryggvi spun on Astrid again. She gritted her teeth, waiting for what he would say. He leaned into her. "You better ask your goddess to protect your brother. If Harald gets a hold of him alone and unprotected, Rikki will get no good death. You better hope he dies like a man, like Jori did."

"Tryggvi," Ingiborg said, her voice soft, but firm. "Astrid is not to blame."

He looked at his wife, his face showing the conflict within as he studied her, before he strode over to her. With some of the anger drained out of him, Tryggvi stood in front of his wife and placed his hand on her cheek. "We must hope the gods will not take from me another son."

She raised her hand to rest it on top of his, and they held each other's gaze.

The thought of Rikki being tortured by Harald ran through Astrid's mind, and she shivered. She hoped her father was right, that the gods would protect Rikki, at least all but the Allfather. He would take her brother as he did Jori. He loved creating chaos.

Dropping his hand and sounding like the argument and the pain had never happened, Tryggvi addressed Gunnar. "Come. Let's find Buri. I would have news about the ships." They threw on their cloaks, Tryggvi's with a dense bear skin at the collar that made him look like a wild animal.

With a quick glance at Astrid, Gunnar followed her father out of the door.

The door slammed, the sound like a crack of thunder, followed by silence. Astrid broke it and asked Emund, "It is true, isn't it? Harald would not give Rikki a good death."

He paused, and she could see the conflicting desires to shield her and to tell her the truth.

"No, he wouldn't." He leaned down so he could look her in the eyes. "Your brother, for all his recklessness, is no fool. Like I told your father, Rikki would not take on Bjorn with Harald's men all around. He will seek him out alone."

"But to sneak up on him and kill him," she said, horrified at the thought. "There is no honor in that."

"Not if Bjorn has his weapon, and it is a fair fight. Rikki wouldn't sneak up on a man and cut him down like an animal. Your father and I have taught him better than that."

Astrid swallowed hard. "Rikki is so angry. What if that gets the better of him?"

He shook his head. "It won't. Your brother also has Short Olaf with, and he has a good head about him."

For a moment, hope bloomed in her, but it was brief. She shook her head. "Olli tries, but he does not get through to Rikki. He hears Galm the loudest."

"Aye." Emund frowned.

"Astrid. We have work to do." Ingiborg interrupted them. "Talking about Rikki will help nothing."

Her voice might not have betrayed her emotion, but Astrid knew it was there. She had seen it before; her mother fought her fears like she would smother a fire, blanketing and burying them.

"Rikki can handle himself, Ingiborg."

"I know," Ingiborg said, and then with a gesture to her daughter she summoned her to work.

Emund left, and no more was said about Rikki.

Ulfdalr

When Bjorn opened his eyes, he saw his father standing next to the bed platform, the elf-bead arm ring on his wrist gleaming in the dim room. Confused, Bjorn squeezed his eyes shut then opened them again. It was not his father, but his foster-father Harald who stood by the bed, a silver ring on his arm, not the elf beads. Disappointment shot through him, adding to the throbbing pain in his head and a multitude of smaller aches and pains that pulsed through his body. He touched his head where the pain was the most severe and found it bandaged. That's right, someone had hit him in the head with an axe. A hiss of pain escaped his lips when he probed the wound with his fingers. At least he wasn't dead.

"Thought we'd never get the bleeding to stop," Harald said, matter-of-fact, but Bjorn could see a flicker of relief in the way his body relaxed slightly.

"I'm thirsty," Bjorn told him as he slowly pushed himself to sitting. His head spun and throbbed even worse upon sitting up, but he hated to be lying down when others stood around him. It made him feel too vulnerable.

Harald motioned for Bjorn's thrall to get him some water. When the woman handed him the cup, the door to his house opened, and Thora entered.

When she saw Bjorn reclining against the wall, she smiled. "I'm glad to see you up."

She carried a plain ceramic cup, steam curling up into the cool air.

Harald blanched at the sight of the tea in Thora's hands, as if he was intimate with the drink and wanted no part of it. "I'll leave you to the women." He clapped Bjorn on the shoulder and steered clear of Thora on his way out.

"Drink this. It will help," Thora told Bjorn, with a smile at Harald's retreating back.

It smelled awful. Bitter, and Bjorn wrinkled his nose and turned away from it. "I'm not drinking that."

"You look like Tanni when you do that," she said with a lilting laugh. Then, more serious. "Drink it."

He took the tea and sipped. It tasted as vile as it smelled. He choked and nearly spit it out. If it hadn't been for Thora's stern eyes watching to make sure he drank it, he would have spit it out on the floor. Dutifully finishing the horrid concoction and hoping that Thora was not poisoning him, Bjorn thrust the cup back into her hand and settled back on the down-stuffed mattress. His stomach churned to go along with his aching head. His cheek hurt, and he reached up to touch it. It was tender, and he could feel a deep cut along the cheekbone.

"Tanni worries about you. Should I go get him?"

"No." He didn't want Tanni to see him like this, stuck in a sickbed, bandaged, cut and bruised. Seeing the boy would also be too much of a reminder of what had happened, of how vulnerable he'd been with his son at his side. How easily Rikki Tryggvason and his men could have killed Tanni, or worse, right before Bjorn's eyes. That his son had done well, had run and raised the alarm that saved him, didn't matter in this moment.

Thora was taken aback. "If that is what you want."

"It is." He hadn't meant for it to come out so harshly, but it did, and Thora raised her eyebrows in surprise. Bjorn usually loved to spend time with Tanni. Thankfully, she did not push.

He turned to his thrall, Eadgyth, who sat nearby with her whorl and spindle. She had dark brown hair, cut short above her shoulders to show her thrall status, brown eyes, and a long thin nose. "Is there food? I'm hungry."

"Cod soup with barley and kale," she answered in accented Norse.

"No meat?" He wearied of fish.

"No," she said apologetically as she ladled out the broth into a wooden bowl. It was not her fault there was not much meat. It was spring, and stores were low.

Bjorn's stomach rumbled, and he ignored it. "Eat," Thora ordered him.

Thora talked quietly to Eadgyth about women's tasks, checking to make sure Bjorn's household ran smoothly, but Bjorn did not listen to them. Despite his fears that Thora had poisoned him with her concoction, Bjorn's headache eased. The soup helped too.

When he finished eating, Thora checked over his injuries, especially the wound on his head.

She gently rubbed some salve on the cut on his cheek. It smelled sweet, like honey, which was likely what she put in it. "That will leave a scar."

He shrugged, then regretted it. His entire body ached from the fight.

"You don't care?" she asked.

"No. Should I?"

"Well, it's just that..." With the color rising to her cheeks, Thora turned away from him and put the beeswax stopper back on the jar of salve.

He sighed, knowing she meant *Pretty* Bjorn. He was not so vain as to be upset over a scar on his cheek.

Done with putting her things away, Thora turned back to Bjorn. Tilting her head as she studied him, she said with a nod, "A scar will make you even more handsome, I think."

"It doesn't matter," Bjorn said, his fingers reaching up to trace the line of the scar, but she swatted them away motherly. He grinned at her before turning serious. "At least my son is safe."

"Thank the gods for that." She settled herself on a chair next to his bed. He studied the carving he'd created on the back; it was the same pattern that he had marked on his arm, his father's design.

"You would have been proud of him. The smithy was the first place he could get to, so he ran straight to Naestr and told him he needed to find Papa Harald. I heard Tanni's shouts and went out to see what the commotion was about. I did not have to look at him twice to know that something was terribly wrong. You were not with him for one. I've never seen him so frantic. We found Harald, and he went straight out to find you. From what I heard, they got there just in time. You have your son to thank for that."

She paused, weighing her words. "Tanni may have been brave, but he is still a little boy and scared for his father. He needs to see you."

Turning his head away from Thora's knowing stare, Bjorn watched Eadgyth as she quietly sat by the hearth fire spinning wool. The expert way her fingers spun and twisted the spindle and whorl soothed him. That, and the horrible tea Thora had forced him to drink. Maybe it was poison, and he was succumbing; he felt tired again and wanted to sleep. He thought of Tanni and how scared he must have been, seeing the armed men surrounding his father, hearing the tortured cry of Bjorn as he yelled at him to run, and then seeing Bjorn collapse, beaten and bloody, at his feet. All Bjorn could think was that *he* was a danger to his son, and as long as he had enemies in the world, his children would never be safe.

"I don't want to see him. Leave me now." He turned his back to her and closed his eyes.

Thora gently placed her hand on his shoulder. He stiffened under her touch.

"You did the right thing back in the woods, protecting Tanni. You are a good father." She gave his arm a squeeze and gathered up her basket.

Bjorn listened as her footsteps walked across the rushes on the floor, then as she opened the door. She paused, and he knew she was waiting for him to say something or ask her to bring Tanni to see him. Bjorn said nothing.

Chapter Eighteen
Storelva

Astrid awoke gasping. Her hair and nightdress were sweat-soaked, and the bed closet she shared with her sister felt close and hot. She shuddered and pushed the heels of her hands against her eyes. Her dream had been about the time when the outlaw had abducted her. Only, in this dream, she did not get away. The outlaw, his face distorted into a gruesome mask, pulled her farther and farther away from her home, her village, and her family. She could see them as they receded into the distance, and she cried out to them, but they couldn't see or hear her. Gunnar did not come to her rescue in the dream either. Instead, she had been pulled right by his lifeless body, Jori's sword sticking out of his chest.

Gunnar. She had not been able to speak to him alone that day, but she had seen by the look on Emund's face and then Gunnar's as they talked, that her father had said no to the marriage proposal. So that was that.

Not able to breathe in the closed-in feeling of the bed closet, she put on her heavy woolen work dress that hung on a hook in the closet wall. The bed closet was built into the wall to provide warmth, but now it felt stifling. She opened the pine doors slowly, thankful the hinges were so well made they opened with no noise, and climbed out of bed, careful to not wake her sister. The longhouse lay in shadows, the light from a low-burning fire giving Astrid enough light to see.

With a sinking feeling, she wondered if her father had cast Gunnar out, angry that he would presume to ask to marry her. Would her father do that? Gunnar was one of his most trusted men, but that could have changed. Her father was filled with grief so big it filled any room he was in. In the best of times,

Astrid could not predict how her father would react, and this was far from the best of times.

The air in the house was thick with the heat and smells of sleeping bodies. The cold outside air took her breath away at first, but it was fresh, and the sky was clear, the frost-covered rooftops and trees gleaming in the full moonlight. Everything was quiet, except for the hoot of an owl that hunted nearby.

As she rounded the corner of the longhouse, she saw a male figure sitting on a bench. He was leaning up against the house, looking up at the moon, his legs stretched out. A small one-handed axe lay across his lap, his hand resting on top of it lightly, but ready. Although his face was in a shadow, Astrid recognized Gunnar's form and the gleam of his hair. Astrid's heart jumped a beat. She put her hand to her chest.

The movement alerted Gunnar that someone was there; his hand tightened on his axe and he sat up. Astrid stepped out of the shadows, holding up her hands.

"Oh...Astrid." Gunnar relaxed the grip on his axe and took a deep breath. "What are you doing out here? It's late. And cold."

"I couldn't sleep." She thought of her terrible dream and shivered. Cradling herself, she turned her face from him and gazed up at the moon. "My father said no." It wasn't a question. She knew the answer.

"He did."

Astrid sat next to him, his body giving out warmth. She rested her hand on his leg and felt the muscles underneath tense at her touch. "We do not have to listen to my father. You have your own wealth. We could leave here and marry without him."

At those words, she felt his entire body tense. "You can't believe I'd do that. I owe your father my life. I owe your father *everything*. I would never betray him like that."

Her father. She wanted to scream.

"Why do you owe him everything? I don't even know how you came to us. I asked mother once, but she said it was not her tale to tell."

He turned and looked down at her, his expression sad. "My father," Gunnar took a breath before continuing, as if the tale would take effort. "Was a brute. He beat me, my mother, and my sisters."

Turning to him, Astrid said, "That is not so unusual. Father has taken his hand to me, and certainly to Rikki. Even Emund has given Rikki his fair share of thrashings, when he was bad or did something dangerous." She paused. "But Emund has never hit *me*. He has not even come close."

Gunnar shook his head. "This was more than taking a hand to a mischievous child. My father beat us viciously, and he liked it. I learned that when I was eight. He had my mother on her knees and was beating her with a mad light in his eyes. It was worse when he was drunk, which was most of the time."

"That is terrible." Astrid took hold of his hand. It was warm despite the chill in the air. He did not resist. She recalled how he never seemed to be drink like the other men.

"Is that why you do not get drunk?"

"*Ja*." He took a breath as if he needed the resolve to finish his tale. "When I was older, bigger, and stronger, I stood between him and the women, but even then, I was no match for him. When I was thirteen, my mother woke me in the dark of night, handed me a small bag of silver she had been hiding in the woods behind our house, and told me to flee."

"Why?" Astrid asked, breathless.

"She thought my father would kill me."

"His own son?"

Gunnar's hand tightened on Astrid's. "She was afraid if I stayed, the brutal bastard would beat me to death." He shrugged. "It was likely."

Thinking of her own family, Astrid could not understand how a father could be so horrible to his own son. Her father may have been severe at times, but he was not vicious, and he did not hit people he was supposed to love and then enjoy it. "So you came here? To Father?"

"*Ja*. Tryggvi had been presiding over a wedding in our area, and my mother asked him for help. He could not interfere with our household, so your father told her to send me to him when I was old enough. So that's what she did."

"Your poor mother. She was very brave to hide that silver away and to help you get away."

"She was. She also..." He stopped. "...put herself between me and my father during that time. Until she sent me off in the night to escape to Jarl Tryggvi. I did not want to leave her, but she begged me to go. To save myself."

"And Father took you in."

"Without hesitation. By the time I arrived here, I was weak, hungry, and heart-sick at leaving my mother and sisters with that brute of a man, and Tryggvi took me in and treated me like a son. He and your mother sheltered me, fed me, clothed me, and your father and Emund trained me to fight." He let go of her hand and leaned down, arms resting on his legs, his hair covering the side of his face. Softly, he added. "That is why I owe your father everything."

Astrid wished she had not heard this story. Instead of explaining why they could not run away and marry, it only made her love him more. She wanted even more to marry him and to create a home for him filled with love, comfort, and children.

"What happened to your mother and sisters?" Astrid asked, not sure if she should ask.

He shuddered and shook his head. "They are all dead. Killed in a fire my father started when drunk."

Wanting to comfort him, Astrid slowly and gently reached out and stroked Gunnar's hair. It was soft and thick. She stroked his head and then brushed the hair back away from his face. As she did this, Gunnar turned his head to look at her. Astrid's breath caught. In that moment he looked like the harvest god Frey, his earthy brown hair gleaming in the moonlight, and his pale green eyes shining.

"You should go back inside. We cannot do this."

She did not leave. She did not move. They sat beside each other in silence, he staring at the ground, she watching him.

After a while, he sat up, taking her hand in his. The warmth of his hand comforted her. Only their hands touched, and yet, she could feel his presence next to her, like an invisible arm holding her close.

"I don't know if I'm strong enough." He said it with a sigh, as if he'd been wrestling with his thoughts.

"Strong enough?" What was he saying? He was one of the strongest men she knew.

"To stay away from you."

He sat up and lightly took Astrid's face in his hands. Her hair was loose and flowed over her shoulders and down her back. Gunnar ran his hand through it, his eyes bright.

"You are so beautiful." His voice had grown raspy.

She whimpered at his touch.

His hands lightly held her face, and he was so close she felt his breath. She leaned into him, wanting to be closer. The kiss was so gentle, a brush of lips together. It was enough to send a thrill through her. She trembled. When his lips met hers again, harder this time and more heated, she melted into him. Gunnar's touch consumed her, his hands on her face, running down her arms, on her waist as he pulled her closer. Wanting to feel him, she laid her palm on his chest. Even through his tunic, she could feel the warmth of his body and the rapid beat of his heart against her hand. She wound her arms around him, feeling his strength, the taut muscles in his back. Responding to her invitation, Gunnar trailed his fingers down the side of her throat and across her shoulders. His lips brushed her throat, and the sensation made her ache between her legs. As his head bent down, she buried her face in his hair. She kissed the soft hair, then bent her own head down, seeking his lips once again. If she could stay there forever, she would be happy.

When they found each other again, Gunnar groaned.

Then he threw himself away from her. "What am I doing?" Gunnar cried, hands up. His breath came in gasps, his eyes wild with desire.

Cold air rushed in and bit at Astrid. Where Gunnar had been warming her inside and out, there was a chilly emptiness. She blinked, trying to focus her eyes, trying to understand what had just happened. Her desire scared her.

She reached out to Gunnar, but he backed away.

Tears burned at her eyes.

"That was wrong." He ran a shaky hand through his hair.

Her mind and body reeled. "Did I do something wrong?"

He blew out a breath and rubbed his face. When he looked at her, it was with tenderness. "No, no." He moved as if to go to her, but then caught himself. "*I* did something wrong. I told you I'd never betray your father, and then..." His hands swept over the two of them. "Then I did just that."

Astrid touched her fingers to her lips, and she could still feel his lips on hers. She blinked back her tears. As she tamped down her tears and desire, another feeling, a stronger one, fought its way through—anger. In that moment, she hated her father. He would keep her from this happiness, only to use her for his own advantage. She looked up at Gunnar, took in the stunned look on his face, and her anger seeped out. And latched onto him.

"Will you not fight for me? You will stand by my father's side as he marries me to someone else?" All her anger at her father, at her helplessness, came out at Gunnar. She couldn't stop it. "It could be Sigmund the Left-Handed. You would stand by while I was married to that beast of a man?"

He blanched at her words. Swallowing hard, he closed his eyes. When he opened them, he searched her face and answered in a choked voice. "I would hate every moment."

That was a yes, then. He would choose loyalty to her father over love for her. Astrid slumped back against the wall and closed her eyes. Her head spun with everything she'd felt that night. Her body felt heavy and wrung out, like a just-washed dress beaten against the rocks of the river. Now that Gunnar was no longer sitting next to her, she was cold, chilled right through to her bones. It was time to go inside. Or maybe she could sit out here until she turned to ice.

She heard his footsteps approach her, but she did not open her eyes until she felt him kneel in front of her. He took her hands in his, and the warmth flowed up her arms and right into her heart.

"I will still love you. Protect you. No matter where I am, you can send—"

She was ready to fling his hands and his words away, but the clop of horse hooves and the murmur of men talking cut him off. Gunnar jumped to his feet and grabbed his small throwing axe from the bench.

"Get down," he hissed at Astrid.

She ducked down next to the bench and made herself small.

The sound of the horses grew closer, and the men did not try to be quiet. That was strange. Men traveling at night, but not needing quiet or stealth as they entered a village? Astrid figured they must be friendly, but she would not move until Gunnar told her it was safe. Then one voice burst out laughing.

Astrid jumped up at the sound and ran past Gunnar toward the voice. "Rikki!"

The relief Astrid felt at seeing her brother and Short Olaf, and even Galm, alive and well, surprised her with its intensity. It was like she'd been holding her breath ever since that day in the barn, when she had given them her blessing to go, and was only now letting it out.

As soon as Rikki dismounted, Astrid threw her arms around his neck, squeezing so hard he let out a choked laugh, "Easy, Asta."

She pulled back and looked at him. He had black circles under his eyes, and his clothes were dirty, but other than that he was fine. A few cuts and bruises. Nothing life threatening.

"What? No hug for me?" Galm said, his feet hitting the ground hard out of exhaustion, as he jumped from his horse. "How about Shortie? He's been thinking of you to keep him warm." Astrid smiled at Short Olaf, happy to see him, but he did not smile back. Instead, he glanced from Astrid to Gunnar and back to Astrid, a frown creasing his face. She blanched. What must it look like to Short Olaf, to catch her and Gunnar out at night together, alone? When she turned back to Rikki, she saw the same frown. His eyes narrowed, and she could tell he wanted to ask her what was going on, as was his right as her brother, but she did not want to explain, so she diverted him.

Gripping his arm, she peppered him with questions. "What happened? Did you find Bjorn Alfarsson? Did you kill him?"

"I don't know."

"Don't know what?"

"If I killed him."

The commotion alerted the household. Gunnar found the stable thralls and told them to take care of the horses. Others were tasked with taking the saddlebags from the horses and carrying them into the house.

If Tryggvi was still angry at his son, he did not show it from the way he rushed out of the house and pulled Rikki into a firm embrace, slapping him on the back. "Tell me," he said when he stepped back.

"They must be tired, hungry, and cold," Ingiborg said behind Tryggvi, a slight chiding to her tone. "Let us go inside. You can talk there."

As Galm made his way to the house, he paused by Astrid's side and whispered in her ear, "I see you and Gunnar have been taking good care of things while we tried to avenge Jori."

She stopped in her tracks. "It's not...we..."

"Galm!" Emund called out from the doorway and waved him over.

Galm laughed a throaty laugh and left Astrid stunned and motionless.

The three young men were safe in Tryggvi's longhouse, eating some barley porridge with such haste that Astrid suspected they hadn't eaten much in a while. The commotion of their arrival had aroused everyone, and it felt to Astrid that the entire village crowded into her house. There was hardly room to move, and the air was stifling and close. Tryggvi, Emund, Buri, Gunnar, and Dyri hunkered over a table and talked to Rikki, Short Olaf, and Galm about what had happened. A frown flittered over Tryggvi's face as Rikki explained something, his hand blurry with motion as he spoke.

Ingiborg, done directing the household thralls with their duties, sat down next to Astrid, and Astrid could feel her mother's relief that her son was safely back in the fold.

"I wish I were a man, so I could hear what they are saying," Astrid said.

"I'm sure Rikki will tell you everything as soon as he has a chance," Ingiborg said. "You two do not keep many secrets. It has been that way since you were children."

With a jolt, Astrid thought of Gunnar. He had been a secret. If her brother or Galm told her father she had been out alone with Gunnar at night, what would happen? He had promised to stay away from her and had broken that promise. She did not think Rikki would do that to her, but Galm might. Her breathing became shallow, and she tried to think of something else.

Rikki also had his secrets, Astrid knew. Like what happened when he was out raiding, and Astrid was happier not knowing. It helped her to keep that part of Rikki's life separate. She could not think of her brother, whom she loved, who had always been good to her, had always been so much fun, being able to kill people. She put those thoughts away, as if in a chest, and she slammed the lid shut, locking it.

Astrid asked. "Does Father tell you everything?"

"No, not everything." Something in her voice made Astrid turn and study her mother. She knew many married men, especially rich men or jarls like her father, had more than one wife, or had taken on a concubine, or several. But her father had no other women than her mother. Or did her father have other women? He must. Astrid chided herself for being so childish. Her father went away for months. How could she think he would remain true to her mother during all that time? At least he had the decency to not flaunt them in front of her mother. With a touch to her Freya pendant, Astrid hoped that her future husband would be discreet.

"It seems you did not tell me everything either." Her mother sounded sad and angry at the same time.

Astrid's heart jumped into her throat. "N-no, I didn't."

"Are you with child? Is that why Gunnar asked to marry you?"

"No!" She flushed, as Ingiborg's knowing eyes flicked over her body looking for signs. Astrid turned her head from her mother's gaze.

"You can understand why I would think that."

"I am not with child." If only she was, then things would be much easier. A thought flickered in the back of her mind, of making it work out so she *was* with child. Hadn't he said he was weak when with her? But an uncomfortable knot formed in her stomach at the thought of doing that to him. An image of him, when he told her how much her father and mother had done for him, the gratitude in his eyes for their kindness and aid in his time of need and distress, was burned into her memory. She could never betray him.

Ingiborg shifted on the bench next to her. "Good. It would complicate your father's plans if you were with child."

"What do you mean?" Astrid had to pull herself back from her thoughts.

"Your father will take you to the King's Island for the council of leaders this summer. He hopes to find a husband for you. All the jarls and chieftains will gather there."

"Will you be going?"

"No. I must stay here and manage everything."

The thought of leaving home and her mother made the knot form again in Astrid's stomach. She understood the time was near when she would leave her family, and it still left her feeling frightened.

Ingiborg placed her hand gently on Astrid's arm. "Do you remember when you were a girl and you'd beg Emund to take you with them to the Thing? You so much wished to see all the people, the merchant's tents, the games, and competitions."

The mention of the festival atmosphere of the Thing brightened Astrid's spirits. She *had* always wanted to go, to see the world beyond her village and the neighboring villages. Merchants with wares from all over would be selling at the summer gathering. All the richest and most powerful jarls and chieftains would be there, not to mention warriors, farmers, and every other kind of person. She might even get to see King Ingjald.

"You will not be alone," Ingiborg continued. "I would like to send Ragnhild with you, if she is willing."

"That would make it better."

Ingiborg nodded. "It is not until the end of summer and much could happen before then. But I want you to make me a promise." Her voice turned serious.

"What?" She was not sure if she would like this promise.

"That you will at least give any marriage proposal a chance. I don't care who it is. Give it a chance. Your father is trying to do what is best for everyone."

"I will."

"Good." She gave her hand a squeeze. "Just because your marriage is being arranged as a political alliance, does not mean it has to be without love or caring. I love your father very much."

"I know." Astrid could not allow herself to hope that she could have a marriage like her mother and father's.

The meeting between the men broke up and Astrid caught Gunnar's eyes. He stared at her, longing etched on his face, but then he shook his head and walked away.

"Oh, no," Astrid said, when she saw Rikki talking to Emund, Emund frowning when he looked her way.

"What?" Ragnhild asked. She looked up as Emund, his ruddy face dark with anger, headed their way. "Does this have something to do with you and Gunnar?"

"Ah..."

"What did you do?" Ragnhild dropped her knitting needles into her lap and turned to face Astrid.

Ignoring her friend, Astrid's mind raced over what she could say to Emund.

Two men walked by Emund, their steps careful in the mud, as they carried a heavy barrel of tar to repair any leaks in the ships. The barrel slipped in one man's grip.

"Careful with that," Emund told him, bristling with irritation. The man's eyes widened in fear. When Emund did nothing, he nodded and strengthened his grip on the rope handle of the barrel.

The sound of men shouting to one another rose from the riverfront where they prepared to pull Tryggvi's ship, *Wave Stallion*, out of her winter storage barn. Astrid hoped something would draw Emund's attention away from her.

Thankfully, something did. Gytha ran toward Emund, a basket held out in front of her, her face radiant. "Emund, look!"

He smiled and squatted to be closer to her level.

She slipped in the mud when she came to a stop, and he reached out to steady her. Not caring if she fell or not, Gytha held up an egg. "Look! The hens are laying again." Gathering eggs was a thrall's job, but Gytha loved the chickens and enjoyed collecting their eggs, so Ingiborg let her do it. If the eggs came out in different colors, she'd arrange them in her basket in a way to make them look pretty and artful. The one she held was a light blue.

"Ah," he said, peeking into the basket. "You know the best way to eat eggs?"

"How?"

He took the egg out of her hand, and it nearly disappeared in his own large hand. Deftly taking it by his finger and thumb, he lifted it to his mouth. "You poke a hole in the end..." He pretended to pierce the egg with something sharp. "And then you suck it all out...like this." He made a slurping noise.

"Ew, I don't like them raw." Gytha giggled and wrinkled her nose at him.

Astrid felt a pang of worry for her sister, who acted so much younger than her twelve winters. She was filling out and men were noticing her. How would they ever find a husband for her? She was so delicate, so innocent, a bad marriage could kill her. A thought entered Astrid's mind, that Gytha and Short Olaf would make a good pairing. They both wanted a simple farm life filled with family and animals.

Emund placed the egg back in her basket, and she arranged it in a circle with the other eggs. "Raw is the best way. But you cook one for me and I'll eat it." He patted his belly.

"I need to talk to Asta now," he said, his voice growling as he straightened up. "Take those inside."

When Gytha went into the pit-house with her eggs, Astrid stood to meet Emund, straightening herself up, smiling to let him see she wasn't afraid of him.

"Come with me," he snapped. He led her to a bench by the house. She was about to say something to lighten the mood, to disarm him, when he came right out and asked. "Rikki says you and Gunnar were out here alone the night he returned. Is this true?"

Not wanting to admit it, she watched several female thralls carrying one of the folded sails for her father's ships over to the women's house. They would check if it needed mending. Her father. She suppressed a groan.

"Has he told Father?"

"No. Is it true?" He extended out the question, so she'd know she had to answer it.

"*Ja*." Her cheeks flushed, and she fiddled with the hem of her dress.

"What did you do?" He took a breath, trying to be calm.

"Nothing."

"Asta...."

"It was just a kiss."

Emund clenched his hands into fists and growled. "I'll cut his lips off."

"No!"

"He promised me he'd keep his hands off you."

She felt hot anger build. "You told him to stay away from me?"

"Aye. For his own sake. I told him that if he continued on with you, we'd throw him out. And that's the best of what would happen."

"You didn't," she breathed, and when she closed her eyes, she saw Gunnar's face at the words, how crushed he would have been. Being one of her father's men meant everything to him.

"Aye, I did. I also told him if he gets you with child, Tryggvi will kill him."

All her anger leaving, Astrid slumped forward, arms on her knees, and put her head in her hands.

"It's not his fault," she said. "He...he told me to leave him alone, but I wouldn't."

Emund was silent for a moment. "Ah, *bjarki*."

At the mention of her pet name, Astrid cried. He wrapped a big arm around her shoulders and let her cry for a while. "If you were my daughter, I'd let you marry Gunnar. He'd be a good husband. But you aren't."

"Can't you talk to Father?" she sniffed, wiping the last of the tears with the heel of her hand, feeling like a child.

"I tried."

"Oh."

"Asta," his voice turned serious. "Don't play with Gunnar. It's not fair to him."

"Fair," she snapped. She wanted to laugh in his face, wanted to spit at him about fairness, about how her life was not of her choosing, how it belonged to her father. That it was anything but fair. But he was right. She could not risk hurting Gunnar. She took a deep breath and nodded. "I will keep my distance."

"Good."

As Astrid rose to leave, she saw he had a bruise on his chin and another on his cheek. "What happened to your face? Did you get in a fight?"

He reached up and touched the bruises. He laughed. "Aye, with your father. His bony elbows are like weapons."

"I noticed he had a swollen lip. Why were you fighting?"

Emund raised an eyebrow and cocked his head to the side.

Understanding dawned on Astrid. "The marriage proposal? You were fighting for me." She put her hand on her chest.

"Aye, my little bear. You know I'll always fight for you."

"But against Father? He's your blood-brother."

"I knew I wouldn't change his mind, but it felt good anyway. He needs a proper thrashing now and then." He chuckled. "Wouldn't want him to get a swelled head, think he's a big jarl or anything."

Joining him in laughter, she threw her hands around his thick neck and gave him a tight hug. Kissing him on the cheek, she whispered '*Tak*' and returned to the house.

Chapter Nineteen
Ulfdalr

The sound of the door opening and heavy footsteps awakened Bjorn. He sat up and reached for his sword that hung on the wall in his bed closet before recognizing Harald's tread. He relaxed, but then anxiety flooded through him. Why was Harald coming into his house at night?

"Get us some ale, woman," Harald ordered Bjorn's thrall Eadgyth. She left her cooking and hurried to get the men drinks.

Wait. Was it day? Bjorn climbed out of bed, wondering how he had lost track of day and night. His body had recovered quickly after the attack by Rikki Tryggvason. His head no longer ached, and the dizziness had subsided. He should have been out of bed long ago, but whenever he got dressed and picked up a weapon to go to the practice area, a fatigue seized him, so bad he could barely hold the weapon. He slept a lot too. Too much.

"Here." Harald thrust a cup at Bjorn. "Drink."

Bjorn took the drink with a grunt and made his way to the oak table. He slumped down and scratched at his face. His beard needed trimming.

He took a pull of his ale. It was strong. He could feel Harald's glare as his foster-father sat down opposite him with a creaking of joints. Bjorn stared into his cup. The two men sat in silence, Bjorn waiting for Harald to speak first. He had come into Bjorn's house, so he must have come for a reason. Bjorn glanced around for something to look at other than Harald, and his gaze fell on

Tanni's rocking horse. The sight was like a punch to the gut. He still refused to see his son, even when he had heard the boy's voice on the other side of the door calling out to him, 'Papa?' Thora came to check on Bjorn every day, and she grew increasingly more demanding and angrier at his

refusal to see his children, poking at the cuts on his head and cheek with no gentleness, telling him he was fine and should be up by now. With a start, he realized she had not been to call on him in several days.

After a long silence, with only the sounds of the men drinking and Eadgyth chopping vegetables, Harald said, without a trace of pity. "You need to pull yourself together."

"What?" Bjorn choked as he tried to swallow.

Harald waved his hand at Bjorn, his face crinkled up in distaste. "Thora tells me your health is fine. No wound sickness. Nothing that should keep you here in your bed."

"I'm tired," Bjorn said, and it sounded weak, like a whining child.

"Tired. From one fight?" Harald leaned in and narrowed his blue eyes at Bjorn. "What happened out there?"

What *had* happened? Bjorn thought of his fear, fear that he'd never felt before when fighting, fear that had made him unsure of where to step, and how to strike. He had felt none of the clarity of vision and movement he usually felt when fighting, but only a muddled blur. The only explanation, Tanni. He had been afraid for his son and could not focus on the threat at hand, and the threat had nearly killed him because of his weakness. That's what it was. His love for Tanni and baby Aud was a weakness. He could not see clearly because of them. An overpowering urge to sleep stole upon Bjorn.

"I'm tired," Bjorn repeated. "I'm going to sleep."

He rose, but Harald grabbed his arm in a grip as strong as iron shackles. "No, you're not."

They stared at each other. Bjorn tried to wrestle his arm out of Harald's grasp and failed.

Harald kept Bjorn pinned to the table. "Your healing is over. We have work to do. The raiding season is almost upon us. My brother will be after us."

Although Bjorn had not heard the sounds before, he now noticed the sound of work. People talking as they walked by. People shouting to one another. The loud clang of the blacksmith's hammer on the anvil as he fixed weapons and prepared horseshoes. The *thunk* of hammers on wood. The grunt of men as they hauled and lugged and chopped. He knew the women's looms would work nearly non stop. Leather was being tanned for shoes. All the sounds that accompany the preparation of the ships and men to leave for raiding and battle.

"I know my brother. We must be ready. *You* must be ready, son. The fight will be hard and bloody." His eyes gleamed.

On top of all the noise of preparation, Bjorn heard children laughing. He knew Tanni would be out there, running and playing, and the thought of Tryggvi's armed warriors bursting in and killing the children made his body tense. His sword arm, the one Harald held in his tight grip, twitched.

Harald snickered. "That's right. Your body knows what to do. It wants your sword to hold." He released his hold on Bjorn and stood to leave, his work done. Bjorn studied his foster-father as he strode toward the door. Harald limped slightly from some old injury, his hair had traces of gray, but his shoulders were still strong and broad, and his legs as thick as tree branches.

Beware of old men where men usually die young.

His hand on the iron door handle, Harald turned back to Bjorn, his eyes narrowed. "Be ready. If you are not, you will stay here..." His gaze flickered over to Eadgyth with distaste. "With the women and children." With that he swept out the door, his blue cloak the last thing Bjorn saw of him.

Like an archer aiming at a target, Harald's words hit Bjorn directly where they had intended. Stung by them, Bjorn gritted his teeth and threw his cup at the door. Eadgyth jumped and let out a squeak, but Bjorn ignored her. Even that small amount of exertion winded him. Harald was right. He was as weak as a woman or a child, and if he did not do something, he deserved to be left behind. In the distance he heard Tanni cry out, 'Papa Harald!'

Bjorn got dressed, buckled his sword to his hip, walked to the door. He would be ready. But he paused as his hand grabbed hold of the handle. Ready for what? More fighting with Tryggvi's men and Tryggvi's son. He remembered the vision he'd had of Tanni just before he'd collapsed from his injury, of his son glowing like one of the light elves. His son had nearly been killed because of him, ambushed in the woods by an enemy *he'd* created. There had to be another way to end this feud, one that did not put his children at risk.

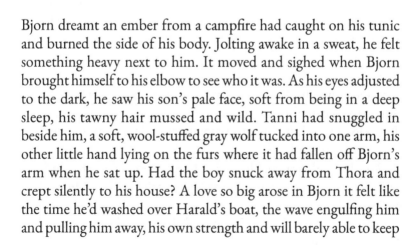

Bjorn dreamt an ember from a campfire had caught on his tunic and burned the side of his body. Jolting awake in a sweat, he felt something heavy next to him. It moved and sighed when Bjorn brought himself to his elbow to see who it was. As his eyes adjusted to the dark, he saw his son's pale face, soft from being in a deep sleep, his tawny hair mussed and wild. Tanni had snuggled in beside him, a soft, wool-stuffed gray wolf tucked into one arm, his other little hand lying on the furs where it had fallen off Bjorn's arm when he sat up. Had the boy snuck away from Thora and crept silently to his house? A love so big arose in Bjorn it felt like the time he'd washed over Harald's boat, the wave engulfing him and pulling him away, his own strength and will barely able to keep him above water. He wrapped his arm around his son and drew him toward him.

Tanni stirred. "Papa?" He murmured in a sleepy voice.

"*Ja*. Go back to sleep."

A small hand reached up and touched Bjorn's face. "You all better?"

Bjorn's heart squeezed tight at the boy's concern. "Soon." It was all he could croak out.

"Papa Harald says you will get the bad men." Tanni held up his stuffed wolf and made him growl. "The bad man who hurt you."

"I hurt his..." His voice trailed off, and he shook his head. Tanni was too young to understand the nature of this fight.

"You were very brave when you ran to get Papa Harald."

"I ran fast!"

Bjorn chuckled, and he swept some stray hair off Tanni's face. "You did. Were you scared?"

Tanni tugged on his stuffed wolf's ear and scrunched up his face in thought. "No. I am big."

"It's alright if you were, son." The thought of Tanni being pursued by Rikki Tryggvason's man sent a jolt of anger through Bjorn. It was the first time since his fight that he'd felt anything at all.

"You were not scared, were you, Papa? You are big and strong and brave! Never scared."

He had never felt fear before, not really, not until someone threatened his child. That was real fear. Before his children, Bjorn only had to care for his own life, and that did not matter much. Tanni looked at him, his eyes big with complete trust and faith in his father's strength.

"No, I wasn't scared," he lied. "Three men? They should have sent ten men, then it would have been a fairer fight." He winked and smiled.

Lifting the stuffed wolf, Tanni made him growl again. "A wolf is not scared of ten men!"

Bjorn studied the stuffed wolf, one of several gifts from Harald on Tanni's naming day. When Harald had laid it on the swaddled boy sitting on Bjorn's lap, he had said, "A wolf for our new wolf." With that he had touched Tanni's forehead and given Bjorn a slap on the back for a job well done. A son was always time for celebration. Once he was old enough to hold anything, Tanni had held on to the wolf, carrying it around, sleeping with it, until the animal took on a life of its own.

"Here," Tanni said after holding up the wolf to his ear, as if listening to a secret, and he pushed him into Bjorn's chest. "Radulf will sleep with you."

When Bjorn took Radulf, Tanni yawned and curled up into his father, closing his eyes. Bjorn adjusted the boy until they were both comfortable, then looked into the stuffed animal's blue beaded eyes. The wolf-head markings on the back of Bjorn's shoulder tingled as if awakened.

"I'll keep him safe. No matter the cost," he whispered to Radulf. He knew it was only stuffed with wool, but something in the animals' eyes made Bjorn think it could really hear him. Tanni's breathing grew heavy, but Bjorn no longer wanted to sleep. He was ready again to do whatever it took to protect his children.

Storelva

The day dawned clear and warm, and Astrid listened to the constant drip of water as the snow melted off the house. Standing at her loom, she wove a blanket in a diamond pattern, with light and dark blue woolen thread. She had worked on it all during the winter, and as it took form she was pleased with it. Two thralls sat with spinning. It was a tedious, never-ending job, and Astrid was glad she did not have to do it all the time. One benefit to being the jarl's daughter. She knelt on the board at the bottom of the loom to weave the dark blue thread horizontally through the vertical thread, and when she finished, she pushed the thread up to join the pattern above. She stepped back to look.

"It is beautiful," Ragnhild told her. She was sewing undergarments for Dyri, and she set the fabric in her lap as she cocked her head from side to side, looking at the blanket. "The dark diamonds stand out from the light background as if they were real. Like I could reach out and touch them. How do you do that?"

Astrid stepped back even farther to take in her work. She shrugged. "I don't know. It...happens. My fingers know what to do."

"A gift from Frigg."

"That's what Jori says when he sees the clothes I make him. Oh." The last word came out in a strangled gasp, and Astrid grasped the frame of her loom. Hot, angry tears came to her eyes. She wished they were fire for then she'd save them for if she ever met Bjorn Alfarsson, and then she'd burn him with them.

"Asta." Ragnhild hesitated. "Dyri says they will go after Harald. Rikki was not sure if he killed Bjorn or not. He thinks so. He hit him in the head with an axe and saw him go down on his knees."

"I don't want them to go," Astrid said. "I don't want them to die. *They* don't care. For them it would be a good death. But what do *we* do? It is always the women and children left behind." Astrid knew she shouldn't be talking like this. Her own words echoed in her mind, of telling her father that Rikki would die a good death if he died avenging Jori, and she believed it. There was a good death and a cowardly death. She wanted her men to have good deaths. But she did not want them to die. How could she have both?

The door to the weaving room opened and Ingiborg slipped in. One look at Astrid and she said, "What is it?"

Astrid looked up at her mother. "How do you bear it?"

Ingiborg tilted her head and studied the two women. "Bear what?"

"When they leave. Many go to their deaths."

She gathered Astrid's hands in hers. "I bear it because I have to. This is my life, and it will be yours too. You must learn to bear it."

Astrid took in a long breath. "They are going out soon. To attack Harald."

"They are," Ingiborg said. Her voice betrayed no emotion.

"Jori left and did not come back. It was his *wyrd*, I know that. What if Rikki is killed or if Father does not return?" She knew she was letting her emotions get away with her again.

"Don't say that," Ingiborg said. "Do not tempt fate." Her voice softened. "Not once have I ever thought Tryggvi would not come back. My faith in him is always rewarded. He always returns to me." Ingiborg tightened her grip on Astrid's hands and held her gaze. "You must stop this. It does not help. The men in our life are warriors. That is what *they* do. We wait for them at home. We provide them with children, food, clothes, and a comfortable home. That's what *we* do."

The three women sat in silence for a long time. The drip, drip from the snow melt continued, and sounds from the village drifted in, reminding them that life continued no matter what.

With a deep sigh, Astrid got up and stood in front of the blanket she was weaving. She ran her hand over it, tracing the diamond shapes. When done, she would put the blanket in her chest to take with her when she got married. It would be part of her marriage bed. She had woven it with Gunnar in mind, but that was not to be.

Without facing her mother or Ragnhild, Astrid said finally, "I'm glad I can't marry Gunnar. I care for him too much." She fiddled with the weights on the loom, and felt something shift inside of her, felt her will harden, like clay put over a fire. "I don't want to love my husband. In fact, I hope I *don't* love him, or even like him. That way I will not care whether he lives or dies."

"Astrid, don't," her mother said.

Astrid turned to her mother and her friend and sent her mother's words back to her. "I will provide my husband with children, clothes, food, and a home, but *I won't love him.*"

"Asta..." Her mother started to say something again and then stopped herself, shaking her head.

Astrid went back to work on her blanket. I won't love him. She sang it to herself like a ritual song. I won't care about him. I won't even like him.

I won't love him.

Chapter Twenty
Hovgarden. August.

Brightly colored tents crowded the grassy, hilly land in between the water and the rock outcropping where the Thing was to take place. Merchants and chieftains had set up tents where they'd live and sell their wares for the duration of the Thing, and the atmosphere was one of a festival with games, feasting, and good fun. In the marketplace, merchants traded metal, furs, and antlers from the north. Cereals, honey, pottery, and silver from the east. Jugs of Frankish wine were also for sale.

Rising as tall as two or three tents stacked on top of one another, the rock outcrop soared above the throng of people, a defensive tower looming over it all, armed men on alert. Astrid had never seen so many people in one place before, and she did not even try to hold back her stares as colorfully dressed men and women walked by her or called out to her from their tents.

Astrid had her arm linked through Ragnhild's and squeezed it when she spotted a red and white striped tent that displayed brightly colored and exotic fabrics. "Let's look." She steered Ragnhild to the tent, the face of the merchant lighting up when he saw the two young women. Astrid was pleased that she'd worn one of her best dresses, a lightweight blue linen. When the fabric had been dyed with woad, it had taken in a strange way, and the dress shifted between the colors blue and purple, changing with her movements and with the light. She had accented it with a double-strand necklace of multi-colored beads strung across her chest and attached by two oval silver brooches. The fabric merchant's eyes brightened with appreciation as he watched her approach; he recognized her wealth.

"More fabric," Dyri groaned. He had offered to accompany the two women for the day, wanting to be with his wife.

Astrid and Ragnhild laughed at Dyri's distress. Ragnhild released her arm from Astrid's and threaded it through Dyri's. "Poor man. I promise we'll go to a blacksmith's next. You can look at the weapons." She kissed his bearded cheek and joined Astrid at the table set up with fabric of every sort. Dyri grunted his assent and hung back, his hand on his belt, while he watched the crowd.

A breeze blew in from Lake Malar, bringing with it the smell of seaweed and fish, and the flaps of the tent fluttered. Astrid sighed as the breeze cooled the sweat on her neck. If she'd known it would be so warm, she would have braided her hair, but she had left it flowing down her back, long and loose, with two small braids wound on each side of her face and laced with blue silk ribbons.

"You young ladies look like you know what you are looking for. And you know quality when you see it." He glanced again at Astrid's necklaces and dress.

"What do you have?" Astrid asked him.

The merchant's hand passed over some plain wool, and although Astrid noticed it was high quality, she went straight to the richly dyed fabric. He pulled out three samples of wool, each an ell in length, one a blue as light as the sky, one dark forest green; the third took Astrid's breath away. A deep red wool the color of rubies. It was a heavy weave made for winter and yet so soft Astrid wanted to rub it on her face. She showed it to Ragnhild and saw the same appreciation in her friend's face.

Astrid took a closer look and ran it through her hands. "How did you get it so red? Ours always turns out much lighter."

The merchant winked. "I can't tell. Trade secret."

His face reminded her of Emund, so she liked him right away.

"How much for eight ells?"

When he told her the price, Astrid dropped the fabric on the table, eyes wide with disbelief, and she heard Dyri snort behind her.

"That is too much. It is not silk." Astrid scoffed and turned to Ragnhild. "Let's go."

The merchant coughed. "I'm sure we can work something out."

That was what she wanted him to say. Keeping her head turned so he wouldn't see her smile, Astrid spied a roll of what looked like tablet-woven silk for edging. It had a black and silver pattern on it and would look perfect as braiding with the red wool.

"I will give you the amount you ask if you include this silk. Enough to edge a man's tunic." She pointed at the silk, raised her eyebrows, and stared at the merchant.

He frowned as he looked first at her, then at the red wool and at the silk braiding. Just as Astrid decided he would not sell to her, he said, as if it caused him distress. "It is yours."

She smiled at him and held back a little squeak of triumph. "They are both beautiful," she whispered.

"Ah, yes. The man who wears this will be a well-dressed man. He is lucky." The merchant's brown eyes twinkled at Astrid and Ragnhild.

While the merchant folded up the fabric for her, Astrid opened the drawstring on her purse and pulled out an arm ring that had been her father's. She handed him the arm ring, and he placed it on his bronze scale. It was too much, so he whipped out a small axe and hacked at it until it was the correct weight. Quickly pocketing the part of the ring that was his, the trader handed Astrid the rest of her silver, along with the wool and the silk braiding. Astrid ran her hands over the soft wool one more time before putting it in her basket with the braiding and covering it with a clean cloth.

"*Tak*," she told the merchant as they moved to leave his tent. Another woman, a woman Ingiborg's age, had edged in and was admiring the green wool. The merchant waved to Astrid and Ragnhild and turned his attention to the other woman.

"Who will the tunic be for?" Ragnhild asked.

"My future husband. That's why I am here." Once she had decided she would not care about her husband, whoever he might be, a great weight had lifted from her shoulders. Let her father marry her to any man, she would not flinch. She would be a warrior with no fear. The basket of goods hung heavier on her arm now, and she smiled at the thought of the beautiful fabric she had acquired. No matter how despicable, her husband would be well-dressed.

A group of little boys ran by them, shouting and jumping on each other like a pack of puppies. They reminded Astrid of Rikki, Short Olaf, and Galm when they had been younger, always together, always on the move. Well, they were still always on the move, only more subdued now that they were grown men.

As if conjured by her thoughts, she saw her brother at a blacksmith's tent, the man's weapons laid out on a large wooden table. Rikki held up a sword, turning it over in his hand and sweeping it from side to side to test its weight and balance. The polished blade flashed in the sunlight and Rikki's eyes lit up; his gaze ran up and down from the blade to the hilt in his hand, like he was looking at a lover. It was the first time in a long time that Astrid had seen him look gleeful, like the light-hearted boy he had always been. Ever since he had returned from his fight with Bjorn Alfarsson, he had not been the same. It was like a curtain had shut down over him, and he allowed no one other than Galm or Short Olaf entry behind it. From the stories told, Rikki had been nearly unstoppable during the fights with Harald's men, killing many. Except for the one he wanted. She was happy to see a light in his eyes and smiled to herself.

"Rikki," she called out and waved. Hearing his name, he glanced up from the sword and gave his sister a lopsided grin.

"Thank the gods," Dyri said under his breath. "Weapons." He pulled the women along with him, giving them no option but to follow, as he wove through a crowd of people toward the blacksmith's tent. When he reached Rikki, the two men let out shouts of greeting and gave each other hearty back slaps. Rikki held up the sword for Dyri's inspection, and the older man's eyes gleamed with appreciation. At the other end of the table, a pair of throwing axes engrossed Galm, who stood talking with a man wearing a funny floppy hat. They were both so intent on the axes they noticed nothing else.

"Put a sword in front of them and they completely forget about us," Ragnhild said.

Astrid threw a quick glance at her friend to see if the neglect upset her, but she was watching Dyri with pleasure in her eyes. With a pang of sadness, Astrid thought of Gunnar. True to his word, he had kept his distance from her, and she felt the loss like a physical ache. That didn't stop her from searching for him in the crowd, even though she knew he would be with her father and Emund. With the death of Buri during the spring raids against Harald, her father needed another man by his side. Gunnar had filled that place and was more her father's man than ever before.

Dyri gestured for Ragnhild to join him, and she took her place by his side, leaving Astrid alone at the table to look at the weapons. She ran her hand over a knife, a stunning work of art, the hilt made of walrus ivory with a carving of a raven in silver.

"Asta," a male voice said in her ear, too close.

She jumped and turned. "Galm," she breathed. "You startled me."

His gaze traveled from her blue-dyed shoes all the way up to the blue ribbons in her hair. "You look fetching. And rich. Looking to attract a husband?" His voice was mean, and the way he looked at her made her squirm.

"Stop it, Galm."

He tipped his head to the side and his stare raked over her again. "Maybe *I* should ask for you to marry me. Do you think your father would agree?" This time he laughed, but the laughter did not reach his eyes. "You know I told Shortie to go off for the winter and come back with grim news. Seemed the best way to get you to agree to a marriage."

Astrid's breath left her at Galm's words. Is that what he thought of her?

He shrugged and rubbed his face. "But Shortie said no. With his fists."

"Good." Astrid's hands balled into fists, and she wished *she* could hit Galm. He had grown meaner since Jori's death, and she suspected he caused her brother's change.

"Asta." The man with the floppy hat approached.

"*Olli?*"

Galm sniggered.

"Do you like it?" Short Olaf asked, touching the brim of the hat. It was made of seal skin and oiled.

Astrid burst out laughing.

"What?" He smiled. "To keep the sun out of my eyes."

"You don't really plan to wear that, do you?"

"Why not?" He tugged it further onto his head, covering most of his eyes. "And if it rains, *I* won't get wet."

She shook her head.

"I bought it off a trader from Iceland." He leaned in close. "Should I get you one?"

"No!"

He, at least, had not changed. But then, the playfulness melted away as he stared at her. He stared for too long, then cleared his throat and looked away from her, his cheeks, what she could see under the hat, beginning to turn pink.

"You shouldn't look at my *systir* that way, Shortie, or I'll have to fight you." Rikki came up behind Astrid and lazily laid his arm across her shoulder.

Feeling her own face flush at all the attention, Astrid changed the subject. "What about that sword, Rikki?"

He shook his head. "Just admiring the goods..." His voice trailed off as he watched a pretty young woman walk by, accompanied by a group of older women. Astrid gave him a nudge in the side. Without asking, he reached down and rummaged through her basket. "What did you get?" He peeked under the cloth that covered her new purchases, and his face fell.

His disappointment made her laugh. "What did you think I would have in there? A sword of my own? A helm, perhaps?"

"A man can hope, can't he?"

In the distance, Astrid saw a flash of yellow hair, and she tensed. "What is it?" Rikki asked.

"Is Sigmund the Left-Hand here?"

"Why would he be here? He is the Danish King Harald's man."

"Oh, right." Astrid's heart slowed down.

Galm snorted. "I heard his *witch* advises him to never attend council meetings."

"His witch?" Astrid felt the blood leave her face. A man who trusted a witch was no honorable man.

"*Ja.*" Galm leaned in closer to her. "When you marry Sigmund, you'll have to make sure you put the witch in her place." He let out a cruel laugh.

Astrid felt sick. "Don't say that."

"Don't listen to him," Rikki said, shooting Galm a warning look, and he backed off. "He's not here."

Astrid took a breath and nodded. Her brother was right. At least she did not have to worry about Sigmund's attentions. Her heart lightened.

Dyri, his eyes bright with interest, approached with Ragnhild. "Foot races at the open field over there." He pointed through the crowd and tents to a large hill that led to a field beyond the marketplace.

"Let's go," Rikki said at once, as he slipped his arm off Astrid's shoulder and grabbed onto her hand. His hand was rough and strong as he pulled her through the crowd.

She hurried behind her brother, allowing him to cut his way through the crush of people as she followed in his wake. As she watched his back, she thought he must cut a handsome figure with his strong, broad shoulders dressed in a light green tunic edged in dark green braiding, his bright hair blowing in the breeze. A sword, newly gifted to him by their father, banged at his side, and he wore two silver arm rings, proclaiming he was a successful warrior. Good-natured shouts erupted, and Astrid knew they were nearing the field. The sun grew warmer as they left the marketplace by the lake where tents and trees shaded the ground. Men and women, from the rich, in their brightly dyed clothes, multi-colored beaded necklaces, and silver and jeweled rings, to the poor farmers, in dull brown rough wool, lined the sides of an open field marked off by ropes. They talked to each other, drinks in hand, while children ran about, laughing and shouting to one another. Men made bets with their pieces of hack silver, coins, or rings.

Astrid gasped, and her eyes widened when she saw the cluster of men who milled inside the roped off competition arena. They were all young, well-muscled, and sweating from the effort of running and wrestling. One man had arms so big he must be a blacksmith, another had blue swirls marked on his back, and the markings moved when he flexed his muscles. Mesmerized, Astrid cleared her throat. She was used to seeing men fight, run, wrestle, and compete, but they were all men she knew and had grown up with. These men were unknown. Her body tingled with excitement.

A jostling at her side made her look away from those strange men as Rikki, Dyri, Short Olaf, and Galm all moved to go join the games, Rikki the first one to reach the men gathering for another footrace. He loped easily out to the group, his arm rings gleaming in the bright sunlight, and they welcomed him. The man with the blue markings on his back gave Rikki a horn of some drink, and he downed it in one go.

"Wish me luck?" Short Olaf asked, hanging back. He'd pushed the hat up on his head a little, and his eyes had an eager look.

"May Thor give wings to your feet."

He flashed her a quick grin. She hoped he would have good luck, that his feet really would have wings, but she knew he would not win. Rikki was much faster.

Her men disencumbered themselves from their tunics, shoes, and weapons belts, dropping their clothes in piles, while setting their swords and axes in a safe place with those of the other men. Astrid groaned when Rikki tossed his tunic on the ground; she had spent hours sewing that tunic, edging it, embroidering the neck, and now it lay in a heap on the dirty ground. But that was her brother; he did not care about that kind of thing.

Ragnhild sidled up to Astrid, and they watched the men line up side-by-side as they prepared for the foot race. An older man walked down the line giving the men instructions, a horn held lightly at his side. She whispered a silent wish to any of the gods that Short Olaf would win.

"Go, Olli!" She shouted.

Short Olaf's head shot up, and he gave her a bright smile, and at the same time Rikki cuffed his friend on the head. He then shot Astrid an aggrieved look and put his hand on his heart as if betrayed.

"By the gods, my brother is such a—"

The sound of the horn blared, and the men all dashed forward. Rikki and the man with the blue markings jumped out in front of everyone as soon as the horn sounded, their arms pumping, their legs relaxed as they took long strides. In the middle of the pack, two men jostled with each other, trying to push their way into the lead. Their feet got tangled together, and they sprawled onto the grass, and two other men right behind them tripped over them and fell too. One man fell right in front of Galm, but he leaped over him and kept running. Astrid was happy to see him too far back to catch the leaders, although it was not a surprise. Galm never was as fast as the others.

"Run, Dyri," Ragnhild shouted.

Astrid looked to the leaders, and spied Dyri to the side of the blue-marked man, his stride matching the other man's. The blue-marked man turned his head slightly, saw Dyri gaining on him, and he threw his hand out to hit Dyri in the chest. Dyri blocked it and tried to push the man over. Running full out, they could not keep hold of their balance, and both went down in a tangle of limbs.

Ragnhild's body tensed as she waited to see if her husband got up. "I hope he's all right."

"I'm sure he's fine." As soon as Dyri got to his feet, Astrid looked away from him to find her brother and Short Olaf. Out in front by a stride's length was Rikki, not distracted by the men falling next to him. His blond hair blew behind him, and his feet kicked up grass as he dug in, determined to win. Seemingly out of nowhere came the blacksmith, and he gained on Short Olaf.

"Hurry, Olli," Astrid said to herself. She could see he would not beat Rikki, but she wanted him to beat this other man.

The blacksmith came up right next to Short Olaf, who shot him a quick glance.

"Run, Olli, fast as the wind." Astrid shouted it this time, hoping Short Olaf could hear her.

As if he had, Short Olaf ducked his head and put on a burst of speed that surprised the blacksmith. He fell further behind until it was clear he would not catch up. Rikki crossed the finish line with a leap, rolling over his shoulder to absorb the momentum, and came to his feet as graceful as a cat, a triumphant smile on his face. He pointed at Astrid, a gesture he always made when he won. Short Olaf came in next, his finish less dramatic. He staggered and collapsed to his hands and knees, his stomach heaving as he tried to gain his breath. The blacksmith fell on his back next to him, his own breathing ragged and hard.

After two more races, Dyri and Short Olaf quit the games, gathered their clothes and gear, and joined Ragnhild and Astrid. The men's chests and arms shone with sweat, and their hair stuck to their foreheads and necks. Short Olaf had the beginnings of a bruise on his cheek where one racer had hit him, and Dyri had a grass rash down his shoulder and upper arm from where he fell during the first race. He gave Ragnhild a sweaty hug, and she squealed, but Astrid noticed her friend did not back away. Instead, she got a look in her eyes like she wanted to be far from the crowd. Feeling like she was intruding on something intimate, Astrid moved away from them and backed into Short Olaf.

She turned as he caught her, his hands hot on her arm.

His dark brown eyes traveled from the hugging couple to Astrid, and she saw hunger in those eyes, the desire to do the same with her. Blood rushed to her face, and she looked down and fussed with the edge of her sleeve. She felt the heat that radiated off Short Olaf as he moved closer to her, and she did not know if the heat was from his exertion from running or from desire. She did not want to know.

"I've worked up a thirst," Dyri said, breaking the hug with his wife and wiping his face with his tunic. "Let's find food and drink." Dyri slicked his sweaty hair back and checked the crowd. When he clasped his belt back onto his waist, he once again looked like a warrior, and not just a young man out having a good time.

Astrid looked back at the competitions, where the men were throwing large round rocks to see who could throw the farthest, Rikki and Galm weighing the different rocks in their hands. The man who had the blacksmith's arms had a huge rock in his hand, and he put it to his shoulder before skipping forward and launching it out over the field. Rikki stopped to watch and looked impressed.

"Rikki is not leaving anytime soon," she said.

"They can always find us again," Dyri said, and he offered his arms to them. "Now, this man needs food."

"I'm staying here," Short Olaf said. "You could stay with me, Asta."

She thought briefly of all the fun she used to have with her brother and his friends, especially Short Olaf, and she wanted to relive it, to feel the freeness of being a child and playing games again, but she knew it was gone.

She shook her head. "No. I'll see you later."

Astrid slipped her arm through Dyri's, and they left the sporting area to find a food vendor.

The three of them talked about the races, and then of the council meeting that would take place in three days' time, the reason they were there.

"At the council meeting, the king and other leaders will discuss the feud between your father and Harald. Your father has been meeting with the King in private, but no one knows what they discuss. I tried to get it out of Red. He's not talking."

"For once," Ragnhild said. "Now is not the time for him to be tight-lipped."

Dyri chuckled. "It will all be resolved at the meeting."

"Father and Harald have been fighting since before I was born. Why is the king bothering with them now?" Astrid asked. A group of young men walked by, the crew of some chieftain, all dressed in their finest clothes, their silver arm rings and weapons sparkling in the sun. One of them caught her eye, a man with short dark hair and no beard, who had stripped off his tunic and tied it around his waist. He arched an eyebrow and looked her up and down as he walked past. A thrill went down Astrid's spine, and she could not resist the urge to look back at him. He had pivoted and was now walking backward, and when their eyes met again, he gave her an appraising look, so full of hunger that she flushed. He winked at her, and with a gasp Astrid quickly turned and clutched on to Dyri's safe arm.

"...complaints and war with his brother-son looming, King Ingjald wants to settle this." Dyri finished.

So struck by the young man, Astrid only caught the end of what Dyri said. "Uh...."

Dyri looked down at her and stopped. "Are you unwell?"

"Um." She ran a hand over her face. "Just hot." Her thoughts went back to the young, beardless man, and she flushed again.

"Dyri's right," Ragnhild added. Two young girls jostled her as they walked by with their family. "Let's find somewhere to sit in the shade."

"I'm fine."

"Nothing a bit of food and drink won't fix." Dyri searched the crowd over their heads. He gestured to a tent not far away and led them to the food vendor.

The merchant greeted them heartily, his crooked-toothed smile welcoming. He had burns, both old and new on both his hands, evidence that he spent his time working with boiling water and hot stones. His wife was in the back of the tent preparing dough on a small pine table, her hands flying over her work area.

"What's this?" Dyri pointed to a small, browned, round of dough shaped like a cup and topped with more dough pinched along the edge. It steamed through three holes poked in the top and smelled delicious.

"Meat pie," the man said.

Astrid leaned over the steam and breathed in. It smelled of meat that had stewed for a long time to release all its flavors. Her stomach grumbled. "Mm. We'll take three." When he told her the price, she pulled out the ring she'd used before and gave it to the merchant. He weighed it on the bronze scale that sat on the table, cut what he needed, and handed over three of the warm meat pies.

With a greedy look, Dyri took a big bite out of his, and nearly dropped the pie. "Hot," he yelped, opening his mouth and waving his hand in front of it to cool his tongue. His eyes watered, and he blinked rapidly to stop them.

Astrid leaned into her friend, the two women picking the crispy dough off the top and nibbling at it. "Now we have a secret weapon against rampaging warriors. Give them hot meat pies."

"Their hunger will take them down," Ragnhild added.

The two women laughed, and Dyri gave them a pitiful look. "I'm glad my distress is entertaining."

"My poor husband," Ragnhild cooed, and she put her fingers on his lips.

Once it had cooled, Dyri quickly finished his meat pie and found them some fresh buttermilk, while Astrid held on to her pie, wanting to savor it. They walked toward the lakeshore where the great longships docked. Finding a shady spot under a tree, Dyri pulled off his tunic and laid it on the grass for the women to sit on.

Astrid took a bite of her pie and let out a small moan of pleasure. The mixture of the floury outside and the thick meaty gravy on the inside came together in an explosion of sweet and savory. Bits of carrots added to the sweet flavor. Gravy dripped onto her chin, and she wiped it off and licked it off her hand. "By Freya, that is good."

Dyri laughed. "When you've been living on the ship and in camp, anything freshly made tastes like the best food you've ever eaten."

"No," Astrid said. "This is simply the best food I've ever tasted. Where is it from?"

Dyri shrugged. "The cook sounded like one of the English."

"The English. Emund does not tell stories about them. Why do you not travel there?" She took a small bite from the pie and ate it slowly, savoring the rich gravy.

Dyri rubbed his arm where he'd gotten the grass rash, then gathered up his long hair and tied it back with a leather thong. "Your father likes to go to the land of the east or to Frankia. But I have heard the English lands are very rich. We have met some of their traders."

Popping the last of the meat pie in her mouth, Astrid washed it down with the thick, tangy buttermilk. "I want another one."

"I don't want to move," Ragnhild said. "Let's stay here a while."

"*Ja*. Astrid, we'll get you another one on our way back to your father's tent. I could eat two or three more myself." Dyri stretched out next to them in the soft grass, his axe at his fingertips, and let out a tremendous sigh. The sound of children splashing in the water was pleasant, and there was a cool breeze under the trees.

"Don't wander off," he told them in a groggy and satiated voice, before closing his eyes.

"Once he's asleep, I will sneak off with the first handsome man I see," Astrid whispered to Ragnhild.

Without opening his eyes, Dyri said, "I heard that."

It didn't take long before his breathing evened out and he was asleep. Ragnhild smiled down at him and ran a hand gently over his face.

"I don't know how he can sleep. There is so much going on," Astrid said as she watched all the activity. Along with the children in the water, others enjoyed themselves, tossing balls or playing tag. Young boys wrestled or pretended to fight with swords. But what really drew Astrid's attention were the massive dragon ships. She saw her father's docked at a pier, its raven banner proudly flapping in the breeze.

"Dyri can fall asleep through anything," Ragnhild said.

"I wouldn't want to miss anything." Astrid watched young children play tag, their squeals of laughter ringing out brightly. The mothers of the children sat in a circle, talking while they sewed or cradled babies in their laps. Every so often one of the tag-playing children would run over to a mother for food or drink or for a soft place to sit for a while. One little girl, about five or six, flopped down next to her young mother, and the mother, without even looking or making anything of it, put her free arm around the girl and pulled her close. The girl relaxed into her mother and wound her hair gently through her little fingers. Watching the ease at which they interacted made Astrid miss her own mother. This was the first time she had ever been separated from her mother and her home.

"Ragna?"

"Hm?"

"I am afraid for my mother."

Ragnhild, who had been leaning next to her husband, sat up and scooched closer to Astrid. "Why?"

"I am afraid she is with child again. Before we left, she had been sick early in the day, she was tired, and there were other signs." The thought that her mother might give birth to another child gave Astrid chills. Screams from the last time her mother tried to give birth echoed in her ears until she realized the screams came from the children playing nearby. She shook her head to dispel the memories.

"I thought Ingiborg...," Ragnhild shifted uneasily. "Took care to keep that from happening."

"She does, but you know the brew does not always work."

Ragnhild laid a hand on her belly in a protective gesture.

"Are you?" Astrid had suspected but waited for her friend to say something.

"*Ja*. I am with child." Ragnhild's smile lit up her face.

"That is good news." Astrid returned the smile.

"It is. Don't worry about your mother. She can take care of herself. Amma is there too. She needs your mother as much as your mother needs her."

"You're right. Poor Amma." When they left to come to Hovgarden, Amma had been grieving for Buri. "It has been a hard spring and summer. So many men lost in the fighting with Harald."

"On all sides. Dyri says King Ingjald has received complaints from farmers and others about the constant warfare and raiding between your father and Harald this season. Farms and flocks destroyed. Too many people killed from raids. He thinks the King will make them settle it somehow."

"Will my father settle it? I don't see him stopping until he has killed every one of Harald's men."

Ragnhild glanced down at Dyri. He was asleep, but she lowered her voice. "Your father took Buri's death hard, especially coming so close after Jori's."

It had been terrible losing Buri, for all of them, and she had still not stopped grieving for Jori. Late winter had turned to spring and then to summer, and it still hurt that he was not around.

"Dyri thinks your father is ready to stop the fighting between the families."

"What about Rikki, though? He wants nothing more than to kill Bjorn Alfarsson."

"Rikki is oath-bound to your father and must do what he decides. We are all here to stop the fighting."

"I'm here for a marriage."

"They might be the same thing."

Astrid froze.

"Have you not thought of that?" Ragnhild asked, nudging her friend.

Why *hadn't* she thought of that? She had innocently assumed her father would not align her with his oldest and most hated enemy.

They sat quietly for a long time, Astrid thinking of what it would mean to marry someone from Harald's household, one of the men responsible for killing her loved ones. She shuddered at the thought.

Catching Astrid's mood turning sour, Ragnhild said, her voice brightening. "It is beautiful here, let's not talk of unpleasantness any longer. Besides, there is nothing you can do to change things." Ragnhild waved her free hand around. "Enjoy yourself. Watch handsome men run. Eat meat pies!"

"Mm. There are some very handsome men here." She told Ragna about the young man who had eyed her earlier.

"That's better," Ragnhild said with a laugh.

Astrid turned her attention from watching the children play to her father's longship *Wave Stallion* docked at the piers. The colorful shields had been removed, so the sides were bare wood, oars stored away, and the red and black striped sail furled, but still the boat looked impressive as it rocked and *thunked* gently against the wood of the pier. It had been thrilling to be on the boat, with its sail up, and traveling so fast she felt like they were flying. Ragnhild had been sick once they hit the open sea, but Astrid reveled in it, feeling like a spirit of the water. Her father's raven banner fluttered in the soft breeze, and Astrid felt a stirring of pride, not only for her father, but for all the women who had worked for many seasons to make the sail. She had embroidered the raven on the banner, working for ages, until her eyes stung with fatigue, to make it perfect. It hung proudly on the mast of her father's massive warship.

Getting to her feet, she cocked an eyebrow at Ragnhild. "Want to join me at the water? I'm going to dip my feet."

"Sounds nice." Ragnhild got to her feet, and with a quick glance down at Dyri, who was snoring, they walked down to the water.

At the edge of the water, they untied their shoes and set them aside. Lifting her skirts, Astrid waded in to cool her feet, kicking the water and swirling the mud at the bottom. Gentle waves moved in and out. Her thoughts wandered to the shirtless, beardless young man she'd seen earlier and the way he'd looked at her.

Looking out at the water as it sparkled in the sun, she made a decision. Her life would never be the same. She would have to marry someone her father chose. Before that happened, she would have a little fun.

Chapter Twenty-one

A speck out on the lake caught Astrid's attention. A ship approached, not one of the massive dragon ships, but a smaller boat, with about twenty men rowing. It drew closer to the pier where Astrid watched, standing with her feet in the chilly water. The boat did not turn to pull into one of the docks but kept traveling in a straight line. The sound of the men singing and carousing traveled over the air. Children waved to them, but the men paid no attention to the people on shore.

One man climbed up onto the edge of the boat at the stern and balanced there, arms out, as he studied the oars.

"Look!" A boy shouted, as he raced up with a group of children. "He's going to run the oars."

The boy's words had just died out when the man jumped onto the first oar handle. The other men kept rowing. He could not linger, and leaped immediately to the next oar, constantly checking his balance, then the next and next until he was halfway down the boat. At that point, he lost his balance, arms flailing in the air as he attempted to catch himself from falling. He looked down before crashing into the swirling water and the mass of oars that did not stop moving.

"Oh, no," Astrid said and lifted her hand to her mouth. Sure the massive oars would injure him as they pounded by where he had fallen, Astrid held her breath, hoping he would appear again. She had once seen a man hit in the head with the oars, and he was never the same after that, wandering off into the woods and never returning.

Moments later, the oar runner's head popped up behind the boat, and he called out to the others. They had stopped rowing, the boat still drifting quickly, but he swam to catch up and threw his hand up. Another man with bright blond hair grasped onto his arm and pulled him over the side of the boat. The first man fell out of view, but Astrid kept her eyes on the blond-haired man.

From the toss of his head, she could tell he was laughing as he shouted for the oarsmen to row again. The boat sped forward as the oars pulled through the water, gaining speed. Once the boat moved at full speed, every oar moving in perfect synchronization, the blond-haired man leaped up to balance on the edge near the stern and shouted something to the man who had fallen.

Astrid could not take her eyes off the warrior on the edge. His hair shone like gold in the bright sunlight, and he had taken off his shirt, so his well-muscled chest and arms gleamed with water spray. Astrid caught her breath and put her hand on her chest to stop her heart from beating so fast.

With a cock of his head, the man watched the moving oars, until, quick as a pouncing cat, he leaped onto the first one. Without even checking his balance, he ran from oar to oar, until he came to the bow where he launched himself easily back onto the boat's rail. He grasped hold of the bow where the dragon head would be on a warship, and lifted his arm in triumph. The other men pulled him down and placed a drinking horn in his hand.

At the same time, the group of children whooped and clapped for him on the shore. Astrid, caught up in the excitement, clapped too, and she continued to watch the handsome young warrior. He ran the oars two more times after that, both times as graceful and strong as the first. The last time, though, he dropped into the boat after he finished.

The others had stopped rowing, and the boat lingered in the water, gently moving with the current, when he popped up from the bottom of the boat and tossed his wet hair back out of his face. Pointing at the first man who ran the oars, he said something. The two men dove off the boat and then swam toward the closest pier.

Astrid admired him as his body sliced into the water as cleanly as a seal.

The children let out a cry of excitement and ran down to the pier to see the end of the swimming race. Astrid scooped up her shoes and hurried after them.

"Asta, wait," Ragnhild called after her. She looked to her husband, who was still asleep, his arm draped over his eyes. "We need to get Dyri."

Still moving, Astrid turned her head and said, "No time. I want to see him finish. It will be fine. Come on!"

Ragnhild shot a glance at her sleeping husband, but Astrid did not give her friend a chance to change her mind. With a shake of her head, Ragnhild grabbed Astrid's hand, and they ran together.

Soon they came to the pier where a crowd had gathered to wait for the racing swimmers.

Beaming, Astrid said, "You told me to enjoy myself."

"I did." Ragnhild frowned at Astrid, but before long the two women giggled.

"I want to get closer," Astrid said, breathless, as she pulled Ragnhild through the crowd to the end of the pier where the men would finish their race.

The children moved aside for her, and she saw the swimmers the moment the blond man reached the pier. Muscles corded through his shoulders and down his arms as he pulled and pushed his way over the edge. As soon as he got a leg up, he jumped to his feet, his hair and trousers soaked and dripping onto the wooden boards. He shook his hair like a dog and laughed as the children ran squealing from the water that sprayed from him. Two thick arm rings circled his upper arms, the silver flashing in the sun when he moved, the green jewel in one of the arm rings throwing sparks on the wet deck. He wore a copper Tyr amulet hanging from a black cord and another necklace of a sharp animal tooth at the end of a brown leather cord. The necklaces stuck to the hair on his wet chest, the light hair glistening in the sun.

One of the little boys said something to him, and he turned, slicking his shoulder-length hair back from his face with both hands. He wore rings on his fingers too. Astrid had never seen a man wear rings on his fingers before, and she found it appealing. Black markings wound their way up his right forearm, and although Astrid could not see what they were, her fingers twitched with a powerful urge to trace along them. Her body burned with excitement, and her breath came in short gasps.

As if he heard her, he turned his attention to Astrid. He held her eyes, his blue eyes so dark they looked like the deepest part of the sea, and Astrid stood as if pinned to the ground by him. Every part of her tingled at the touch of his stare. He arched an eyebrow and smiled at her, his teeth so white and straight his smile flashed like the sun reflecting off a calm lake.

Astrid knew she should walk away from him, should probably run away from him, but she stayed where she was. She had decided to enjoy herself and returned his smile with her own.

The blond warrior inclined his head, and he gave her a teasing grin that emphasized a scar on his cheek as he walked toward her. His wet trousers clung to his legs, showing the definition of every part of his body. He stopped before her, and she could feel the cool from the water on his skin, could smell the scent of the lake on him. Drops of water trickled down his chest and over his arms.

Astrid looked up at him. He was too close, close enough to touch, and she had to grab on to her dress to keep herself from touching him. His eyes held hers again, and he continued to smile at her. She pulled in a breath.

Gathering up her nerve, she said, "That was, ah, well done." She held in a groan. Why couldn't she think of something better to say than that? She did not know how to talk to a strange man, especially one who took her breath away.

He chuckled, a rumble that vibrated through Astrid and made her feel tingly.

"*Tak*," he said. He had a deep voice, rich and smooth. "I won a bet. But your smile would have been reward enough."

Astrid felt Ragnhild's hand on her arm, tugging at it to get her away from this man, but she stood firm.

The blond warrior noticed with a lift of his eyebrows and said, "I am Bjorn—"

"Bjorn!" A man ran up to him, not even paying attention to Astrid. "If you want your winnings, you'd better go now. That *gloggvingr* is trying to sneak away without paying. Here." He whipped a dagger out of his belt and shoved the hilt into Bjorn's hand.

Bjorn gave Astrid a look of regret, but then he leaned in close to her, a drop of water from his hair dripping onto her arm. "I will find you again..." he whispered as he gently touched her cheek. It sent a shock through her, and though his fingers were cold, she felt she'd been burned.

She watched him disappear into the crowd, hoping he would keep his promise.

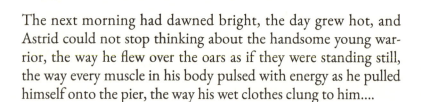

The next morning had dawned bright, the day grew hot, and Astrid could not stop thinking about the handsome young warrior, the way he flew over the oars as if they were standing still, the way every muscle in his body pulsed with energy as he pulled himself onto the pier, the way his wet clothes clung to him....

She dropped the deer-bone comb she ran through her long hair. She reached down to pick it up, but Ragnhild was there first.

"Here, let me do it," Ragnhild told her as she took a handful of Astrid's hair and combed it. "You've been clumsy since yesterday. Would you like me to braid it?"

Astrid thought of the blond man. Would he like her hair loose or bound? Why was she even thinking of what he'd like? She remembered his soft, deep-throated whisper in her ear, and the touch of his fingertips on her cheek, and she suppressed a shiver of excitement.

"I don't know. What do you think?" Astrid cleared her throat and tried to focus on what she was doing.

Running her fingers through Astrid's hair, Ragnhild said behind her, "Let me try something new. Three small braids on each side that then join into one bigger one at the back."

"I've done that before."

"I promise this will be different and stunning."

She gathered up some of Astrid's golden hair and braided it. "Where is your blue silk ribbon? I'll weave it in."

"In my new jewelry box." Astrid pointed to a small birch wood box that Rikki had made and decorated for her. He had carved sixteen interlocking circles and swirls all over the sides and cover during the winter and given it to her on her name day. "Ragna?"

"Hm?" Ragnhild answered, absently, as her agile fingers worked her way through Astrid's hair, pulling it into tight braids along the side of her head.

The edge of the ribbon tickled Astrid's neck, and she giggled, but tried not to move, so it would not mess up her hair. "Did you think the man who ran the oars, Bjorn, was handsome?"

Ragnhild did not stop weaving. "*Ja*, he was handsome, but..."

"What?"

"You should stay away from him."

"Why?"

"*Why?*" Ragnhild stopped braiding. "You know why. He looked at you too hungrily. And you...you liked it too much." She gave the braid a little tug.

Astrid held in a groan of longing. She *had* liked it. No one had ever looked at her the way he had. This man had walked right up to her, as if to claim her right there on the pier.

"His name is *Bjorn*," Ragnhild added.

"So," Astrid said more forcefully than she meant. "It's a common name. There must be a hundred Bjorns here."

"True," Ragnhild sighed. She stepped behind Astrid and began working the hair on the other side of her head.

"Do you remember when we played that game when I imagined my perfect husband?"

"Oh, no."

"Oh, yes. I've changed my mind. He does not have brown hair, but bright blond hair and dark blue eyes." She giggled, and Ragnhild laughed with her.

The flap to the tent opened and bright sunlight washed in, only to be blotted out when a dark figure entered, followed by two more. "Ladies!" Rikki announced. "Get yourselves ready or you'll miss it."

"Miss what?" Astrid asked her brother. She could only see him out of the corner of her eye, since Ragnhild still worked on the back of her hair.

"Wrestling! Most of the others are already at the field. We came to get you."

Ragnhild patted the back of her head to let her know she'd finished the braid, and Astrid turned to see who the 'we' was who came in with Rikki. Her heart leaped when she saw Gunnar standing near the tent flap, looking her up and down and stopping at her face. He seemed ready to take the three steps across the tent and take her in his arms. She wanted him, too. She remembered the touch of Gunnar's lips on hers, and the feel of his hands on her body, but then the memory of the blond warrior invaded her thoughts, leaving her confused. She dropped her head and brought her hand up to run it over her new braids, just to have something to do.

Clearing his throat, Rikki looked between her and Gunnar.

They all filed out of the tent, Gunnar holding the flap open. The smell of meat roasting over open fires, and the sounds of people talking and laughing, hit Astrid as soon as she stepped outside, and she stopped and took in a deep breath, smiling. Music from a lyre drifted from a tent nearby. She could get used to all this activity. So many new faces, smells, tastes.

When he exited after her, Short Olaf put on his floppy hat.

"Really, Shortie, must you wear that ridiculous thing?" Ragnhild said. She walked past him to meet Dyri.

"I'm with Ragna," Rikki added.

"I like it," Short Olaf said. "You will wish you had one the next time it rains."

Rikki snorted a laugh and jogged ahead to catch up to Gunnar, Dyri, and Ragnhild. As soon as he joined them he told Ragnhild, with a vicious glee in his voice, that a group of Harald's men would be there.

"Someone could get killed," Astrid said to Short Olaf. She looked up at him and then had to look away. The hat *was* ridiculous.

"It happens," Short Olaf said.

"Even Red will be in on the action," Rikki said over his shoulder. He jangled his purse. "My silver's on him, no matter who he wrestles."

"Mine, too," Gunnar said. "He's old, but nearly impossible to take down."

"He must be like fighting against Thor." Astrid tried and failed to imagine what it would be like to fight with Emund.

"That's exactly what it feels like," Rikki answered. He spied a tent selling food and ale and pointed at it. "We need a drink."

They all wound their way through a crowd of people who walked, talking loudly, toward the wrestling field, Short Olaf grabbing Astrid's hand so they wouldn't become separated. Rikki hurried ahead, but Astrid slowed down, wanting to linger, not hurry.

"Are you enjoying yourself?" Short Olaf asked, as they watched their friends disappear into the crowd.

When she nodded, he gave her a shy smile, and squeezed her hand. His face was shaded by the brim of his hat. "You used to cry every summer when your father and Emund left to come here, you wanted to go so bad. Remember?"

"I remember."

His brown eyes shone with the memory. "Then you, Ragna, me, and Rikki would set up a pretend market and we'd buy and sell goods."

"We'd get Jori to play the king and hold a council meeting." When they'd played, Jori was always a good king, laying out justice fairly, and he even let the girls come to the 'meeting,' though women were not allowed at the real one.

"I miss Jori," Short Olaf said. "He was like my brother. I wish I had been there when Bjorn killed him. Maybe I could have saved him." His voice was raw, and he looked at the booth where Gunnar bought food and drink. "Gunnar was there..." Short Olaf said. "Forget about that. It is done and we are here, right?"

"Right," Astrid said. "You can take it out on Harald's men when you wrestle."

"*Ja.*" With a gleam in his eyes.

As Short Olaf led the way, as they moved in and out of people to catch up with their friends, Astrid felt a prickle up her spine, like someone was watching her. She shivered and looked around. And there he was, standing at a carpenter's tent, a small toy horse in his hand, the blond warrior from the pier. Bjorn.

When she caught his eyes, he smiled at her. Just like the day before, his smile nearly took her legs out from under her. With a slight gesture with his head, he indicated the space between the tents and out of view. Her breath quickened. She could not do that, not at all. It was dangerous. She shook her head, just enough so he could see her. At least Short Olaf had turned away from her.

Bjorn shrugged and went back to paying the merchant for the toy horse, and she wondered who the horse was for. A younger brother? Or his own child? Done with his purchase, Bjorn turned back to Astrid, and she jumped from being caught still staring after him. He laughed, and although she could not hear him, she imagined the sound caressing her. It made her want to be with him. He held her stare with his dark blue eyes, and then he slowly disappeared behind the tents.

She turned away from Bjorn and looked at Short Olaf's back, at the floppy hat that dangled over his neck. She did not want him there, her brother and Gunnar either, their very presence suffocating her, and she longed to go after her handsome warrior.

"Olli," she said to get his attention. "It's too crowded for me here."

He turned around to face her.

"I'll be right over there." She pointed to a bench under a few birch trees, between the two tents where Bjorn had gone, her heart banging in her chest so fast and hard, she feared Short Olaf would notice it.

He gave a quick study of the area before letting her go, his face shadowed under the floppy hat. And Astrid felt bad about her deception. "Be right back," Short Olaf said lightly, and he worked his way to the front of the food seller's tent to join Rikki, Gunnar, Dyri and Ragnhild.

As soon as his back was turned, and making sure the others were not looking either, Astrid hurried to where Bjorn had disappeared, her heart racing.

He waited for her, leaning up against a tent pole, while he turned the toy horse over and over in his hands, a jewel in one of his rings winking in the dappled sun. When he heard her footsteps, he looked up, and his gaze once again made her feel unsteady on her feet, like a newborn foal. If she was the foal, did that make him a wolf? He had lured her from the safety of her family.

He was wearing a sapphire blue tunic, the same color as his eyes, edged with yellow braiding, and cream-colored trousers. On his waist was a belt with a silver buckle, a sword clipped onto it, the silver hilt with a Tyr rune carved into it visible from the sheath. His shoes were soft leather with silver buckles. He had on the two arm rings he'd been wearing the day before, and he still wore the Tyr amulet and boar tooth necklace. His blond hair was shoulder length with one side tucked behind his ear.

She couldn't breathe. He was rich, and the most handsome man she'd ever seen.

He looked past her toward where she had come from. "Your brother...? The one with the hat? Keeps a tight rein on you. I don't blame him." He gave her a wolfish smile.

"That was not my brother," she stammered, looking behind her, hoping that Short Olaf or Rikki would appear, and hoping even more that they would stay away.

At this, he glanced down at her hand. "Husband?"

"No."

"Whoever he is, he will miss you soon." He pushed off from where he lounged against a tent pole. The movement was so quick and easy, it reminded Astrid that this man was a warrior, if the sword hanging at his side was not enough of a reminder, and could hurt her easily and quickly.

"Yes."

Her voice came out shakier than she wanted, and it stopped him.

"You don't need to fear me. I do not hurt women." He soothed, like he was talking to a skittish horse. When he raised his hand, his sleeve fell to his elbow, exposing the black marks that decorated his arm in a knotwork pattern that looked like vines traveling up his arm. She studied them.

"I...I am not afraid you will hurt me." She meant it too. The trembling of her body and shakiness of her voice was not fear of him, but something else. Was it desire? She wanted him to touch her, but was afraid that if he did, it would consume her. She took a step back.

Bjorn gestured to her with the toy horse, his face softening, his eyes bright. "A gift for my son. Do you think he will like it?"

His son. Of course it was for his son. How could a man this potent not have a child? He tilted his head in question, waiting for her answer.

Determined not to let it upset her, she gave a small laugh, "Is that why you called me over here? To ask me about a gift for your son?"

"Do you have a better reason?" He arched an eyebrow.

Astrid's eyes went wide. "Um...how old is he?"

"Five."

She liked the way his face softened when he talked about this son, it made him look young, like he was a child too. A vision of him on the floor, playing with his son and the new toy horse, went through her mind, making her feel warm all over. Gesturing to the horse, she reached out for it, but when she took hold of the toy, he held on to her hand for a moment, and the touch sent shivers down her back.

"He will love it." Astrid rubbed her hand over the smooth wood. The horse was painted a deep crimson with black for his mane and tail.

He stepped closer to her, so close she smelled mint on his breath. "Do you know how to ride?"

"Y-yes." His closeness made her skin tingle. "My father has horses."

He gave her an arched look and then studied the beaded necklaces strung from the heavy silver brooches that pinned her apron to her dress. She thought about pulling her Freya pendant out from under her dress, but she left it nestled in her bosom where Freya could protect her heart.

"I'm going to look at a horse I want to buy. Would you join me?" He gestured his head toward the food tent, a strand of his hair brushing his cheek. "You can bring your protector with you."

The thought of Short Olaf, or even worse, Rikki, joining her to look at horses with this man, made her nearly laugh out loud.

"They are going to wrestle." She choked out instead. "Why aren't you there?" She looked at his arms, the strength of them showing through the lightweight tunic he wore.

A dark cloud of anger passed over his face, and he clenched his jaw. "There are men there I do not want to see."

She feared for those men, for Bjorn looked like he would tear them to pieces if he got the chance.

"Asta?" A man's voice called out from not far away, and she whirled, heart racing. She could not see Short Olaf, but she knew it would not be long before he came this way.

"Your protector." The anger that had flashed over Bjorn vanished, and he smiled at her, the force of it hitting her so hard, she couldn't breathe. "Meet me at the horse trader's corral if you wish."

He strode off and disappeared behind a tent. Astrid realized she still held his son's toy horse in her hands, and she started to go after him, but Short Olaf and Rikki rounded the corner.

"What are you doing?" Rikki searched the area.

"What's that?" Short Olaf asked her, pointing to the toy in her hand.

"Um," A lie popped into her head. "I saw it lying on the ground and was trying to find whoever dropped it. I'll keep it, and if I see a little boy missing a toy, then I'll know it's his."

"You shouldn't run off like that. Father would skin me if anything happened to you." Rikki told her.

"Or Red," Short Olaf said.

"He'd just tear our arms and legs off." Rikki took hold of Astrid's arm. "Let's go, *systir*, I want to destroy some of Harald's men."

They met up with Ragnhild, Dyri, and Gunnar, and the group of them started back to the wrestling field, Astrid planning how she could escape them all.

Chapter Twenty-two

At the wrestling field, the men were already in action, with two wrestlers engaged while the others watched in a circle surrounding them. Astrid followed Rikki, who gripped her arm, making her bristle with irritation. He found an open spot near the edge of the circle, and Astrid saw that Emund grappled with a much smaller man, although he was agile and darting around. Emund lumbered like he was made from stone, swiping out at the man, who then laughed at him and danced away.

"What's wrong with Emund? Why is he so slow?" Astrid pulled her arm out of Rikki's grasp.

Rikki snickered. "Red is playing with him. Men always think because he's big, he's slow, so he plays it up, blundering like a drunk troll."

"It's his way of punishing them for underestimating him." Gunnar chuckled. "The man must have insulted him. It's the only time he does this and..." He shrugged. "It works. Watch."

Astrid watched, but she could not focus well on what was before her with Gunnar standing next to her, his arm brushing against hers, the closest they'd been to each other all summer. She longed to have him wrap his arm around her, or to take her hand in his, but she knew he could not. And would not. She also wondered how she would get away to meet Bjorn. With Rikki on one side of her, Gunnar on the other, and Short Olaf behind him, she had no chance to break away. Why was she even considering it? What drew her to this man?

"Not long now," Gunnar said, his lips so close to her ear that his breath tickled her neck. She wished he were not so close. It confused her.

"*Ja*," Rikki said, his tone full of anticipation, like a boy about to be given a gift. "Red's bored with him now."

The smaller man continued to dance around Emund, giving insult to Emund's size and apparent slowness, comparing him to a dumb troll. Unfazed by the taunts, Emund lunged at the man, not reaching him, which only added to the verbal abuse, until the other man got too close. Lashing out much more quickly than he had up to that point, Emund grabbed hold of the man, one arm around his neck and the other around his waist and picked him up as easily as he picked up a child, and then slammed him onto the ground. When he straightened back up, red hair loose and wild, Emund walked away from the motionless man on the ground.

Rikki whipped his arm off Astrid's shoulder and surged forward to meet Emund.

"See? Red always wins," Gunnar said.

"Are you going to wrestle?" Astrid thought back to when he'd wrestled at Ragnhild's wedding feast, of how he had beaten Sigmund Ketilsson that day. She wanted to see him do the same thing with Harald's men.

"*Ja*. Me, Rikki, Dyri, Short Olaf." He nodded to Short Olaf, who had hung back, a cup of ale in his hand. "You will cheer for us?"

"I will."

He smiled at her, his eyes glittering in a way that left her feeling unmoored. She wanted him to take her in his arms, to whisper in her ear that they could run away and marry, to forget about her father and the others. He leaned toward her.

"Here's your drink." Short Olaf stepped in between them and held up the cup he'd been holding.

Without another word, or even a glance her way, Gunnar turned and went to join Emund and Rikki. She watched him walk away over Short Olaf's shoulder. Her heart sank.

"Asta." Short Olaf cleared his throat to get her attention.

She blinked and looked down at the drink she had asked Short Olaf to get. While the knowledge that he'd held on to it for her should have made her grateful to him, all it did was make her angry at his constant attention. The desire to flee them all, Gunnar, Rikki, Short Olaf, took hold of her, and the plan to meet with Bjorn solidified in her. Snatching the cup out of his hand, she drank deeply of the strong ale. "Shouldn't you be with the others?" The words snapped out like a flag in the wind.

Eyes widened with surprise, Short Olaf stiffened. "*Ja*."

Astrid waited for his usual wave and 'wish me luck,' but he made his way to the others, leaving her alone in the crowd of onlookers. This was her chance to leave, if she acted quickly. Erasing any guilt she felt over hurting Short Olaf, she checked the crowd to make sure none of her family were watching. The men were so busy discussing the wrestling they paid her no mind, and Ragnhild worked to put Dyri's blond-streaked hair up in a knot on top of his head, so she was not aware of her friend.

Astrid ducked past a large man and his wife and made her way toward the pasture where the horse traders had their horses. As she got to the edge of the crowd, Astrid glanced back and spotted Galm staring in her direction, a half-smile on his face, eyebrows raised. A shot of fear hit her, and she froze, not knowing what she should do. Go back? Galm could have no idea where she was going, could not know she planned to meet a strange man, so why did he look at her as if he *did* know these things? Her mind raced, trying to figure out what to do, but Galm did not move to get Rikki or Emund; he continued to watch her, like a hunter waits and watches his prey. It was as if he wanted her to leave. Would he follow her? Just then, a group of men from some chieftain's household strutted by on their way to the competition. Their bulk shielded Astrid from Galm's view, and she used the moment to slip away.

Breathless at her escape, Astrid resisted the urge to run. Instead, she forced herself to walk normally, and soon the weight of her family's attention lifted off of her; she held her face up to the warm sun and took in a deep breath. She still held the toy horse in her hands, and the realization made her smile; she needed to get this back to Bjorn, or he would miss it. That's why she was meeting him.

She smelled the horse trader's corral before she saw it, the familiar odor of horses, manure, and hay. The corral, nestled in a small grassy valley, under the shelter of birch trees that provided shade for the animals, was surrounded with a pine log fence to keep them from straying. Since so many of the jarls and chieftains and their men were at the competitions, it was quiet but for the horses' nickers, the stomp of their heavy hooves on the grass, and the swish of their tails as they swatted at flies. A duo of voices floated over to Astrid, and she headed toward them. She should have been afraid, or even tentative, to be here meeting a man she did not know, but it felt good, and her shoes lightly touched the soft ground as she walked.

Bjorn and the trader did not hear her approach and were talking and intent on examining the animal, so she stopped to watch as Bjorn ran his hands gently, but with firmness, over the back and withers of the light dun stallion, its skin twitching and quivering. Astrid quivered too, at the thought of Bjorn running his hands over her, skin to skin, and before she could stop it, a little sigh escaped her lips.

The horse trader stopped mid-sentence, and gave her a quick look, before walking toward her.

"*Velkomin!*" He cried out heartily.

Without removing his hands from the horse's leg, Bjorn glanced up, catching her with his knowing stare. He grinned and straightened up, telling the trader, "She's with me." A thrill went down Astrid's spine at those simple words.

He gave a quick glance over her shoulder.

"I am alone," Astrid told him, and as the words left her mouth, she fully understood the impact of her actions. She was truly alone with this man, and no one knew where she was or who she was with. Her mouth felt very dry, and she swallowed hard. "You forgot this." She held out the toy.

He strode over and took it from her and set it on a fence post. His hands were strong, and his rings gleamed. As if sensing her disquiet, like he had earlier, Bjorn turned his attention away from her and back to the dun stallion. With that movement, Astrid had an image of Bjorn in the crimson wool she'd bought earlier.

"What do you think of him?"

Happy to focus on something other than the way Bjorn made her feel, Astrid walked up to the horse's head and laid her hand on the spot above his eyes. His white and brown mane fell loose and long over one eye, and he nodded toward her, nosing her, looking for something to eat.

"I don't have anything for you," she whispered, and stroked his head. The horse nudged her again, tried to nibble at her sleeve, but she gently pushed him away. "That's not for you." He stomped his foot, and she laughed, moving to his side, and patting his neck.

"He likes you," the trader said, pleased.

"What is his name?" She asked him, as she moved along the horse's side and ran her hand over his sleek back.

"Grani."

"A good name." Bjorn walked around the animal's other side from Astrid, mirroring her movement, like they were in a dance and the horse was a part of it. He caught her eyes, and she held on to his gaze.

"A hero's mount," Astrid recited. "'Sleipnir's kin. The best of all horses.'"

Bjorn arched an eyebrow at that, and once again gave her the crooked grin that emphasized the scar on his cheek.

"The young lady knows her stories," the trader interrupted the moment. "Old One-Eye himself led Sigurd Dragon Slayer to his treasured horse, but it took a great warrior to subdue the wild beast, Grani. Sigurd was up to the task. After Sigurd slew the dragon Fafnir, Grani carried the treasure, the 'beauteous burden.'"

Bjorn ran a hand through his hair. "Trader, if this horse rides like his name, you have a deal."

"You will think you are riding Odin's eight-legged Sleipnir himself, so fast and smooth is Grani's gait," the trader said, with such earnestness that Astrid had to stifle a laugh.

"Saddle him up."

"I thought you'd never ask. You will not regret it." The trader walked over to the fence where he had slung the saddle and harness.

When he came back and saddled Grani, talking all the while about the animal's breeding and prowess, Bjorn sidled up to Astrid and asked, "You know where Sigurd rode Grani after retrieving Fafnir's treasure?" His voice sounded like the mulled wine she had once had—rich, warm, and soothing.

"I do!" Astrid said too loudly.

His dark eyes sparkled with amusement. "Sigurd rode to the castle where Brunhild was held in an enchanted sleep from Odin's sleep rune." The horse stomped as the trader slid the harness over his head, and Astrid patted his neck. "Only the bravest warrior on the bravest horse could make it through the fire that surrounded the castle. Sigurd and Grani jumped right through it."

"And he woke Brunhild from her sleep. They fell in love, and she taught him all of her magic. She was the most beautiful woman in the world..." Bjorn's gaze traveled over Astrid's face, hair, and down her body.

She inhaled sharply, the heat rising to her cheeks.

"There," the trader said, breaking the spell. "He's ready." He whispered into Grani's ear, loud enough for Bjorn to hear. "Show the man what you can do." With a pat on his neck, the trader handed the reins to Bjorn.

Astrid didn't want him to ride off. She wanted him to stay with her, talking about the brave Sigurd and the fallen Valkyrie Brunhild. The words, 'don't go' lay on the tip of her tongue, but she could not speak them.

Instead of mounting the horse, Bjorn turned to Astrid, a playful grin on his face. "Ride with me?"

She looked at Bjorn, at the saddled horse, and then the corral, before turning back to him. His eyes, the color of dark sapphires, were wide with anticipation. The ground below her felt unstable, like when she stood on the beach and the waves pulled the sand away. In the distance, she could hear the shouts of the people watching the wrestling competitions, and the smells from the food tents carried over along the soft breeze from the lake. Her safety, in the form of her brother, was back there. She shouldn't dare ride with this man.

He held out his hands to give her a lift. By doing this, she knew her father's wrath would be as awful as one of the gods, but at the moment, she did not care. "Let's ride."

When his strong hands circled her waist, they sent an ache to the core of her body that made her think she might not manage to sit atop the horse. He lifted her with ease and settled her behind the saddle.

"Good?"

"*Ja*," she croaked out.

He swung himself up easily to sit in front of her, his presence so overwhelming it made her lightheaded. The leather of the saddle creaked underneath him as he settled himself.

With a glance back, he asked, "Ready?"

She thought of her family, of how they hovered over her, smothering her. She couldn't wait to get away from them.

"Ready," she said.

He started off slowly, leaving the corral with a wave to the horse trader, Grani's gait smooth. They rode in silence for a while, enjoying the warmth of the midday sun, listening to the birds chattering in the trees; soon they left the shelter of the corral and trees and made their way further inland until they came to a rise just before it dipped into a grassy valley. Bjorn stopped Grani to take in the view, the deep green grass blowing in the breeze. The horse shook his head, the harness rattling, his shaggy mane whipping around.

"I'm going to let him run," Bjorn told Astrid over his shoulder.

She was so close to him she felt the vibration of his voice, and it resonated through her like a lyre string.

"Hang on."

With a gulp, she looked at his back, muscles shifting as he held the reins of the horse, then down at his legs, as they gripped onto Grani. If she hung on to Bjorn, she was afraid she'd never want to let go. Taking a breath, she slipped her arms around his waist and held tight. The muscles in his stomach tensed when her hands touched him, and he shifted in the saddle, but then he relaxed, and put one of his hands on her clasped hands and squeezed. His touch, the feel of his muscular body up against her chest, of his firm stomach on her hands, made her lightheaded, and she pressed her forehead against his back, breathing him in. He smelled like horse and sweat, like a man, and the smell kindled a heat inside of her like when she'd drunk something warm and smooth. Lifting her head, she grasped onto him tighter, and he responded with a soft inhale that she could feel.

"Let's run," she told him, her voice finally under her control.

He turned his head to her, and she caught his bright smile. She was about to say something more when he clucked to the horse, and they tore off down into the valley. Astrid let out a squeal of excitement, and had to grab on to him even more tightly, to keep from falling off. They raced down the hill and through the valley, the wind blowing through their hair and clothes, pieces of Astrid's hair coming undone from the braids by her face and tickling her cheek. All thoughts and worries flew from her mind; she relished the feel of Bjorn's body as she clasped her arms around him, the strength and movement of the horse beneath them, and the valley as it flew past in streaks of yellow and green grass, bushes, and trees. The barley was high in the fields, and it was a golden-brown blur.

When Bjorn reined in Grani, Astrid cried out, "Don't stop." She could have run forever.

"I have to give him a rest," Bjorn said with a laugh, shifting in the saddle to turn toward her. "He's strong, but he is carrying both of us. What do you make of Grani now?"

She leaned back and patted the horse's rump. "He's wonderful. Like his namesake." Without thinking, she wrapped her arm back around Bjorn's waist, even though she no longer needed to hang on. "I think he could ride through a magical ring of fire."

"I think you're right."

Grani snorted and shook his head, which made them laugh. "He thinks so too," Astrid said.

"The man who called to you earlier, he called you Asta?"

"Yes." She didn't want to think of Short Olaf.

"A pretty name. Let me guess. You are here with your father to find you a husband."

Astrid tensed at the mention of her father, but then took a breath to shake off the feeling of foreboding. "And you are here to...what? Lure young women away from their families?"

"Not *any* young woman. Just you."

She was suddenly very aware that her hands were on this man's, this stranger's, body. The sun had warmed his tunic and heat radiated off of him.

"When I saw you standing on the pier after I ran the oars, do you know what I noticed first?"

She shook her head and then remembered he could not see her. "No, what?"

"You were barefoot, holding your shoes in your hand." His voice grew soft and slow, reminding Astrid of honey pouring out onto porridge. "And your hair, it was shining in the sun, like gold, like Sif's. But that's not what drew me. It was loose and messy, as if you'd been running to meet me."

Astrid did not move, and took tiny breaths as she listened to him, afraid that if she made any noise, he'd stop.

"That's how I always imagined...hoped...my wife would come to greet me when I returned, hurrying to meet the boat, her hair long and loose, blowing in the wind. Expectant. Happy for my safe return." He cleared his throat. "You looked like that."

She did not know what to say to that, or how to tell him she *had* been rushing to meet him. Her mouth opened to reply, but nothing came out. Everything about the moment was too big for her; even the sun was shining too hot and bright, as if the sun goddess Sol was focusing all of her attention on the two of them.

"We should go back, or the trader will think we've stolen his prize horse." Bjorn hesitated before turning Grani around. "Although, the thought of riding away has its appeal."

His tone caught Astrid off-guard; it was wistful, and so unlike what she had heard from him so far, the cocky confidence gone in one simple statement.

"Yes, it does."

"It would not work," he said.

"No, it wouldn't."

Bjorn clucked at Grani and turned him so they could return to the trader's corral, to the Thing, to their families and obligations. They did not run this time, but let the horse walk at an easy pace.

"When I was a boy, and wanted to escape the wrath of my father's wife, I would run away to the woods and find a clearing that looked like Frey or the elves enchanted it. I would wait, hoping someone would come take me away. Gods, elves, dwarfs, it did not matter," Bjorn said, his voice as warm as the sun. He paused, as if waiting for her to laugh at him or tell him it was silly. When she didn't, he continued, "At least until it grew dark. Then I got scared and ran back home."

"It's hard to imagine you afraid of the dark."

"Well, I'm not *now*." He laughed.

"Did they ever come to you?"

"No." He said it with such regret Astrid gave him a squeeze, forgetting herself, and he leaned back into her. It felt good.

"I used to think my mother was a goddess." Astrid had never told anyone this, not even Rikki, and it felt right to share it with Bjorn, like he would understand. "One of the healing goddesses, like Eir. My mother is a skilled healer."

"Healing is a gift from the goddess."

"It is. She would always let me help when she collected her herbs, and watch as she created her healing salves, and I believed she was magic, creating something that would heal out of ordinary plants." Astrid thought of her mother, with child again, in danger again, and her heart squeezed tight. When she returned to her tent, she would ask her father if she could go to the house of the gods to give an offering to Frigg for her mother. When she got back. Her body turned to ice. What would happen then?

"She sounds like a good woman."

"Y-yes," Astrid choked out. Needing to change the subject of their conversation away from her family, she grasped on to the first thing she could think of. "So, you have a son?"

"And a daughter."

Astrid did not like that he had a woman somewhere who gave him these children, and she wished that she had never asked him. "And their mother?" She needed to know.

"Dead." His voice was flat, emotionless.

"I'm sorry."

"She died giving birth to our daughter during the winter. It is a woman's bane, childbirth. But I have a beautiful daughter, Aud."

His voice softened when saying his daughter's name. This man loved his children. It drew her to him even more than his handsome face.

The birch trees under which the corral nestled, rose into view, reminding them that their ride was over. Astrid didn't want it to end, wanted to tell Bjorn to turn around and keep going, but she knew she could not. She felt his hesitation when the corral came into view, as if he did not want to return either.

"Ah! You were pleased, I can tell," the trader called out.

Astrid removed her hands from Bjorn's waist, and despite the hot sun, she felt the loss of him like a cold burst of air.

Reining in, Bjorn slung his legs over the horse's neck and jumped down.

"He is sturdy and strong," Bjorn told him, not letting his voice betray anything as he reached up to help Astrid down.

She put her hands on his shoulders to steady herself as he lifted her down. It was the first time since before they had ridden that she faced him. She found his presence a little less overwhelming, but still her feet felt unsteady.

As Astrid settled on the ground, she leaned over to straighten her dress, and her Freya pendant swung out, the purple bead flashing in the sunlight. It caught Bjorn's attention, and he reacted to it as if it had punched him, taking a step back, all the color leaving his face.

"What?" She held up the pendant. "It is Freya."

"I need to take you back." His voice had grown hard. "Now."

"Why?" Her head spun. What had happened to him? "It is not dark magic." She tried to lighten her tone.

"Come." He did not touch her but led the way out of the corral with such determination she did not question to follow. So many questions flew through her mind, she could barely see where they headed. One look at his face, once so kind, but now turned to stone, silenced her.

"Wait!" the trader called after him. "What about Grani?"

Bjorn turned to the man. "I will be back."

When he caught Astrid's eyes, he stopped and said, "Astrid Tryggvisdottir." It was not a question, but a statement, and stated with such detachment that Astrid stumbled.

She righted herself. "Yes. Wha—?"

"You must go back." Without another word or explanation, Bjorn spun and strode back toward the festivities, leaving Astrid reeling as she lurched after him.

Chapter Twenty-three

Astrid Tryggvisdottir. How could he have been so stupid to not ask her name? It had been fun to not ask names, to avoid the family ties that complicate matters, but now he regretted it. He glanced back at her as she followed him, her lovely face marred with hurt and confusion, brows furrowed, lips pulled down in a frown, and he sighed. It was not her fault. All the same, he did not want to be seen with her, and wanted to see nothing more of her. The Freya pendant gleamed in the sunlight, like a beacon, and he searched the area as if the purple bead could call her male family members to her. He recalled the first time he had seen that pendant and its unique purple bead in Gunnar's hands, while the man told him about how much he loved this woman, this woman who walked behind him and endangered him and herself.

Bjorn stopped when they reached the edge of the marketplace and turned to Asta...Astrid. "You must go. We can never see each other again."

She blinked her lovely blue eyes in confusion. "What is happening? What did I do?" She clasped the Freya pendant as if it could protect her.

"Just go." The part of him from moments ago, when they had been alone, wanted to take her in his arms and pull her close to erase that confusion and hurt. He raised his hand to touch her face, then dropped it. The part of him that wanted to protect her was stronger than his desire, and he kept his distance. If her male kin caught her with him, she'd surely be punished. "Go."

She didn't move and he could see that she was getting ready to ask questions, questions he did not want to answer, and did not have the time to answer.

"There she is!"

"Asta!"

It was too late. He could not get away without anyone seeing him with her, and he would not run away like a thief or outlaw. Putting his hand on his sword hilt, he waited for whatever came, putting distance between Astrid and himself.

It was worse than he could have expected. Her brother, Rikki Tryggvason, the two men who had ambushed him, another man and a woman, all hurried toward them. Bjorn could not take his eyes from the one named Galm, the one who had threatened Tanni, and he felt hot anger surge through his veins. Tryggvi's son looked like he had dressed hastily, and his hair fell over his shoulders in a mess. He had dirt on his face, a cut on his chin, and an abrasion on the side of his head near his ear. He must have been wrestling and thrown down not long before someone noticed his sister had gone missing.

Tryggvi's son stopped short when he saw who stood next to his sister. He glared, and his hand reached for his sword. Bjorn's hand grasped onto his own sword even tighter. They stared at each other for a tense moment.

"What's going on? Rikki?" Astrid put her hand on her brother's arm, but he shook her off with such force that she jerked back. The woman who had come with the men hurried up to Astrid, her face set in a grim frown.

"What are you doing with *him*?" Rikki asked Astrid without breaking the stare.

Bjorn could see in her eyes the moment she realized that she had never asked him for his family name and that he had never given it. She turned to him, hurt etched in her face. "Who are you?"

The man with the hat stepped up to her, and Bjorn could see now it was the one who had tried to protect his son when the boy made his escape.

The young man's face flashed with hurt and anger. "You went off with this man not knowing who he was? How could you do that?"

"Olli, who is he?" Turning from the one called Olli before he could answer, she looked at Bjorn. "Bjorn—?" she started, but then caught herself. Her eyes grew wide, and she stumbled away from him, as if he were a snake. She pointed at him. "You are Bjorn *Alfarsson*?"

She looked like she might be sick.

He gave her the quickest of nods, before turning back to Rikki and the others. They were a threat. She was not.

"You killed my brother." Her voice was filled with so much confusion, hate, and anger on the surface that it surprised Bjorn, and then a tinge of sadness crept in as if she could not believe it. "*You* killed Jori?" She sagged, and Short Olaf reached out to steady her, but she shook him off and continued to stare at Bjorn.

Better to get this over with. He looked into her eyes deeply and said with as much detachment as he could. "*Ja*. I killed Jori Tryggvason."

"No." She shook her head. "No. That can't have been you." Her eyes pleaded with him to take back what he had said.

"It's him." Rikki said, but his voice had lost some of its edge as he noticed his sister's distress. "What did he do to you?"

"He took me riding. That's all. He was..." She let out a sob. "Kind."

Someone smirked, and they all turned toward the sound. "*Kind.*" Galm said. "He put a sword through Jori's heart. Why do we stand here talking? Kill him, Rikki."

When she heard those words, Astrid gasped, and Short Olaf stepped in. "Not in front of her!"

"Why not?" Galm asked, and he walked up to Astrid.

Bjorn's hand clenched into a fist. He did not want Galm near Astrid, and he had to hold himself back from going to her, to protect her. It would do more harm than good.

Instead, Short Olaf moved between her and Galm. "Leave her alone." He sounded deadly.

Galm shrugged and backed off, not intimidated by his friend, but not willing to fight with him either. They had a common enemy and would stand together. "She should see it done. She wants him to die." He faced Astrid. "Remember? You told Rikki to do it, to defend the family name. You told him to kill Bjorn Alfarsson. Now's your chance."

She had gone still and silent at his words. They all waited for her to speak, to do something. Her face showed an internal struggle, and in the end she gritted her teeth, and her body stood as rigid as if she'd turned to stone.

Everyone froze when Astrid took the few steps to stand in front of Bjorn. His hand still grasped his sword hilt, but he did not move it. He did not move at all, except to look down at her, waiting to see what she would do. Would she try to stab him with the knife she carried in her belt? Stand by his side against her kin? A trickle of sweat threaded its way down his back.

She met his eyes, and he drew in an involuntary breath. They were cold as ice, and it hit him in his heart, as surely as if she had stabbed him.

When she placed her hand on his chest it took him by surprise, and he recoiled as if she had hit him. He lifted his sword hand to touch hers and was about to say something when she spoke up, her voice as cold and deadly as her ice-blue eyes that no longer held kindness. "Do what you have to do, Rikki."

Bjorn stepped back from her, shocked by her deadly pronouncement.

Someone snatched her out of the way, and she fell out of his view. Bjorn reached for his sword, but his arm felt heavy, like sand filled it. No, not again. He could not have this heaviness hit him again, like it had the last time he fought young Rikki Tryggvason.

Two voices bellowed out, "Enough!" and "Stop!" at the same time. Loud voices honed from years of shouting on wind-swept ships and battlefields.

Bjorn froze and Rikki did the same, both of them trained to heed those voices.

A heavy hand came down on Bjorn's shoulder. "Not today, Bjorn," Harald said.

Across from him, Rikki dropped his arm as Tryggvi said, "Son."

The two enemies glared at each other as they held back their sons, and Bjorn recognized the same confusion on Rikki's face as he felt. Why did the old men stop them? He looked at Tryggvi, the first time he had ever seen the man up close, and found a face etched with pain and anger, his eyes flashing at Bjorn, his hand twitching by his sword. Tryggvi wanted to kill him, Bjorn could feel it wafting off of him like a hot breeze.

Harald noticed it too, for he said, "Brother" as a warning, and Bjorn felt his foster-father shift as he put his own hand on his axe.

With great effort, Tryggvi dropped his hand by his side. "Our agreement."

"*I* mean to hold by it," Harald said.

"I do as well."

Bjorn frowned. An agreement?

At that moment, the red-giant strode up and took in the situation with a discerning look. He studied everyone quickly, Bjorn and Rikki facing off, their fathers behind them, and then he turned his attention to Astrid, who had retreated. She held onto herself, as if needing to hold her body together, and Bjorn hated to see her in distress. His carelessness had caused this trouble, had caused her pain. He wanted to brush the loose strands of hair out of her face, erase the pain etched there with a kiss. But then he remembered the way she'd looked at him when she'd delivered what she thought would be his death sentence, and the need to ease her pain drained away.

The red-giant walked right up to her, put his massive hands on her arms, and bent down to look her in the eyes. "What happened, *bjarki*? Did they hurt you?" Straightening up, he looked like a bear about to tear apart its prey.

Tryggvi walked into the space between both groups and put up his hands. "Leave it, Red." He turned to Harald and Bjorn. "Go."

The big man looked at Tryggvi with confusion, but he stepped down all the same.

Bjorn hated to leave Astrid with them. He did not know what kind of father Tryggvi Olafsson was, and Bjorn hoped he would not beat Astrid for this. As he left with Harald, he gave her one last look; she stared after him, her blue, teary eyes filled with hatred and disgust.

"Meet me at my tent," Harald ordered Bjorn, and he stalked off without waiting for a reply.

It must be about the 'agreement' that Tryggvi and Harald mentioned. Curious to know what had transpired, Bjorn hurried to his own tent to collect himself before talking to Harald.

Astrid watched Bjorn walk away with his foster-father. Bjorn Alfarsson. Her brother's killer. She had a face to go with the name, and he was not the monster she had built up in her mind, not at all like she had imagined. It changed nothing. He was the enemy, and when he looked back at her, she straightened and stared back. All of her anger at what he had done to Jori, how he had tricked *her*, lured her away from the protection of her family with his pretty face and his pretty words, aimed at him like an arrow. She saw him flinch, and a spark ignited in her, the slightest flicker, that she had the power to hurt a man in a way other than fists and swords.

Footsteps sounded next to her and then her father's face loomed in front of her, his mouth set in a thin line, his jaw clenched. He took her chin in his firm hand and stared into her eyes. "What did he do to you?"

The silence of the others was so loud she wondered if they could all hear her heart beating. Her mouth went dry.

"Nothing," she croaked.

She lied. He *had* done something to her, but not what her father thought, not what he was demanding to know. Under the anger, her body remembered how safe she'd felt with Bjorn, how much she wanted to keep riding with him, how his nearness made her feel soft and warm. She felt heat rising to her cheeks.

"I don't believe you, *dottir*." Tryggvi held onto her chin for too long. "It's no matter. You are to be his, anyway."

The silence broke like a thunderclap, as Emund, Rikki, and Short Olaf cried out.

The air left her, and she grew as cold as if submerged in the river in winter.

"No."

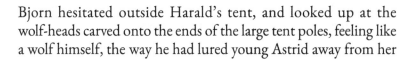

Bjorn hesitated outside Harald's tent, and looked up at the wolf-heads carved onto the ends of the large tent poles, feeling like a wolf himself, the way he had lured young Astrid away from her family. The girl had gotten under his skin, and even now that she despised him and wanted him dead, he still desired to see her, and wanted to be sure she was all right. He waited, not wanting to face Harald, but then a thrall, a tiny girl, pulled back the red wool tent cover, a basket slung over her arm. She jumped when she ran into him, and then shrank back, her head lowered.

"So sorry. I did not see you," she stammered in halting Norse.

He waved her concerns away.

"I am to—" she said in a squeaky voice as she pulled her basket closer to her body.

The thrall's eyes darted back and forth between Bjorn and the inside of the tent, like a spooked rabbit, uncertain of what to do. She must be a recent addition to Harald's household, for she looked at him as if she expected him to take her right there. The other thralls knew better.

With an exasperated sigh, for he did not have patience, Bjorn said, "Move aside." He brushed past the girl, stepped inside the hot, dark tent and found his foster-father at a table talking to Styrr.

At his entrance, Harald and Styrr both stopped talking and looked up toward him.

"Bjorn," Harald said in his deep, gravelly voice. His voice, which carried so well on board ship or during a battle, for it cut through all other noises, felt inappropriate in this small space. It was too gruff, too ferocious, like someone had let a beast in, one that meant to devour them all.

"I hear you nearly got into a fight with several of Tryggvi's men. Too bad you didn't kill them," Styrr said, but then his face broke into a nasty smile. "Caught with Tryggvi's daughter, alone. Delicious. Nothing like a ripe young virgin."

Bjorn glared at him, but Styrr was undaunted. "I hear she is beautiful. But is she as pretty as you? I bet the little virgin spread her legs for *you* willingly. Not that it matters."

Bjorn took a threatening step toward Styrr, but the other man only laughed. "You did us a favor."

Frowning, Bjorn turned to Harald. There was something they were not telling him, and he did not like to be kept waiting.

"Have a drink, son," Harald told him, and snapped for a thrall to pour Bjorn some ale.

Bjorn took the cup, downed the ale in one long drink, and then held his cup up for her to pour him another drink. Being drunk seemed like a good idea.

"Styrr is right," Harald told him. "You taking Tryggvi's daughter will work in our favor."

"Nothing happened with the girl." Something *had* happened with her, but not what they thought.

"I don't care what you did to the little cunt." Harald leaned forward, resting his arms on the table. "I have no living sons, Bjorn. You are my son, even if you are not blood."

With a sudden understanding, like the spark that ignites a fire, Bjorn knew why Harald had wanted to talk to him. The way the two old enemies had stopped him and Rikki from fighting, the 'agreement' mentioned, this talk of sons made perfect sense.

"You want me to marry Tryggvi's daughter," Bjorn said.

"*Ja.*" Harald stood up, his bulk too big for the tent, and paced over to where his shield leaned against a tent pole. "King Ingjald threatened to banish both me and Tryggvi if we do not end this feud. People have been coming to the king all summer with complaints, the small-minded peasants." He spit. "The king is not happy, and he has to deal with his own troublesome family. He suggested this marriage alliance as the best way to bring peace. You marry Tryggvi's precious daughter, and we stop the fighting."

"You have agreed?" Bjorn asked.

"I only wait for you to agree before I make it official. I will talk to Tryggvi for his daughter, on your behalf, since I am the closest you have to a father. The wedding will be in Autumnmonth."

Bjorn thought of the way Astrid had stared at him earlier, with enough hatred to knock down a horse. "She wants me dead."

"Are you afraid of a girl?" Styrr asked, scorn in his voice.

"Women may not wield swords and spears, but they have other ways. Killing me in my sleep. Poison." He leaned his elbows on his legs and swirled his drink, watching the liquid as it spun in the cup. It would be simple for a wife to kill her husband with poison; she was in charge of the brewing and food. Simple, but not easy. It is no easy thing to kill a man when you are not trained to do it. His thoughts returned to Astrid as she had been when they rode together, the way she had clung to him even when she did not need to, the way her eyes lit up when he smiled at her. If he married her, would that affection win out over the anger she felt over her brother? He did not blame her for her hatred; he had felt the same thing once.

Harald's hand clasped his shoulder. "Her anger is no concern. Keep her on her back with her legs spread, and she won't have time to plot." He barked a laugh. "Once she's thick with your child, she will forget about her blood feud with you."

"It shouldn't take long," Styrr laughed. "You already have two children and who knows how many more out there..." He waved his hand toward the tent flap to encompass the outside world. "We know you are able."

Bjorn gritted his teeth to not punch Styrr in his leering face. This was different, this girl was different. He looked at Harald, who had put up his hand to silence Styrr.

"You and Tryggvi could stop fighting," Bjorn told him.

Harald sniffed and picked up his battle axe, running his hand along the blade to check for nicks. "I do not trust Tryggvi. The only way he will stop fighting me is if we hold his daughter's life in our hands. Even better, if his daughter's *son's* life is at risk."

"I'll marry her," Styrr blurted, a nasty gleam in his eyes. "Then Tryggvi will have good cause to worry."

Both Harald and Bjorn jerked to attention and stared at him. Bjorn's limbs turned to ice, like someone had doused him with a bucket of cold water. They stared at Styrr for a long moment, and Bjorn saw the eagerness in the other man's eyes. He understood then that Styrr had wanted him to balk, to come up with a reason to not marry the girl. He wanted her for himself, that's why he had been asking about her, how he knew she was beautiful. The thought made Bjorn feel sick.

"No," Harald said finally, "as much as I'd like to see the look on my brother's face when I threw his daughter to one of my men..." He and Styrr shared wolfish smiles. "...it has to be Bjorn. He's the only one with enough status to *appease* Tryggvi."

No matter how much she despised him, Bjorn could not allow Astrid to fall into the hands of Styrr and Harald. If at all possible, Styrr treated women with even more disdain than Harald.

"I'll do it," Bjorn said. He finished his drink and slammed the cup on the table. "I will marry Astrid Tryggvisdottir."

Chapter Twenty-four

"Asta, how could you go off with a man you do not know?" Short Olaf shouted, again.

She grew tired of his outrage, but bit back a retort. It would do no good, and she *had* been in the wrong. She faced Short Olaf, Galm, and Rikki; Dyri had taken Ragnhild back to their tent, saying that Rikki needed to talk to Astrid, as was his duty as her brother. The three men looked bigger than normal, hulking around her, asking questions she did not want to answer. All she wanted was to retreat to the tent and crawl under the blankets, hide away from everyone. But she understood she had to face her family. She had made the choice to go off with Bjorn, and she had to suffer the consequences.

"Was he so handsome you couldn't resist?" Galm added. "They call him *Pretty* Bjorn." His voice dripped with scorn.

Rikki rounded on them both. "I will talk to Asta alone."

Galm opened his mouth to say something more, but Rikki grabbed the front of his tunic. His knuckles were white, but his tone was clear. "Not another word. She is my *systir*."

The fierce protectiveness of his words made Astrid want to sink to her knees. What had she done? What was she going to have to do?

Wresting Rikki's hand from his tunic, Galm said, with a tone that could freeze water, "Harald and his men are our enemies. *All* of them." He glared at Astrid, then back at Rikki. "Don't forget. Harald killed my father."

"I have not forgotten," Rikki said, bristling at Galm's tone.

"No marriage will make that go away. I will not forget. I will not forgive." He stepped away from Rikki and lifted his axe, running a finger along the blade, and he grew agitated.

Astrid watched him uneasily.

"There is only one thing we should give Harald Olafsson and Bjorn Alfarsson. It is not your *systir*. It is this." He slammed his axe into a tree.

Astrid jumped at the ferocity, and Rikki stepped in front of her. Galm hit the tree again. One strike for each man. When he pulled the axe out the last time, he was breathing hard. He rounded on Astrid. "Don't do it, Asta. Don't agree to marry him. He is our enemy. He is *your* enemy."

"Galm..." Short Olaf stepped forward with his hands out like he would to calm his horse.

"*Laesa*, Shortie." Galm pointed his axe head at Short Olaf. "Don't try to fix this like you always do. They need killing. That's it."

Knocking the axe head out of his face, Short Olaf spat back. "I know that."

"You've wanted her for as long as I can remember, Shortie. Now is the time to do something."

"Not like this," Short Olaf said, and he looked at Astrid. "I don't trust her now."

His words hit her like a physical blow. She deserved it. But then, what did she owe Short Olaf? He was not her brother, not her husband. It was not his place to question her actions. Except that he had been like a brother to her, and she knew she owed him more than she wanted to admit.

She stepped forward, so she was next to her brother. His body was tense, ready to fight both Galm and Short Olaf if he had to.

"Go," she told them. "I want to talk to my brother. This is not your concern."

They looked at Rikki, but he did not answer them. Instead, he gestured to Astrid.

"I said go," she repeated more forcefully. Like a jarl's daughter.

Galm and Short Olaf exchanged a surprised look. Galm held up his axe and said, "Bjorn is still out there. We can take care of this now." They moved to leave.

"Father said to leave him alone," Rikki told him.

Galm snorted. "Your father. Tryggvi grows old. He will not be in this world much longer. Who will lead us then? The man who avenges the deaths of his family and his Brothers? Or the man who uses women to get what he wants?"

"What are you saying?" Rikki's eyes narrowed.

"There are other jarls and chieftains here." He waved his axe in the air, encompassing the entire assembly at the Thing.

Short Olaf inhaled sharply. Rikki tensed.

"You are oath-bound to my father."

"I am."

"My father is a generous ring-giver." He pointed to the rings Galm wore on his arm and neck. "He is a great warrior, known all over the land for his battle prowess."

"Tryggvi has been all of those things. But does he still have the will to fight? To avenge those who have been killed?"

"Are you calling my father a coward?" Rikki said, his voice so low it made Astrid think of a dog about to bite.

He moved so quickly that Astrid felt him as a rush of air, and then he was on Galm, taking him by surprise as he wrapped him up by the waist and took him down, Galm's axe falling out of his hand. Rikki punched Galm in the face before he could react, but Galm was strong and moved to the side before the next punch landed, and he hit Rikki on the side of the head. He used the momentum to scramble out from under Rikki. While Rikki righted himself, Galm kicked him in the side.

Astrid started to say something when Short Olaf stopped her. "Let them do this."

After what felt like ages, Rikki and Galm faced off, both breathing heavily, stumbling, their faces bruised and cut, their clothes torn.

"My father...is no...coward," Rikki said, and he wiped sweat out of his eye.

"He is not doing...what needs to be done."

The fight had gone out of them both, and Galm rested his hands on his knees and took in a gasping breath, wincing as he did so. Astrid waited for Rikki to defend her father some more, but he remained silent, watching his friend.

"Help me, Rikki. Help me avenge my father. Jori. Our Brothers."

Silence hung over them all.

"Buri...Thorkell the Steersman..." Rikki added.

"Erik Ale-Lover. Olvir Bent Leg." Short Olaf released Astrid and joined his friends, and the three of them clasped arms. "Our lost Brothers."

They continued to call out the names of men, their brothers-in-arms, whom they had lost in fights with Harald Olafsson.

So strongly she could not resist, Astrid joined another name to theirs. "Sitha."

They turned to her, startled, as if they had forgotten she was there. "Sitha," she said louder. For a moment they looked like they did not know what she was saying. "Emund's wife."

She continued walking into their circle, naming the *women* who had died in raids, while Rikki and the others watched her, silenced. When she finished with the women killed, she kept going, her voice growing stronger as she named all the women who still lived but did so without their husbands or sons. "Amma. Lufja."

"Gytha." Short Olaf's voice was soft.

A knot formed in Astrid's stomach. Gytha. Her sweet sister who had never been the same since the summer when Harald raided their village.

"Gytha," Astrid and Rikki repeated together. She was by her brother's side now, and he laid his arm across her shoulder and pulled her to him.

"Harald and Bjorn are the enemy," Galm said.

They all agreed, but in calling out Gytha's name, Astrid felt a stirring, a tugging at her heart, that she needed to do what she could to help and protect her sister. Her mother's words came back to her, that she was afraid the feud would take away all of her children, like a blazing fire left unchecked. With her brother's arm heavy on her shoulders, with the smell of blood still clinging to him, Astrid knew she had to make a decision. She just didn't know which one was the right one.

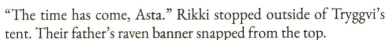

"The time has come, Asta." Rikki stopped outside of Tryggvi's tent. Their father's raven banner snapped from the top.

She felt her knees weaken and dread washed over her. On the walk over, she had thought about what she would tell her father. She thought of her sister. After the attack on their village by Harald, Gytha had gone in search of her pets, only to come across the body of one of Harald's men, a big man, his skull cleaved in two, and a local farmer, eviscerated. Ravens pecked at the men's eyes and other soft spots. Astrid could still hear her sister's horrified screams that did not stop even after their mother carried her away, thrashing, from the carnage. If marriage with Bjorn would help protect Gytha from ever having that happen again, Astrid would do it. But then, every time she looked at Bjorn, she knew she'd see the man who killed Jori. How could she live with that every day? That the sight of Bjorn made her heart flip did not help her decide. It made everything worse. She nearly groaned out loud in her confusion.

Rikki turned to face her. "I will be by your side."

The words took Astrid back to a day when she had wanted to play with the foal of one of her father's best mares and let it out of the stable, only to get distracted, which allowed the foal to wander off. The foal was not hurt, but their father was furious with Astrid, and she ran away to hide in the woods rather than face his wrath. Rikki found her and brought her back by promising to stand by her side. He did, and knowing that he would be there with her had made her braver.

"Wait," she told him. She unbound the large braid in her hair, ran a hand through it, and then redid it neatly. She straightened her dress and refastened one of the brooches that held on her apron. It had jiggled loose when riding with Bjorn.

When she finished collecting herself, Astrid gave her brother a once over. He had bruises and abrasions on his face and arms, and the imprint of a boot on the side of his tunic.

"You've looked better."

"I've looked worse too."

He shrugged and stuck his head in the tent flap. He was about to ask permission to enter when Tryggvi waved him in. Giving his sister a quick wink, Rikki disappeared inside the tent.

When he closed the flap, Astrid heard Emund ask, "What happened to you?"

"Galm." He gave no more explanation and neither Emund nor her father pushed.

A long moment passed. She absently picked up the hem of her dress and picked at the corner, watching as two women, likely farmer's wives from the plainness of their dresses, walked by talking. What they said Astrid could not hear, but one lifted her head and laughed loudly. Astrid felt a pang of envy at the simplicity of their lives. She'd wager her father's sword neither one of those women had to marry her worst enemy.

The sound of a cup hitting a wooden table brought her attention back.

"Astrid is outside," Rikki told his father and Emund, his voice betraying no emotion.

"Get her," Tryggvi said.

When she entered the tent, her father and Emund had their heads together and talked in low voices. Her father's blue eyes flashed at her, as if he wanted to say something, but then he stepped back at a nod from Emund, who approached Astrid like she was a skittish horse about to bolt. She stood straight and tall and did not flinch. She was glad she had tidied her clothes and fixed her hair.

Rikki moved to stand by her, and a pang hit Astrid's heart that they needed to stand together against Emund. He had always been her protector.

Without a word, Emund led her to sit down on the bench. He had to duck his head to keep it from hitting the top of the tent. The feel of his big callused hand encasing her small one assaulted her with memories of when she was a little girl. But she was not that girl anymore, and as soon as they sat down she slipped her hand from his grasp. He grunted as if she had hit him.

"Asta," he said as gently as he could.

"Don't do it, Red," Rikki spoke up, looking from their father to Emund. "Not you, too."

Astrid could sense how hard this was for Emund, but she did not care. He was not the one being asked to spend his life with the enemy.

Rikki's hand went to his sword hilt, the sword their father had given him. "Bjorn needs to die, not put in a marriage bed with Asta. Father, let me kill him now."

"Rikki, stop," Astrid said. The power in her voice surprised even her, and Rikki stopped. Everyone went still.

Emund took the opportunity and said to Tryggvi and Rikki. "Let me talk to Astrid alone."

When they assented and left, he turned to her, his face soft and caring, but before he spoke, she spat out. "*You* want me to marry Bjorn Alfarsson?"

"Aye." He paused, as if unsure of what to say. "*Bjarki*—"

"Don't." She held up her hands and shook her head. "You too will tell me to marry Bjorn Alfarsson. You would make me share a bed with...have children with..." Her emotions had taken hold, and she stuttered. "The man who *killed Jori*."

He reached for her hand, but she snatched it away. "Your father is right, *bjarki*—"

The pet name was too much. She jumped to her feet and moved away from him. "Don't call me that. Not anymore. You said you would always fight for me. You have not kept your word."

Emund flinched, and he no longer looked like a mighty warrior, but a man hurt by a woman. What had been unleashed when she had turned on Bjorn flickered again within her. She had the power to hurt this man as she had with Bjorn. It gave her courage. She crossed to the table and picked up a cup, although she did not fill it. What she wanted to do was fling it at Emund's head.

"Astrid." He said her birth name slowly. "Do you think your mother is a wise woman?"

The mention of her mother took her by surprise and she set the cup back down. Blinking off her confusion, she said, "I do. Why?"

He took in a deep breath and started to stand, but then lowered himself back down. Astrid was glad. She would have more courage without him towering over her.

"Before we left, Ingiborg came to me and asked that I do whatever I could to ensure her children not carry on this fight between Tryggvi and Harald."

"Did she know…?" If her mother had betrayed her to the enemy too, Astrid did not know if she could stand it. Why was she to be the sacrifice to right all the wrongs her father and Harald had created? Her body coursed with anger, and she balled her hands up into fists to keep from throwing something.

He nodded. "I think she and your father had planned something like this marriage." He rose slowly, and in the movement he looked like the old warrior he was, one who had seen many battles. A lump formed in Astrid's throat as she watched what he would do. He hefted a shield, the strap too small for his arm, and stood in front of Astrid.

"That's Rikki's shield," she said.

"Your father and Harald hate each other and will not stop fighting, not until one or both of them breathe their last breaths. Your brother hates Bjorn Alfarsson as much and continues on the blood feud."

"As is right," she reminded him.

"Aye."

Something in his voice made her bite back what she was going to say. She put her hand on the shield and traced the raven's wings. Her brother's wild energy flowed from the raven and into her fingers. Something called to her from it, and her way became clearer.

Emund continued, "He is wild with his anger. Reckless. I will be honest with you, Astrid. He will not live much longer if this feud continues. I do not know what would happen to your father if he were killed. Rikki is strong and fast but—"

"I know," she blurted out, not wanting him to finish the thought. "I know what you would say. I am the shield."

"Aye. You can be the shield that protects your brother, your sister. Everyone."

She placed her palm down on the cool wood that Rikki had so carefully crafted and painted. "What if the shield is too heavy for me to carry?"

At that moment Tryggvi ducked into the tent, his eyes quickly taking in the scene. Rikki followed right behind him. "Enough talking." Tryggvi moved to stand before Astrid. "Give me your answer."

Despite the three men waiting for her decision, Astrid turned her back on them and slowly removed the Freya necklace. A ray of sunlight filtered into the tent through the flap, and she held the pendant up to it, the purple bead catching the light, throwing off sparks. She rotated the pendant in the light, and as she did so she imagined the faces of her loved ones. Then, without warning, she heard Bjorn's voice, the way it softened when he spoke of his children, and she saw a picture in her mind of two little blond-haired babies that looked like him. A marriage to Bjorn would also protect *his* children from this blood feud. Could she bear the burden? Bear the shield? She would have to be with the man who killed her brother, who had a hand in killing men like Buri and Thorkell, leaving behind grieving widows and children. She had been there by Amma's side when the men had returned, and Buri was not with them. Astrid had felt the cries of grief, as if they had been her own.

When Bjorn touched her would she see the hand that drove a sword through her brother's heart? When he talked to her, would she hear the battle cry that terrified her so much when she was a girl it froze her in her tracks? Would she hear Gytha's screams when she saw the carnage left from Harald's raid, a raid that Bjorn was a part of? If she did not marry him, they would continue to fight, and more people would die. She glanced at Rikki as he waited for her to decide. He wanted her to refuse. He ached for a chance to fight with Bjorn again, to kill him, but she did not think she could endure the death of another brother. If her father and Harald kept up the feud, they would be banished, and it would tear apart her whole world.

Palming the pendant and bead, Astrid closed her eyes and asked Freya to guide her. An image of Rikki's shield flashed in her mind before quickly dissolving away like ashes. In its place, she saw the blanket she had woven as part of her marriage gift, the different colors, and separate threads at first, wove in and out until they became a complete blanket, with nothing to distinguish the threads from each another. It was not as a shield, something to hold up as a barrier between the bearer and the enemy, but as a *weaver* that she could protect everyone. She could weave the two families together. She opened her eyes and turned back to her father.

"I will marry Bjorn Alfarsson."

Rikki made a movement toward her. She caught his eye and held it, pleading with him to understand why she had chosen this path. He clenched his jaw, and she knew he wanted to tell her no, but after a brief struggle with himself, he nodded.

"You have done what is best for our family," Tryggvi said.

"I have." She slowly returned the pendant to her neck and tucked it under her dress, so that its warmth touched her bare skin. Whether it would be best for her would remain to be seen.

Chapter Twenty-five

A rivulet of sweat trickled down Bjorn's back as he listened to the law speaker recite the laws of the land. Thorgny Thorgnyson was known as the wisest man in the land, and probably the oldest, Bjorn thought, as he watched the ancient man lift his arms along with his voice, so it would carry over all the men at the council. Even old and blind, Thorgny had a loud, clear voice, honed over so many council meetings that Bjorn's father's father might have heard him.

King Ingjald sat on a high-seat, the wood oiled to a brown so dark it shone in the sun as black as onyx, while the king wore his finest red tunic with gold trim, gold and silver rings inlaid with jewels circling his arms and fingers. Several of his *hird* lined up behind him, fully armed, their hands firmly on their spears. Surrounding the king, sitting in a circle, so that no man could be put above another, were the jarls and chieftains of the land, Harald among them. The jarls were so colorfully dressed, they looked like the peacocks Bjorn had seen once at a menagerie in the east. The chieftains and their men who stood behind them, all dressed in their finest, most costly, tunics and armor, all to display the chieftain's wealth and power. As Harald's closest men, Bjorn and Styrr stood behind him, ready for anything should it happen. If only he could protect himself against the boredom.

More sweat trickled down Bjorn's neck, and he resisted the urge to wipe it away. The late summer sun burned down on the council meeting; the dark rock outcropping where they held the Thing radiated heat. It was so still, even King Ingjald's banners flopped limply on their masts. As the law speaker continued on, Bjorn eyed Rikki Tryggvason, who stood on the opposite side of the circle as him. He couldn't get the image out of his mind of how Rikki had ambushed him when he was with his son. He had

wanted to call out Rikki to a *holmgang*, hoping to end this feud with one-on-one combat, but he had promised Harald that he would not. King Ingjald must have really threatened Harald and Tryggvi to make them so amenable to his wishes.

The law speaker finished reciting the laws, and he called forth the first dispute for himself and the king to mediate. Two farmers stepped into the circle and faced King Ingjald, Thorgny Thorgnyson at his side. Both farmers appeared nervous at being before the king, but, as free men, they knew he would hear and treat them fairly. The first farmer's thrall had been caught trying to steal a sheep from the other farmer's field and had been killed for the attempted theft. The thrall's owner claimed he had no knowledge of the thrall's actions and demanded the other farmer pay him for his lost property. King Ingjald awarded him the nominal compensation for the thrall as lost property. The price was not high, and both men went away satisfied.

More disputes were presented before King Ingjald and law speaker Thorgny as the day wore on, and they handled the disputes with fairness.

"Will this never end?" Bjorn muttered, shifting from side to side, his body thrumming with pent up energy. He did not like standing still for so long.

Styrr snickered and muttered his own agreement.

"One of you might sit here one day," Harald said, although his voice belied his own weariness at the long proceedings.

Bjorn and Styrr straightened and stared at each other. Something flickered in Styrr's eyes, like a predator seeing prey, then he grinned.

"Or..." Harald laughed. "Even better. Bjorn will sit in Tryggvi's seat."

Bjorn looked over at Tryggvi, who had turned his gaze to Harald. He glared at them, and if it had been possible to freeze with a stare, they would have been turned to ice. Behind Tryggvi stood the red-giant and Rikki Tryggvason. When their eyes met across the circle, Bjorn's fingers twitched, wanting a weapon in them. Rikki did the same, his gaze darting to the circle, daring Bjorn, calling him out.

"Bjorn." Harald's voice cut through. He leaned in. "Once you *take* the daughter, you kill the son." He let out a bark of laughter before noticing that the sound of voices talking, and the clink of weapons had stopped.

Law speaker Thorgny had walked into the middle of the circle again.

"I well remember Olaf Haraldsson. He was a powerful chieftain and warlord who hosted hundreds of men and a fleet of twenty ships. He ravaged the coasts. Olaf Haraldsson fathered two sons, mighty warriors both."

At this, the household guards of both Tryggvi and Harald, who remained outside of the circle, proclaimed 'Tryggvi' and 'Harald'.

"Mighty warriors, yes. But they have ravaged the lands and people that King Ingjald, son of King Anund Hringsson, has sworn to protect. Free men from all over the land have traveled many leagues through harsh land and much peril to bring their grievances before the King. Grievances about Harald Olafsson and Tryggvi Olafsson. We have brought these brothers before this assembly to settle the dispute and to return peace to their lands and people."

With this, Thorgny called Tryggvi and Harald to step into the circle.

King Ingjald rose slowly and approached the two chieftains. "Harald Olafsson and Tryggvi Olafsson, you have disturbed the peace in my kingdom. No more. You will either submit to my judgment." He paused. "Or I will banish you from these lands forever."

A hiss went through the crowd. Banishment was a harsh punishment. The law speaker lifted his arms, and the crowd quieted again to hear what he had to say.

King Ingjald spoke again. "I have proposed a marriage between the two families to settle this with no more bloodshed to my people and destruction to my lands. With this marriage, Harald Olafsson and Tryggvi Olafsson have agreed to cease their fighting."

King Ingjald nodded to Bjorn. "With no living sons of his own, Harald has spoken for his foster-son Bjorn, son of Alfar, son of Bjorn, to ask for Tryggvi's eldest daughter Astrid in marriage. Tryggvi has agreed to the joining and Astrid Tryggvisdottir has given her approval. The marriage will take place this Autumnmonth at Storelva and at Tryggvi's expense."

Bjorn felt the movement and muttering from Rikki and Gunnar at the king's words. It was almost worth the marriage to see how much Rikki hated it. Bjorn stared at him and turned his mouth up in a cruel smile. Let him think the worst.

After it was all over, King Ingjald left the circle, his men flanking him. The jarls and chieftains made their way back to their own camps; much of their talk was about the marriage between Bjorn and Astrid.

Rikki approached him. "This is not over. Astrid may be forced to marry you, but I have not agreed to anything."

With a laugh, Harald swatted his hand toward Rikki. "What you do means nothing to me."

Red-Beard put a big, heavy hand on Rikki's shoulder as if to hold him down.

Rikki glanced down at Emund's hand on his shoulder. "I will abide by what my father, my jarl, has arranged, but I will be ready. If you..." He got closer to Bjorn, his blue eyes, so much like Astrid's, burning with hatred, "hurt Astrid in *any* way, I will be there."

Emund relaxed his grip and laughed. He made a slashing motion with his huge hand. "If Bjorn hurts Astrid, I will be there by your side, Rikolf. He will feel the bite of my axe across his pretty neck."

"That would be too quick," Rikki added.

"Aye." Red eyed Bjorn, his eyes glittering with menace. "We'll have to take apart his pretty face first."

They both walked away before Bjorn could say anything.

He felt Harald behind him. "Red," he spat. "He is Tryggvi's dog, doing what his master tells him to do. He will do nothing to you." His hand gripped Bjorn's shoulder hard. "Tryggvi's daughter will soon be yours, and you can do whatever you want with her."

Bjorn watched Tryggvi Olafsson as the man, his soon to be father-by-law, left the tent. They had made the marriage announcement in front of witnesses and worked out the private arrangements, and Bjorn would wed Astrid Tryggvisdottir in Autumn-month in Storelva.

He thought about the way she'd turned him over to her brother, knowing well that one of them would die. It was a brave thing to do, standing up to him. He smiled as he remembered how fierce she had been; he had been as eager for vengeance once. He could respect that fierceness, except he'd have to be wary around her, at least at first.

"Tryggvi's daughter is ripe for the plucking," Harald said as he sat back down with a grunt. "She's almost as pretty as you!"

Harald slapped Bjorn on the back so hard he nearly toppled off the bench. With his other hand, Harald signaled his thrall to him. "You should be able to get her with child with no problem. Be enjoyable too..." The thrall approached, and Harald grabbed her hand and yanked her into his lap. He grabbed her breasts. "I had a mistress once who was so ugly I usually rutted with her from behind, in the dark. But she did anything I demanded without talking, so I kept her. Women don't need to talk." He gave the young thrall a long, hard look. "They just need to open their legs."

The girl's face had a gray tinge to it. It made Bjorn feel sick, but there was nothing he could do for the unfortunate girl. Harald was a powerful man, and she was a slave. That was the way the world worked.

"The marriage to Astrid is a suitable match," Bjorn said, refusing to rise to Harald's bait.

From the other side of the table, Styrr asked, "Still worried she'll try to kill you?" He had his hungry gaze on the girl with Harald when he spoke.

Bjorn shrugged. "I will sleep with one eye open."

Harald took his attention away from the girl he was groping. "Tryggvi's daughter had some spirit. I thought she would gut you with her knife."

"She pulled a knife on you?" Styrr asked, eyebrows raised in disbelief, finally taking his eyes off the girl.

"No." Bjorn gave Harald a pointed look. "She never pulled it out—"

"She looked ready to."

"Pretty Bjorn stabbed by an angry woman. It would surprise no one," Styrr said.

Bjorn propped his elbows on the table. "Astrid has good reason to gut me. I did kill her brother."

"You've killed many brothers, Bjorn. Fathers, husbands, sons." Harald pointed at Bjorn, a cup in his hand. "That girl's father and brothers have done the same. Tryggvi has left wives without husbands, sisters without brothers."

"I don't think that matters to Astrid. She will only know that *I* killed Jorund."

"In that case, have a thrall test your food before you eat and your brew before you drink," Styrr told him with a chuckle, his greedy gaze back on Harald's thrall.

"You want her so much, you can have her," Harald told Styrr, removing the girl from his lap and shoving her toward Styrr. "She's too skinny, anyway."

Getting to his feet, Bjorn finished his drink and banged his cup on the table.

"Where are you going?" Harald asked him, a frown creasing his weathered face.

"I have someone to see."

It was a lie. He needed to get away from them. He threw the tent flap aside and stepped out into a bright summer day. A cool breeze blew in from the lake, a welcome respite from the warmth and closeness of the tent.

As he walked, he was more aware than ever of the covert stares of the younger women and thralls and the sometimes outright stares of the married women and 'camp women'. Normally the looks washed over him, and the only acknowledgment was an occasional smile aimed at a pretty girl; he liked to see the pink blush that rose to their cheeks, the way their eyes widened and then fell to the ground, the flickering shy smiles. This time he did not smile at a shy young girl who peeked up at him under her lashes, nor did he nod to her mother who stared openly at him.

Out of the corner of his eye he saw a familiar form and turned to see two of Astrid's companions making their way through a group of people with meat pies in their hands. The young woman carried two, and Bjorn suspected the extra one was for Astrid. An idea came to him. He hurried to a copse of trees where he'd seen a few Freya's flowers and picked some, then ran back to the main square, glimpsing Astrid's companion as she turned at one of the merchant stalls and headed toward the strip of land along the shoreline where the jarls had their tents pitched. Bjorn followed the man and woman until they entered a modest tent set up next to a large red and black striped one with a raven banner flying from the tent pole. The big one must be Tryggvi's. Bjorn paused, not wanting to encounter Tryggvi, his giant right-hand man, and especially not Rikki.

Two soft, feminine voices carried outside the tent, one of them Astrid's. Bjorn rapped on the heavy wool, took a deep breath, and stepped back. The voices stopped. The man pulled back the flap and could not hide his surprise at seeing Bjorn.

"What do you want?"

Bjorn was not expecting a warm welcome, but the coldness in the man's voice took him back. He gripped the flower stalk so hard he bent it, and regretted his decision to come here, but he would not back down.

"I am here to see my future wife."

"That's not a good idea. Better to keep apart until the wedding." The man folded his arms over his chest and leaned in close enough for only Bjorn to hear. "Tryggvi has ordered no harm come to you, but if it were not for that, I would run you through. My spear is right here." He gripped the spear that leaned next to the flap and showed Bjorn enough of it to make his meaning perfectly clear.

"Then I must thank Tryggvi." Bjorn smoothed his tunic. "This is a new tunic. I'd hate to get blood on it."

The man scowled at him.

"It's all right, Dyri. I will see him." Astrid appeared at the man's side, her blond hair loose and looking so soft, Bjorn longed to run his hands through it. Her face was flushed from the heat, making her glow with youth. But her eyes were cold.

Dyri disappeared inside. Astrid said nothing and stared into the distance, waiting for Bjorn to talk. The smell of the meat pies wafted out, the aroma making him hungry.

"Will you sit with me?" Bjorn gestured to a bench nearby.

They sat, and Astrid kept herself as far from him as she could get without falling off the end. When she saw the flowers, she raised her eyebrows and said, "It is late for Freya's Hair to bloom." As soon as the words were out, she closed her mouth tight, as if privately chastising herself for speaking to him.

"It is. A good omen for our marriage." He offered them to her.

She kept her hands firmly locked together in her lap. If she held a bird, she would have crushed it to death. "I do not want them."

He felt like a fool sitting there with his hand outstretched, flowers hanging in the air. Coming to her was a mistake. Seeing Harald and Styrr with that thrall had made him feel a tug on his heart for Astrid, a tenderness and protectiveness he'd never realized he possessed. Unfortunately, he'd let that emotion carry him here, to her. To this woman who wanted him dead. He needed to leave and to tamp down any feelings he had toward her.

Astrid stood, the abruptness taking him by surprise. "If you mean to flatter me, it won't work. Do you think flowers will make me forget you killed my brother?"

"We are to be married. Whether we like it or not." His voice sounded cold now. He rose, but she took a step back, as if he meant to hurt her. He dropped his hands to his sides.

With a narrowing and flashing of her bright eyes, she said, "I know that, Bjorn Alfarsson. But it is nothing more than a transaction. Trading me for peace between my father and your foster-father. So be it. That is all it is. All I want it to be."

"If that is your wish."

"It is."

He could agree to that and hardened his own voice. "I will not bother you again. I leave with Harald when the tides turn in our favor."

He waited for her to say 'safe journey' or something, anything, but she remained silent, and he laughed to himself. She was most likely praying that he be taken down to Ran's hall, drowned and captured in the sea goddess's net.

He walked away from her tent and her harsh words. When he came to a path that led to the water, he took it until he saw a jumble of rocks that jutted out over the water. He climbed onto them, and when he got to the one farthest overhanging one, he tossed the flowers into the lake. Bjorn watched them as they floated on the surface until the petals became so waterlogged they sank beneath the surface, the deep purple turning black as they disappeared into the depths.

Astrid did not want him or his offering of peace. He remembered how her arms felt as she clutched onto him when they'd let Grani have his head, and how she had not let go even when she no longer needed him to steady her. But whatever that had been, she buried beneath hatred and anger. The thought of a woman's arms around him spurred him to leave behind the flowers, and his feet took him toward King Ingjald's camp. If Astrid Tryggvisdottir would not give him what he desired, he knew a woman who would.

With a contented sigh, Bjorn rolled off Selime and ran his hands through his hair to get it out of his face. He closed his eyes and enjoyed the feeling of relaxation that flooded through his body.

After a long moment of silence, Selime spoke up. "Bjorn."

He did not want to talk.

She rested her hand on his chest, but he pushed it away, sitting up to fetch his trousers.

"Take me with you. Buy me from Ingjald."

As he pulled on his clothes, he thought of Astrid and how she'd pushed him away. Turning back to Selime, he saw the look of longing, even passion, and he hesitated. He would not get this from Astrid. She hated him. He should buy Selime and keep her for himself.

She ran her hands over his back, wrapping them around his chest, pressing her breasts onto his bare skin. "Please, Bjorn." She accentuated the way she said 'bee-oorn,' knowing he liked it.

He stood so abruptly Selime fell back onto the pallet. An image of Astrid invaded his mind, as she was when he first saw her, breathless, shoeless, standing on the pier, waiting for him to finish his swimming race, her hair loose and blowing in the sea breeze. A lump formed in his chest, and he pushed it down.

"I will marry in Autumnmonth."

Selime gave him a husky laugh as she lay back, running a hand over her body. "So?"

It shouldn't matter. He could have as many women as he wanted. Harald did. He had a wife, but since Bjorn had been in his household, Harald had gone through so many mistresses, sometimes several at once, it was impossible to keep track.

Somehow it mattered to him. His wife was to be his for his whole life. His mind went to the happy marriage between his mother and father. With a sigh, he reminded himself his wife-to-be had made it clear that to her this marriage was an arrangement between their two fathers, and she would not bring any love or affection to the joining. He felt the pressure of Astrid's hand on his chest when she had discovered who he was and given her brother permission to kill him. It felt like a heavy stone pressing down on him. He would find no love with his wife.

Selime looked so tempting, like ripe fruit ready for picking. He looked at her hungrily, and when she saw it, she smiled, her hazel eyes flashing in triumph. She reached out for him.

"Come to me, Bjorn. I can please you. You are a man..." With that she eyed his growing hardness, licking her lips. "Men can do what they want."

Instead of Selime lying before him, he saw Astrid. He thought of his children, who he would make safe by this marriage alliance.

He turned away from Selime. "No."

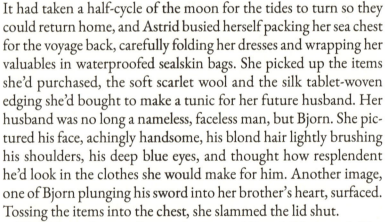

It had taken a half-cycle of the moon for the tides to turn so they could return home, and Astrid busied herself packing her sea chest for the voyage back, carefully folding her dresses and wrapping her valuables in waterproofed sealskin bags. She picked up the items she'd purchased, the soft scarlet wool and the silk tablet-woven edging she'd bought to make a tunic for her future husband. Her husband was no long a nameless, faceless man, but Bjorn. She pictured his face, achingly handsome, his blond hair lightly brushing his shoulders, his deep blue eyes, and thought how resplendent he'd look in the clothes she would make for him. Another image, one of Bjorn plunging his sword into her brother's heart, surfaced. Tossing the items into the chest, she slammed the lid shut.

The flap on the tent fluttered open, and Ragnhild entered. The sounds of people packing up their tents and goods and preparing to leave grew louder with the flap open. "Do you need any help?"

A horn blew and Ragnhild stopped to listen.

"Dyri said Harald leaves today," Ragnhild told Astrid. "That might be them."

"Ran can take them to her hall. All of them," Astrid choked out, but as soon as she said it, she thought of Bjorn again. The way his face glowed with love when he talked of his children. It was too much. She wanted to scream.

"That would solve your problem." Ragnhild glanced around the tent to see if Astrid had missed anything. When she moved, she winced and placed her hand low on her abdomen.

"Ragna?"

"What?" She looked down at her hands and let out a nervous laugh. "I'm fine. Just a little cramp."

"I'm taking you to a midwife."

"It's nothing. It happens."

Astrid took Ragnhild by the arm and pulled her outside. She had seen some healer's stalls, but people had been leaving for days, and she wasn't sure if any midwives would still be around. Taking the lead, Astrid led her friend past the docks where the massive longships moored, men crawling all over as they loaded up the boats with their sea chests and weapons and checked the sail, rigging, and lines. Above all the shouts and laughter, she heard Emund's unmistakable deep voice as he called orders to her father's men.

Once past the docks, a flash of red out on the water caught her eye, and she turned to see dragon ships with red sails speeding across the water. Against the blue of the water and green of the surrounding islands, the sails looked like gashes of blood. A wolf-head banner flapped from the mast of the biggest ship, and a jolt of fear hit Astrid before she remembered that Harald and her father were at peace. All because of her.

Ragnhild noticed her pause, and she stopped walking to watch the fleet pull away. "I suppose Bjorn is on one of those." Her voice was soft and hesitant. The subject of Bjorn was a tricky one.

Squinting her eyes to see better, Astrid searched for his golden hair, but they were too far away. All the bodies looked the same from the distance. With a glance at the nearly cloudless sky, Astrid said. "I feel like the gods are playing with me."

"A cruel trick if they are."

"Do you want to know the worst part?"

Ragnhild turned to her, but Astrid kept her gaze on the longships as they disappeared on the horizon.

"When I went riding with Bjorn…" she hesitated when she heard Ragnhild's intake of breath. "I enjoyed it. He was gentle and kind. At one point I thought maybe the goddess had sent him to me." She smiled, embarrassed.

"That complicates things."

Tearing her gaze from the ships, Astrid looked her friend in the eyes. "It felt so very good to be with him. How can that be? How can that man have killed Jori? How can he be the enemy?"

"He is not the enemy anymore. He will be your husband."

Astrid sucked in a deep breath. "I know. For my entire life Harald Olafsson has been our enemy. He has killed my father's men. He has attacked our village. He killed Buri! Bjorn Alfarsson has been a part of that killing. Am I supposed to put that all aside? I don't know if I can."

"Do you remember when you told me and your mother that you would marry who you were told to marry, but you would not love him?"

"Yes."

"You do that now."

Astrid hated having her words thrown back at her, but she knew Ragnhild was right. She had consented to marry Bjorn Alfarsson; there was no reason she would have to forget what he had done. No reason to love him. Except…another image of him came up, of the way he'd shared his memory of hiding from his father's wife, the longing in his tone when he'd talked about running away, the way he'd keenly seen her distress and put her at ease. His flashing smile.

"A lot can happen before the wedding," Astrid said.

"Bjorn could drown at sea, get thrown from a horse, or fall sick," Ragnhild said.

"That's not what I meant."

"Isn't it?"

The thought of Bjorn dying gave her little comfort, even though there were moments when she missed her brother, and she wished Bjorn would die. Astrid touched her Freya pendant. The feel of the cool, smooth bead and silver amulet between her fingers soothed her, as it always did.

"Mother told me before I left that I have a part to play in all of this, not to kill, but to heal and weave."

The red sails of Harald's ships shrank until they looked no bigger than the head of a needle.

"We cannot know what fate the Norns have woven for us. Maybe the goddess sent Bjorn to me that day, and kept his name from me, for a reason. I do not know."

A breeze blew over her, whipping her dress around her legs, her hair over her shoulders. Astrid watched until the ships disappeared in the distance.

Chapter Twenty-six

The ship rolled and yawed; the wood creaked with the movement, and the sail snapped in the wind. Astrid heard her father shout something to Dyri the helmsman, and Dyri's shout as he replied. They made their way home from the Thing, and so far had had fair weather and smooth sailing. Dyri was an expert steersman, and she felt the ship changing course under her. She gripped the edge of the sleeping pallet set up for her and Ragnhild inside the ship's tent. The tent was so low she had to stoop when she stood up. The only time she wanted to be in there was when they slept, preferring to be on deck to feel the wind and sea spray in her face.

Ragnhild, though, was a different matter. She had been sick for much of the journey. Astrid huddled in the tent, cradling Ragnhild's head as she was sick into a bucket. Another wave hit the boat, this time rocking them up and over, and they were both nearly tossed off their sleeping pallet. It sprayed up, dousing the already wet deck with frigid water. Astrid gripped onto Ragnhild tightly with one arm, and with the other she held onto the pallet. Ragnhild shivered in Astrid's arms.

The flap opened and a head with wind-blown brown hair appeared. "How are you doing?" Short Olaf asked. His eyes flicked to Ragnhild, and he frowned.

The wind that blew in the opening was a welcome relief, washing the tent of some of its stench, and Astrid took in a deep breath.

She would prefer to be on deck with the others, but Ragnhild needed her. She ran a hand over her friend's matted hair. Ragnhild stirred and struggled to sit up, her tired, black-ringed eyes blinking in the light that Short Olaf had let in.

"Can you get Dyri? I need him," Ragnhild asked. Her voice came out weak and childlike.

Short Olaf shook his head. "He is steering."

Ragnhild mumbled something before she lay back down, tucking her knees to her chest.

Pulling a rough wool blanket over her friend, Astrid put out her hand for Short Olaf to help her up. Between the fatigue and the cold, she did not trust her legs to stand on their own.

He grasped her hand and pulled her up with such ease she felt like a cloth doll. When she got to her feet, she wavered, and he held tight to steady her.

"I need some air." With a quick glance at Ragnhild to make sure she would be all right, Astrid grabbed her cloak and stepped out onto the deck. Short Olaf followed her.

Once outside, she stopped and took a deep, cleansing breath. The air was wet and cool, but she didn't care, as long as she did not have to smell sick and unwashed bodies. The wind whipped at her hair and clothes.

She gathered her cloak in her hands and wrapped up tightly as she took stock of all of her men. A quick survey of the boat assured her that all was well. Rikki played dice with Galm and three others, her father talked with Dyri, while Emund and Gunnar were both rolled up in their cloaks, asleep on the rowing benches.

"I'm worried about Ragna," Astrid told Short Olaf, as quietly as she could over the sound of the wind and swells smacking against the boat. "She has grown so thin and pale. It can't be good for the—" She stopped herself. No one knew Ragnhild was with child. "Good for her."

"I don't know what we can do." He glanced back toward the tent. "How bad is it?"

"She barely eats or drinks and grows weaker by the day. How long before we reach home?"

He looked steer side at the land that they always kept within sight and then to the left. "It depends on the weather and on the Oresund."

Brushing her hair out of her eyes and holding it back, Astrid swept the horizon to her left, and saw that land was coming into view. A chill, not from the sea spray, shivered up her back. The Danes often prowled and raided through this narrow strait between the two land masses. She reached for her Freya pendant and intended to send up a prayer to the goddess to protect them, but touching the purple bead reminded her of Bjorn, and she let her hand fall.

"Don't Ketil and Sigmund control these waters?"

Short Olaf looked away from her and bit his lip. "Sigmund is unhappy with your father. He sent a messenger to your father at the Thing. It was not good."

"Over the marriage to me?"

"*Ja.*"

"It may not be safe for us?"

"No."

Her eyes searched the horizon. What if Sigmund came for her? She did not want to marry Bjorn, but at least she didn't think he would hurt her. Sigmund, however... She let the thought fade away.

"But it should not be long. Three or four days?" Short Olaf said, trying to soothe her. "You could ask your father or Red. They have made this journey so many times, they could do it with their eyes closed."

"No." She was firm.

"Do you plan to be angry with them forever? Even Red?"

Her stomach clenched at that. She had never been angry with Emund before, but she could not even look at him without thinking of how he had betrayed her. He had always said he would protect her, but she now understood that his protection and love came with conditions—as long as she did what her father said.

"They sold me to my worst enemy. I will never forgive them for that." She turned her back to him. "Not even Emund," she choked out.

"You said yes to the marriage," he mumbled. He stepped closer to her, and she could feel his warmth, and how much he wanted her. "They were only doing what was best for everyone. If Rikki had been asked to marry one of Harald's daughters, he would have done it."

She barked out a bitter laugh. "But he can do what he wants. It does not matter to the man. Rikki could go off raiding for weeks, months, even years. He could be with other women, father other children."

"Not all men are like that. *I* would never do that."

"I'm not marrying you, am I?"

Short Olaf recoiled at the harshness of her words, and Astrid felt sick for saying them. She did not take them back.

"I need to get back to Ragna," she said brusquely.

Dyri studied the water, the sky, and the land intently with both hands on the steering oar. Astrid considered telling him that Ragnhild grew worse, but at that moment he said something to her father, who nodded and answered. One man hurried over to her father, his face filled with concern, and he pointed in the direction they headed. Her father frowned. They all looked so serious and intense that Astrid did not want to bother them; there was nothing they could do to help, anyway.

Instead, she threw back the flap to the tent, stepped inside, pushing the unpleasant smell away, and went to sit next to her friend.

Ragnhild stirred. "Dyri?"

"No, it's me, Asta."

"Asta?" She rubbed her belly. "I think something is wrong."

Astrid thought if this baby survived, he would either be sickly or incredibly strong, like metal forged in fire.

"Would you like me to check?" She did not know what she could do. It was too early, and the child had not yet quickened, so there would be no way for her to tell if it was alive or not. She knew she had to do something to make her friend feel better.

"Yes."

Pulling back the blanket and lifting Ragnhild's dress, Astrid laid her hands on the swelling belly, pushing gently to determine if she could feel anything. "Does it hurt?"

Ragnhild winced. "No."

"That's good." Astrid saw the intake of pain but acted as if she had not noticed it. Instead, she tried to imitate her mother's calm and knowing nature, although her heart raced. "Maybe I should tell Dyri you are with child—"

"No!" Ragnhild scrabbled to sit up and pushed Astrid's hands away; the small exertion tired her out, and she slumped back. "What good would it do?" She turned her head to the side and said so softly Astrid had to lean in to hear her. "I don't know why I had you check. I can feel it slipping away. It won't be much longer."

"Dyri would want to know."

"I don't want him to see it. Stay with me?" She turned back to Astrid, her eyes pleading. A pang of pain hit her then; she gritted her teeth and let out a soft groan.

"Where else would I go?" She laughed, but it came out all wrong, high-pitched and frantic. When she looked down, she noticed a spot of blood staining Ragnhild's dress and the bedding under her. Astrid met her friends' tired, sunken eyes, saw the despair in them, and she had to swallow down her own fear. She was not sure she could do this, help her friend through this without her mother or any other women around, surrounded by warriors, trapped by the sea. Her mind raced with what to do. Should she ask her father to make landfall so they could find a midwife or some other healer? No, making landfall and finding a midwife would take much too long. Steeling herself with a breath, Astrid took her friend's too-thin shoulders in her lap, and brushed Ragnhild's matted hair away from her face.

"We have seen this before. We have to let it happen," Ragnhild said.

"I'm sorry." She pulled the Freya pendant over her neck and placed it in Ragnhild's hand. "It's not Frigg, but—"

Ragnhild gripped it. "It will help. *Tak*." A spasm wracked her body, and the blood stain on her dress grew wider.

A male voice shouted an alarm that rang out from the deck.

Astrid tightened her grip on Ragnhild and listened. More shouts followed, and then the sound of thumping feet and the clang of metal as men gathered up weapons and put on armor. Both women sucked in a breath and looked at each other. Astrid eased herself out from under Ragnhild.

When she poked her head out of the tent flap, she saw what she had feared the most. Warships bearing down on them.

They were under attack.

She could hear her father's voice bellowing to his men, to the archers to get ready, to the warriors to arm themselves, to Dyri to steer them away from the approaching ships. Rikki ran up to the tent as he secured his sword belt. Before Astrid could ask him anything, he said, "Get inside and stay there. I mean it." He did a quick search of the tent where he found an extra shield. Handing it to her, he added. "Don't come out. Not for anything."

The look in his eyes told her everything, not that she needed a reminder of what would happen if the raiders found her and Ragnhild.

He took hold of her arm. "Do you understand? Stay hidden."

"We will." Her voice caught out of fear, not for herself, but for him. "Be careful."

He snorted. "A careful warrior is a dead one." When he saw the distressed look on her face, he added, "I will do what I have to do. Don't worry about me." He gave her a grin and ran off.

"They are coming!" Someone shouted.

"Let them come," another voice growled. "My axe is thirsty for blood."

A quick look at the approaching ship made Astrid's stomach flip. Dozens of Danes lined the sides of the dragon ship, armed with swords, axes, and spears, colorfully painted shields held in their arms, while they banged on them with an intimidating *thump, thump, thump*. The sight of them made her knees weak, and she lugged the shield back into the tent only to find Ragnhild in the grips of a cramp, her face wracked with pain.

"Ragna." Astrid rushed to her side, forcing her mind to forget about the battle that would soon rage outside, and to focus only on her friend. "Here. Hold on to my hand." Ragnhild gripped Astrid's hand tightly until the cramping subsided.

"What is happening?" Ragnhild asked.

Astrid did not want to tell her, but there was no way to hide it. "We are under attack." She hauled the shield to their pallet. "We need to stay under this."

Ragnhild nodded and curled up as much as she could, and they both huddled under the heavy shield. As they adjusted themselves, Astrid's father called for his archers to ready, and she held her breath, waiting.

"Loose!"

Astrid imagined dozens of arrows flying over the water to strike the Danes and envisioned one of them flying straight into the throat of the leader, of him dropping to the deck.

"Please let that happen," she whispered, knowing that spoken words had power.

Moments later she heard another cry. "Arrows! Shields up!" and she folded herself over Ragnhild's body, both of them protected as much as possible under the shield.

Arrows *thwopped* into the boat and onto shields, one of them ripping through the tent and piercing the bed next to them. Astrid instinctively jerked back, but Ragnhild was cramping again, and did not notice. Screams from the deck of the ship made Astrid's heart race with fear. Who had been hit? The bedding grew damp with Ragnhild's blood, and Astrid took a breath to calm herself. "They will stop the Danes. Father, Emund, Rikki, Dyri. They are out there, Ragna."

The sounds of the Danes grew louder, their shouts, their insults, the thumping of their shields, and Astrid had a hard time breathing, the air in the tent closing in on her. She could hear her father shouting to Dyri, and Dyri's voice yelling back to be ready. A loud crash rocked the boat, and she and Ragna were nearly flung to the boards. Ragna cried out in pain. It was followed by the sound of metal hitting wood, and the boat listed to one side. It could only mean one thing. They were being boarded by the Danes.

Astrid had heard the men talk of sea battles, had listened to the tales of epic battles with vast fleets of ships, the men fighting in the close and cramped space of two boats lashed together. She had heard the tales, but nothing prepared her for the terror of being in the middle of one. The Danes screamed as they flooded over the sides of the boat, and her father's men screamed back. They sounded like demons, possessed by battle rage.

The boat rocked viciously, and Astrid could hear the sounds of men yelling, the tramp of footsteps, the cries of agony as someone died. A man's scream cut off, and his body fell into the wall of the tent and slumped down, his blood trickling underneath and toward Astrid's feet. She watched it, transfixed, as if she had never seen blood before. Please be the blood of an enemy.

Ragnhild groaned, and she gripped onto Astrid so hard that she feared her arm might break. With a final spasm, something slipped out from between Ragnhild's legs, and then she lay back, breathing heavily. It was a small mass of blood and tissue that looked nothing like a baby, and Astrid rose to get something to cover it up, when a man screamed in agony and the tent flap flew open.

"Women!" A Dane ducked his head in and leered at them. Another warrior joined him and smiled, his teeth shockingly white in his blood-spattered face. A quick glance told Astrid that he was in charge; he had rich armor and carried a bloody sword.

Astrid stared at him, knowing the blood on his face and sword belonged to a man she knew. She had to fight back a wave of nausea. The leader took a step into the tent, his sword in his right hand and his shield hanging from his left. He surveyed the bed, the bloody mess, and the two women.

With the tip of his sword he pointed at Ragnhild and told his man, "That one's all used up. Kill her."

"No!" Astrid screamed. She clutched onto Ragnhild with one hand, and with the other she scrabbled at her side to reach her knife. They would not kill her friend.

The leader looked Astrid up and down, and he smiled at her. "I see why the yellow one wants you. Too bad." He chuckled at a joke she did not understand. "I'm taking you. You're mine now."

Her fingers shook so much, she could barely unclasp her knife sheath. The leader laughed at her. "Think that little knife will help you?"

His laughter tugged at a place deep within her, an anger at being so helpless. "It will if I stick it in your neck."

This time he let out a loud laugh. It sounded wrong here, along with the continuing shouts and screams of pain. Why had no one noticed these Danes had breached the tent? Unless they were all dead or dying. Astrid swallowed hard and took a deep breath, shoving those thoughts out of her mind. She needed to keep her wits. She stared at him.

"I'm *definitely* keeping you for myself," the leader said, his dark eyes showing his approval. "He will have to fight me for you."

"He has a witch," the other Dane said.

The leader waved that away.

The other Dane took two steps toward the bed, and as soon as he got close, Astrid lashed out at him with her fists. He easily knocked her arm away, and then, just as easily, he grabbed her and threw her to the leader.

She stumbled, and he caught her by the arm in a grip as strong as an iron band.

"Ragna! No!" She struggled to get away, but he was too strong.

The other Dane held his axe at his side as he approached Ragnhild. She tried to scrabble away from him, but she was so exhausted she had a hard time even rising to her elbows. Her black-ringed eyes stared at him in terror. He put his big, bloody hand on her face, and then felt down her body while she whimpered.

He looked back at his leader. "She's worth keeping. Just needs to recover."

Astrid thought she might be sick.

"I won't waste food on her. Kill her."

"Dyri!" Astrid screamed so loud it scratched her throat. The leader grasped onto her more tightly and clapped his hand over her mouth. It tasted of sweat, dirt, and blood. Astrid gagged.

The Dane turned to face his leader, his axe pointing down at Ragnhild. "No, this one is mine." There was something desperate in his eyes.

A surge of hope bloomed in Astrid's chest. Maybe they would fight and forget about her and Ragnhild. Kill each other. She went still, waiting. Hoping.

"Dyri!" This time the cry came from Ragnhild. She had roused herself when the Dane had his back to her, and she reached for the clay water bowl that Astrid was going to use to clean up the blood. The bowl would do nothing against his leather armor, but it was all Ragnhild had to hand.

The leader's eyes must have flicked to her, for the other Dane turned, but he did not finish.

Dyri came crashing into the tent, axe at the ready. "Ragna!"

He did not see Astrid and the leader but went straight for his wife. His helm was missing, and blood matted his brown hair so it looked black. Blood stained his right leg, and Astrid could see a hole in his thigh where a spear had hit him. He could not put much weight on that leg and his movements were awkward, the axe looking too heavy for him to wield. But his eyes were determined, and when he saw Ragnhild lying in a bloody mess on the bed, he attacked the Dane looming above her.

The leader wrapped his arm around Astrid's waist and picked her up to drag her out of the tent. She thrashed and kicked at him, but she might as well have been kicking a tree, for all the hurt it did him. Instead, it amused him. She heard the moment Dyri and the other Dane met in combat, the hard clatter of metal on metal. She heard Ragna call out Dyri's name, her voice weak and quavering. What would happen to her friend if Dyri should fall? Ragna could not fight back; she could barely move or speak.

When Astrid saw what waited outside of the tent, she screamed. The hull of the boat filled with blood. Bodies of men were strewn where they had died, limbs severed, a man groaning near her, who had his hands over his stomach as he tried to hold in his innards. Nausea rolled over her. The two boats, locked together, swayed under them, so it was hard to walk without stumbling, but the big Dane had good sea legs, and he held on to her tightly as he moved toward his own boat.

A female scream pierced the air from the tent. Astrid put all her strength into getting away from the big Dane, so she could make her way back to Ragnhild. Another scream. Astrid needed to know what was happening. Had the Dane killed Ragnhild? Dyri? Was he ravaging her friend who had just been through so much?

"Let me go!" Astrid screamed at the Dane leader, and she struggled to reach her knife. If she could get to it, she'd plunge it into his belly and make him regret ever putting his hands on her.

She felt rather than heard his laughter again. "I'll let you go when you're bound up on my ship."

Astrid went slack and, with her fingertips, slipped her knife from its sheath, thanking the gods she had unclasped the sheath before now. In his arrogance, the Dane leader had not disarmed her, and was more concerned with dodging the fighting men on board her father's ship than paying attention to her movements.

Lines and wicked looking hooks lashed the two boats together. Deep scratch marks marred the side of *Sea Serpent* and for a moment, Astrid was furious that these raiders had damaged her father's magnificent ship. It added fuel to her rage at this man who carried her like she was a child. Astrid knew that she needed to do something before the Dane leader got her onto his ship. Once there, he could detach the ships and carry her away.

Fighting down her panic, she gripped the knife as firmly as she could. She wanted to gut him, but he wore mail that covered him from neck to waist. He stopped and adjusted her in his powerful arms, tightening his grip. He held her so tight her breath came in gasps, and the stays on the leather gauntlet he wore on his arm dug into her ribs.

He halted as two men crashed in front of him, fighting. All she could see was their legs. Astrid recognized her brother's shoes and *winingas*.

"Rikki!" She plunged her knife into the Dane's thigh.

He roared with pain but did not drop her. "Little bitch!"

Over his curse, she heard her brother cry out her name.

A man dropped in front of them, the one Rikki had been fighting, blood gushing out of his leg, and the metallic smell of the blood made Astrid gag. So much blood.

The Dane's grip relaxed on her, and she thrashed in his arms, trying to get away. He grunted with pain as she sent an elbow into the hilt of her knife that still lodged in his thigh.

"Asta!" Rikki rushed up, sword in hand, and the Dane dropped Astrid. She fell next to the dead body of the man Rikki had just killed, and she let out a scream. His blood soaked into her dress and got on her hands. A stray foot kicked her, and she toppled over.

She tried to crawl away, but she could not escape their feet, they both moved too much and too quickly. Even with a knife in his thigh, the Dane leader was a ferocious fighter, and Astrid looked up to see him pushing Rikki back. No, no, she could not lose another brother. She found the side of the boat and curled up, making herself as small as she could, watching her brother fend off the big Dane. Out of the side of her eye she saw Emund fighting with one of the Danes, his battle axe swinging in an arc as it removed most of the man's head. Emund lifted his bloody axe to the sky and let out a terrible battle cry, and Astrid closed her eyes. She did not want to see this, did not want to see her brother fighting for his life to protect her, did not want to see Emund celebrating to the gods after killing a man, did not want to see the carnage and the blood. Squeezing her eyes shut tight, she sent a song to Freya, asking her to keep Rikki safe.

"Goddess of war
Beautiful and fearsome
Protect my brother
My only brother.
Freya, shield my brother.
Freya, shield my brother."

By the last line, Astrid was crying out the words.

The Dane leader howled in triumph, and Astrid snapped her eyes open in time to see him back Rikki up against the side of the boat. Rikki shot Astrid a look, and she saw in that quick glance that he regretted not being able to save her. His attention went back to the Dane as the big man raised his sword to bring it down on Rikki's head. Rikki blocked it with his own sword, but the Dane trapped him between the side and a dead body.

As if struck by lightning, Astrid felt a surge of energy flow through her. Her breath grew ragged, and all the sounds of the raging battle grew dim and muted. The Dane leader raised his sword to slice off her brother's head. She saw everything with clarity. She moved with more speed than she realized she had, jumped up, and rammed into the Dane. It was like running into an oak tree, but it made him stumble. His blade slashed across Rikki's neck.

Astrid screamed as she saw Rikki's eyes grow wide with shock. He grabbed his neck and opened his mouth to say something before slumping to the deck.

With a roar of rage, the Dane snatched Astrid again, crushing her against his body. "You will pay for that." His breathing came in quick gasps, and she knew the knife in his leg pained him.

She fought him, angry at being caught once again. "Rikki, Rikki...," she cried out.

"He will not help y—" He choked on the last word, and she fell from his arms as they went slack.

Two strong arms picked her up, and she screamed and struck out at the body behind her, thinking it was another Dane to take her to their ship.

"Easy. It's okay," Emund's voice soothed in her ear.

Astrid nearly fainted with relief.

A man shouted. Emund dropped her and spun around, and the clang of metal on metal rang out.

Without Emund to hold her up, Astrid fell to the deck, and she saw Rikki's body move. He was not dead. Picking herself up, she staggered over to her brother and dropped next to him. His blood-covered hand held his neck, but he moved and when she knelt next to him, he looked up at her and smiled a weary smile.

"My brave *systir*," he whispered.

"Don't talk."

Astrid found a piece of her underdress that was not wet with blood and tore it off. As soon as she lifted Rikki's hand away, she quickly pressed the fabric to his wound. He winced as she pressed down and squeezed his eyes shut. The fabric soaked through with blood, and Astrid had to rip another piece of her dress.

So focused on her brother, the sounds of the battle dimmed, as if she were underwater and it was raging above her.

An anguished female scream sliced through the air, louder than the clanging of weapons, the shouts of men as they taunted one another, the agonized groans of their dying. The sound pierced Astrid's heart. Her friend was alive, but what had happened?

Rikki's eyes flew open, and he relaxed when he saw Astrid hovering over him. His eyes were so much like hers, it was like looking into a pool of clear water and seeing her reflection. She heard Emund howl in triumph again. How much longer could this last?

"Asta," Rikki whispered, and she had to lean close to hear him.

"Don't talk. It will bleed."

"If I die…"

"I won't let you die."

He closed his eyes again, and she peeked at the wound. It was not as deep as it could have been, but it was still bad. If she could stop the bleeding and keep it clean, he might not die. She glanced down at her own dress, soaked with blood, dirt, and saltwater, and her heart fell. Keeping a wound clean in this mess would be hard.

"Make me a promise," Rikki said, surprising her. She thought he had fainted.

"What?"

"If I die…you will…avenge Jori."

"You're not going to die." Not if she could do anything about it. She thought of the prayer she'd made to Freya, right before the Dane hit Rikki. Would the Dane's sword have killed him if she hadn't said those words?

"Promise me *systir*."

"Bjorn will be my husband."

"Asta, you will be the last one who can do it."

Anger swelled up inside of her, at being asked to make this promise. She wanted to avenge her brother. She did. But she did not think she could kill her husband. She wanted to say the words 'I promise' to Rikki, to appease him, but a lump had formed in her throat, as if *she* had been slashed there and she could not speak.

From across the boat she heard a familiar voice cry out, "Rikki." She looked up and saw Galm running toward them, covered in gore, bruises, and cuts. He had lost his shield, but still carried his battle axe. Where was Short Olaf? Didn't they fight together?

Brushing that out of her mind, relieved that someone was coming to help at least, Astrid told Rikki, "Galm is coming."

He gave a slight nod. "Tell him...to get you...to safety."

Safety? There was no place for her to go that would be safe.

"It will be fine." She lifted the bloody cloth at his neck and saw the bleeding had subsided. A good sign.

A new voice called to her over the din of fighting. Gunnar. She nearly wept to hear his voice. Thank the goddess. He was alive. He would come to her, help her, protect her. He said he would always protect her.

She spun around. "Gunnar. I need you!"

"Asta," he called again, his eyes frantic with worry.

"Gunnar! Get down!" Galm shouted, closer now, but then his shout turned to a howl of rage. He thumped his shield with his axe. "Danish dogs!"

What Astrid saw appeared as if she were dreaming a horrible nightmare. Gunnar did not move fast enough. A throwing axe hit him on the back of the shoulder that carried his shield. Astrid heard the impact, heard the tearing as the blade ripped through his leather armor and into his muscles and bone. Gunnar staggered, his arm falling to his side, lifeless and useless. He fell to his knees and worked to get the shield off his arm as blood ran down his arm and soaked his tunic. Astrid watched in horror as he fought to be free of the shield that weighed down his left side. His movements grew slower and more desperate, like an animal fighting to escape a snare, as blood continued to soak his tunic.

The Dane who had thrown the axe stalked over, stepping over a dead body with as little attention as stepping over a fallen tree branch. When he saw Astrid, his face lit up as if he could not believe his luck. He licked his lips.

He hulked over Gunnar as he finally got loose from his shield; Gunnar stumbled to rise.

"Is she yours?" The Dane asked Gunnar, his voice mocking, and he kicked Gunnar back down. "Mine now. Maybe she'll cry out your name when I take her."

Gunnar remained still before the man, his breath ragged and shallow, his fingers trying to hang on to his sword.

"I'll let you watch." The Dane said, and he stepped toward Astrid.

With his left arm hanging useless at his side, Gunnar gave a great cry and lunged at the Dane. In his weakened state, he was too slow. The Dane blocked the strike and ran Gunnar through the chest with his spear.

Astrid screamed. She watched, her body frozen, as Gunnar collapsed to his side on the ground.

Galm, having dispatched his enemy, let out a fearsome battle cry, rushed in and swung his axe, smashing the Dane's head in one awful blow. Blood went everywhere and the man fell where he stood. Galm then ran to Gunnar, skidding to a halt next to the body and dropping to his knees.

Astrid barely registered any of this. All she could see was her beloved Gunnar's body, broken and bloody, lying on the bottom of the boat.

All at once, Astrid's limbs freed, and she rushed to him, shoving Galm out of the way with a growl of 'move,' and she dropped to her knees next to Gunnar. His left arm lay lifeless at his side, blood pooling under his shoulder where the throwing axe had struck him. He covered the chest wound with his right hand. Blood seeped through his tunic and stained his leather armor.

She put her hand on his sweaty forehead and brushed his hair off his face. At the touch, his eyes fluttered open, and he looked at her. His pale green eyes had a faraway cast to them, as if he was already on his way to the hall of the Allfather. Once again the shouts of the men, the smell of blood and death, all swam as if she was underwater.

"My..." he took a labored breath, "sword."

With an effort, his hand, wet with blood, gave hers a feeble squeeze.

Astrid looked up, but before she could move, Galm knelt, and with an agonizing gentleness opened Gunnar's right hand and put his sword in his palm, brushing his fallen friend's fingers closed over the hilt.

Gunnar sighed and grasped the sword, his bloody fingers staining the hilt. Galm helped Gunnar rest the sword on his damaged chest.

"...*Tak*...Brother," Gunnar rasped. His face scrunched in pain as he tried to take in a breath. Blood continued to drip and stain the wooden planks.

"We will meet again in the Allfather's Hall," Galm said, his voice thick and choked.

Astrid turned to him. "I need some clean cloth to bandage the wound. Hurry!"

But Gunnar shook his head slightly, grunting with the pain and effort. "No..." He closed his eyes and took a shallow breath, his face white with pain. Every breath caused him distress, and Astrid wondered how long he could hold on. He spoke again, his voice so soft she had to lean close to hear him. "No...too late."

Astrid choked on a cry. Her father's raven banner flapped on its mast above them, and she looked up at it, her own eyes filled with tears, knowing this would be the last time Gunnar saw the banner flying proudly over the ship, or even saw the sky. She thought of all he'd never see again, and a lump formed in her chest so big she could barely breathe or swallow.

Galm knelt by Gunnar's side. "We will feast for you. We will all raise the ale cup in your honor. We will remember you for your deeds here today. We will sing for you." He raised his right arm and slapped himself on the chest in salute.

Gunnar did not answer, could not move his arm, but gave them a weak smile. His breathing continued to labor, and his skin had taken on a gray tinge. He turned to Astrid.

"Astrid," he rasped. Taking the cue, Galm backed away.

"See to Rikki," she told Galm, and he hurried over to his other fallen Brother. Astrid knew in her heart Rikki was not dead and would not die this day.

"Asta," Gunnar whispered again. At the sound of her name on his lips, the rest of the world fell away.

"Gunnar," she whispered, touching his face. It was cold and clammy.

"My love."

He had only ever called her love once before, and hearing the endearment made her cry and her tears fell on him, mixing with his blood. How she wished there were healing properties in her tears, for she could let them loose with abundance and heal him in a moment.

Putting her hand on the hand that held his sword, Astrid leaned over him and looked into his eyes. They were drifting even farther away. Wondering if the war-maidens were hovering over the ship to take him to Valhalla, Astrid kissed him on the lips before it was too late. She wanted the last thing he felt to be a kiss rather than a spear.

He rallied. "Asta." His voice sounded like it came from a great distance. He shivered as the life-sustaining blood drained out of his body.

"Gunnar," she answered.

"My...dagger..." A racking breath rattled in his chest.

"You want your dagger?"

He nodded once, so faint it was nearly imperceptible.

Astrid moved to search his belt and found his sheathed dagger. Her father had gifted it to him after he had rescued her from the outlaw when she was a little girl. The hilt was silver and embossed with the runes of Tyr. The god of war had not saved Gunnar this day, but at least he would die a good death. He would have that much.

"Here it is." She lifted it so he could see.

His eyes had closed, but he opened them to look at the dagger. "I...want you...to...have it."

Astrid held it next to her heart. "I will keep it with me always."

He closed and opened his eyes in agreement and gave her a weak smile.

"I want...to always..." but before he could finish a great heaving pain wracked him. He cried out, grunting and writhing.

"Gunnar." Astrid cradled his head in her lap.

When the spasm finished, he looked back at her, his eyes wet with the tears of pain and he finished what he had begun to say, "To always...be there to...protect you."

He took a short, labored, painful breath that seemed to rattle his entire body. Then, holding Astrid's eyes he said, "love."

Placing her hands on his face, she held him as he drifted away. With his last breath his eyes grew dim. Astrid watched as life left him.

Chapter Twenty-seven
Storelva

The pyres burned so hot, Astrid's tears dried immediately on her cheeks. She closed her eyes, and black spots danced before her in the shape of the flames that consumed Gunnar and Dyri. A high-pitched keening sliced through the air, the sound rising to the sky, aiding the spirits of the dead men on their way to Valhalla. A body fell next to her, and the keening rose to an even higher pitch, the voice of a heart shattering into pieces.

Astrid dropped to her knees and held her friend tight as she grieved for her fallen husband. If she held onto Ragnhild, it helped keep her own grief at bay, a grief she could not show. She could grieve for Gunnar, but not the way she wanted to and needed to. The more she kept it back, the more it grew, until she felt she would burst.

She looked across the funeral pyres, through the flames that rose so high they disappeared in the black sky, at her father who, as jarl and *godi*, had said the words to send off the men. Gunnar and Dyri died fighting. They would go to Valhalla, to the Allfather's hall, where they would feast and fight with their ancestors. The men of her father's *huskarls*, all praised their fallen Brothers, but the words left nothing but bitterness in Astrid's mouth. What good would the praise do for Ragnhild? What little comfort would knowing that Dyri was feasting in Valhalla, give the wife who was bereft of her husband? The words would not hold her in their arms. They would not give her a life, a child, a home. She was alone in *this* world.

Gunnar's dagger hung heavy on Astrid's belt, its weight a constant reminder of the man she'd lost. She had loved him, had wanted nothing more than to be his wife. She thought of the night they'd sat outside her house under the full moon and kissed. She could still feel every moment, but then the heat of

the pyres and the wracking sobs of Ragnhild brought her back to the communal grief.

The sobbing became unbearable, and Astrid rose to her feet, wanting to get away from this scene of death. As if sensing Astrid's distress, Gytha slipped up and put her hand in her sister's, squeezing it tight. The desire to run away subsided, and Gytha's presence comforted her.

"Gunnar and Dyri are in Valhalla now," Gytha said. "Odin only allows brave men into his Hall."

Black smoke curled its way into the sky, where it disappeared. Astrid imagined Gunnar and Dyri feasting at the Allfather's enormous table, plates piled high with roasted pork, cups filled to the brim with mead, as they boasted to their friends and ancestors about their feats in battle. Buri would be there, and Thorkell the Steersman. And Jori. How glad they all would be to see each other again. It helped a little. Astrid wanted them here in *this* world, not in the Hall of the Slain.

"They were so brave," Astrid choked out, and squeezed Gytha's hand. "They were fighting to protect Ragna and me. I will miss them."

"Listen," Gytha whispered.

Emund's voice rose above the crackling of the flames and the logs that shifted as the fire consumed them. He sang about his fallen Brothers.

During the last refrain, the other men joined in, all of them lifting their weapons to honor their fallen friends. The blades of axes, swords, and spears shimmered with the reflection of the flames.

Astrid felt, rather than saw, her mother as she knelt down on the other side of Ragnhild and drew her to her feet. Amma was with her, Amma who had recently been the one keening for her lost husband, Buri. The two older women wrapped Ragnhild in their arms and moved her away from the pyre. She did not fight them. They would put her to bed, give her a draught to help her sleep, and sit by her for comfort. They all knew the bitter sting of grief.

Astrid caught sight of Rikki and was so glad to see her brother alive and standing among the other men, his sword aloft. A large bandage circled his neck, and a cord tied his long hair to keep it out of the wound. But he was alive, and that was all that mattered to Astrid. He sensed her stare and turned to her. He mouthed 'brave systir' and lifted his sword toward her. Her stomach soured. She had not been brave. If she had, she would not have called out to Gunnar to protect her. She had done that out of selfishness; she'd needed him and wanted his protection. If she hadn't, if he hadn't focused on her need, he would still be with her.

As the song died away, the men quietly left with their comrades or joined their wives and children to go back to their homes. The *huskarls* were taking turns to watch the flames, Galm and Short Olaf taking first watch. Astrid was happy to see Short Olaf there, alive and mostly well, the left side of his body battered and bruised after having his shield torn from his grasp, the muscles in his arm up to his elbow torn and sprained, his knee still swollen from when it had twisted under him.

"Are you terribly sad? You do not say much," Gytha said.

"It was too horrible to talk about."

It had been a grisly business afterward. Not long after Gunnar fell, the battle ended, and with that thought, Astrid's heart tightened in her chest. If only she hadn't called out to him, had waited longer, then he would be alive. Hot tears threatened again.

With their leader dead, the Danes had been dispatched, many of them by Emund. Astrid shivered, remembering how her father's men had rifled over the bodies of the slain Danes looking for booty, taking any armor, jewels, silver, and weapons. Then had come the business of dumping them overboard with her father saying a few words to Ran, the sea goddess. She must have been pleased with her bounty. Father had given her many men for her watery hall.

Without warning, Gytha broke away from Astrid and moved to Rikki, hugging him.

"Easy. You'll break my ribs." Rikki patted her back.

After hugging Rikki, she ran to Emund and did the same thing. "What is this for?" The big man kissed the top of her brown curls.

"I am glad you are alive."

"Huh," he grunted. "Me, too."

"I liked Gunnar and Dyri. They were nice to me. Asta says they were brave and died protecting her and Ragna."

"They were very brave. A Dane was trying to carry Asta o—" He stopped when he saw Gytha's face turn pale.

Despite the heat from the fire, Astrid shivered as soon as she heard his words. She could feel the way the big Dane's arms had held on to her as he carried her to his ship. Images of what had happened raced through her mind until it was a jumble of horrifying sensations overwhelming her. The pyre's oppressive heat turned into the Dane's body as he pressed against her, but then he turned into Gunnar as he smiled at her. She wanted to smile back, but he jerked and fell at her feet, an axe in his back, his blood spilling over her shoes. Her ears rang.

She swayed and pressed her hands to her head.

"What's wrong with Asta?"

Gytha's voice was muted, and Astrid tried to respond, but the pit of her stomach swooped, and her head felt as light as a leaf fluttering in the breeze. She heard Emund call to her brother, and the sound of feet shuffling on the ground.

Strong hands took hold of her, and she collapsed into them. "Sit down," Rikki said.

She sank right where she was standing, Rikki guiding her down. "I think I'm going to be sick."

"Take a deep breath," Emund said from above, his deep voice cutting through her haze.

Astrid did as she was told, but smoke, ash, and the smell of burning flesh filled the air, and she gagged. It also reminded her of the stench that permeated the ship after the sea battle, of blood and dead bodies.

"Maybe not too deep," Rikki said, with a slight chuckle.

His attempt to make her feel better worked, and her head cleared. Once she felt able to stand, she offered her hand for him to help her up. "I wish to visit my Freya shrine. Will you go with me?"

"Now?"

It was near dark, and Astrid did not want to walk to her shrine, which was in a grove by a stream that ran by the village, by herself. She knew she needed to be at the shrine, that being with the goddess would ease her aching heart.

"Now."

Rikki shrugged, and then winced in pain, although he tried to keep it hidden.

"I want to go too," Gytha spoke up.

Emund looked between Astrid and Rikki and then shook his head. "No, you're coming with me."

Before he got far, he turned back and said to Rikki, "You armed?"

Rikki scoffed. "Always." He patted the sword that hung at his belt.

A loud snap of the fire echoed in the air, followed by the sloughing of a large log falling to the ground. The flames roared up, and a puff of black smoke rose into the star-crusted sky. They all remained still and quiet as they watched it rise.

Gytha broke the silence. "Emund, tell me about the ghost of Hrolf. Is it true he haunted his farmhouse because he did not get a proper burial?"

In the firelight, Emund's bulky form shuddered, and he searched around, spooked. "Sh. We must not speak of ghosts out here. Wait until we get inside. Better yet, wait until daylight."

They left, and Astrid looked at her brother. He grinned, his teeth shining in the dark, and they walked to the shrine, the night air wonderfully cool after the stifling heat of the pyres. Astrid's heart relaxed too, once away from the oppressive atmosphere of death. The closer they got to the shrine, the better she felt. Her nausea and lightheadedness diminished, as did the horrible images of the death-filled sea battle.

"One time when we camped in...I don't know...near Novgorod, I think," Rikki said. "Galm and I came on an old abandoned farmhouse when out scouting. I am not afraid of ghosts, but something about that old house was creepy. Galm had to explore it..."

"Was there a ghost?"

"No. Nothing."

"What did you do then?"

"Galm decided he wanted to play a trick on Emund. You know how afraid he is of ghosts."

She let out a little laugh. "He's as skittish as a kitten when it comes to ghosts and revenants."

They were almost there, the gentle gurgling of the stream, the smell of damp earth filling the air. It was a soothing tonic to Astrid's senses. She took in a deep breath.

"Galm told Red about the farmhouse, and how he thought a ghost lived there. His face went so pale! So, Galm wagered two silver Frankish coins that Emund the Red could not spend a night in that farmhouse."

"Emund cannot resist a wager."

"You should have seen him." Rikki laughed. "He was as scared as a little girl, but he accepted the bet. He could not back down. Not in front of everyone."

They had come to the shrine, a collection of small stones, shaped into a circle in the middle of a grove of ash trees. Rikki stopped at the edge of the stream, picked up a rock and tossed it into the flowing water, black in the darkening gloom. They could not see the rock, but heard the soft *plunk* as it hit the water.

She sidled up to Rikki, both of them quiet for the moment. After it passed, she brought them back to the conversation. "Did Emund make it the whole night?"

Rikki glanced at her out of the side of his eyes, the whites glowing in the dark. "He said he did. But Galm, Shortie, Gunnar, and me, we watched him from the woods. It took him three tries to go into the house, he was so scared. Once he got inside, we waited for him to settle, and then Galm threw some small rocks at the roof of the house. We heard Emund moving. When we knew he was awake, Gunnar sneaked to the back of the house and made a scary whistling sound. Remember how he whistled?"

Astrid could. She hoped he could whistle in the Allfather's Hall.

"That was too much for Red. He crashed through the house like a bear, and then we saw him run out dragging his bedroll, his pack half open over his shoulder. We nearly gave ourselves away, we were laughing so much. I thought Shortie was going to piss himself! But Red was so spooked, he would not have heard a pack of wolves."

"Poor Emund!"

Rikki guffawed. "He threw his bedroll on the ground, wrapped up in it tightly, and pulled it up over his head, tucking his axe in with him. I don't think he would have come out for anything, like a turtle in its shell. Gunnar made some more whistling sounds, but Red did not come out."

Astrid smiled when she imagined the four young men hassling the older man, so big, people joking that he was a half-troll, taking his measure and poking at a silly weakness.

"Did he pay up?"

"*Ja*. When he found out we knew he slept outside."

"Was he mad?"

"As mad as a hungry bear when its hibernation is disturbed. When Gunnar taunted him with the whistling sound he'd used the night before, Emund went after him, yelling 'I'll rip your tongue out', but Gunnar outran him. He didn't come back until the evening meal."

Rikki impersonated Emund's voice, and they both laughed. He picked up another rock to throw it in the water. "I hate it when one of my Brothers falls, and Gunnar was more of a Brother than most."

"Thank you for telling me that story."

Rikki put his arm over Astrid's shoulder, and she slid her arm around his waist. They hugged in silence.

"At least you are alive, my brother. I don't know what I would have done, had you died too. It would be too much to bear."

He stared up at the half-full moon. "No point worrying about something that didn't happen."

"When that Dane's sword sliced across your neck, I—"

"Stop."

She wished she *could* stop thinking about it, but the image of that Dane's sword, of Rikki collapsing, of the blood seeping through his fingers as they clasped his neck, played over and over in her mind, as did the image of Gunnar's desperate race to tear his shield off of his injured arm. Gunnar's eyes as his life left him was the last thing she saw when she went to sleep at night.

"I can't, Rikki." She pushed the heel of her hand into her eyes, as if she could squeeze out the offending pictures.

"You have to. It's the only way. Put it out of your mind."

"It's not that easy." She was on the verge of tears again, feeling frantic.

"I didn't say it is easy. I said it is the only way." Rikki had lowered his voice and spoke firmly. He put his hands on her arms and turned her toward the shrine. "Do what you need to do, *systir*."

He walked away from her and settled on the grass next to the stream, resting his back against a rock. When his eyes closed, she could see how pale he was, the dark rings under his eyes like bruises. He had not been sleeping either.

Astrid entered her little shrine and knelt before a small stack of stones draped with a piece she had woven in respect to Frigg, the goddess of weaving. Beside the weaving, she'd placed a small figurine of Freya, something Rikki had carved for her out of a branch from an ash tree they'd discovered in their secret place. The figure was only as tall as one of her fingers, but intricately carved with spirals in Freya's belly. The earth was cool under Astrid's knees and her toes where they touched the ground. She lifted her Freya necklace over her head and draped it on the stones; a lump formed in her throat at the sight of her pendant. Tears burned her eyes. The pendant had been through so much—had been with her during her coming-of-age ceremony, had been with Gunnar when Jori was killed, had been the means by which Bjorn Alfarsson had discovered her identity. She ran her hand over it. It wove through her life and those of her loved ones. What more would it see?

She let her tears fall onto the ground for Gunnar and Dyri, for Ragnhild, for herself. As they hit the earth, her tears became an offering to the goddess. But she wanted something more. Without thought, or even much understanding, Astrid unhooked Gunnar's dagger from her belt and unsheathed it. She held it up, and the blade gleamed in the moonlight, sharp and fierce, well cared for and deadly. Then she placed it on the altar stones, where it looked alive, ready, waiting. With a slightly shaking hand, she rolled up the sleeve of her dress, exposing the tender white skin underneath. Her hands were callused and tough from long hours spent weaving and sewing, but her arms were as soft as a flower petal. With her arm exposed, she picked the dagger back up, and with a fortifying breath, she drew the blade across the skin. She hissed in a breath of pain and watched, transfixed, as blood seeped to the surface of her arm. Her blood stained Gunnar's dagger. She plunged it into the soft ground in front of the altar and held her arm over it, allowing her blood to mix with her tears in offering, not knowing what she was offering, or how it would help, only that she needed to do this. Needed to give up her tears and her blood, to let it go.

Astrid did not know how long she knelt before the altar stones. It could have been the barest wisp of time or all of eternity. The sound of Rikki shuffling and taking a drink of water from the stream brought her back. Blinking her eyes to clear them, she rolled her sleeve back down, the blood dry now, and she pulled the dagger from the ground and wiped it on the grass. She slowly slipped the Freya necklace back on, and though it should have been cool from the night air, the pendant was warm when it touched her chest.

She left the shrine without a backward glance. Rikki looked up at her approach, his eyes filled with a question he would not speak, and she would not answer. There was no need. She merely nodded. He jumped to his feet, and they returned home in silence.

As they returned to the village, she heard the bleating of the goats, and her thoughts went to the feast that would happen the following night. Her father would sacrifice the goats to the gods to further ensure that Gunnar and Dyri reached Valhalla. The meat would be roasted, and everyone would feast in honor of the two fallen warriors. She would serve the men at the feast, listen to the words and tales of Gunnar's fellow warriors, tales of his prowess in battle, of how he fell bravely in the service of her father, how he was protecting Astrid, even as he died. She would let the stories and songs sing away her grief.

Chapter Twenty-eight
Storelva. October.

"Astrid, go check the stores of mead," Ingiborg told her amid a flurry of activity. Women and thralls rushed to prepare food and lodgings for the wedding guests. In addition to Harald and his household, people from all over the countryside would be in attendance. They would all feast and drink for several days to celebrate the marriage of Astrid and Bjorn.

"Mother, I have already checked several times. We have plenty."

"I've forgotten." Ingiborg's face was pale, and she took the moment to lean on a table, her exhaustion etched in the dark circles under her eyes. She gave Astrid a tired smile. "We still have to finish the last touches on your wedding dress."

It was unlike Ingiborg to be forgetful or flustered when preparing for a feast, and Astrid worried about her mother's health. For a woman four months with child, she was much too thin.

"You should rest. I will ask Ragna to help with the dress."

"I don't think that is a good idea..."

"It has been two months since Dyri was killed," Astrid said, swallowing the lump in her throat at the thought. It had been two months since Gunnar had been killed too, and she thought about him every day, kept expecting to see him in the house or village, to have him stand too close to her when they talked, the excitement of his nearness making her shiver. "Ragna does not leave her house. Maybe giving her something to do will help."

"But a wedding dress. That might be too much."

Determined, Astrid said, "I know my friend. She needs something."

"Your dress is in my sewing chest."

Astrid pulled the neatly folded dress out of the chest and held it up. The wool was of the softest, most expensive blend, and dyed the deep blue of a sapphire. The silk trim was as light as a cloudless summer's day and shimmered like liquid. She remembered the day the summer before, when her father had brought the silk home, and how stunned she and her mother had been. As soon as her fingers touched the luscious fabric, Ingiborg had decided they would use it to trim Astrid's wedding dress. They had set thralls to work to spin the thread used for the dress, as only the thinnest, most delicate thread could be sewn into the silk.

When Astrid arrived at Ragnhild's house, she found her friend still abed, the fire in the hearth burnt out, a pot of cold barley porridge sitting on the table with a bowl next to it. Astrid placed the basket with her dress and thread on the table and saw that porridge filled the bowl. Amma must have been there earlier to make it, although Ragnhild had eaten nothing. A slight breeze touched her through a crack in the wall and Astrid shivered, clutching her cloak to her body. She would need to talk to the carpenter and ask him to shore up Ragnhild's house for the winter so she did not freeze. She stoked and relit the fire to bring some warmth back into the house. Astrid rarely had to do these kinds of tasks, so it took some doing to get the fire started.

Astrid went to Ragnhild's sleeping platform, the curtain open to the chilly air. "Poor Ragna," she whispered. Ragnhild's face was etched with grief. To lose her child in a miscarriage, followed so quickly by the death of her husband in front of her, was a terrible burden. Astrid knew she had to shake Ragnhild out of her grief, or else she would die of it. She would not last the winter this way.

She put her hand on Ragnhild's thin arm and shook her gently but firmly. "Ragna."

Ragnhild's eyes fluttered open and took a moment to adjust. A brief flicker of anticipation in her eyes was followed by the sinking realization that Dyri did not wake her, that Dyri was gone forever. She gave a heavy sigh. "Asta."

"I need your help." Astrid did not want to waste time.

"I don't want to help you. Get someone else." Ragnhild rolled over so her back was to Astrid.

"No," Astrid said firmly, and she grasped hold of Ragnhild's shoulder. It was as thin as a child's. When was the last time she had eaten? Astrid leaned in closely. "I need you, my friend. Please."

"Leave me alone."

"No." Astrid settled herself on Ragnhild's bed and told her all the village gossip, everything they would normally discuss when they spent the day together at their work. A long time passed, but Astrid would not leave until her friend got out of bed, no matter how long it took. In time, Ragnhild turned over toward Astrid to inquire after everyone, a little life blooming in her pale face.

"Emund caught Galm coaxing young Hak to saddle Hrimfaxi and ride him. You know how that horse is when anyone other than Emund gets near him."

A slight smile flittered over Ragnhild's face. "What was Hak thinking, listening to Galm?" Her voice came out harsh from disuse.

"That boy will do anything Galm or Rikki tells him. He treats them like gods."

"Hak's not a child. He's nearly twelve. Old enough to know better." Ragnhild scooched herself up to sitting.

"Let me get you something to drink." Astrid found some soured milk to pour in a cup. She hung the pot of porridge over the fire to warm it up, hoping Ragnhild would be hungry too.

Ragnhild drank deeply of the soured milk, leaving a small milk mustache on her upper lip. She wiped it away and asked, "What did Red do to Galm when he caught him?"

"That's the best part," Astrid said, taking the cup over to the table and then fetching one of Ragnhild's combs. When she returned to the bed, she gestured for Ragnhild to sit up so she could sit behind her. Astrid slid in and ran the comb through Ragnhild's tangled bed-hair.

"Emund got Galm in a headlock, marched him out onto the jetty, and then threw him in the river! Galm, a grown man! He fought the whole way, but he could not get out of Emund's grip. He's too big and strong."

"I wish I could have seen that."

Finally, some life was returning to Ragnhild. Astrid kept going.

"Galm was furious, but when he came up from the water…I'm sure it was freezing…Emund warned him, if he ever messed with Hrimfaxi again, or put a young boy in the beasts' path, he would drown him."

Ragnhild let out a small laugh. "Galm deserved that."

"He did. Hak is a good boy." Astrid was about to tell her that Hak would begin his training with a real weapon and shield but held her tongue. She did not want to remind Ragnhild of weapons and battles.

Astrid worked a braid into Ragnhild's hair and changed the subject. "I need help with something and Mother is busy overseeing the wedding preparations."

Ragnhild blinked a few times. "Is it so near?"

"Yes." Astrid hesitated. She wished her mother were with them; she'd know what to say to Ragnhild.

"I will be of no help." Ragnhild sighed and slumped into herself.

"But you will. It is my dress. I have to finish Bjorn's tunic and there is little time. Please, Ragna, I need you."

She felt Ragnhild stiffen at the mention of the dress, but before she could refuse, Astrid got up. "Let me show it to you. You remember the blue silk father bought last summer?" Quickly, Astrid unpacked the dress and held it up so Ragnhild could see it.

Her friend's eyes widened. She pushed herself to sitting again. "It is more beautiful than I could have imagined."

"So you will help me?"

Ragnhild's gaze flicked over Astrid's shoulder to something on the wall. Her eyes went dark, like something shuttered them closed.

"No. You will have to tell me about the marriage after it is done. I will stay here."

"No," Astrid cried. "You can't leave me alone to marry Bjorn."

"You won't be alone."

"You know what I mean. I need my friend with me."

"My husband is dead."

Tears burned at Astrid's eyes. "I watched the man I love die, too." The words came out so softly, she wasn't sure if Ragnhild would hear them. "And now I have to marry my enemy." Her eyes blurred as tears fell onto her hand.

"Oh, Asta." Ragnhild put her hand on Astrid's. "In my grief, I forgot about yours."

Eyes filled with tears, Astrid felt Ragnhild shift on the bed and put her arms around her. They held each other without words for a long time.

It was Ragnhild who broke the embrace and the silence. Her breath was ragged and yet her voice was firmer than it had been. "Come tomorrow." She studied the dirt under her fingernails. "We will share a morning meal, and I will help you."

Two days later, Astrid finished the final stitch on the embroidery for Bjorn's tunic. She had used the scarlet wool she bought at the marketplace at Hovgarden, and with gold colored thread had stitched two dragon heads across the chest, their heads meeting in the middle. It was one of the best pieces she had ever done, and she hoped he would like it. Her hands paused as she folded the tunic to pack it away. Why should she care if he liked it? She did not care for him. He was to be her husband, and she wanted him well-dressed, that was all.

"I am nearly done," Ragnhild said. As she had worked on the dress, Ragnhild's face had gained back color, and her eyes showed some life. Astrid had made her stop to eat and drink.

Astrid moved to stand at Ragnhild's shoulder and looked down at the dress in her friend's lap. It was perfect, as she knew it would be. "Ragna? I have something else to ask of you."

"What?" She kept her attention on her sewing.

For the past two days, as they worked quietly together, the idea had taken form in Astrid's mind. The more she thought of it, the more she needed it to happen.

"Will you come live with me when I am married? I will..." Astrid paused, not sure she wanted to admit to such weakness, but the prospect of leaving her home, her family, and her friends to live with Bjorn, away from everything she knew, made her stomach tight. "I will need a friend with me."

At this Ragnhild stopped, her hand lingering over the silk. She looked up at Astrid hovering at her shoulder, her brown eyes surprised, but not enough to cover the grief she carried.

Astrid continued, "I was going to ask mother if Gytha could come, but Mother will need her now that she's going to have another child, and...well..." How to broach the subject?

"Now that Dyri is dead, I have nothing left here?" Ragnhild finished it for her, her voice as harsh as a crow's caw. Astrid flinched and stepped back.

The air grew heavy as Ragnhild gazed around the house, no doubt thinking of Dyri when she looked at his cloak, as it hung on its peg by the door, and a pair of his shoes he'd kicked off in the corner and never put away. The hooks where his battle axe and shield had hung were empty, a cobweb strung between two of them, the shield and the axe taken with him to Valhalla. She carefully put the dress in the basket and moved through her house, touching Dyri's cup and pulling out one of his tunics and holding it to her.

Astrid swallowed a lump in her throat as she watched her friend. She was afraid to speak.

With a moan, Ragnhild picked up Dyri's cloak and pressed it to her face. She was like that for so long, Astrid wondered if she should leave her friend alone. With a long inhale, Ragnhild turned to Astrid. "I will come with you. There is nothing left here for me. You need me more than this empty house does." Her voice broke, and she crawled into her bed with the cloak.

"*Tak*," Astrid whispered. While her heart broke for her friend, she was relieved to have her by her side.

"Now, please leave me," Ragnhild said. "I will be there to help you prepare for the wedding."

As Astrid slipped out the door, she let out a sigh. If she was to weave the two families together, she needed someone to help her with the burden. It was too much for her alone. At least for now.

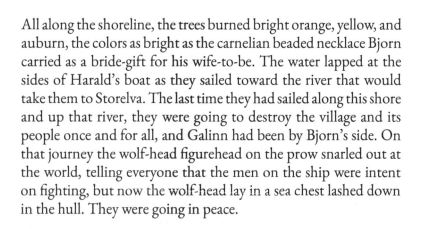

All along the shoreline, the trees burned bright orange, yellow, and auburn, the colors as bright as the carnelian beaded necklace Bjorn carried as a bride-gift for his wife-to-be. The water lapped at the sides of Harald's boat as they sailed toward the river that would take them to Storelva. The last time they had sailed along this shore and up that river, they were going to destroy the village and its people once and for all, and Galinn had been by Bjorn's side. On that journey the wolf-head figurehead on the prow snarled out at the world, telling everyone that the men on the ship were intent on fighting, but now the wolf-head lay in a sea chest lashed down in the hull. They were going in peace.

While two men played tafl next to him, Bjorn pulled the treasure necklace out of his bag and lifted it to the sun, the carnelian beads glowing in the light, the blue glass beads reflecting the sea below. The green glass beads were the color of the moss that covered the rocks along the shore. He ran his finger over the silver medallions spaced evenly throughout the necklace: two gold coins from Miklagard that had been hammered down, a silver spindle, a spiral, and a small Thor hammer. In the middle, a loop with three jade beads hung down, forming the centerpiece. His new wife might hate him. *This* gift she could not refuse.

An appreciative whistle made Bjorn look up. Styrr stood there, his eyes gleaming as he looked at the necklace.

"Care for a game of dice? You could wager that." Styrr stared at the carnelian beads hungrily, like a dog begging for a meaty bone. He shook the bone dice in his hand.

"No," Bjorn said. "I might offer it if someone would bring me your head."

Styrr narrowed his eyes. "Not so loud. These dogs would do it."

The crew Harald had chosen to accompany them was done with the purpose of intimidating Tryggvi. Bjorn had asked for Rekja and Vefinn to attend, and Harald had refused without giving a reason. Sometimes Harald said no to make a point that he was in charge.

"You would cut off your *own* head for this reward if you could."

"Tempting." Styrr continued to stare at the necklace. "A rich gift for a wife who would kill you, given the chance. You could have refused. The little virgin cunt might have been more...receptive...to *me*."

The thought of Styrr in Astrid's bed, of him even touching her, made Bjorn's sword hand twitch.

"She will be my wife. Remember that." The air between them crackled.

Styrr stepped back as Bjorn rose to his feet and dropped the necklace into its bag.

The lookout shouted that they had reached the river. Men who had been sleeping jumped up, games and dice stored away, and everyone moved to furl the sail. They would have to row up the river. Styrr went to join them, but Bjorn stopped him with a hand on his arm.

"If I see you sniffing around Astrid..." He gripped Styrr's arm so tight that he flinched. So quick the other man did not see it coming, Bjorn grabbed his crotch. "I will slice off your balls."

Styrr's eyes watered, but he gritted his teeth and nodded.

Releasing him, Bjorn hurried to help with the sail, taking hold of a line to lower it down. His anger toward Styrr surprised him, and the hard work to lower the sail and stow the mast helped get that anger out. Once they stored the sail and mast, he slid his oar through its hole and took his place rowing.

The rhythm and steady pull of the boat through the water calmed Bjorn, but he did not like his reaction to Styrr's taunts. Would this woman be one more weakness? One more way someone could get to him? He had never felt attached to a woman before. A wife, though, that was different. Astrid Tryggvisdottir was different.

Chapter Twenty-nine

The warning horn blew once, the sound echoing off the trees and the houses. Astrid stepped back from her loom and waited for the subsequent blasts that would tell them that the incoming ships were friendly. Across the women's house, Gytha and Ragnhild stopped their work, both going rigid at the sound. The deep bellow from the horn blasted twice more, and they all relaxed.

Astrid met Ragnhild's eyes. Her friend had finally come out of her grief seclusion. "They have arrived. Harald and Bjorn." A lump formed in her throat as she said his name.

Although she could not admit it to anyone, Astrid wanted to see Bjorn again, but she knew what she wanted to see was the Bjorn she had been with for that short time when they went riding. Before she knew who he was. With his arrival at her shore, she did not know what to do. He would be her husband, and she would have to live with him. She thought of the day he had brought her the last of the Freya's Hair bloom, and she had rejected him. Would he remember that and punish her for it when they married? Her mouth went dry.

"You will be married soon," Gytha said, her eyes alight with excitement. "I am so excited for you. Is Bjorn as handsome as everyone says? You will be the prettiest bride." She said it all in one breath.

Astrid shared a look with Ragnhild before turning to Gytha and giving her younger sister a hug. "Yes, my sweet, Bjorn is very handsome. You'll soon see for yourself."

With a quick glance, Ragnhild took in what Astrid was wearing. "You should change your dress and put on your best necklaces," she said, while putting her knitting in a basket that

sat at her feet. Gytha did the same. Before they left to return to Astrid's house, Ragnhild took her by the arm. "You want him to see what he is getting. How beautiful *you* are."

As they walked back to the house, Ragnhild continued, "What I would like to see is a line of your father's men behind you, their spears bristling as a warning to Bjorn."

Astrid snorted. "My father is more likely to serve me to him on a platter."

When they arrived at the longhouse, it was full of activity, people rushing to check all the arrangements they had made to house, bed, and feed the wedding guests. People from the surrounding area had already arrived and set up camps outside the village.

After donning a more formal dress and necklaces, Astrid walked with her mother and Gytha, Amma, and Ragnhild, to meet the incoming ship, but her legs felt weak, and her feet felt as heavy as if they had stones attached to them.

When they came into sight of the ship and she saw the wolf-head banner flapping in the breeze, she stopped, her heart hammering in her chest so hard she thought it might burst right through. Her mother walked a few steps before she realized that Astrid was not at her side. She stopped and turned around.

"Astrid?" She saw what Astrid stared at and nodded, understanding dawning on her face. "They come in peace this time. Because of you."

Astrid had to suppress the urge to run and hide in the woods or the cave. But she was not a little girl. She would be a married woman soon. Harald's ship, with its wolf-head banner flying proudly, was simply docked at their pier. Squeezing her eyes, she opened them again and saw that Harald's men climbed off the boat, their eyes studying the area, as her father's household men waited for them on the shore. Even though they had sheathed their weapons, they were all armed, and stood at the ready. It wouldn't take much to start a fight.

Then she saw him.

Bjorn bounded out of the boat and onto the dock in one fluid motion, just like the first time she'd seen him. Only this time he was not dripping wet. Thinking of him with droplets of water sliding down his bare chest and arms caused her to flush, and she put that out of her mind. Thankfully, he wore a tunic.

He must have felt her staring at him, for he straightened and spun in her direction, catching her with his deep blue eyes. Unlike the first time they met, he did not walk to greet her, and he did not give her an enticing grin. This time, he nodded in her direction. She flushed again, but from humiliation, not desire. What did she expect? She had made herself clear when she'd rejected his overture of peace. Theirs would be a marriage to bring their two families together, nothing more. Gritting her teeth, Astrid reminded herself of the reason she hated this man. She ran her hand over her necklace until it came to the green beads that Jori had given her. She thought of her brother, dead at the point of Bjorn's sword.

"Asta." Gytha pulled her down so she could speak into her ear. "You and Bjorn will be the most handsome couple ever."

"I…" Astrid began, but then she faltered.

Bjorn pulled someone out of the boat. A little boy leaped up lightly as Bjorn helped him, and he stood gawking at all the activity. A boy about five winters old, his tawny hair tousled from the wind, and his hazel eyes wide with excitement. He stumbled when his feet touched solid ground, which made him laugh. A few of the other men laughed with him, so he played it up, stumbling around, giggling, until he got too close to the edge of the pier. One man whisked him up. This man tossed the squealing boy to Bjorn, who caught him with ease and practice.

"Bjorn's son?" Ingiborg asked Astrid.

"He said he had a young son." Now that it was a reality, she did not know how to handle it.

"Look at the cute little boy!" Gytha gushed. "Asta, he will be your new son!"

"Frigg help me..." Astrid whispered.

"We need to greet them all," Ingiborg said. Astrid heard the undertone of distaste in her voice.

They joined her father, Emund, and Rikki at the end of the dock, Ingiborg taking her place next to Tryggvi, and Astrid next to her mother. After Harald had barked orders to his men, and Bjorn had given his son over to an older woman, they approached the welcoming group. Harald looked back to a young woman and called her over to him so harshly it made Astrid grit her teeth. The woman stood behind him, her head down, but her eyes boldly studied Astrid.

The two parties came together.

"Harald," Tryggvi said using his jarl voice. "*Velkomin.*"

"Brother. Ingiborg," Harald replied. The way he said her name, it sounded like some old anger had risen to the surface. His gaze lingered on Ingiborg. She shifted slightly under his stare, and if Astrid had not been watching so carefully, she would have missed it. Her father put a possessive arm around Ingiborg and held onto her, even moving her back a little, away from Harald.

Harald noticed the movement and laughed. "What do you think I will do, brother? Snatch her up and whisk her away?"

Everyone bristled, Tryggvi the most. "You tried that once before."

Ingiborg put a steadying hand on Tryggvi's arm.

Harald leaned in close to Tryggvi. "She is no use to me now."

Before Tryggvi, Emund, or Rikki could react, Harald threw his empty hands in the air and laughed. His gaze went to Astrid. "I come in peace, brother. For you to give your daughter to my foster-son." He sounded like he'd won more than peace between the two brothers, like he knew he was taking something from Tryggvi that he did not want to give.

When Harald's gaze landed on her, Astrid had to hold back the desire to flee. She reminded herself he was standing on her father's land, on the bank of her river, with no weapons drawn and no army. She met his eyes instead, and would not look away, however unnerving it was to have eyes that looked so much like her father's study her in such a way, as if he were checking to make sure the prize he'd won was to his liking.

Bjorn broke in with a smile, showing straight white teeth. "Tryggvi. Ingiborg. Thank you for your hospitality." He stepped over to Astrid and took her hand. "Astrid."

She could not tell if he was being serious or putting on a pleasant face in front of her father and his household. It didn't matter. She could barely think; he was so close. He was wind-blown and his beard untrimmed, but that was normal after sailing for days. It made him look even more attractive, less pretty, more dangerous. His strong hand was warm as it took hers, and the touch sent a shiver through her that went from her fingers all the way to her toes.

"Bjorn," she said, surprised at how calm she sounded, despite the pounding of her heart. "*Velkomin.*"

He dropped his hand and moved over to Rikki. "Rikolf Tryggvason." Bjorn held out his arm and Rikki paused for a tense moment and stared at him, his jaw clenching and unclenching, his arms at his side.

Astrid stared at her brother. She wished for him to put aside his anger and at least take Bjorn's offered arm. Rikki blinked and glanced over at Astrid as if he'd heard her silent plea, and he slowly raised his hand and clasped Bjorn's forearm.

When Bjorn stepped back, Astrid sent a thank you to whatever god she could think of. Rustling among her father's guard, who all stood behind the small party, told Astrid that she was not the only one who had been anxious to see what would happen between Rikki and Bjorn. Short Olaf caught her eye, and he winked at her. She smiled, but it faltered when she turned and saw Bjorn watching them, a frown on his face.

"Did you not bring your wife?" Ingiborg spoke up, looking at Harald and the woman who came with him.

"Sigrun?" Harald guffawed. "She does not like to travel. She also has no love for Bjorn!" At this he clapped Bjorn on the back. "Besides, she runs things while I am gone." Done with discussing his wife, he gestured to the woman who had come with him. "That is Katrin. I found her in Gotland. She pleases me."

Not showing her distaste for Harald, Ingiborg nodded. "Astrid and I will show you where you will sleep, and my women will take care of your men. People have been arriving for days and things are crowded."

Not trusting herself with Bjorn, Astrid fell into step with Harald's concubine. Up close, the woman looked older than Astrid had thought, but still not much older than her. She was well dressed, and the brooches attaching her apron to her dress were bronze and a necklace with a few beads was strung between them—a valued mistress.

Astrid asked about her name. "Katrin? I have never heard that name before."

"I was born Katherine and a Christian." Her Norse was accented in a way unfamiliar to Astrid.

Astrid had never met a Christian. They were people with strange beliefs in Emund's stories. "Are you a Christian?" She hoped the woman would tell her about their ways, so different from her own.

The young woman threw a quick glance at Harald before answering; he paid her no attention. He and Tryggvi were in a tense and forced conversation. She stared at Astrid, anger flaring up in her eyes, and snapped, "No."

The woman's reaction took Astrid aback. Why had she snapped?

"I worship the Aesir, same as you. Harald will have it no other way."

Astrid thought she heard a slight tremor of fear in Katrin's voice.

"How long have you been with Harald?" Astrid could not believe she was speaking to Harald's mistress, while the hated man himself walked with her father. Could not believe he walked on her father's land and would sleep in her father's house as a guest.

"Long enough," Katrin said in a clipped voice.

Long enough to hope to be with child, Astrid suspected. Long enough for that to guarantee her some safety. An image flashed in Astrid's mind, of the day when she was kidnapped by the outlaw. What would have happened to her if Gunnar had not saved her? Or if she'd ended up with the Dane who had attacked their ships? Would she have ended up like Katrin, sold and passed from man to man, only to end up far from home as the mistress of a brutal man, her only hope to be carrying his child?

"I do not remember seeing you at the Thing," Astrid said.

"I stayed at home to help care for Bjorn's children. Their mother died."

Katrin searched for something until she spotted Bjorn, who talked with one of Harald's men. Her brown eyes briefly lit up when she saw him, only to turn back to indifference. She arched an eyebrow at Astrid. "You know he has two children?" Her voice betrayed her as well.

Did she have a rival with this woman? If so, Katrin was playing a dangerous game. If she was Harald's favored mistress, she would be at grave risk to do anything with Bjorn. Unless they shared women.

Unless this woman already shared Bjorn's bed. Astrid's stomach churned at the idea of Bjorn with Katrin.

"I know of his children," Astrid said, catching sight of the boy. Gytha got hold of the boy and coax him away from the woman in charge of him. The two were hand-in-hand, and Gytha answered the boy's questions.

"I am surprised the boy is here."

"Tanni begged Bjorn and Harald to travel with us. Bjorn has a hard time saying 'no' to the boy, and Harald has a soft spot for him."

"So, here he is," Astrid said, trying to be light. Once she married Bjorn and went to live with him, these women would be her new family. A wave of sadness washed over her at the prospect of leaving her mother and sister, Amma, and all the other women of her home behind. If Katrin was any indication, the women in Harald's village would not give her a warm welcome.

"Yes." Katrin eyed Astrid. "Tanni's mother may be dead, but he already has women to look after him. He has no need of another."

"In my experience," Astrid snapped back. "Children can never have enough people to love them." She hoped the boy would like her. If he did not, it would make her life difficult. As she watched her sister and Tanni, she vowed to be good to the little boy, even if he was the child of another woman.

"Katrin, I see you have a rival."

The deep voice startled Astrid, as she had not heard Bjorn approach them. She looked at him, and his eyes sparkled with teasing as he spoke to Katrin. Rival? Was he talking about her? Astrid's stomach flipped. She took a step away from them.

Katrin gave a quiet laugh, and it showed off how attractive she was. "You know how Tanni likes a new friend."

Astrid followed their attention to Tanni and Gytha. The rival had been Gytha, not her. Still, she did not like the way Katrin acted toward Bjorn.

"*Ja,*" Bjorn said with a stiff laugh.

"Papa! Papa!" Tanni ran to them, Gytha's hand still in his as he pulled her along behind him. Asleifr had joined them. Gytha's face was lit up, as it always was when she had the opportunity to care for someone or something, and the more children she had the better.

They stopped and Bjorn squatted down as the boy ran up so they were eye to eye. That little movement, that he instinctively brought himself down to Tanni's level, tugged at Astrid's heart. Bjorn was making it hard for her to hate him.

"Papa! I made new friends! Geetha and Leif."

Bjorn gave him a big smile. "Go play with them. You look like you are in good hands." He winked at Gytha as he said this, and she blushed at his praise.

They scurried off, Gytha herding them in front of her, like a mother hen.

"Gytha is your sister?" Bjorn asked Astrid. He had placed himself in between her and Katrin.

"Yes." His closeness was like the crackle right before lightning struck. She moved away just enough so she could think straight.

"Tanni likes her."

Focusing on her sister, Astrid said. "All children and animals love Gytha. She has a kind heart." Astrid sighed at the last words.

"You sound sad about that," Bjorn said.

She met his eyes. "It is easy to be kind to children and stray animals. They do not lie to you and they do not kill your loved ones. Life is too hard for an overly kind heart."

He lifted a brow. "Astrid—" he started, but a shout of greeting cut him off.

"Astrid!" A woman waved to her from the opening of her tent, a spoon in her hand, as she walked over to the cauldron hanging over the campfire. She had her baby strapped to her back, and a little girl played on the ground near the tent.

Astrid waved back with a smile.

They had come to the outskirts of the village where people had pitched tents and set up little makeshift villages of their own. Campfires burned, and the smell of boiling or roasting meat filled the air. Children and dogs ran around. More people called out greetings to Astrid and wished her well with the wedding. She could see that some women stared openly at Bjorn. She would have to get used to that.

Tryggvi, Ingiborg, Rikki, and Harald were already at the longhouse when Astrid walked up with Bjorn and Katrin. "There you are, woman," Harald barked at Katrin as he waved her over to his side. He put a proprietary arm around her shoulders and pulled her close roughly as they followed Tryggvi into the longhouse. Ingiborg had already gone in, Tryggvi using his body as a barrier between his wife and Harald.

Rikki walked up and stood in front of Bjorn at the door to the house. The two men bristled with distaste for each other.

"Where are your friends?" Bjorn taunted Rikki. "They usually flank you, do they not? Your brave men, who chase after a child."

"What?" Astrid gasped. She looked from Bjorn to Rikki, but the two men ignored her outburst, they were so intent on each other. From the furious look on Bjorn's face, it must have been his son they talked of. Astrid knew it could only be one person. Galm. Short Olaf would never intentionally hurt a child. Or would he?

"They are around. This is *my* home and Asta is my *systir*. We will watch you, Bjorn Alfarsson. We will never be far."

"In two days' time she will be my wife. She will live in my home, far from you, Rikki Tryggvason." He had taken a step closer to Rikki.

"I will know if you hurt her. I will know and you will regret it," Rikki said.

Both men faced off like dogs protecting their territory, their hands near the swords at their sides.

Astrid stepped closer and put her hands on their arms. She could feel the muscles tight and twitching, ready to pull their swords out, ready to kill. "Stop," she said. They did not move, nor did they relax. "Please."

Bjorn surprised her by meeting her eyes and giving her a terse nod. He backed down and let his hand fall to his side.

She gave him a forced smile. "You will stay here with the men. I will be with the women u-until the wedding night." A spark of fear raced through her, making it hard to breathe. The wedding night. What was she going to do? She could not refuse him. Yet, how could she let him touch her? Her brother's blood tainted Bjorn's hands.

He leaned down and kissed her cheek gently, his whiskers tickling her. The touch of his lips on her skin made her shiver in anticipation. Her breath caught.

The moment broke when Bjorn straightened and turned to go into the house. He met Rikki's eyes, and his face grew hard as the two men glared at each other again. Bjorn stepped over the threshold and closed the door behind him.

"What are you doing?" Rikki asked Astrid.

Astrid could feel the anger radiating off him like steam. "What are you talking about?"

"I saw the way you looked at him just then."

She ran her hands over her face. "He will be my husband. What would you have me do? Spit in his face?"

Rikki laughed, and some of his anger dissipated. "*Ja*. That is exactly what I'd like to see you do." He moved closer to her and grabbed hold of her arms. "Remember who he is, *systir*, and what he has done."

She looked into his eyes. "How could I forget..." she raised her voice, but then lowered it again, not wanting anyone to hear, "...with you and Galm always at my side, whispering for me to remember? I cannot murder my husband." She spat out the last words.

"You won't need to. There are other ways."

Astrid felt sick. She took a breath. "Stop. I will marry him in two days. I will hear no more of this." She took his hand from her arm and led him away from the door. "I understand your anger and your need to take revenge for Jori. I loved Jori. More than *you* did." She stressed this with a jab to his chest. "I will not plot against Bjorn."

Rikki started to speak, but Astrid waved her hand for him to be silent. "You do what you have to do brother, but you will not sully my house or the peace I am buying with my life."

Understanding spreading over his features. "You are doing this for me."

"Yes. And Gytha. For all of us."

"No, you are doing this for *me*. I can see it in your eyes. You are afraid if I go up against Bjorn, I will be the one to die."

That arrow hit too close to the mark. "No," she lied. "I am afraid because your anger burns so hot, like a fire that rages out of control. Remember, I felt it too. When Gunnar told us how Jori had died, I wanted Bjorn to die slowly, in agony, for what he'd done. I wanted to do it myself. My only regret then, was I couldn't go with you."

She moved to a bench and sat down, ignoring the bustle surrounding them. Rikki followed and sat next to her. He radiated so much heat, it was as if he really was made from fire.

"What changed?" Rikki asked, calmer now.

"Mother and Emund planted the seeds. But they sprouted that day on the ship when I thought you might die."

He rubbed his neck where he still had a wicked scar. "That had nothing to do with Harald or Bjorn."

"I love you more than anyone else in the world. If I can take away one enemy, I will. I will give my life for that."

Rikki looked stricken. She leaned into him and rested her head on his shoulder.

"Aw, isn't this sweet," Galm called out as he approached them.

Rikki tensed. Astrid sat back up and glared at Galm.

He put his foot up on the bench next to her, leaning in. "It's not too late. Still time for you to run away with Shortie." Galm gave Rikki a pointed look.

Astrid looked from Galm to Rikki and back to Galm. They were up to something. "What is going on?"

Rikki jumped to his feet. "Nothing." He shoved Galm aside. "Galm has been in the ale, that's all."

Astrid narrowed her eyes and studied them. She'd knew them well enough to know when Galm was drunk. Rikki was lying.

Before she could say another word or do anything, Rikki kissed her cheek. "I would give my life for you too." He gestured to Galm, "Let's go."

They walked off, leaving Astrid feeling confused and stunned. And wondering what they were planning.

The next day, Astrid found herself at her father's corral watching the horses graze. She should be ensuring the thralls had cleaned and prepared the women's house, where she, her mother, Ragnhild, and Amma would stay until the wedding. But her feet had led her here.

She rubbed the Freya pendant. It was here that Emund had given her the purple bead she cherished, the one attached to the pendant. If Bjorn had never recognized it, would their lives have been different? But he *had* recognized it, and the thread of their *wyrds* would be woven together.

A flash of movement out of the corner of her eye startled her. Kis-Kis jumped onto the railing and meowed at her. She petted the cat's soft head.

"Kis-Kis, I will have to leave you behind," Astrid said, near tears. "You don't care though, do you?"

"That vicious cat is not the only one you will leave behind," a voice said.

Astrid spun around.

Emund approached, his green eyes misty with unshed tears.

All at once, Astrid felt like a little girl again, and Emund had come to fetch her home. Without a thought and leaving behind all the anger she felt over him pushing the marriage with Bjorn, she ran and threw herself into his outstretched arms. Those arms, big as tree branches, hugged her tight, lifting her off her feet. He did not let go for a long time, and neither did she.

When he put her down, she had tears running down her cheeks and her heart felt like it would crack.

The sounds of the wedding guests swirled around them as people talked and laughed. The shouts of men and boys at play, wrestling and fighting. Mothers calling after their children.

"I will miss you, my *bjarki*," Emund said, his voice breaking with emotion.

Astrid did not answer right away. She would miss him so much. She did not know if she could even speak without the tears coming hard and fast.

He took her silence the wrong way. His face fell, and he sighed. "I need to get back before your father and Harald kill each other. Not that I would work hard to keep Tryggvi from killing Harald." He gave her a conspiratorial wink, bringing back his usual smile.

The smile broke her, and she let out a loud sob. "I will miss you, too," Astrid snuffled.

He pulled her back into a hug and held her tight while she cried. She did not know what she would do without this man, who she loved more than her own father, there to take care of her hurts and ease away her cares. The outrage she had felt toward him over the marriage arrangements flowed out of her, and she imagined it sinking deep into the earth at her feet. She had lost too many men she loved, and she would not let herself lose Emund because of her anger.

When her tears subsided, he kissed the top of her head. "We should go back. They will think you've run away." He laughed.

She snorted. "Galm tried to convince me to run away with Olli."

"Was he?" Emund's eyes narrowed.

"It's nothing. It's just Galm," she said, although she was not sure it was nothing. "You keep Father and Harald from killing each other, and I will do my best to keep Rikki and Bjorn from doing the same."

"The gods help us. It will not be easy. Call us the Peacekeepers," Emund said.

She looked up at him, with shoulders and chest as broad as a bull, and laughed at him being a peacekeeper.

Emund laughed with her, his green eyes twinkling, and they walked side-by-side back to the village.

Chapter Thirty

Steam filled the bathhouse as Astrid entered, enveloping her and the women who attended her with the scent of herbs. The thick door closed behind her and with it her life as an unmarried girl. The married women would wash her and dress her in her bridal dress. She took in as deep a breath as she could in the heat, allowing the scents to relax her.

Her mother's gentle hands removed Astrid's dress while Ragnhild unbound her hair. Amma sprinkled more water on the heated stones, and a rush of steam hissed into the air. As she worked, Amma sang to the goddess Frigg and set a small stone statue of the goddess on a wooden shelf that they used as an altar. Naked and stripped of everything, Astrid stepped into the steaming bath where she sank down into the hot water.

She sighed as she dipped back her head to wet her hair.

"Enjoy it while you can," Ingiborg said, a smile on her tired face. She had worked hard with the wedding preparations, to make sure everyone had a place to sleep, and that there was enough food and drink for them all. If they ran out, it would reflect badly on her and Tryggvi. This wedding celebration would last at least three days.

"Once you are married, with your own household and children, there will be little time to enjoy a bath," Amma added.

"But," Ragnhild ran a comb through Astrid's wet hair, her voice happier than it had been since Dyri died, "find a way to share a bath with your husband. It will keep things heated."

"What?" Astrid wiped her hair back to squeeze out the water and looked at the women. They all had the same faraway look on their faces, the same slight smiles.

Astrid would have blushed if she had not already been so hot from the steamy heat. She closed her eyes and imagined Bjorn next to her, his hair wet and slicked back, his hands soft on her skin as he whispered to her in his deep voice, his breath tickling her neck. In a rush, her body flooded with heat that had nothing to do with the steaming water and air.

The smell of lavender scented soap filled the room, and Astrid felt her mother's hands work their way through her long hair, her mother's deft fingers rubbing her head. Astrid had forgotten how wonderful it felt to have someone care for her in this way. She melted into the water, all the fear of the upcoming wedding and wedding night draining out of her. Right now, there was only this hot, steamy room with the women who loved her the most taking care of her. Once she left the comfort of this bath, she would have to care for others. For her new husband, for their children, even for the children he already had.

As Ingiborg washed her hair, the three women talked to her and between themselves about men, marriage, and children. The tears of loss and laughter fell in the water, blessing Astrid as they told their tales to the newest woman to join them in the sisterhood of married women.

When Ingiborg finished with her hair, Astrid got out of the bath and they went into another room, smaller and colder, where Astrid plunged herself as quickly as she could into a bath of cold water scented with herbs. She shrieked when the cold hit her warm body. This time she submerged herself, dunking her head under the water, letting her hair swirl around her. She stayed under as long as she could stand it, for she knew that when she left this bath of water, it would be the end. She would have to get dressed and leave this room and these women. When she could no longer stand it, she got out, her body steaming with the mixture of heat and cold, and Ingiborg wrapped her in a soft towel.

As the women dressed her in her wedding dress, Amma sang, Ingiborg and Ragnhild joining in on the last line.

"In Frigg's name, bless this marriage."

Astrid's hair, unbound and loose over her shoulders, hung down her back.

Ingiborg combed it one last time and then ran her bare hand over it. "It glows like gold, *dottir*. You will shine as brightly as any gold arm ring. I hope he will value you, Astrid, daughter of Tryggvi, daughter of Ingiborg."

"I hope so too."

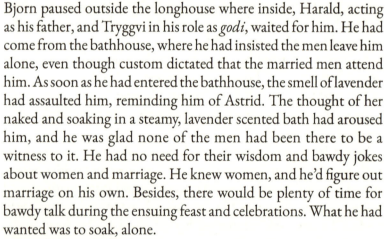

Bjorn paused outside the longhouse where inside, Harald, acting as his father, and Tryggvi in his role as *godi*, waited for him. He had come from the bathhouse, where he had insisted the men leave him alone, even though custom dictated that the married men attend him. As soon as he had entered the bathhouse, the smell of lavender had assaulted him, reminding him of Astrid. The thought of her naked and soaking in a steamy, lavender scented bath had aroused him, and he was glad none of the men had been there to be a witness to it. He had no need for their wisdom and bawdy jokes about women and marriage. He knew women, and he'd figure out marriage on his own. Besides, there would be plenty of time for bawdy talk during the ensuing feast and celebrations. What he had wanted was to soak, alone.

Finished with the bath, he entered the longhouse. Tryggvi's longhouse was bigger than Harald's, the pillars painted red and black and carved with images of Odin. Animal skins, shields, and two beautifully woven tapestries hung on the walls. One tapestry caught Bjorn's eye, and he went to look more closely at it. It had crimson and a mustard-yellow knotwork with four spirals with a black raven emerging. Tryggvi's raven. Along the edge, the weaver had woven red flames. The spirals, the ravens, and the flames were so alive they looked like they were moving. Bjorn reached his hand to touch it, when he heard footsteps. Figuring it was Harald, he turned abruptly and was surprised to discover the red-haired giant standing behind him.

"That is Astrid's work," Red-Beard told him, his voice gruff, as if he'd like to cut off Bjorn's hand for touching it.

"It is fine work," Bjorn answered, keeping his tone even. Crossing his arms over his chest, he turned back to the tapestry, admiring it. "My father...." He stopped before he explained that his father Alfar had been a silversmith, one of the best, and he knew fine craftsmanship when he saw it. His grandfather had also been a smith. Family lore told that the family's ability to create beautiful work was a gift from the elves. His father had died before Bjorn had had a chance to learn anything for himself. All he knew was how to fight. And how to bed women.

Red-Beard leaned in closer to Bjorn and said so no one could hear him. "If you hurt Astrid, I will come after you, and kill you slowly. One piece at a time." He looked Bjorn up and down. "Starting with your pretty teeth. Pop, pop, pop."

Bjorn clenched his jaw and took a breath. He had killed Jori in a fight, in revenge for killing his friend. It had not been murder, it had not been dishonorable, and he had no intention of hurting Astrid. He grew weary of her male kin threatening him.

He glared at Red-Beard. "I am no beardless boy, to be frightened by your threats. Come after me if you want. Rikki too. You will regret it."

With that, he walked away from Red-Beard before the other man could say anything more.

Harald had moved to stand next to Tryggvi, who sat in his high-seat. Bjorn's eyebrows shot up. It was odd to see the two brothers together. Harald, looking pleased with himself, waved Bjorn over.

When he got close enough, Harald gestured for him to take a seat on the bench in front of the high-seat. Married men stood all around, waiting. Emund Red-Beard walked over to take his place at Tryggvi's side, and he scowled at Bjorn.

Tryggvi nodded to Harald, who pulled something out from behind his back. A thick silver torc, the metal polished as smooth as glass, each end worked to form the head of a wolf. The eyes, made of onyx, gleamed in the firelight as Harald held it out in his hands as an offering. Bjorn's breath left him. He'd know his father's handiwork anywhere.

"Bjorn. You have no living male relatives. I have no surviving sons. Not yet. And none I am likely to live to see married," he chuckled. "I give this to you."

Bjorn traced his fingers over the smooth silver, the intricate detail of the wolf head. It was magnificent. He had to swallow hard, as thoughts of his father invaded his head. He grasped the torc in his hand and held it up. Then he placed it around his neck, the metal cool on his skin.

"*Takka fyrir*," Bjorn told Harald, and he saw his own pleasure reflected in Harald's face.

"Bjorn, son of Alfar," Tryggvi spoke up.

Reluctantly, Bjorn turned to face Tryggvi. He did not like hearing the name of his father on Tryggvi's lips, but he did not show it. The man looked so much like Jori up close that Bjorn caught himself thinking Jori had returned to walk the land of men again.

Tryggvi held up a hammer carved with the rune of Thor. "You are to marry my daughter. May it be a fruitful marriage." As the ceremonial hammer exchanged hands, Bjorn stared hard at Tryggvi. Much passed across the other man's face. All the hatred of Harald, the grief for his son, and the burning anger toward Bjorn.

After accepting the hammer, Bjorn tucked it into his belt and thanked Tryggvi.

"Now!" Harald boomed. "What do you need to know about women?" He clapped Bjorn on the back and barked a loud laugh. The other men followed, and as they left the longhouse to walk to the sacred grove for the wedding ceremony, they gave him advice on what to do with a wife.

Chapter Thirty-one

This was it. Time for the wedding ritual. Ingiborg placed the bridal crown on Astrid's head, the wreath woven with straw and wheat and garlanded with dried flowers. It rose high above her head, the same bridal crown that her mother had worn on her wedding day, kept stored away until this moment. Ingiborg fixed it, tucking a flower that had fallen off, back into place. Amma had woven blue silk ribbons into the crown, the same silk that trimmed the dress. The ribbons trailed down Astrid's back, like a cascading waterfall. Ragnhild fluffed out Astrid's hair, making sure it fell loosely over her shoulders.

One of the village women poked her head in the women's house to tell them that the men and all the guests waited for the bride.

Ingiborg laid a gentle kiss on Astrid's cheek. "You are a lovely bride."

Each of the married women also kissed her cheek and gave her their blessings.

Astrid managed a weak smile for them all, but inside she felt sick, until Ragnhild came to her turn. She ran her hands over Astrid's arms and whispered, "You can do this. You are strong."

Taking a deep breath, Astrid nodded to Ragnhild, and then hugged her.

"Careful!" Amma said. "Your dress and crown."

They met young Hak outside the door. The boy would lead the procession and carry the sword that would be a part of their marriage ceremony. After the deaths of Gunnar and Dyri, Tryggvi took in young Hak, to train him in the ways of war. Since none of Astrid's kinsmen would be in attendance and Rikki was too old, Hak stood in as the sword-bearer, and he puffed up with pride as he waited for the bridal procession.

One of Tryggvi's household men helped Hak with the sword.

"Don't let it drag on the ground."

"He looks very strong to me. You will not have any trouble, will you, Hak?" Astrid asked the boy. He was nearly twelve; the sword was a little heavy for him, and he had such a tight grip on it that his knuckles were white.

The household man laughed and clapped Hak on the back before leaving to join the wedding guests.

Astrid thought briefly to the night before, when her father had shown her the sword used for the wedding ritual. As soon as she saw the sword, she had the slightest glimmer of a thought. Bjorn would be unsuspecting. She could take that sword, and instead of holding it blade down, she could plunge it right into his heart, just as he had done to Jori. Then, horrified at her own thoughts, she had stammered out thanks to her father. He had given her a look that told her her face betrayed her. For a moment, she thought she saw a hint of a smile, but she looked away and when she looked back, he had reverted to his usual stony stare. It was as if Odin had showed himself in her father's face, and then, just as quickly, had disappeared. She had to suppress a shiver.

It was not far to the sacred grove where the ceremony would take place, but it felt like she walked all the way to Asgard. When they reached the outskirts of the grove, Astrid stopped and felt her neck for her Freya pendant. She sighed when her hand touched the pendant and purple bead.

"The goddesses are here with us," Ingiborg breathed. "Look around."

An autumn sun filtered through the grove of pine and birch where the wedding guests waited. Thor's sacred oath ring glinted on the stone altar, two gold finger rings resting inside the Thor ring's spiral, the gold gleaming in the low sunlight.

Had it only been last Autumnmonth since she had stood here for Ragnhild's wedding? It seemed like much longer than that. She searched for Rikki and found him with Short Olaf and Galm, but this time, instead of bouncing on the balls of his feet with impatience for the feast to start and joking with her, he stood rooted to the ground, distaste for what was about to happen swirling around him like a bad storm. He sensed her stare, and when he caught sight of her his eyes widened in shock. Next to him Galm nudged Short Olaf, who could not contain himself; he looked at her with such longing that a heaviness weighed on Astrid's chest. Galm's words about running away with Short Olaf spun in her head. Life would be so easy with Short Olaf. He loved her. He would care for her. If she married him, she knew he would even stop raiding with her father and remain at home. She would not lose him. He turned away as if watching her was painful.

The crowd shifted and parted for Hak, who preceded Astrid, and she saw the two sacred elm trees that grew over the altar stone, holding it like two enormous arms. Yellow leaves littered the ground around the sacred stone.

Her father, acting as *godi*, stood under the sacred trees, but Astrid's vision narrowed, and she saw only one person—Bjorn.

Astrid's breath caught and her step interrupted as she nearly tripped.

Bjorn waited for her, his blond hair combed back from his face, allowing his deep blue eyes to shine out as he watched her. His beard was trimmed and neat, exposing the white scar on his cheek. His eyebrows raised in appreciation as she came into full view, and he smiled, his lips full, his teeth straight. She remembered how his lips had felt on her cheek, and she took a deep breath to keep the heat from rising to her face.

He wore a tunic of the deepest blue, trimmed with silver tablet-woven edging, a perfect complement to her own blue dress. His trousers were blue, and the *winingas* wrapped around his calves were silver, like the edging on his tunic. A red cloak was held together with a thick silver clasp in the shape of a wolf-head. Under that, a stunning silver torc on his neck. He had a finger ring on the middle finger of each of his hands. The ceremonial Thor hammer was tucked into his soft leather belt.

When she got near him, her heart fluttered as he gave her a reassuring smile and reached his hand out to take hers.

Her father spoke, his voice loud and commanding, but she barely heard what he said. The feel of Bjorn's hand on hers, the closeness of him, overwhelmed her. He smelled faintly of lavender, and she thought again of what it would be like to have him in the bathhouse with her. Her thoughts were cut off when the sacrificial goat's bleating jarred her as someone brought it forward. Bjorn gave her hand a squeeze. For a moment, she was glad he was by her side and not an old lecherous man like Ketil, or a brute like Sigmund, who would not have cared about her distress or would even have laughed at it. But then she remembered that she would not love him.

Holding up the sacred bowl, plain and unadorned, but stained a dark red from blood sacrifices, Tryggvi said:

"Before these witnesses, may Thor bless this marriage!"

With his ornate, sacrificial dagger, he slit the goat's throat in one quick, practiced motion, catching the blood in the bowl. After the blood drained, Tryggvi placed the bowl on the sacred stones and picked up a bundle of fir-twigs that he dipped into the blood. He turned to face the couple. Astrid closed her eyes, knowing what was to come. Tryggvi touched her forehead with the stick, and Astrid felt the warmth of the blood. She opened her eyes when she heard the next animal brought forward—a sow in honor of Freya. Tryggvi repeated the sacrifice, calling out Freya to bless the marriage and to make it fruitful.

When the sacrificial animals had been removed, to be prepared for the feast, Bjorn let go of Astrid's hand and took a step to the side. She felt the loss of his presence, and she wanted to reach out for him again; he was the only thing holding her up. Then she heard Ragnhild's voice in her head, 'you can do this, you are strong.' Astrid looked at the sacred elms, standing ancient and strong, when she saw a falcon soar in the sky above them. Freya was here. The thought gave her strength.

With a nod from Tryggvi, Young Hak carried over the ceremonial sword. Astrid smiled at how proud the boy looked at his part in the ceremony. Tryggvi took it from him, and Hak stepped back. Tryggvi held the sword between Astrid and Bjorn, the tip pointing down. He nodded to them.

They placed their hands on the hilt. Bjorn's hand covered Astrid's smaller one, and the pressure was reassuring. She started to smile at him, but then a cold wave washed over her. That was the same hand that had wielded the sword that killed her brother. She was giving herself to Jori's killer. Pushing down the urge to rip her hand off the sword hilt, Astrid gripped the sword even tighter, as if it were a tree branch growing from the ground and bolstering her. She felt the blood leave her face.

She turned away from Bjorn and searched for her mother. Ingiborg stood watching with the other married women, and although she did not have the smile of joy that she should have at her daughter's wedding, she looked pleased. She gave Astrid a reassuring nod when she caught her eye.

Astrid focused on how Bjorn had been when they'd met, before she knew who he was. It helped a little.

Her father moved to the altar and picked up the Thor oath ring, a gold arm ring that spiraled three times, and on the end, held a large Thor hammer amulet. The two gold wedding bands had been placed inside the oath ring before the ceremony.

Tryggvi took the smaller ring and placed it on the butt of the sword with a nod to Bjorn. He picked up the gold band, and Astrid held out her left hand so he could slide the ring over her finger. The touch of his hand as it slid the ring on made her shiver, but the ring felt heavy, as if it were pounds of gold rather than a sliver. This was it. The ring on her finger signified she now belonged to this man.

It surprised her she could lift her hand to take the wedding band that her father held out for her. Bjorn's wedding band. It was smooth and perfectly round. She hoped the smoothness of the gold meant their marriage would go smoothly, but she doubted it. How could it?

She placed the gold band on Bjorn's hand to signify the joining of their two lives. As she did so, she noticed he had nice hands, strong with long elegant fingers. She slipped the band over his finger. It felt so intimate, touching his hand.

Now the wedding bands were on their fingers, Astrid and Bjorn gripped the hilt of the sword again.

Tryggvi spoke. "Astrid, daughter of Tryggvi. Before the gods, before Thor, Freya, and Freyr, and before those assembled here as witness, will you swear an oath to give yourself to Bjorn, son of Alfar, to honor him as your husband?"

Astrid looked at her father, stern and serious, and then she turned her gaze to Bjorn. He was so handsome and had treated her well, so far. It was too late, anyway. She could not back out now. The assembled guests were so quiet, she heard the *shush* of the trees that surrounded them. A cool autumn breeze blew in, ruffling her dress around her legs. Everyone waited for her answer.

"I will," she said.

"Bjorn, son of Alfar. Before the gods, before Thor, Freya, and Freyr, and before those assembled here as witness, will you swear an oath to give yourself to Astrid, daughter of Tryggvi, to honor her as your wife?"

"I will," Bjorn answered with no hesitation.

Tryggvi held the oath ring above their heads, the gold shining in the weak sunlight. "Bless this joining."

The guests repeated, 'bless this joining.'

Tryggvi took the sword and handed it back to Hak.

With that, Bjorn took both of Astrid's hands in his and leaned down to kiss her. As he leaned in, she smelled a hint of lavender from the water in the bathhouse, and his breath smelled like mint. When his lips touched hers, a spark raced through her like a flash of fire. His lips were gentle and when he broke the kiss, she had the desire to pull him back down to her. Chastising her treacherous body that would not let her hate him, Astrid lowered her head as the wedding guests cheered.

"To the feast hall!"

Harald clapped Bjorn on the back. "The *brudhlaup!*"

Bjorn didn't think he needed to worry about beating Astrid to the feast hall, no worry that he and the men would end up serving if the women got there first. He was glad the ceremony was finished. The poor girl looked so unhappy and confused, he wanted it to be over for her sake. He had tried to make her more comfortable, but every time he tried, she looked even more unsettled.

"Sorry, wife," Bjorn said with a grin, trying on the word. "The women will serve at the feast. No one beats me in a race."

That perked her up, and she raised her eyebrows, her pretty face lighting up. Perhaps Astrid liked a challenge?

Her blue eyes widened at something behind him, and he turned around, but he saw nothing. At the same time, he felt a ruffle at his sleeve as Astrid ran, her friend Ragnhild at her side. Astrid let out a shriek of laughter as they got their head start.

"You can't let a woman win," Harald growled.

Bjorn laughed. "Let her have her lead. It will be more fun when I pass her."

The thought of catching Astrid, of sweeping her up in his arms, of her light laughter, made him think of what she would be like in bed, and the force of his desire surprised him.

The other wedding guests, except for the older men and women who could not run, and the women who cared for the babies, had all taken off in the race.

"Now I will go," Bjorn said, and he took off, running easily and quickly, soon passing the slower women and the young children. It felt good to run after the tension of the wedding ceremony.

Up ahead he saw a tawny head running as fast as he could go. As he ran up to his son, Bjorn slowed, so they were running side by side. Tanni beamed at him.

"Go, Papa! Catch her!"

"Think I can?"

"Yes! You are the fastest!"

Bjorn liked the person he was in his son's eyes. He sped up, leaving them behind, and soon he saw Astrid ahead. She held her dress so it would not encumber her, and she was faster than he had thought.

He deliberately made noise when he approached them from behind. Astrid looked back and let out a squeak and tried to run faster, but she was at the end of her endurance.

Bjorn laughed. "I told you. No one beats me." He whirled to run backward, teasing her.

He felt, rather than saw, the movement to the side and he pivoted, but he was too late, and three dogs shot behind him, barking and jumping, as they joined in the excitement. One of the dogs cut him off at the knees. His feet taken out from under him, Bjorn fell.

Astrid cried out his name.

Lucky for him, he had trained his entire life on how to fall and get up again. Instead of fighting it, he tucked his head and rolled on the ground, popping up, barely breaking his stride.

The men urged him to hurry. Whoever lost the *brudhlaup* had to serve the others, and so far, Bjorn had never been to a wedding where the men had lost. His would not be the first.

He saw the feast hall not far ahead and the guests who had already arrived. Some of the younger men already held drinks. Putting on a last burst of speed, Bjorn reached the hall. The men congratulated him and clapped him on the back. He brushed dirt and grass from his hair and clothes from when he had fallen. Unsheathing his sword, he laid it across the entry-way, barring his new wife from entering. Then he waited for Astrid to catch up.

It did not take her long. She arrived breathless, with a pink glow to her cheeks. She had taken off the bridal crown for the race and her long, golden hair was loose around her face. The sight of her like that made him want to pick her up and take her somewhere far away, where he could slowly discover her body. Given time, he could make her forget she hated him.

He must have let his thoughts show on his face, for Astrid's eyes grew wide, which only made her more beguiling. She lay a hand on her cheeks, her new gold wedding band glowing like a beacon that she was taken. In three strides he reached her and swept her up into his arms. She gasped when he did it and clutched onto his neck. He could feel her heart pounding against his chest, and her breath came in short gasps. The feel of her against him aroused him, and he had to take a breath to tamp it down. It was like he was a boy with no control of himself, not a man of twenty, who had his first woman at fourteen.

People hooted when he took her, and they crowded the couple, ready to watch as he carried her over the hall's threshold. Carrying his new wife, he paused before they entered.

Atli called out, "If you trip Pretty Bjorn, your wife will turn into a shrew to pick at you night and day!"

A female voice added to the din. "Asta! If he trips, your new husband will not give you sons."

"Careful Bjorn, don't drop her or you'll never have a moment of happiness in your marriage!"

That one was grim, and Bjorn searched to see who had said it, but it was impossible to discern any one person. Everyone shouted out their favorite dismal outcomes for him tripping or dropping Astrid.

He shifted her in his arms for a better grip, and she hissed in a breath.

"Don't worry," he whispered as he lightly kissed her cheek. "I have you. We won't fall."

Stepping over the threshold, he easily carried his new wife through the door.

"To the luck of our marriage!" Bjorn plunged his new sword into the main pillar of the great hall.

Everyone watched as the new bridegroom performed the next ritual in the ceremony. The men shouted encouragement, some of them already on their way to becoming drunk.

Tryggvi stepped up to the oak pillar and checked the depth of the thrust. Bjorn had sunk the sword deep into the wood. Tryggvi raised his eyebrows at his new son-by-law, as if recognizing for the first time what kind of warrior he was.

"This marriage will be fruitful. You will have many sons," Tryggvi proclaimed. He said it proudly, but his face looked like he'd eaten something sour.

Everyone praised the new couple.

Bjorn sought his son in the crowd. The boy was with Katrin, hanging on to her skirt in the large throng of unfamiliar people. Thinking Thor had already blessed him with such a stout, healthy son, Bjorn gave Tanni a wink. If he could fill his house with children, he would.

With that thought, he wrapped his arm around Astrid's waist and pulled her to him. The guests cheered, thumping their cups on tables. She did not resist, but he felt her trembling. Was it from nerves or desire? Only one way to find out. He leaned down and kissed her, her sweet young lips soft, and he felt her relax into it. He could hear people making bawdy comments and ignored them. She pressed her body to his, and he pulled her even closer. But then she tensed, her lips tightening up, and she put a hand on his chest and backed away from him. It reminded him too much of the day they'd met, when she had done the same thing, ready to give him over to her brother.

"'Gonna have to do better than that to please your new wife, Pretty Bjorn!" Styrr's voice carried over the laughter of the guests.

Bjorn forced out a laugh and tried to contain the anger he felt at her rebuff. If she wanted to hate him, fine, but not in front of everyone.

"I'm sure Pretty Bjorn has coaxed out more than one virgin!" someone else shouted. "He'll rise to the challenge."

Their bawdy laughter made Astrid pale, and Bjorn rested his hand on the small of her back. Angry or not, she was his wife, and he would protect her, even during the inevitable talk of virgins and deflowering that would last until he took her to bed.

The smell of various meats and vegetables, stews, and mead wafted through the hall, and thralls entered carrying trays of food and pitchers of mead. They brought roasted meats, the skin crackling from where the fire had browned it. Thralls carried in bowls of rich boar stew heavy with white carrots, turnips, kale, and wild onions and set them at the tables, the steam rising. They brought out more platters and bowls of roasted root vegetables cooked with onion and covered in butter, and bitter greens tossed with cloudberries. Alongside the vegetables came the platters of hard cheeses, rounds of wheat-floured bread as well as barley and oat bread. Little hazelnut and honeyed cakes topped with tart cherries were saved for after the main meal for a treat. At the high-table sat bowls of exotic walnuts. Female thralls wound their way among the tables, constantly filling cups with meadowsweet mead and ale. Even the children got watered down mead.

"Let the feast begin!" Tryggvi called out.

Bjorn took Astrid's hand and led her to the head table and the two chairs that were for them, Tryggvi's raven carved into the backs and painted black. As the married couple, they sat just next to Tryggvi and Ingiborg, while Harald and Katrin sat to Bjorn's left. The other guests sat accordingly, with family members next to the head table, and then the household men of both Tryggvi and Harald. At the far end were the villagers and other guests, including the children. Bench companions who shared the barley bread trenchers began talking and laughing as they waited for the rest of the ceremony.

Once seated, Bjorn leaned into Astrid and whispered, "Do not do that to me again."

Her eyes flashed at him.

"Hate me if you must, *wife*, but not in front of witnesses."

"I—"

She was cut off by her mother leaning across Tryggvi to tell her it was time for her to serve her new husband. Bjorn wished that Astrid had said whatever it was she was going to say. The girl was confusing, one moment leaning on him as if he were the only thing holding her up, and then the next pushing him away as if his touch repulsed her. Did he want the challenge, or did he leave her alone, only visiting her long enough for her to get with child?

At her mother's reminder, Astrid stood and went to pick up the ceremonial drinking bowl in front of her and Bjorn. But Bjorn's words had unnerved her, and she had to stop to steady her hands. What had she been thinking, pushing him away like that in front of everyone? He was right, and she had angered the man she would have to share a bed with that night.

"Astrid," Ingiborg whispered.

Her mother's voice shook her out of her panic. She took a breath and focused on the ceremonial bowl. It had seen many weddings, and her mother had served her father with it at their wedding feast. It was a large oval shaped bowl, made from elm, stained and sanded until it shone like glass. On both ends of the bowl were two horse heads, their eyes large, mouths open. Astrid poured mead infused with drops of the blood from the wedding sacrifice into the bowl and picked it up by the two horse heads. As she did this Bjorn shoved his chair back, so he could stand to receive the offering. Her physical reaction to him surprised her as she watched him unfold himself with ease and grace. If he had only been a hateful, lecherous old man, it would be much easier to hate him. Easier to stay away from him. As it was, she found herself drawn to him, wanting his touch, only to be repulsed when reminded that he had killed her brother. Then she could feel the blood on his hands as if it was seeping into her dress, staining her body.

She lifted the cup.

"I bring you mead, my husband
Mixed with honor and pride;

Mixed with mighty songs and runes.
Drink it and be well."

He took the bowl, his hands touching hers, and he held it up. His voice was as thick and rich as honey.

"Thor! Bless this bride!
May she bear many babes, brave, hale, healthy, wise and
Sharp as the blade."

He took a sip, and the guests cheered him. They all drank from their own cups.

It was Astrid's turn, and she steadied herself to make sure her voice rang out over the hall loud and clear.

"Freya! Bless this union." She knew she should have said more, but she could not bring her thoughts together. It would have to do, and no one seemed to care.

The wedding guests all drank and hailed her, and everyone again raised their cups and took a drink to toast the new couple.

She and Bjorn each took a handle, and they placed the ceremonial bowl on the table. Glad she could take a seat, Astrid sat down with a quiet sigh of relief. She had once attended a wedding where the wife had spilled the ceremonial mead right into her husband's lap. It had not been a good start for their marriage. The woman died from illness the next summer. Astrid thanked Freya for a steady hand.

Bjorn stood up again and pulled the Thor hammer out of his belt. He knelt before Astrid and placed the hammer in her lap. It was warm from being next to his body.

"On my wife's lap I lay Mjolnir,
The hammer to bless the bride
In Frigg's name, we bless the marriage."

After he finished, the guests all raised their drinks and yelled out their additional blessings for the marriage. Men banged on the tables with their cups. If all of their blessings came true, she and

Bjorn would have so many children, it would take a house as big as the great hall to hold them all.

Chapter Thirty-two

Astrid collapsed onto a bench to catch her breath. After the feast, the trestle tables had been broken down, and the benches pushed against the walls. She had been dancing with Bjorn and, it seemed, everyone else. It was well into the night, and so far everyone had been getting along, or at least, the two camps had kept their distance. At one end of the feast hall, some of Tryggvi's household men gathered with a group of Harald's men. The mead was flowing generously, so the men were all good and drunk. One man told a story and from the blustery way he spoke and the more he waved his arms, Astrid knew they were taking part in *flytings*, bragging about their own prowess in fighting or with women, while insulting the other men. It surprised her to not see her brother among them; Rikki usually loved to *flyt*. He was either staying clear of Harald's men, or he was with a woman.

A woman squealed and laughed, followed by a deep male voice. In a dark recess of the hall, a man had a woman up against the wall. The sight of them together reminded Astrid that she would soon be put to bed with Bjorn. The thought made her quiver with anticipation and dread.

The feel of a small hand patting her leg made Astrid jump, and she turned away from the couple in the dark to find Tanni standing at her side, trying to get her attention. She looked for the boy's nurse, or Katrin, or even Bjorn, but the thrall had disappeared, Katrin was in Harald's lap, and Bjorn was dancing. Gytha had gone to the women's house to look after the babies; at twelve, she was too much of an attraction to drunk men.

The little boy stared at her with piercing hazel eyes that Astrid worried he could tell she had been thinking about what Bjorn would be like in her bed. But that was silly. He was a child.

"Hello, Tanni," Astrid said. "You are up late. Why are you not with the other children?"

He didn't answer right away, but kept studying her. "You are my new mama?"

She did not know what she had expected him to say. Not that. She searched again for a rescue, but none came.

"My mama is dead." The boy said it so plainly, Astrid wondered if he even remembered his mother.

"I know." She put her hand on his back. "I am sorry."

He scooted closer and leaned into her. "Papa married you."

"Yes."

"You will live with us?"

"Yes."

The boy nodded as if the world suddenly made sense and proclaimed. "You are my new mama."

"You can call me Asta." She felt like she was walking through a stream with slippery rocks at the bottom.

Her senses prickling, Astrid looked over at where Katrin sat with Harald. The woman glared at her, her glance flicking between her and Tanni. Possessiveness was in her eyes.

Astrid stared back and ran her hand over Tanni's messy tawny hair. Eyes narrowed, Harald's big hand then distracted Katrin when he put it on her thigh.

Her spirit lifted when she saw her mother coming over to her, a smile on her tired face as she took in the little boy leaning on Astrid's legs.

"I see you have made a new friend," Ingiborg said, as she lowered herself slowly to the bench next to Astrid. She smiled at Tanni. "A good thing."

An image of a young Jori, his red-gold hair shining in a midsummer sun, rose in Astrid's mind. "Were you married to Father when Jori was conceived?"

Ingiborg nodded and stroked her belly that was showing signs of the baby. "Jorund was a by-blow from when your father was away."

Astrid winced at the crude term coming from her mother. She watched Bjorn as he danced and laughed with the guests, many of the women having flocked to his side. He was brighter and more colorful than every man in the room, so it was natural for the women to fly to him, like moths to a torch. His blond hair stood out in contrast to the dark of the red and black striped tapestry that hung on the wall. In the flickering firelight, the stripes seemed to sway in time to the music.

"I suppose I will have to get used to that."

Ingiborg glanced down at the boy who was was fiddling with one of Astrid's necklaces. She let him.

"You will." Ingiborg's gaze traveled around the room until it landed on Tryggvi. "You cannot do anything about when they are traveling. It is to be expected." She turned back to Astrid and took her hair in her hands, gently smoothing it down. "But take control of what happens at home, *dottir*. Do not allow him to bring a concubine into your home."

Astrid shuddered at the thought of Bjorn doing that to her, but men did it all the time. They set up thralls as concubines and made their wives live with them in the same household. Her eyes flicked over to Katrin. Harald's wife seemed fine with Harald parading his mistress around.

"How can I do that?" Astrid asked. "Bjorn is not a weak man who can be controlled by a wife."

"Like The Crow?" Ingiborg said with a smile.

Astrid started. "How did you know about that name?"

"You and Rikki are not as sly as you think. Did you think I wouldn't notice that you called the tanner's wife The Crow?" She leaned into Astrid and gestured toward the woman who drank with the men, easily holding her own, while her husband snored in the corner. "She does peck at him, doesn't she?"

"*Ja.*" It was nice talking to her mother like this, like a married woman gossiping, sharing secrets.

"You will find your way with Bjorn." Ingiborg returned to the original thread and took Astrid's Freya pendant in her hand. "Let the goddess guide you."

"Pretty!" Tanni said when he saw the pendant with its purple bead. His little fingers reached out for the bead. He got hold of it and tried to pull it down to look at it closer. The cord dug into Astrid's neck. She grabbed him under his arms and slid him into her lap so he could reach better.

As she settled him, she glanced up at the dancing guests. The rhythm of the drums had sped up, and she jiggled her legs to the beat. Bjorn caught sight of her, and a genuine smile broke over his face at the sight of his son in her lap. His eyes were glassy from all the mead he'd been drinking, his hair mussed from dancing, but he looked even more handsome, if that were possible. Her heart fluttered, and she quickly looked away to avoid his eyes.

She looked for someone safer. Guests had settled at tables and benches to tell lygisogur, stories mostly about weddings and marriages, each storyteller trying to outdo the others. Some guests would even come with their tales prepared. Emund and Short Olaf were in the circle of storytellers, both of them gesturing with their hands. From the way Emund moved, she could tell it was the story of Thor and Loki, the one where they dressed as bride and bride's maiden and stole Thor's hammer back from the giant Thrym.

Astrid took in the happy faces of the people in the hall, all of them sated with excellent food, drunk on mead, and enjoying themselves with dancing and games. There had even developed a tenuous peace between some of Tryggvi's and Harald's huskarls. This was why she married Bjorn, to bring about this peace. To ensure that when Harald's men were at her door, it was for a peaceful celebration, and not to kill the men and carry off the women and children.

Bjorn walked over and swept Tanni up into his arms. He swayed a little but caught himself before stumbling. "What are you still doing up?" He asked his son. Bjorn's eyes shone with excitement. His lips looked so inviting, Astrid wanted to kiss him.

"Don't want to leave." Tanni's lips pressed together in stubbornness.

Bjorn leaned over to Astrid. "I was the same. I never wanted to leave a feast."

She liked thinking of him as a little boy and could see him pretending to be grown-up, with his play sword and shield. She knew she would have liked him. But it was impossible to keep that picture of a little boy for long with him, very much a man, standing next to her.

Nodding at what he'd said, she said. "Once when we were young, Rikki, Jori and I snuck back into the hall during a feast. We should have been in bed, but we wanted to know what the grown-ups were doing. It all sounded like so much fun. So, we snuck in and hid under a table with my father's dogs."

Bjorn chuckled and shifted Tanni in his arms. Tanni had tired. "Did you get found out?"

"Ja. We thought we were in trouble." Astrid smiled at the memory. "Father laughed at us, and when he pulled me out from under the table, he swept me into his arms and took me out to dance. He said as long as I was there, I might as well have some fun. Emund and Buri taught Rikki and Jori how to play jomswikinger. It was a good night."

The pained look on Bjorn's face surprised her.

"You were well loved," he said.

"Yes." She tried to meet his eyes, but he had looked elsewhere, to find Harald, and he absentmindedly rubbed his cheek.

It reminded her that Harald was his foster-father. She wondered how well loved the young Bjorn had been.

His gaze leaving Harald, Bjorn shook his head and looked around. "Where is your brother?"

A quick search of the great hall, and Astrid discovered that Rikki was still not there. Galm was also missing. Thinking about it, she realized she had not seen her brother for a long time. A further study showed that several of her father's *huskarls* were also missing, those closest to Rikki. A wave of unease swept through Astrid. Something was wrong. She reached up to touch her Freya pendant.

Instead of giving voice to her unease, she laughed it off and told Bjorn. "Probably off gambling."

Bjorn's eyes went to her hand as she touched her pendant, and he frowned. "*Ja*. I'm sure that's it." He rubbed the back of his neck.

He looked down at Tanni. "Time for you to go to sleep. Where is your nurse?"

"Some man..." Tanni mumbled, drooping in his father's arms.

Astrid froze.

"Something wrong?" Bjorn asked her.

"No," Astrid said, although she had begun to sweat. The heat from so many bodies closed in on her.

He hefted Tanni. "Let's go find her."

As soon as Bjorn wound his way through the crowd, Astrid hurried over to Short Olaf, who had just finished telling his tale with Emund.

"Do you think your new husband will let you dance with me?" He said it in a teasing way, but she heard the catch as he said the word 'husband.'

She pulled him aside and asked, "Where is Rikki?"

Short Olaf looked around. The lyres and flute played again, and a circle formed for more dancing. He had to raise his voice over the din. "I don't know."

Astrid's unease grew. Was he in a fight with Harald's men? If so, someone would have alerted Tryggvi or Harald, and they were both here in the hall. Harald was drinking and talking boisterously with some of his men, while Tryggvi lounged in his high-seat. Ingiborg had rejoined him. If something was wrong, he would not be so relaxed.

"Do I need to look for him?" Short Olaf asked.

"No." This was a feast. So her brother and others were missing. They could be outside dicing or gambling or anything.

"I'm sure he's with a woman. You know him," Short Olaf reassured her, leaning down to speak to her more quietly. "Rikki would have told me if something was going on."

That made her feel better. Rikki, Galm, and Short Olaf were inseparable, and had been since they had all been old enough to walk. Short Olaf would know if the other two planned something. She needed to stop letting her mind run away like this.

As she searched the feast hall one last time, she caught Bjorn watching her with Short Olaf, his eyes focused on the hand she still had resting on Short Olaf's arm. Her heart flipped, and she jerked her hand away. Bjorn's stare burned into her and fear of him flickered in her stomach. She had not figured her new husband would be a jealous man, but what did she know about him? She would have to be more careful to not allow her actions to hurt either her or Short Olaf. He had been a part of her life for so long, it would be hard to shut him out

A thrall hurried to Bjorn, taking his attention away from Astrid. It was Tanni's nurse, and she looked flustered as she approached Bjorn. Her dark red hair, cut close to her head to signify she was a thrall, was tangled, and her eyes glowed with satisfaction. He glowered at her. Astrid waited, watching to see how Bjorn would treat the thrall who had disappeared. She hoped he would not strike her.

The thrall spoke to Bjorn and he handed her the now sleeping Tanni, speaking to her through a clenched jaw. He did not raise his hand to her, but he appeared angry. The nurse shifted the sleeping boy in her arms and quickly left the feast hall. She would take Tanni back to the women's bower to sleep with the rest of the children and their mothers and nurses, something she should have done long ago.

As the nurse exited with Tanni, Rikki and Galm walked through the door, both of them more serious than they should have been during a wedding feast. Galm pushed his way in, as if he did not see her or the boy, but Rikki stepped aside to let the nurse pass with her sleeping cargo. An exchange that only Astrid could interpret happened between Rikki and the nurse in that brief encounter. Rikki made the slightest eye contact with the woman, and the smallest flicker passed before his eyes. It happened in the beat of a heart, but Astrid knew it for what it was. Rikki had been with a woman, as she had suspected—Tanni's nurse. It did not help rid her of her unease. But why would she feel like this? It was perfectly normal for a man to bed a thrall. It would be unusual if some man hadn't taken her. The girl was lucky it was Rikki and not someone else, someone much worse. But she was Bjorn's thrall. Was Rikki trying to prove something?

Astrid's distress eased when Rikki's face lit up with a smile as he strode over to her. He kissed her cheek.

"You are the prettiest bride, *systir*. Too bad it's wasted on *him*." He tossed his head, his blond hair flopping in his face, and indicated Bjorn.

She narrowed her eyes to study him. He was not drunk, which itself was suspicious. "Where have you been?"

He tilted his head and gave her his mischievous grin. "You don't want to know."

Galm sauntered over with two cups in his hands. He handed one to Rikki, who took a drink.

"What were you doing?" Astrid asked.

Galm snorted. He looked Astrid up and down, waggling his eyebrows. "You make a pretty bride. You'll be a pretty widow too." He laughed.

"Widow?" she exclaimed.

Galm shrugged. "Bjorn is one of Harald Olafsson's *hird*. He has many enemies. It is only a matter of time."

Once, Astrid would have liked to think of Bjorn dead, and herself as a widow. Now she was not so sure. She searched for her new husband, who had migrated to a corner where Harald and his men had started an arm-wrestling contest. He had rolled up the sleeve of his tunic, and the black knotwork marking that wound up his forearm stood out as his muscles strained against his opponent. They appeared evenly matched, until the other man tired, and then it took only a moment before Bjorn slammed his hand down on the table. He grinned and leaned back, flexing his hand, the muscles in his arm still pumped up. Astrid remembered how those powerful arms had felt when he lifted her into his arms to cross the threshold.

Another man took the place opposite Bjorn, and the arm-wrestling continued.

"By Tyr, I hate it that Harald Olafsson and his men are in my father's feast hall," Rikki said, teeth gritted.

"They eat our food, drink our mead, swive our women," Galm added, his voice growling with hatred. "When what they deserve is steel in their bellies. Harald first."

"Bjorn first," Rikki said.

They clinked their silver cups together and laughed.

Galm noticed Astrid's face. "Don't look so upset." He pointed to Harald, who played dice with several of the men, Katrin on his lap. One man rolled the dice, and Harald threw up his hands in disgust, mead slopping out onto his and Katrin's lap. He laughed drunkenly and licked the mead off her throat while the other men snickered. Katrin laughed along with him, and she angled her body toward him. Astrid looked to her mother, who frowned at the display.

"Harald killed my father. How often has he tried to kill *your* father? And Red? If he had found you or your mother or Gytha, he would have taken you for slaves. At best."

As he knew it would, Galm's point hit the mark. Even though the feast hall was hot from all the bodies, she shivered as she remembered the times that her father and Emund had had to fight Harald. What would have happened to her and her mother if Harald *had* killed her father? And the thought of Emund killed made her feel sick.

Galm nodded toward Harald and Katrin. "That could be one of *our* women."

"That's enough, Galm," Rikki broke in.

"Here," her brother handed her his drink, and she drank deeply of the strong mead.

When she had finished her drink, he took it from her and shoved it at Galm. He gave his friend a hard look.

Rikki grabbed Astrid's hand and pulled her out into the middle of the floor of the hall where people were dancing. Her brother was a good dancer, and he led her in the circle, spinning in time with the music. Normally, they would dance together easily; this time, he held himself tense and alert. It would be harder than she thought to weave the two families together.

Chapter Thirty-three

"Time to find out if Bjorn can hit the mark with his arrow!"

"Sheathe his sword!"

More talk of swords, of forging his steel, of taming mares, flew through the hall as the drunk men took delight in the tradition of ribbing the new groom.

Although she could see that Bjorn took it with ease and laughed, Astrid, in a panic, sought her mother and Ragnhild. He had experience, while the only intimacy Astrid had ever known were the few stolen times with Gunnar, and those only involved kissing. In secret. Everyone would be on hand to see her put to bed. Her only consolation was that they would not stay to watch the actual deed. She hoped.

Astrid could not find her mother, but Ragnhild came to fetch her.

Ragnhild recognized Astrid's distress. "It will be fine. You said yourself Bjorn would not hurt you."

She had said that, but she was not so sure anymore. She thought of the agitation on his face when he saw her touch Short Olaf, or how angry he'd been when she pushed him away. Across the hall, the men had surrounded Bjorn, and plied him with drink while mocking him about his manhood. He laughed with them, and even though he took a cup handed to him, he did not drink from it. Astrid did not know if that was a good thing or bad.

As if in answer to her unspoken question, Ingiborg walked up with the bridal crown in her hands. Her eyes were on Bjorn. "If he is deep in his cups, then you might be spared this night, *dottir*."

Ragnhild chuckled. "Bjorn would not be the first groom to not perform on his wedding night."

"It is a surprise that any wedding night is completed, with everyone so drunk," Ingiborg added.

"Dyri..." Ragnhild said with a wistful sigh. Tears filled her eyes, but she wiped them away quickly.

A boisterous group of men carried Bjorn along in their wake, their bawdy talk getting worse as the time for the bedding drew closer. Noticeable for their absence were Emund, who remained outside of the huddle of men, and Rikki and Galm, who had disappeared again. It was just as well. Astrid did not think she could bear the burden of her brother's hatred of Bjorn right now.

At the head of the crowd, Tryggvi approached his wife and daughter. "It is time." He gave Astrid a long look. In an undertone meant for her alone, he said. "Do your duty, *dottir*."

Anger flashed through her like lightning. She had married Bjorn, the enemy of her family, her brother's killer, and her father was telling her to do her duty? Not for the first time, she wished she were a man and could lash out with her fists. But she was not. Instead, she narrowed her eyes and looked her father full in the face. "I will." She was about to add a retort, that she expected him and Harald to do their duty and cease fighting, but she bit her tongue.

The married women joined them, and with Ingiborg and Amma leading the way, they took Astrid out of the feast hall. At the door, thralls met the women with torches. Here they left the men behind and proceeded to the *kvenna hus* that they had arranged for the new couple to share for the night. With good wishes from the other women, Astrid and her three attendants entered the house. Astrid gasped. Her father and mother's bed dominated the chamber.

Two posts reared up from it, both of them mare's heads. A large eiderdown pillow rested against the headboard. Astrid and her attendants had woven the bed linens specifically for her wedding. It was part of her bride-price, her heiman fylgja. The blanket was the one she had so carefully woven to take with her into her marriage. In a short time, Bjorn Alfarsson and the wedding guests would converge on this room, with their talk of sex and fertility, and she would be arranged in the bed like an offering.

When the door closed behind her, Astrid jumped.

"Relax. You are as skittish as a cat," Ingiborg told her, talking in the voice she used when soothing birthing mothers. She fussed with the linens, folding the blanket down and making sure everything was in place and clean.

"Being nervous will only make it worse," Ragnhild added as she picked up the nightdress Astrid would wear and shook it out. Astrid looked at it as if it would bite.

"Ragna is right," Ingiborg said.

As she straightened the bed, Ragnhild hummed to herself. "Such luxury to be with a husband in this soft bed."

"Do you want a drink?" Ingiborg asked. There was a pitcher of mead and two ornately decorated silver cups on a table in one corner of the chamber, along with a platter of cheese and raspberries. Astrid and Bjorn would drink the honeyed mead every day for a full cycle of the moon.

"It might calm you." Ragnhild gestured for Astrid to move closer so she could begin the undressing.

"But you loved your husband," Astrid said, her voice squeaking, and her legs felt like stone, so reluctant was she to take this final step.

As the women talked, Amma walked around the chamber, blessing it with a song. When finished, she pulled three figurines out of a bag she carried at her waist and placed them on a small altar. First she set down a figure of Thor, his hammer in his lap, next a statuette of Freya, wearing her necklace and finally, Frey. His figure had always made Astrid laugh, but tonight it did not seem so funny. The seated Frey had an enormous erection. So big it reached up to his beard.

Astrid felt all the blood leave her face as she stared at Frey.

Ingiborg laughed when she saw Astrid's face. "My dear. Don't worry. I've never seen a man that big."

"We would have noticed if Bjorn was that well-endowed," Ragnhild teased. "He'd be unable to sit down properly. And he'd walk with a limp."

Astrid let out a nervous laugh. He might not be that big, but it had to hurt.

The fire sputtered and spit as Amma threw fragrant herbs on it. The scent of sage permeated the room. "All women must do this," she said as she stoked the fire.

Ingiborg ran her hand down Astrid's arms. "Amma is right. You will be fine."

"Ja," Ragnhild teased. "Think of the rest of your new husband. Everything is well put together. I'm sure it is there, too."

Astrid yelped, sounding to herself like a dog whose tail was stepped on.

"Stop it, Ragna, you are not helping," Ingiborg chided, shaking her head, but her voice was light.

With a gulp, Astrid tore her gaze away from the figure of Frey. They had finished preparing the space, and it was time to prepare her. Ragnhild removed her necklaces and looped them over the bed posts. The three women helped her out of her wedding dress and into the night dress. Ingiborg had embroidered knotwork in red thread along the neckline but had left the rest of the dress plain and white. Despite the fire that burned, Astrid shivered in the lightweight dress. Ragnhild brushed out her hair again until it was as shiny as glass.

When they finished, Astrid climbed into the bed, the bedclothes cool on her bare legs and feet. It was softer than any bed she'd ever been in, and she luxuriated in the richness for a moment. For the final touch, Ingiborg settled the bridal wreath back on Astrid's head.

They were just in time. Astrid heard the commotion of the procession of the men and the other wedding guests as they made their way from the feast hall to the bride's house. In her mind, Astrid could see the torchlight flickering in the dark so Bjorn, the new groom, could join his wife in the light. She had taken part in many such processions, enjoying the joking and teasing that went with it, but now, on the other side of the festivities, she was as jumpy as a deer at a watering hole. In moments, they would all be at the door, Bjorn leading the way.

Before that happened, Ingiborg, Ragnhild, and Amma all surrounded Astrid and linked hands. Amma had taken her own Freya amulet and placed it in Astrid's lap.

"Freya! Goddess of sexual union
Bless this bride
Bless the groom
Bless this night
May it bear fruit."

Their quiet moment ended when the guests and groom arrived. Ingiborg and Amma both gave Astrid's hands a quick squeeze before they let her go.

A gale of laughter erupted outside, the door banged open, and Bjorn was shoved inside. He had removed most of his clothes too, and only wore his linen under-trousers and a short, plain tunic. He stumbled and stopped short when he saw her. She had a flash of what she must have looked like to him, sitting in the bed, her blond hair spilling out over her shoulders and down her back, the white nightdress with its shockingly red trim barely covering her nakedness. Her body naked of any jewelry or ornamentation, except for the bridal crown that rose high above her head. She looked into his eyes and knew what an animal must feel like the instant before the hunter releases his arrow.

People crowded into the bride house, Tryggvi and Harald right behind Bjorn. Ingiborg moved to stand by Tryggvi's side. A few of the guests made jokes about Astrid and Bjorn, but their talk sounded far away to Astrid, like they were down in a well. Her blood pounded in her ears, and the room grew heavy with the odor of so many people and of the mead and meat on their breaths. It made Astrid feel queasy, and she hoped they would all leave soon. Panic hit her like a burst of lighting. What if they didn't leave? This was an important match. What if the witnesses stayed to make sure she fulfilled the marriage oath?

Bjorn strode over to her, steady on his feet, and he knelt on the edge of the bed. She quivered with him so close to her, and she closed her eyes. He gently removed the crown from her head, the last symbol of their union. The wedding guests hooted and whooped.

"That's not the only thing you'll remove tonight, Bjorn!" someone shouted, and that evoked laughter.

"The other won't be so easy..."

"But he'll push through!"

"Shut it," Emund boomed over the snickering. The remarks and laughter quieted but did not stop. Part of the fun of a wedding was the crude jokes at the bride and groom's expense. Everyone had to endure it.

Eyes closed, Astrid only felt it when Bjorn moved from the bed. She peeked to see him place the crown on the table and giggled as she watched him walk, thinking of the earlier conversation with the women.

She gestured her friend over to the bedside. Surprised, Ragnhild went to her. Astrid waved her to lean down so she could whisper.

"What?" Ragnhild asked.

Astrid cast a quick glance at Bjorn, and he watched her, his head cocked. She looked him up and down and giggled nervously. A ripple of murmuring went through the witnesses and the guests.

To Ragnhild she whispered, "He does not limp."

A loud laugh erupted from Ragnhild and that made Astrid laugh too. Once started she could not stop.

"Hold on to that, and who knows? You might even enjoy it."

Astrid remembered how it felt to have her arms around Bjorn's waist, his muscular stomach under her hands, his broad back pressing into her chest. Yes. She might enjoy it.

Chapter Thirty-four

Laughter and shouts from the wedding guests died down as they made their way back to the feast hall, leaving Astrid alone with Bjorn. Despite the bride's house being warm from the scented fire, Astrid shivered, the nightdress too thin and light, although it was not the lightness of the nightdress that made her shiver. She was alone with Bjorn Alfarsson. She stared down at her hands and fussed at the gold wedding ring that circled her finger.

The fire crackled and popped, and the scent of sage infused the room. It was hard to breathe, and Astrid wanted to throw open the door to let in some air, but if she did that the wedding guests would come back to watch, and that thought kept her firmly in the bed. The sound of liquid being poured brought her attention to the man in the room with her. Her husband. Bjorn picked up the two silver cups and carried them to the bed. He sat down next to her, his weight pressing down on the goose feather filled mattress, making her body shift toward him.

"Here," he said, his tone gentle as he offered a cup to her. "I think you need this."

She nodded and took the cup, grateful. The honeyed mead burned her throat as it went down, but she took a long drink of it, anyway. Aware of his gaze on her, Astrid held the cup in both of her hands, as if it were a shield.

"*Tak*," she choked out.

Bjorn chuckled and took a small drink of his own mead. "You can relax, Astrid, I will not hurt you. We don't even have to do this." He gestured to her and the bed. "Not tonight anyway." He got up and walked over to the fire, the cup dangling in his hand. His light linen tunic and trousers clung to his body, showing the muscles in his thighs and arms.

She watched him as he knelt in front of the fire, her heart hammering in her chest. Did he just give up his right and duty as her husband?

Astrid pulled her legs under her. "Do…do…you not want me?" Her voice came out weak, and she wished she could take it back.

Bjorn spun around, his eyes clear, and she could see he was not drunk anymore. The neck of his tunic fell open, revealing pale chest hair. His gaze traveled like a caress from her head down to where the bedcovering covered her legs, then rested on her breasts. Astrid felt heat rising in her body where his gaze touched her.

"That is not the problem," he said, his voice deeper than usual. It sent a tremor through Astrid's core.

He stood and returned to the bed, sitting next to her. His closeness made her heart race, although she was not sure if it was because she desired him or was afraid of him. He had done nothing for her to be afraid of him, but she was afraid of her desire too. She did not *want* to want this man.

Bjorn picked up her left hand, his touch gentle, but firm, as he ran his finger over her wedding ring. "I take my oaths seriously, especially those made before the gods. You are my wife now. I know what my duty is tonight, but if you wish, it can wait."

Astrid looked around the room, anywhere but into her new husband's eyes, afraid of what might happen if she did. Her eyes rested on the Freya statue Amma had placed in the room. Freya would not shirk from coupling with Bjorn; in fact, the lusty goddess would enjoy it. Out of habit, Astrid grasped for her Freya pendant for reassurance, but it was not there. She never took it off, not even when sleeping or bathing. She felt a moment of panic at its absence and searched for it.

"Do you want your necklace?" Bjorn leaned over her to reach it, and she smelled in his scent. He smelled like mead and a hint of mint. And something else, something that was just him, an earthy smell, like the forest after a rain. Fresh and new. The smell made her heart catch in her throat. "Here," he said, and he leaned toward her to loop the necklace over her neck. His face was close to hers, and his hair brushed up against her cheek.

She felt the closeness of him, his warmth, his strength, his scent, and she wanted him to gather her into his arms.

Bjorn pulled back, the pendant secure on her neck, but his hand lingered on it, gently touching the Freya figure. It warmed under his touch and Astrid's heart beat faster until she was afraid he'd be able to feel it. His face, though, was unreadable. Was he remembering the scene at the Thing when seeing her pendant had given away who she was?

She looked down at Bjorn's hand and at the black knotwork markings carved into his forearm, the muscular arm that wielded a sword.

A sword that had killed her brother.

All at once, the room tilted, and her breath left her. His hand that had held her own so gently had killed Jori. She closed her eyes and tried to catch her breath. Instead, images of Jori crashed into her.

"Astrid?" Bjorn's voice was concerned, but it sounded dim, competing with the images of Jori. Her head swam. How could she have believed she could marry this man? He would always remind her of Jori, of their families and their hatred of each other. There was too much bad blood between them. It flowed like the river swollen after the rains, heavy, rough, and dangerous.

"Astrid?" Bjorn asked again, and he took both of her hands in his, but she pulled them away. His hands felt slick with blood, and she rubbed her hands on the bedclothes. "What is it?" He sounded sincerely concerned.

She took in a breath and dispersed her thoughts of Jori, scattering them like the hens when she entered the henhouse.

Focusing on Bjorn's eyes, Astrid asked him, aware that her voice came out shaky. "You know that marshy place at the edge of a lake? Where it is hard to tell where the lake ends and the land starts?"

"*Ja.*" He said slowly, furrowing his brow.

"I hate the marsh, hate not knowing if my next step will be on land or if my foot will sink into the mud." She paused, not knowing if she should go on.

Bjorn waited for her to continue, to explain herself.

"That is how I feel now."

The house grew so quiet, Astrid could hear the wedding guests as they continued their celebrations back at the feast hall.

Bjorn broke the silence. "So I am the marsh?" His jaw clenched as he talked.

"Yes...no..."

He raised his brow.

"Yes." She sighed. "You are the marsh." She worried at her wedding band. "The ground underneath me is not stable. I am on edge with every step I take, fearful it will be the wrong one."

He stood, and she recoiled, sliding away from him on the bed, afraid that what she'd said had upset him.

It surprised her when he sighed and ran his hand over his face. "I will not hurt you. Have I not made that clear? Have I given you cause to fear me?"

Not trusting her voice, Astrid shook her head.

He moved to the table and poured himself another cup. She watched as he drank deeply, understanding from the way he clenched the cup she had upset him.

When he finished, he set the cup down on the table a little too hard. "I know you do not want this marriage. If I had been mistaken to think otherwise, it would have become clear by the way you barely made it through the ceremony." He paced back and forth, his long legs making it so it only took him a few strides before he reached the wall of the house and had to turn around. In his bare feet, his stride was as silent as a cat.

Her heart raced. She had insulted him.

"You said this is a business agreement between your father and Harald. The deed is done. But if you want to turn back and divorce me, I will not stop you. Go tell the others, make it public. Everyone is already here to be your witness." He swept his arm toward the door, as if inviting her to leave.

It felt like all the air left the room. Bjorn crackled with irritation.

Instead of leaving, Astrid pulled the bedcovers up to her shoulders. She had to see this through. She had married this man, had made an oath before the gods, and she did it for good reasons. To protect her family. Even, she knew now, to protect *his* family. The feud between her father and Harald had to stop with the two brothers. They could not pass it on to a sweet child like Tanni.

Bjorn stopped pacing and waited for her reply. When she said nothing, he leaned against the wall, looking at the ceiling. "I understand why you hate me. I would hate me too if I were you."

"Don't," Astrid said, with more force than she knew was in her. "Don't say anything about that." She would not discuss Jori with him.

He nodded and held up his hands, his gold wedding band gleaming in the firelight. It was the only ring he had on. Like her, he had been stripped before being put to bed. Astrid studied him while he was not looking at her, or sitting by her so intimately it muddled her brain. Without his fine clothes and rings, he appeared young, and her heart softened. He hadn't chosen this marriage either.

"I do not want to divorce you," Astrid said. Not only did she still need to do it for the sake of their families, she also could not bear the shame it would bring on her father. He had negotiated this marriage in good faith. He would be angry with her, and he would have to marry her to someone else, someone much, much worse. Her father and Harald would go back to fighting one another. On it would go until they were all banished from their homes, their lives torn apart, more than they already were.

"Then you need to treat me like your husband. And you need to believe me when I say I will not hurt you. I don't abuse women." At the table, he picked up a platter that had a bowl of raspberries and a hunk of dill-flavored cheese and brought it back to the bed. "Hungry?"

Astrid was not hungry, but appreciated the effort, and gave him a smile when he cut a piece of cheese and offered it to her on the edge of his knife. The salty cheese melted in her mouth.

"The only way to eat raspberries." Bjorn picked one up by sticking his finger into the end of it and then popping it into his mouth. He looked like a young boy when he did it, and Astrid let out a little laugh.

He grinned and popped one in his mouth. It eased the tension.

They talked of inconsequential things, never veering into conversations of her family or Harald until they grew more comfortable with each other.

"More mead?" he offered.

"Yes," Astrid answered, so eagerly that Bjorn laughed.

She liked his laugh. It came from deep in his chest and filled his whole body. His smile was nice too, with straight white teeth and full lips. When he smiled and laughed, he lost some of his warrior look and became a young man who liked to play and have a good time. She thought of the first time she'd ever seen him, the blond-haired warrior running the oars. He'd been laughing and joking then.

When he handed her the cup, she did not drink right away, but watched him as he flopped down on the bed close to her. Her body tingled, remembering the way he'd so easily pulled her up to ride behind him on the horse. He'd wanted to ride off with her that day, and she would have, too. Now here he was, in her bed as her husband.

"How is Grani?" She asked.

Bjorn choked on a berry he'd been swallowing. "My horse?"

"Has he led you to any castles protected by a wall of flame? Have the two of you found any Valkyries in an enchanted sleep?"

"That is all we ever do." He gave her a playful grin. "Another day, another castle of flame, another Valkyrie. I grow weary of it."

"Did they at least share their magic with you?"

"Magic? That's for women, not warriors. The only magic I can do is make food and mead vanish." With that, he grabbed a handful of berries and threw them into his mouth. The berries stained his lips red, and Astrid wanted to kiss them.

"I have a feeling you know more magic than that," she breathed, as she reached out and touched his lips.

He took hold of her hand and kissed her fingers. The kiss shot through her fingers, and raced down her body, making her feel like her legs had turned to liquid. Her own breath caught, and the sensation was overwhelming, making her want to pull her hand from him.

The fire crackled and spit, sending up a burst of herb-scented smoke, distracting them, and Bjorn let go of her hand. He went to check on the fire, and when he did, he moved with the ease of a man who was completely comfortable in his body.

As she watched him, his every move and her reaction to his movements seemed heightened, like she was in a dream. The firelight lit him up like he was glowing from within, the loose-fitting clothes giving him an unearthly look. A spark from the fire popped, and the light flashed across Bjorn's face; in that moment he seemed like what she imagined the *alfar* to be.

"Son of Alfar," she whispered as if she had just understood the name.

Bjorn turned and tilted his head to the side and gave her a crooked grin. He looked pleased, like he liked the way the word sounded coming from her.

"*Ja.*"

She kept staring at him, unable to speak what was in her mind. It sounded too silly.

Astrid shifted on the bed and ran her hands over her hair. As she did so, he watched her, his gaze hungry. "When I was a girl, my—" She was about to say brother, but stopped, not wanting to bring him up here, unsure of how Bjorn would react to hearing Rikki's name. "I wanted to find the *alfar.*"

She hesitated, wondering if she should tell him this. "I was warned against it, told the light elves were cruel and would take away a girl like me. My little brother Olaf had just died, and I hoped he was not dead but with the *alfar*..."

Her face flushed. This was a ridiculous thing to be talking about on her wedding night, but Bjorn did not stop her. If anything, he seemed interested. He never took his eyes off her.

"I did not want him to be dead. I hoped that they had taken him, even though he died next to me." Why was she mentioning her dead brother?

Instead of telling her to be quiet, or that she was being a silly woman, Bjorn gave her hand a gentle squeeze. She looked at where his hand held hers. He had a scar on the back of his hand, and she traced her finger over it. He frowned, deep in thought, as if remembering something or someone. She was not the only child touched by death.

"Did you find them, the *alfar*?" he asked quietly, with no teasing in his voice.

She shook her head. "I don't think they come when you are looking for them."

He ran his thumb over the back of her hand. The touch sent a shudder through her. "Hm. You're right. I have searched for them, too, and did not find them."

Her head shot up, and she looked him in the eyes. He held her gaze, making it hard for her to breathe.

"My father told me we are descended from the *alfar*," Bjorn told her.

"Really?"

"*Ja*." He shifted to the end of the bed and laid down, sighing, and lifted his hands above his head in a stretch. His tunic rose, exposing his stomach, the light sprinkling of hair glistening in the firelight.

Astrid wanted to reach out and touch it, to feel the warmth of him. But he moved again, turned over on his side and propped himself up, resting his head on his hand. He did not bother to pull down his tunic, and his trousers had slipped low over his hips. She felt her face grow warm. His eyes widened, and he took her hand again and kissed the palm. The feel of his lips on the soft part of her palm made her ache in a deep part of her.

"T...tell me about the elves?" She stammered, finding it difficult to talk with him so close, so intimate.

He released her hand, and she relaxed, pulling her legs up and resting her chin on her knees while he talked. As he talked, he ran his hand through his thick hair, but he kept his eyes on her, the blue as deep as a sapphire. The firelight flickered across his face, making him look soft and young.

"You never found the elves?"

He frowned. "No."

Astrid held her breath.

"I have something for you," Bjorn said, and he leaped from the bed and strode over to the chest that stored his belongings. He rummaged in the chest, pulled out a plain bag, and then walked back to the bed.

Astrid propped herself up on her knees in anticipation. "For me?" When she moved, her nightdress slipped off her shoulder, and Bjorn froze when he saw it. His eyes grew dark with desire as he stared at her, and she felt like the very surface of her skin tingle with sensitivity.

"For you," he said, his voice raspy.

She quickly fixed her nightdress. "I love gifts."

As she said it she clapped her hands, and Bjorn laughed at her delight. "I will remember that." He sat down again and turned to her.

"Not so fast, wife." Bjorn teased when Astrid reached out for the bag. Instead, he opened the drawstring and drew out a necklace.

Astrid gasped.

"This is your wedding gift, but I don't want to wait until morning."

She reached out and ran her fingers over the necklace, needing to touch it to make sure it was real. It was the most exquisite gift anyone had ever given her. The carnelian beads glowed in the firelight, as if they had a fire burning within them, and the other glass beads, the blues and greens all glimmered as brilliantly as jewels. She touched the silver Thor's hammer and another amulet that looked like a spindle.

"Is that...?" She took it in two fingers and held it up to see it better.

"I was told you are an exceptional weaver. Now I know it is true."

That he'd thought to ask about her, that he'd created a necklace designed for her, took her breath away. Then she remembered her gift for him. She had thought about him when she'd made it, remembering the knotwork markings he'd had on his arm, and tried to copy them, knowing he would look handsome in the red wool and gold silk edging.

"Do you like it?"

She was so engrossed by the necklace and her own thoughts that she'd forgotten he was sitting so close to her, and his voice startled her. "Yes," she said, but it came out as a whisper. "It is beautiful. When I was a child, I wanted a necklace like Brisingamen."

"Does it compare?"

"Yes," she breathed out.

His face lit up in a boyish smile. As he had done before, he leaned in to loop the necklace over her head, and she closed her eyes, drinking in his scent.

Sitting back, Bjorn nodded appreciatively and said, "It suits you. My wife will be the most beautiful, most richly dressed woman around."

"I have something for you, too." She left the warmth of the bed, and walked over to her chest, where she had stored his wedding gift tunic. She heard an appreciative hum from Bjorn as she made her way across the small room, and it made her aware of how little her nightdress covered her. Looking down, she saw that it was nearly see-through with the firelight shining on her. She knelt down to retrieve the tunic from her chest and was afraid to stand up again, to show herself to Bjorn in her near nakedness. She ran her hand over the tunic to smooth it, and took in a deep, fortifying breath before standing. Holding it in front of her like a shield, Astrid hurried back, aware of Bjorn's gaze on her every movement.

She unfolded the scarlet tunic and showed it to Bjorn.

"You made this?"

"Yes. I designed the edging along the collar to match your..." She gently traced over one of the knotwork patterns with her fingers. "Your markings."

The muscles in his arm tensed at her touch, but she did not take her hand away.

"You remembered what it looked like?" Bjorn asked, a little shocked.

"Uh...yes," she said, embarrassed to admit that she had remembered much about her new husband's body.

"Only one way to see if it matches." He whipped his tunic over his head and dropped it on the floor.

Astrid froze at the sight of his naked chest and arms, the patch of light hair that covered his chest and trailed down his well-defined stomach muscles to the top of his trousers. But she quickly brought her gaze back up to the muscular swoop of his shoulders and his strong arms. A rugged scar ran along the side of his chest, just below his arm, and she wondered what had happened. It was much too jagged to have been a sword or axe cut.

Astrid reached out and gently traced over the scar. She felt the hitch in his breath when she touched him, and he shifted on the bed.

"How did you get this?" She asked. His bare skin was softer than she had expected, and he was so warm.

In response, he grabbed her hand and kissed her palm again. He brought her fingers to his lips and gently kissed the tip of each finger. The slight touch of his lips and tongue made her wet between her legs.

She gasped, but she did not pull her hand away. "The...the tunic..." She could not think clearly, his kisses on her fingers still lingering.

"It can wait," Bjorn said, his voice thick with desire, and he gently moved it to the side.

He set her hand down in her lap, and ran his hand up her arm, his fingers trailing along her skin, and everywhere he touched, it sent shivers down her back. When he reached her face, he cupped it lightly, running his thumb over her cheek. She leaned into his touch. He ran his hand through her long hair slowly, looking at it as it slid through his fingers.

"Like gold." He took his other hand and ran that through her hair too. "Or like the sun."

She rested her hand on his thigh and felt him twitch at her touch.

Bjorn let go of her hair and cupped both cheeks with his hands. They were callused and rough, but Astrid did not mind. He touched her with as much gentleness as if he were holding a delicate flower. He leaned in, his lips brushing softly on hers. It was the barest of kisses, and Astrid's body responded as if he'd set her on fire. She gasped and felt Bjorn smile, his lips still against hers.

One of his arms slid down to her waist, and he pulled her closer. His lips kissed her again, this time more deeply, and she softened, kissing him back, and her arms wrapped around him. She wanted his body closer to her, wanted to touch him, feel him.

He kissed her jaw and her neck, his tongue gently licking her skin, and she let out a moan. He slid the nightdress off her shoulder and kissed the skin there, too, while his hand slid up her waist to cup her breast, his thumb brushing across her nipple through the fabric of her dress. It hardened, and she leaned into him, her hands running up his strong back. His fingers brushed over her shoulders and down her arms, sweeping her nightdress off, exposing her breasts. The sensation of the air and the closeness of his bare chest to hers took her breath away. He trailed his hand down her back as he pulled her to him, the press of skin so intoxicating, it was like she'd drunk a pitcher of mead.

Bjorn leaned her back on the bed until she was lying flat, and he rose over her, his face so close she could smell the mead on his breath. It made her want to lick his lips, and his blue eyes met hers. "We can still stop." His voice was so husky and deep, she wondered if he really could stop.

"N-no."

He held himself just above her. He was still while he watched her, but when she said nothing more, he leaned in and kissed her. This time it was with more urgency, and when she felt his tongue flick across her lips, she parted them and met him with her own.

When they touched, she raised her body to meet his, and she felt his hardness. It sent a jolt of excitement through her, but then a thought rose unbidden in her mind.

She giggled, breaking their kiss awkwardly as she remembered the conversation with the women earlier.

Bjorn rose on his elbow. "What is funny?" He looked a little stunned; no doubt women did not laugh when he was kissing them.

She tried to stop, but the more she tried, the funnier it became. All she could do was to point at the Frey statue. When Bjorn saw what she was pointing at, he laughed and gave her a look of pleasure before he rose from the bed. The light fabric of his linen under-trousers did nothing to hide his own excitement, and the sight of it made Astrid gasp. He arched a brow as he picked up Frey and held the little erect figure next to him, moving it suggestively.

Astrid let out a squeal of laughter that turned into a gasp when she saw the look in Bjorn's eyes, and the effect she had on him.

"I can't compete with the god." He untied his trousers and let them slip to the floor. "But I will do my best." He gave her the bright smile that drew her to him the first time she saw him.

If anyone could compete with a god, it was her new husband. He was as magnificent without his clothes as he was in them.

Bjorn set the Frey figure on the floor next to their bed. He leaned over Astrid and kissed her on her lips, her neck, and down, until he kissed her just above her nipples. He pushed her nightdress off her body with one practiced move and threw it onto the floor.

Her breath came quickly now, and she was no longer laughing.

When he flicked his tongue over her nipple, she whimpered. He took her other breast in his hand, rubbing his palm over it and over her nipple so lightly, she thought she might scream. The sensation became so intense she grabbed his face and pulled him back up to her, kissing his soft lips hungrily, their tongues intertwined. His hands never stopped stroking her body, and his touch felt like fire rushing over her.

Bjorn worked his way down to her breasts again, murmuring something about how perfect they were, and she arched her back toward him. She ran her hands through his hair, and he looked up at her, his eyes flashing with desire and happiness that he was bringing her pleasure.

His hand tickled over her stomach and down to her cleft, and when he touched her there, she cried out, so intense was the pleasure. He rubbed her and kissed her breasts, her neck, her stomach, until she thought she might scream. His fingers explored her where no one had ever touched her before. When he slipped his finger inside of her, she moaned in pleasure. Her hips moved on their own to meet him.

Her eyes fluttered open when he kissed her lips, their tongues meeting, and her excitement grew. He met it with experienced hands.

Desire and pleasure at her excitement filled his eyes. He gave her a lazy smile.

"I-I..." She panted. "It...feels..."

He quieted her attempts to talk with another kiss. "I'm not done yet."

Good. She didn't want it to stop, she wanted him to kiss her and touch her like this forever. The movement of his fingers on her, in her, made her breath come in gasps, and she felt a welling up inside of her like a wave, building. It felt too good, and she panicked, pushing at him.

"Relax," he soothed, rising to meet her eyes. "Let it happen." He murmured, but his fingers never stopped. He kissed her lips again, the touch of them pushing her over the edge. The wave that had been building crashed into her, engulfing her entire body, and cracked her open with such pleasure that she cried out. Her body rose to meet his hand again and again as the wave rolled over her.

When it subsided, every inch of her body tingled, and she collapsed against the bed.

Before she could catch her breath, Bjorn had risen above her and eased her thighs apart, his hardness pressing against her. It aroused her more, and she clutched onto his back, pulling him closer. He was sweaty, and she licked his chest. He tasted of salt and sweat, and it only further inflamed her. Him, too.

He kissed her so deeply, it was like he wanted to consume her. Her body was so fluid, she could barely feel her arms and legs, but when he pushed into her, she welcomed it, pulling him to her.

She cried out when a shock of pain hit her, and she clenched her legs together.

Bjorn stopped and trailed his fingers over her cheek and down her neck. "It will only hurt for a moment."

He kissed her again, and she relaxed, and as soon as she did, he thrust past the barrier and deeper into her. It hurt. Tears came to her eyes, but then Bjorn was there, his lips brushing the tears away.

He slowed down, but did not stop, his own breath starting to come in gasps now. The pain subsided and Astrid met his movements. She pushed his head down, so he could lick her nipples again. With a raspy chuckle, he obliged and when his lips met her breasts, she arched into him.

His movements grew more fevered, his breath more ragged, and her body reacted by wanting more of him. She moved with him and arched her back as he groaned and exploded into her. The weight of his body was on her, and she grasped onto his hips, pulling him even closer.

When he finished, he lay still on her, their two sweaty bodies entwined. She ran her fingers through his hair and down his back. With a sigh, he rolled off her and threw his hands up over his head. His chest glistened with sweat, and he stared up at the ceiling, satisfied.

Astrid pulled the bedclothes up over her breasts; she felt shy and exposed. A wetness had formed between her legs, but she did not want to look. Her insides ached with pain, but it was muted by the lingering satisfaction she felt from what Bjorn had done to her before that.

"Don't," Bjorn said, and it surprised Astrid to find him watching her. He rolled onto his side and pulled the bedcoverings back down, so her breasts were exposed again. He caressed them gently but did not seem to want to do more than that. He seemed content to run his hands over her breasts and down her stomach. Astrid was relieved. She did not think she could do that again so soon, even though she had enjoyed it. It would hurt too much.

Bjorn gathered her in his arm, and she rested against his chest, her arm slung over his waist. It was nice.

"Did it hurt very much?" he asked.

"No." She did not know what to say to him now. How did people do this? They had shared something intimate, and she did not know what to do now.

He yawned and let out a contented sigh. Astrid knew that men often fell asleep soon after coupling. She was glad. She did not want to talk.

It didn't take long before she felt the steady rise and fall of his chest. She relaxed. She turned her head to watch him sleep. In sleep, he looked so harmless. She brushed a few stray strands of hair out of his face. If she had felt confused before, now it was even worse. Her body still tingled from the way he touched her, and the hatred she needed to feel for him was getting more difficult to find. The deeper she buried the hatred, the more she felt like she was betraying her family and her brother's memory.

She rose on her elbow, careful not to wake Bjorn. As she watched him sleep, Astrid wondered if he was descended from the alfar and had enchanted her. Her enemy. Her lover. Her husband. Bjorn Alfarsson.

Chapter Thirty-five

Astrid lay nestled in Bjorn's arm, her head on his chest, his fine chest hair tickling her nose, as she listened to him breathe deeply. Tired beyond belief, she still could not sleep, not after everything. She had not expected her wedding night to be so enjoyable, or for Bjorn to be so attentive to her needs. When he was not around, it had been easy to hate him, to think of him as her enemy, but his presence muddled everything she believed and wanted to hang on to. That he had fallen asleep so easily with her beside him, spoke of his trust in her. Either that, or he afforded her little respect in her ability to hurt him or arrange for him to be hurt. She played with the hair on his stomach, heat rising in her body again, but all he did was shift in his sleep, and take hold of her hand.

The chamber was warm, even though the fire had burned down. The smell of sage still lingered lightly, as did the smell of their love making. If this is what it was like, she could get used to it. She smiled at the thought.

Shouts rose from the direction of the great hall and her father's longhouse. Some of the wedding guests were taking the celebration late into the night. She heard more shouts and the sound of footsteps running back and forth. That did not sound like people were celebrating. Astrid's smile faltered, and she looked at Bjorn to wake up, but all he did was inhale and stir. Should she wake him? He was a trained warrior, surely he would rouse if he heard something that concerned him.

The noise grew more worrisome, with more men shouting and calling out to each other. The footsteps continued, more of them. When the sound of ringing steel carried over the village, Bjorn jolted up, nearly spilling Astrid over the side. A woman screamed, her voice panicked.

Bjorn leaped naked from the bed and instinctively reached for his sword, but it was not there. He had left it at the hall when he'd bedded Astrid. He cursed and looked for something, anything, he could use as a weapon. He hurried to the table and picked up the eating knife. It looked so small and inadequate in his hand.

"Who is attacking us?" Astrid asked him, as she quickly threw her nightdress back on.

Bjorn pulled on his trousers, while Astrid hurriedly grabbed his tunic and threw it to him. He gave her a look of gratitude.

"I don't know," he said, then frowned at her flimsy clothes. "You should hide."

"Where?" She held out her arms to encompass the small room. There was nowhere to hide, not even under the bed.

Bjorn grabbed her hand and pulled her behind him, so he was between her and the door.

This couldn't be happening again. Visions of the Dane, who had tried to drag her away, collided with images from her childhood when they'd been under attack by Harald and had to retreat into the woods. Astrid put her hands on Bjorn's waist for reassurance and got it when he slid his left hand back to take hold of hers.

"Whoever it is will have to kill me to get to you," Bjorn told her.

That did not make her feel any better.

"I've been fighting with a knife since I was ten. I can hold my own, even against a sword."

She did not have time to respond, for the door to their little room banged open, bringing with it the sound of chaos and violence.

Rikki walked in, his sword in his hand.

"Rikki!" Astrid ran to her brother. She had never been so happy to see him. "What is going on? Are we being attacked?"

He looked her over. "You are unhurt?" Then he turned an angry gaze toward Bjorn, who stared back.

"Yes, they have not come here yet."

"That's not what I meant. Did *he* hurt you?"

He meant Bjorn. "No."

She grabbed her brother's sleeve and forced him to turn toward her so she could look him in the eyes. What she saw took her breath away. This was not her brother. His eyes had a dark tinge to them, as if he was in a dark room, and as they studied her from her tousled hair to her bare feet, they grew so angry they looked murderous. He looked over her shoulder and let out a growl. She turned and saw the bed all rumpled with the bedcoverings askew and a small stain, like a red scar staring at them in accusation.

Shouts from the feast hall and out in the village yard continued, and Astrid heard her father's voice rise above them all, yelling at Galm to stop what he was doing. Astrid didn't have time to wonder why her father would tell Galm to stop, when Rikki took a step toward Bjorn. Bjorn shifted to make himself ready for an attack, the knife held lightly in his hand.

"Rikki," Astrid said, fear rising with her understanding. She tried to be calm, although she felt far from it. "He is my husband."

"Not for much longer."

The floor underneath Astrid grew unsteady, and she grew light-headed. "Did you cause all of this?" Her voice came out squeaky. "What have you done?" She needed to sit down to unravel what was happening, but she couldn't. Whatever it was, was happening now.

Rikki gave her a quick shake of his head. "Doesn't matter. I'm here to finish what I started."

"I don't think so." It was the first Bjorn had spoken, and it shook Astrid to her core. This could not be happening. Her brother and her husband fighting here, in the room where she had become a wife, the sheets still warm from their bodies.

"Rikki, don't." She grabbed his sword arm, but he shook her off. The force of it, the physical force and the hatred in every part of her brother's bearing, made her stumble.

"Get back," Rikki said.

"Step back, Astrid," Bjorn said at the same time.

Neither man took his eyes from the other as they gave her orders. She had to stop them before they fought, because once the fight began, they would not stop until one of them was dead. She did not want that to happen.

Emund's voice boomed over the din outside, followed by her father's, and she desperately wanted to know what was going on. Her heart raced with panic.

She had watched her brother fight for as long as she could remember, so she knew when he was about to lash out. She rushed forward to grab his arm, but she was a moment too late, for he had already begun his sword strike. At the same time, Bjorn crouched and moved to the side to avoid the strike, his knife slashing out at Rikki's leg.

Astrid felt a body crash into hers, and the stinging burn of a blade as it sliced her arm. White-hot pain flashed through her arm and she stumbled backward and crashed into the bed. Both men shouted her name, but instead of stopping, it made them even angrier, more determined to kill one another. Warm blood ran down her arm, staining her white dress. She pressed her hand against it to stop the flow and took deep breaths to control the pain.

Bjorn and Rikki had resumed their silent circling of one another, both waiting for his chance to strike.

She let out a wail to distract them, and then rushed in to stand in front of Bjorn, blocking him from Rikki. Rikki stared at her, and the look in his eyes scared her.

"Get out of the way."

Bjorn tried to push her aside, but she was expecting it, and grabbed on to the floor with her toes as tightly as she could to keep from getting knocked over.

"No." She told them both.

Her arm throbbed with pain. Applying more pressure to the wound, she stood tall, almost as tall as her brother, and stared him down.

"He killed our brother. Move aside," Rikki said.

"No."

"Move," Bjorn growled behind her. "I do not need a woman to shield me."

She ignored Bjorn and continued to stare at her brother. "Rikki, don't do this. For me."

He still held his sword, the knuckles on his hand turning white with the force of his grip. He glanced quickly at the bed and then back to Astrid. "One tumble in bed and you forget your duty to your family? Did it only take one night of pleasure to make you forget that you want Bjorn Alfarsson dead?"

His words made her reel. The pain in her arm continued to rage, but it was nothing compared to the pain and confusion in her heart. Perhaps Rikki was right. Ever since Bjorn had arrived, his closeness and her attraction to him had confused her.

As if sensing her thoughts, Bjorn shifted behind her. Astrid tensed, thinking of the knife in Bjorn's hand. It was too late for second thoughts, and she stood her ground, sending up a prayer to the warrior goddess Freya that she would not be killed between these two men.

She should step aside and let her brother kill Bjorn. A brief flash of the day at the Thing when Rikki had discovered her with Bjorn emerged in her mind. She had given Bjorn over to Rikki then. She could do it again now.

Everything fell silent as they waited for Astrid to move or speak. She hesitated. She could not decide what to do, to whom she owed her loyalty. Her brother or her husband? She wanted to avenge Jori and let Rikki kill Bjorn. But she had also sworn herself to Bjorn before the gods. The noise from outside the bride's house matched the confusion in her head.

"Rikki!" Short Olaf ran into the room.

Rikki's strong hand took Astrid's arm, gripping her tightly as he went to move her out of his way.

Then Short Olaf was next to Rikki. "Not like this Brother," he said, his voice calm. "Bjorn is her husband. He is a guest under Tryggvi's hospitality."

A loud voice that boomed like Thor's cried out, "Bjarki!" and Emund ducked into the house, battle axe in hand. He took one look at the scene in the bedchamber and his face turned red with anger and then concern, when he saw the blood on Astrid's arm. "You're hurt," he said to Astrid and walked across the room in two strides.

"It was an accident. I don't even know who did it." She heard Bjorn start to say something when he was cut off.

"You will answer to Tryggvi for your oath-breaking, Rikolf," Emund growled, placing himself where he could stop Rikki from attacking Bjorn. "You and Galm and the others."

"Red. You know what I do is right." Before anyone could do anything, Rikki pushed Short Olaf aside so hard it made him stumble, and stalked out the door.

With her brother gone, with the immediate conflict over, all of Astrid's strength left her, and she shook. Strong, familiar arms grabbed her and helped her to sit down. Her head resting on Emund's chest, she heard him tell Short Olaf to get her a blanket, and for Bjorn to fetch her a cup of mead. When Emund settled her on the bed, Short Olaf gently placed the blanket over her shoulders, being careful to avoid her injured arm. But Bjorn did not bring her a drink.

He remained where he'd been, the knife still in his hand as he stared at Astrid, his blue eyes cold and hard. Short Olaf, seeing that Bjorn would not help her, poured Astrid some mead. He wrapped his hands around hers and helped her take a drink. His hands were steady and strong.

"What did Rikki and Galm do?" Her voice sounded dead, even to her own ears.

No one said anything.

"Emund?"

He scratched at his red, scraggly beard. "Rikki and Galm, along with some of your father's men, plotted to kill Harald and Bjorn. Once everyone was drunk, and you and Bjorn were alone, they made their move. Galm and the others attacked Harald, hoping to catch him asleep, while Rikki came after Bjorn."

Astrid thought she might be sick. She took a drink of the honeyed mead. "Was anyone killed?"

"No," Emund shook his head. "Galm was hurt. As was one of Harald's men."

"I need to find them," Short Olaf said, and he hurried out.

Astrid looked at Bjorn, whose eyes burned with anger. With a start he said, "Tanni." and hurried to the door.

"He's safe," Emund assured him. "I checked on him myself."

Bjorn stopped mid-stride, surprise showing on his face.

Nodding, Emund said, "I thought Galm might go after the boy. The boy's nurse had Tanni tucked away. She'd been told to keep him out of sight tonight."

Astrid pulled her legs up and rested her forehead on her knees. Rikki had been with Tanni's nurse earlier. He had planned to keep Tanni safe. Maybe all was not lost. Her brother still had the mind to protect a small child.

"I must see him," Bjorn said, and headed to the door. He did not get far.

Tryggvi burst in. "Where is my son?"

"You don't know where he is?" Emund rose to meet him.

"No. They have disappeared."

Astrid looked up to see her father in his night-shirt, his sword gripped tightly in his hand, his face a mask of fury and betrayal. It was too much for her. "You drove him to this," she spat, rising to her feet, and she felt all the air leave the room at her outburst as everyone held their breath. "You!"

He stepped toward her, and she was suddenly aware of her father's size, his strength, the sword in his hand. He could kill her as easily as he had sliced the throat of the sacrificial goat. She gulped. There was no turning back. She had said the words, and they hung in the air.

"This is your fault," she said. "When you allied with Harald, the man who killed Galm's father. When you *sacrificed* me to Bjorn Alfarsson, the man who killed my brother." She moved aside to expose the blood on the sheets.

Her father's face paled, and he clenched his jaw. A flash of sadness? Regret? Washed over his face, but it was too late for regrets. The deed was done.

"That's right," she went on, not knowing where she got the strength to speak to her father like this. "There is the blood of my sacrifice."

The room crackled with tension. No one spoke.

The tension broke when Ingiborg and Ragnhild arrived. Their very presence changed the atmosphere, Ingiborg bringing with her the calm she brought to every crisis. She quickly surveyed the room, and with one firm touch to Tryggvi's arm, she made him relax the grip on his sword. She hurried to Astrid and wrapped her in her arms, and Astrid breathed in her mother's comforting scent of herbs. Ingiborg hugged her tighter, making Astrid wince in pain.

"You're hurt," Ingiborg said.

Feeling like a child with her mother there, Astrid nodded, tears forming in her eyes.

Ingiborg moved the blanket aside and examined Astrid's arm. Ragnhild walked to the other side of the bed and took Astrid's hand. "I was worried for you when the fighting started."

"I am fine."

Ingiborg caught sight of the stain on the bed and looked into Astrid's eyes. "Oh, my *dottir*."

"It is done. I have done my *duty*." Astrid averted her eyes from everyone. Outside, it was still dark, the night punctuated by bursts of flame as people went by with torches.

A torch appeared, and one of Harald's guard stood in the doorway. He looked at Tryggvi, Bjorn, and Emund before turning to Tryggvi. "Your son and his men have fled." With that, he gave both Tryggvi and Emund a pointed look.

"He is not your concern," Tryggvi said.

The man nodded toward Astrid, Ingiborg, and Ragnhild, letting Tryggvi know that he did not want to talk in front of the women. "Harald waits for you in the feast hall."

"*My* feast hall," Tryggvi spat.

The man shrugged. "You, too, Bjorn." He did not wait for them to reply and left.

Ingiborg went to Tryggvi's side, sliding her arm through his. "We will find him and we will make it right." She took his face in her hands.

He rested his forehead against hers and then spun and walked out the door.

Bjorn looked down at Astrid, his own face showing betrayal and disgust. She opened her mouth to say something to him, but had no words.

"We will see if your 'sacrifice' was worth it," Bjorn told her, his voice as cold as a morning frost. "I almost believed you, *wife*. I never suspected your treachery."

He spun away from her and followed her father out into the night. Astrid watched his back, her heart breaking with everything that had gone wrong.

"*Bjarki.*" Emund said. "I will do what I can for your brother." And then he left, too.

Once the men were gone, Ragnhild shut the door behind them, throwing down the bar to lock it. Astrid sank onto the bed that she had so recently shared with Bjorn and closed her eyes. The events of the night swirled in her head. From the moment she heard the shouts and cries of the wedding revelers, it had all gone wrong, like a nightmare.

The look on his new wife's face when she'd told Tryggvi she'd been a sacrifice burned into Bjorn's mind. Disgust, fear, anger, had all flashed over her open face, but he could not tell if she aimed those feelings at her father or at him. It didn't matter. She'd made herself clear. Rikki's words also echoed in his mind. Astrid *wants* him dead. Not in the past, as in wanted him dead, that he could understand; no, Rikki said *wants*. Astrid had hesitated, too, for much too long, when her brother had told her to get out of the way, and that hesitation was enough for Bjorn. She'd had to think about whether she wanted Rikki to kill him, and it had not been the first time. He could not trust her.

He kept his distance from Tryggvi and Red-Beard as they stepped over the threshold into the feast hall. It had only been earlier that day that he'd entered here with Astrid in his arms, but it felt like an age had passed. Harald's people gathered in the hall to make sure everyone was alive and unmolested. Bjorn was searching for his son when Red-Beard let out a strangled growl. On alert, Bjorn looked to where Red-Beard had his attention.

Harald sat on Tryggvi's high-seat. Bjorn burst out laughing at the blatant disrespect his foster-father showed for his brother. It relieved him to see Harald alive and well and harassing Tryggvi.

"Get out of my seat, brother," Tryggvi snapped, throwing a quick glare at Bjorn, and he strode across the hall toward the high-seat.

"Are you still in charge here, Tryggvi?" Harald smirked. "I thought perhaps your son tried to kill you too."

"I am still alive, as you will find out if you don't move."

Red-Beard moved to stand behind Tryggvi, while the household men from both leaders arranged themselves around the hall, their hands near their weapons. Styrr approached Bjorn and handed him his sword. It felt good to have it in his hand again.

"I will vacate this seat, *brother*, if you admit that your son has done me and my men a grievous wrong..." Here Harald paused and gestured to Atli who huddled on a bench, a bloody bandage covering his torso. His angry words were betrayed by an undercurrent tone of glee at the attack. Harald only arranged the marriage to placate King Ingjald, and now he had reason to continue to harass his brother.

Harald searched the room until he found Bjorn. They exchanged nods. "He even attacked your son-by-law in front of your own daughter."

Tryggvi had held himself erect and steady during this brief exchange with Harald. When he spoke, it was with authority. "My son did not act on my command. He is within his rights to call out Bjorn to fight."

"Not when Bjorn is within your protection of hospitality."

Tryggvi stared at Harald. "A minor matter."

Out of the side of his eye, Bjorn saw people shuffling, and he turned to see Tanni working his way through the adult legs to get to him. The nurse followed, trying to grab his little arm and drag him back to where he had been. Bjorn held up his hand to stop the nurse and reached out for his son. He had never been so glad to see his boy as he did in that moment. Tanni's little hand grasped on to his.

"Papa?" For once, Tanni was subdued, his gaze darting among all the armed men.

Seeing his son frightened made Bjorn's blood boil in his veins. Rikki Tryggvason had caused this, and he should pay for it. He lifted his finger to his lips to keep Tanni quiet, and he stepped forward.

"I want Rikki Tryggvason and his men banished and declared outlaw. They are *niding*."

A collective rumbling, whispering, and hissing traveled through the hall. To be declared a *niding* was the worst thing that could happen to a man.

"No." Tryggvi rounded on Bjorn, his eyes flashing with anger.

As quickly as if they were on a battlefield, Bjorn's other brothers-in-arms closed in behind him, facing Tryggvi.

Red-Beard joined Tryggvi at his side, while Tryggvi's men surrounded him. His face looked murderous. A flicker of fear ran down Bjorn's spine. The man was enormous and could do a lot of damage in the enclosed space.

Stepping forward to meet Tryggvi, Bjorn said, "Your son wants to kill me. He has ambushed me twice, once while I was with my wife. *His own systir.* He would have killed me in front of her." Bjorn paused, but Tryggvi's face showed nothing. "I gave you *wergild* for Jori. I want payment for Rikki's actions and demand he be declared *niding*."

He had not expected to say so much, but his anger was burning hot. What he wanted to do was to shove his sword into Tryggvi's gut, to strike him down, the red-giant next, and rid the world of them all. Calling the man's son *niding*, though, was nearly as good. His hand gripped his sword.

"Rikolf." Tryggvi measured his words. "May have acted rashly, but he did not murder you in secret, did he? There would have been witnesses, it would have been public. That is not the action of a murdering *niding*."

"You deserve to die for killing Jori," one of Tryggvi's men called out.

His other men shouted at Harald's men, who bristled and shouted back, until the two groups were on the verge of an all-out fight.

Tryggvi held up his hands for his men to step back. Harald threw himself out of the high-seat, strode over to his men, and did the same. He stood shoulder to shoulder with Bjorn as they faced Tryggvi.

"You will pay the *wergild* for injuring Atli. You will give Bjorn more for his *bride-price*."

Tryggvi nodded and waved his hand dismissively, as if money meant little to him.

"I also want your son found and brought before King Ingjald next summer. He will decide what is to happen to them. Do you agree?" Harald asked, but the way he said it sounded less like a question and more like a demand.

Bjorn started to say something, but Harald's firm hand clamped down on his forearm to quiet him. Gritting his teeth, Bjorn thrust his arm out of Harald's grasp, but he said nothing.

"I agree," Tryggvi said. "The King will decide."

"Good." Harald gave Tryggvi a wicked smile. "Next summer...if young Rikki survives that long." He laughed, and with a swoop of his arm, he gathered his men to him.

Bjorn smirked at Tryggvi when he saw the man pale at Harald's thinly disguised threat. In that moment, Bjorn saw an old man, past his prime, who could only sit by and watch as younger men like his son and son-by-law wrested control from him.

"We need to find Rikki," Bjorn told Harald as the men clustered to hear what Harald had planned next.

"It is already in motion. Styrr is handling it." He nodded to Styrr, who grabbed a few men and hurried out of the feast hall. "It is dark, and we are unfamiliar with the land. We might have to wait until first light."

"He will be long gone by then." He glanced over at Tryggvi and Emund, who had their heads together. Tryggvi waved one of his men over and spoke to him. The man nodded and hurried off. They would look for Rikki, too.

"You're smarter than that, boy. I know you want his blood, but where would you go? You don't even know which direction to head first."

Bjorn gritted his teeth. He needed to do something. To find Rikki Tryggvason and kill him for what he'd done. A brief thought of Astrid rose in his mind, of how she would react if he killed her other brother. But she had made her choice clear. She would choose her brother over him, and Bjorn would give her no more thought.

Harald grabbed his arm. "Styrr will shadow any of Tryggvi's *huskarls* who leave the hall, to discover what they plan and where they go. If they reach Rikki before you, he will get away." He gestured to Tanni with a warning in his eyes. "Do not get distracted. Be ready."

Bjorn knelt down, and Tanni threw himself at his father. Bjorn picked him up, relieved more than he'd believed possible that he was unharmed.

"You need to go with your nurse or Katrin. Stay with them. Only leave them if Papa Harald or I come for you. No one else," he told the boy.

"Why?"

Bjorn shook his head. "No questions. Just do as I say. Do you understand?"

Tanni's eyes showed fear as he nodded, and it made Bjorn so angry he wanted to tear the walls down around them. "Go now." He set Tanni on his feet and the boy ran to Katrin.

He turned to Harald. "No matter what happens, no one harms Astrid."

"Was it that good?" Harald's mouth turned up in a mean smile, the scar on his lip white against his ruddy skin. "One dip in the virgin's cunt and you are attached?"

"She is my wife now." Bjorn clenched his fists.

"Don't worry. We won't hurt your little wife. We may need her." He flashed a look at Tryggvi and gave his brother a satisfied smile.

That assurance had to do. Astrid was with her mother, and Bjorn knew the red-haired giant would remain in the village to look after her. With that he prepared to find Rikki Tryggvason.

Chapter Thirty-six

Astrid slipped out of the bed where her mother and Ragnhild slept on either side of her. She had not slept, as the events of the night raced in her head, like two dogs chasing each other around the table. Her arm throbbed, but it would heal. Not her heart. Quietly, so as not to wake the other women, Astrid got dressed in the dark, and slowly opened the door to the bride's house. A light drizzle fell, so she pulled her cloak and hood over her head. She paused and took in a breath of the clean, wet air, allowing it to fall on her upturned face.

She needed to find Rikki, and she knew where to go. Hearing men's hushed voices coming from close by, she crept closer.

"I want to hunt him now. He will get away if we delay." Bjorn's voice.

He meant to hunt her brother like an animal. The thought made her shiver, and she huddled inside her cloak, the drizzling rain dripping off the edge of her hood.

"We have to wait until Tryggvi's men make a move. They know we are watching them, and they hesitate," the one named Styrr said. "They don't want to lead us to him."

Bjorn muttered something under his breath she could not hear. He sounded angry and frustrated.

Good. Bjorn and his men did not even know where to start to look for her brother. Astrid smiled to herself. Rikki knew her father's land like he knew his own skin. She did too. And she knew Rikki.

Whatever the price to her own safety or to her marriage, she had to see Rikki again. Leaving Bjorn to stew in his waiting, Astrid slipped around the corner of the house and into the woods. Harald's men may have been watching her father's men to see where they went, but they would not think to keep watch over her. They would not suspect a woman to lead them to their prey. The thought, that their inability to see her as an asset, made her smile. Men often overlooked and underestimated women, to their own disadvantage.

Astrid's feet were silent on the mossy, grass-covered path that led to the hidden grove and waterfall. At one time they had marked it with notches in a few trees, and stones left in particular spots, but in the dark she could not see the tree marks, and undergrowth covered the stones. At one point Astrid tripped over some vines, falling to her knees, the wet earth soaking into her dress.

When she rose, she looked around, panic rising. She did not recognize where she was. It had been many seasons since she and Rikki met here. The trees were taller, their branches heavy with yellow and orange foliage, and the undergrowth was thick and wild and slick with water.

She tipped her head back in frustration when she saw the three enormous pine trees that marked their grove, their shadows black against the moon. When she stopped to listen, she could hear the soft gurgling of their little waterfall as it splashed into the pool.

Astrid came across the boulder she and Rikki used as the entry point to the grove. She rubbed her hand over it, wiping away some water that had accumulated, as she looked for the runes they had marked into it the spring after baby Olaf died. Rikki had always looked after Astrid, Olaf, and Gytha, protecting them from anyone who tried to hurt them. He was always more careful with their lives than he had ever been with his own.

She placed her hand on the carvings for baby Olaf. Searching to make sure no one had followed her, Astrid pursed her lips and whistled. It was their secret greeting. She waited, holding her breath. The drizzle let up, and Astrid wiped her face with the sleeve of her dress.

The answering whistle came back so quietly that Astrid would not have heard it if she had not been listening so closely.

She walked into the clearing and nearly ran into Rikki. He grabbed her arm, and she gasped.

Trying to regain her composure, she searched the grove. Besides Rikki and Galm, at least four of her father's men were there, and likely two or three more who were on guard or out scouting. Rikki and Galm must have been working since before the wedding to convince these men to take arms against Harald and Bjorn while they were guests in her father's house. Short Olaf was not among them. So Rikki and Galm had not trusted Short Olaf with their scheme. Astrid was both relieved and angry.

"What is this?" she asked.

Rikki raised his arms to encompass the men standing around. In the shadows, they looked menacing. "We decided to take action while we had the opportunity. They have killed people in our families. Our Brothers. We could not stand by and allow Father to make nice with Harald."

The men in the grove nodded their heads, some of them looking at Astrid as if she were the enemy. A ripple of fear ran down her spine. The men were treating Rikki like he was their leader. They had defied Tryggvi's orders to keep the peace, and they had violated their oaths to him. She did not want to talk in front of them, so she led Rikki away.

"You have broken your oath to our father. I understand your anger, I do. But to do this? To rouse Father's men against him? To ambush Harald and Bjorn during my wedding night?"

He shut his face down as easily as their father did. He was more like Tryggvi than he wanted to believe.

Unwilling to push, Astrid found a log that had fallen and sat down on it, suddenly too tired to remain on her feet. It was wet, but she did not care. "Why did you not do this before the marriage or before...?" She thought of Bjorn's lips on her body, the way she'd felt when he'd kissed and caressed her. It was all simple for a while.

Rikki turned his head away from her. "That was Galm's idea. He convinced me you would be better off as a widow."

It was true. She would have more rights and power as a widow, but the calculating way in which Galm planned it unnerved her.

She let out a bark of laughter. "Thank him for thinking of me. I saw them, Bjorn and some of Harald's personal guard. They are coming for you."

He nodded. "I knew they would. We wait for someone. He needs to hurry, or we will leave him behind."

Astrid jumped to her feet and grabbed hold of Rikki's arm. "Emund warned me that your anger was too reckless. He was right. You—"

"Red," Rikki spat. "He is as bad as Father. They are old men. Their time is past."

The stranger who had once been her brother rose again, and Astrid did not recognize him. Tears welled up in her eyes, and she blinked to get them to stop.

Rikki noticed and softened. She took the opportunity. "Come back with me. You can pay a compensation to Bjorn—"

"No." He jerked back from her, as if her touch burned him.

One of their father's men, one Astrid had not noticed before, hurried up to them, giving Astrid a look as if she might try to stab her brother. It shocked her. She had known this man a long time. They were no strangers.

"Rikki," the man said. "We need to leave. The sun will rise soon. It will not take them long to find us here."

"Get ready to move."

"We need to get to our horses. Now."

"Wait. You have horses waiting?" Astrid asked.

Rikki nodded. "We've been planning to go out on our own. Ever since father and Red arranged this marriage." His gaze went to the wedding ring on her hand. "I wish we could have killed Harald and Bjorn, but that does not change things. We are leaving."

Astrid's heart and mind raced. This could not be happening. "Where will you go?"

"Come with me." Rikki gripped her by the arms, and she winced in pain when he touched the wounded spot. A flicker of remorse flashed through his eyes, and he lightened his grip.

Gray clouds passed over the half moon, blocking most of the light, and the overhanging trees closed in on her.

"We have always stuck together. Protected each other. I will find you another husband, one who is not our enemy."

Astrid stared at her brother, the face and eyes so like her own, and her heart broke into pieces. She could not go with him. It would be madness. But neither could she let him go. She threw her arms around his neck and held him close. He was wet and cold, as she was herself. She did not care. He hugged her back. She clung to him, like a drowning person fighting to keep from going under.

"No," she whispered, barely able to get the word out.

Rikki stepped away from her. "You will go back to him."

"You have undone everything I sacrificed for this marriage."

"Then come with me."

Astrid shook her head. "I have to think about more people than you." She studied his face for any signs of him changing his mind. She saw none.

"What Harald and Bjorn have done to our families cannot be forgotten," Rikki said. "We cannot be friends with them. Or lovers."

"I could be with Bjorn's child."

Rikki recoiled.

She remembered the day on the ship when she'd thought she lost him. How terrified she'd been to face life without him. She could not turn her back on her brother now. How could she let him leave, not knowing if she'd ever see him again?

She took a breath and her words came out pained, like each one was a splinter being stuck into her. "I am a weaver, brother, and it is my duty as a woman to weave these families together. You are a thread that is out of place."

"So you will cut *me* out."

Looking away so she could not see her pain reflected in his face, she answered in a quiet voice. "You made the choice for me when you betrayed our family's hospitality and tried to kill my husband in front of me."

"Rikki," Galm said, throwing a nasty look at Astrid. "Time to go."

Another man threw Rikki his pack. Rikki caught it and swung it over his shoulder.

He turned to go, but Astrid grabbed him by the sleeve of his tunic. "I love you, brother. More than anyone. Take that with you."

"But you choose Bjorn Alfarsson."

The air between them was charged, like a storm was on its way.

"Yes. I...have to."

He did not have time to answer her, if he even wanted to. The men were hurrying him away, but the look on his face told her everything. Her brother took her answer as a betrayal of their bond as brother and sister. Rikki joined the men as they made their way out of the clearing, leaving Astrid alone and shaken to the core.

The world lightened, the black sky turning gray with tinges of pink. How could the world be coming to life when the life she knew had ended?

Rain spattered on her head, and she pulled her hood back up. It would be a gray, wet, cold, miserable day. She started to leave the clearing, wanting to never see it again, when a rustling in the bushes alerted her.

Rikki hurried to her, and her heart flipped. He had changed his mind!

Without a word he hugged her again, holding her so tight her back cracked. "I love you more than anyone too, *systir*." He pulled back, and she saw in his eyes he had not come to stay. Her heart sank.

"Trust Shortie," Rikki told her, his voice earnest. "He will look after you."

With that, he kissed her cheek and ran off again. The waterfall sounded loud in her ears, like it was mocking her and all the times they'd spent there. Her beloved brother was gone, not much better than an outlaw, and she had to return and face her angry husband. She had to go live with him, their new life beginning with treachery and anger. She blinked back tears, not wanting to let them start, lest they never stop. Her heart was torn into shreds.

With a meow, Kis-Kis crept out of the bushes and stalked over to her, butting her head against Astrid's leg. Astrid sat back down on the wet log and pulled Kis-Kis into her lap, burying her face in the cat's thick fur. She smelled of pine and earth. The cat put her paw on Astrid's chest, and the silver of the Freya pendant grew warm to the touch, a reminder that the goddess was present, still with her. Overhead, birds began their welcome of the day with their song. The new day was breaking, and the trees emerged as shadowy outlines, the slightest hint of the sun making the dew on the leaves sparkle.

She sat there for too long, petting her cat and watching the sunrise. With every passing moment, Rikki got farther away, and she risked being found by either her father's men or Bjorn's, and she didn't know which was worse. Astrid rose to her feet and walked back toward the village, back to Bjorn Alfarsson, her feet so heavy, it felt like she was walking through mud. She thought of the good things about Bjorn, the way he looked when he laughed, young and without worry, the way his hands felt on her when they'd danced. Thoughts of their night in bed were too intense, too confusing, and she had to push them aside.

So deep in her thoughts, she had forgotten to pay attention to her surroundings. Leaving the woods near the great hall, she did not see them until she heard her name.

"Astrid?" Bjorn said. Four men filled in around him.

"Bjorn!" Her heart raced so fast and loud, she was sure he could hear it. He was dressed to trek through the woods, brown tight trousers, soft leather shoes up nearly to his knees, and a short green tunic without adornment fitted for quick movement. He wore his sword at his belt and held a spear ready in his hand, a reminder that he hunted her brother.

Kis-Kis hissed at them, her back arched, fur standing up. One man looked down at the cat with disgust.

Bjorn's eyes roved over her, lingering on her sodden cloak, the wet knees of her dress, her tear-stained face. "Where have you been?"

"I..." She hesitated. It was obvious where she'd been, and Bjorn knew it. Her mind raced for something to say. "I couldn't sleep, and I needed some air. Kis-Kis ran off into the forest, and I went to get her. I tripped." Here she lifted her dress to show the wet mud stains on her knees.

He arched his brow. "You went into the forest alone, before dawn, to get your cat?"

Now that he said it, it sounded ridiculous. "I needed air."

Bjorn stepped closer to her. "Where is Rikki?"

"I don't know." She straightened up, glad that she didn't know where her brother had gone, so it wouldn't show in her eyes.

"But you went to meet him, didn't you?"

Should she continue to lie to him? She studied his face, the way he looked at her, as if he could sense what she knew. Her hesitation gave her away, and she told him. "*Ja.*"

One of Bjorn's men shifted toward her, his face menacing, and a shiver of fear raced down Astrid's spine. Kis-Kis hissed at him again. Bjorn stopped the man with an arm across his chest. "No closer."

"Bjorn. This is a waste of time," Styrr said. He pointed his spear into the woods. "That's where she came from. We start there."

Bjorn nodded. "Go. I will catch up."

The men left, following the disturbed path from where Astrid had come. She cursed herself for her inattention, for leading them toward Rikki. She wished she had a pair of ravens, like the Allfather, who she could send to her brother to warn him to be quick and careful.

Bjorn turned to Astrid. "What did you and your brother discuss? How you are disappointed that I'm not dead?"

"What? No. I had no part in what happened last night. I have no more control over Rikki than I do the moon."

He stared at her for a long time. His body softened toward her, and she hoped that meant he believed her. He turned to follow Styrr and the others.

"Bjorn."

He stopped and faced her, his hand tightening on his spear. His face showed her nothing, not even anger.

"What did my Father and Harald..." she swallowed hard. "Decide about Rikki?"

If her father or Harald declared Rikki a *niding*, an outlaw, he'd be on the run and anyone could kill him with no punishment. Men could hunt him like an animal. A thought of the outlaw who had tried to kidnap her when she was a child came to her mind, how horrible he was, how desperate to sell her for as much silver as he could get. The thought of her brother being brought that low made her feel sick. She wrapped her arms around herself.

In a voice that may as well have been reading the rules of law at a council meeting, he said, "Your father is paying a *wergild* for the injuries Atli sustained in the attack. He is also paying me more for your bride-price."

To know that all she was to these men was pieces of silver to exchange should not have come as a shock, but it made her stomach turn over. She thought Bjorn was different, that he cared for her more than for her bride-price. He had loved her so gently last night. But that was probably how he was with all women. She did not matter to him. Hardening her heart, she asked. "But what about Rikki? What will happen to him?"

"Do you mean have we declared him *niding*?" Even hearing the word made Astrid wince.

"No, we have not."

She closed her eyes and let out a long breath. She wanted to sink to the ground with gratitude.

"I demanded he be declared *niding*," Bjorn said, barely containing his anger.

Astrid felt as if he'd hit her in the stomach. "But he is my brother!"

"Who has tried to kill me twice. I will not let that go."

"You killed our brother," Astrid shouted, and took a step back from him, nearly tripping over her cat, who had laid down by Astrid's feet.

Bjorn did not raise his voice. "I paid the *wergild* for Jori."

She wanted to hit the calm right out of him.

"Jori's life was not an exchange of silver. Not to me." She choked out the last words.

His face softened, and he took a step toward her. As if some unseen hand pulled him back, he stopped. Looking over his shoulder to where the others had gone, he said, "If I find Rikki, I will kill him for what he has done."

"Or he will kill you."

"Is that what you want?"

"No. Either way, I lose."

His blue eyes were dark with anger as he tried to understand her part in all of this.

"Asta," Ragnhild's voice called from the house. She and her mother must be worried at her disappearance, especially with armed and angry men stalking around.

"Go back to your mother. Stay close to your father too," Bjorn told her.

Was there concern in his voice? Was he afraid Harald would do something to her? Would she never have peace?

All that raced through her mind as he swept his cloak around him and hurried after the others. She watched him disappear before going to find her mother and Ragnhild, dread seeping into her at the thought of what would happen between Rikki and Bjorn.

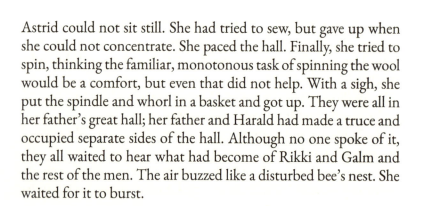

Astrid could not sit still. She had tried to sew, but gave up when she could not concentrate. She paced the hall. Finally, she tried to spin, thinking the familiar, monotonous task of spinning the wool would be a comfort, but even that did not help. With a sigh, she put the spindle and whorl in a basket and got up. They were all in her father's great hall; her father and Harald had made a truce and occupied separate sides of the hall. Although no one spoke of it, they all waited to hear what had become of Rikki and Galm and the rest of the men. The air buzzed like a disturbed bee's nest. She waited for it to burst.

Thralls had cleaned up the hall, so that the remains of the food and drink from the wedding feast the night before were gone. Like it had never happened. As Astrid rose to her feet to walk again, the soreness between her legs reminded her that the wedding had happened. She knew women sometimes got with child on the wedding night. Resting a hand on her belly, she considered what would happen if she was with child.

Short Olaf sat off by himself in one corner of the hall, nursing a cup of ale. Astrid joined him.

"They told you nothing?" she asked.

"No." He took a drink and turned to look at her, his dark brown eyes hurt. "I should have known. They had been acting strange since the Thing. They kept to themselves and always got quiet when I approached them."

She laid her hand on his arm, feeling the muscles twitch at her touch. Leaning in close, she asked, "What would you have done?"

"I would have stopped them. They could have hurt you."

The door to the hall banged open, revealing Bjorn and Styrr and the other men. The frown on Bjorn's face and the disappointed look on Styrr's, told Astrid everything she needed to know.

She let out a sigh and closed her eyes.

When she opened them again, Bjorn was staring at her and taking in her closeness to Short Olaf, her hand on his arm. His already dark face grew darker. She removed her hand from Short Olaf's arm and put it in her lap.

Bjorn took the few steps to Astrid, his eyes flicking between her and Short Olaf. "We did not find your brother."

She rose to face him, her hands balled into fists. "Good."

Despite their anger with each other, Astrid could feel it, the way she was drawn to him and him to her. In a flash, she remembered him on the dock the day they'd met, how, despite all the people crowding around, he had walked straight to her as if he were an arrow finding its target.

Bjorn lingered, as if he sensed her thoughts, his dark blue eyes boring into her.

Harald approached and laid a hand on Bjorn's shoulder. "What do you want to do now, son?"

"Leave."

"What? No," Astrid cried.

"Prepare your things."

He left her open-mouthed, staring at him as he stalked off. She watched as he spoke to Harald, his blond head shaking in answer to Harald's questions. When Harald eyed her, she turned away, not wanting to meet his cold blue eyes.

Ragnhild and Ingiborg approached, Ragnhild giving Bjorn a look full of menace.

"He blames me for Rikki," Astrid told them.

Ragnhild leaned in close, her eyes wide in question. "Should he?"

"No." She lowered her voice when others looked over at her. "I knew nothing about it."

"Of course you didn't," Ingiborg said, her voice sad and tired.

"I believe you," Ragnhild said. "Now you'll have to figure out how to get *Bjorn* to believe you. That won't be so easy."

Astrid sighed. "I'm glad you'll be with me. I don't know if I could face leaving with him alone."

"Some men are quick to anger," Ingiborg said. "And are equally quick to forgive."

"Like Rikki," Astrid said.

"And your father. Well, except with his brother. Bjorn may be the same." Ingiborg pulled her aside so no one could hear. "Give him time, Asta. He is angry and has a right to be."

Astrid wanted to argue, but her mother shook her head.

"He does. Once his anger subsides, he will know you are not to blame."

"I hope so. What am I going to do? How can I be his wife when he looks at me like I'm going to stab him in his sleep?"

"You could stab him in his sleep. Get it over with," Ragnhild joked.

"Ragna," Ingiborg chided.

"I thought about it," Astrid whispered, her gaze sweeping the hall to ensure no one could overhear.

"What?"

Astrid nodded. "When father showed me the ceremonial sword. I had a brief thought of stabbing Bjorn in the heart with it, like he did to Jori."

Ragnhild sucked in a breath.

"Oh, Asta," Ingiborg said.

"He killed my brother. How can I ignore that? Maybe he is right to mistrust me."

Ingiborg took hold of one of Astrid's golden braids. "Last night...did he...?" For once, she struggled for words.

Knowing what her mother meant, Astrid shook her head. "He was gentle."

"I thought so." Ingiborg looked over at Bjorn. "I've seen the way he looks at you, and you him. If you can get past what happened with Rikki and Jori—"

Ragnhild scoffed. "That isn't a small matter."

"I didn't say it was."

"You will know what to do," Ingiborg said, touching the Freya pendant that rested on Astrid's chest.

"I'll have to."

Ingiborg swept her gaze around the room. "Let us go pack your traveling chest. You need to be ready."

Ready. Her mother's words banged in her head. Ready to leave her home. Ready to live with Bjorn, the man who had killed one of her brothers, and who wanted to kill the other. Ready to be with a man who mistrusted her. How could she be ready for that? She watched her father and Harald and knew she had to do this, for if she didn't, they would fight again and more people would die. She was the weaver who had to hold it all together. Straightening her dress, and with a touch to her Freya pendant for strength, Astrid went to pack her chest for the journey to her new life.

"Did you enjoy Warrior and Weaver? Continue Astrid and Bjorn's exciting story in Sword and Story, the second book in the Norse Family Saga

You can get a free copy of *By Their Wits*, a Warrior and Weaver prequel story, when you sign up for my newsletter."

Go to www.ksbarton.com sign up for my newsletter and receive your free book. You can also find information about the other books in this series.

Please consider leaving a review on Amazon or wherever you purchased this book. Reviews from readers help support indie authors. Thank you!

www.ksbarton.com

www.facebook.com/ksbartonauthor

www.instagram.com/ksbartonauthor/

www.twitter.com/ks_barton

Also By

Other Books in the Norse Family Saga Series
Sword and Story – Book Two
Hero and Healer – Book Three

Books Related to the Norse Family Saga Series
Raven Marked – Book 1 of the Helgi the Marked Duology
Raven Tempted – Book 2 of the Helgi the Marked Duology

Historical Viking Fantasy
A Deal with Odin

Author's Note

My fascination with Vikings came to me in about 2009 when I did research for a non-fiction book I wrote for kids that included information about mythology. I already knew a lot about the Greek and Roman mythology I put in the book, but not so much about Norse mythology. This was before the Marvel Universe started pumping out movies every year with their fictionalized Norse gods and stories. When I dug into the stories of the Norse, I felt a strong tug towards these gods and their worlds and the stories that went along with them. It was like a homecoming of sorts. Getting into the mythology of the Norse led me to the sagas and my interest grew from there.

When I started reading fiction about Vikings, I found a lack of stories about ordinary women, the women who were not shield-maidens or women who dressed like men so they could fight. If these stay-at-home women were in stories, they were bit characters and not the protagonists. Most Viking fiction at that time was written by, about, and for men. That's to be expected, since the Viking culture was highly masculine. Of course, actual "Vikings" were the people who went raiding and fighting and colonizing other lands. To go "viking" meant you actually left home. Most women did not. I wanted to tell a story of a woman who stayed home while her menfolk sailed off time and time again, never to know if they would come home or not.

Since the Nordic people of the Viking Age did not have a written language, other than runes, it is hard to know how women felt. The written information we have about the Viking Age comes either from the sagas that were written hundreds of years later, or from the Eddas that are incomplete. They still give us a good vision of how strong the women were, and not necessarily in a physical sense. These women, like Unn the Deep-Minded, were intelligent, resourceful, independent, and strong-willed. Her story is more extraordinary than most, but her inner strength was what I latched onto. When we think of the Viking Age, we tend to think of burly men jumping off ships and wielding battle axes, but I wanted to show the strength of women.

Another place I wanted to focus on was relationships and not just romantic relationships between a woman and a man. I wanted to dive into the relationships between parents and children, brothers and sisters, and friendships not only between men but between women as well.

I tried to remain as true as I could to the research that's been done about the Viking Age. Of course, this is a work of fiction, so I did what I felt was appropriate for the story. All of my characters and most of the places are fictionalized, except for Birka Island, Hovgarden, and the Oresund. Even so, the events of this story took place over a 1000 years ago, and things have changed since then.

One thing I learned after I'd already started writing was that Viking age people may have slept sitting up, their backs propped against the wall. How strange! Research shows that their beds were made too short for a grown person to lie down on. Or they slept on a platform or bench while propped up against the wall. I found that too different and decided to take artistic license and have everyone sleep lying down.

Many of the men in Warrior and Weaver own swords. Men like Tryggvi, who was a jarl and wealthy, most likely would have owned a sword. But swords were extremely expensive and not many men would actually own one, unless they defeated someone in battle and took the sword as booty. More men fought with spears and axes than they did with swords.

Bjorn Alfarsson has a tattoo on his arm and back and all of Harald's men have wolf tattoos on their backs. There is not a lot of information about whether Vikings had tattoos or not. Since skin deteriorates, we have no archaeological record of tattoos. We do have the account of the Arab chronicler Ibn Fadlan. When he described the Rus (the Vikings who settled in what is now Russia and the Ukraine) he said, "Every man is tattooed from finger nails to neck..." He thought the designs were "trees" but they were probably the knotwork pattern favored by Vikings in their art. Fadlan also described the markings as dark green or black, but they were most likely dark blue. Other than his description, there is not much to go on. However, other cultures tattooed their skin, and the Vikings came into contact with so many cultures that they would have seen tattoos on others. So I figured, why wouldn't some of them do it themselves?

In Warrior and Weaver I've included a wedding, something I've not ever seen in a fictional book about Vikings (if you know of one, please let me know!). From the research I've read, we don't know that much about weddings during Viking times. It could be because weddings were a commonplace event that people of the time did not think to mention in detail. Or perhaps, a wedding is a ritual more associated with women and not mentioned in the sources. One source we have for a wedding and wedding feast is the Thrymskvitha, a story in the Poetic Edda. In it the god Thor has lost Mjolnir, his mighty hammer to the giant Thrym and when Thor asks for it back, Thrym demands payment in the form of marriage to the goddess Freya. What results is a funny story in which Thor and Loki dress up as women--Thor as Freya and Loki as her handmaiden. In the Warrior and Weaver wedding feast scene, Bjorn places a Thor hammer on Astrid's lap as a symbol of fertility. I took that from the Thrymskvitha story. In that story, when Thrym places Mjolnir on Thor's lap (he's still dressed up pretending to be Freya), Thor takes the hammer and kills Thrym and all the other giants attending the wedding feast. For the other aspects of the wedding ritual, I used the website The Viking Answer Lady for guidance. She has gone through the sources and compiled them to determine what might have happened during an actual Viking Age wedding. Anything else, I made up.

One unpleasant fact about the time period is that the Norse people, at least the ones who had enough wealth, owned slaves. Viking warriors who went raiding captured slaves and either took them for themselves or sold them in slave markets. It was a very profitable endeavor for them, although it is distasteful to modern sensibilities. In the Rigsmal, an Eddic Poem, a god named Rig names the different classes of men. The three classes are thralls, a class of freemen (mostly farmers), and then the class of jarls. My belief is that this story came after the Vikings started taking slaves in their raids as a way to justify the behavior, by saying one of the gods had deemed it this way.

Astrid, as a daughter of a jarl, would probably have had a slave girl who attended her, someone who saw more specifically to her needs. I wanted Astrid to have a female companion, someone with whom she could confide and who would go with her when she married Bjorn. It might have been her thrall who went with her. But, even though it would have been very probable, I didn't like the power dynamic of her best friend also being her slave. That's why I created Ragnhild.

One thing I feel strongly about is that, even though we have the sagas, stories, myths, and archaeological finds, we don't know everything about everyone during the Viking Age. It was, after all, 1000 years ago. We can't know how every group of people in every district spoke or believed or dressed or ate. And that's where artistic license comes in as well. In my story, I have Ingiborg tell

Tryggvi that in their household they do not abuse their slaves. Even if there is no story about a woman who is like that in the sagas, that doesn't mean one didn't exist. Just because we don't have evidence that a warband would be tattooed with the same image (like Harald's wolf-head) doesn't mean it couldn't have happened somewhere.

The wergild was a real Viking Age transaction. Men did meet before a jarl or godi or at a council meeting like the Thing to air grievances against each other. Disputes about the killings of men, women, thralls, or animals were often settled through paying a fine. Of course, the fine for killing a jarl's son would be much more than killing a man's wife, slave, or cow. Even though it was commonplace, I still imagined that a young woman might react in the way Astrid did, angry that her brother's life was reduced to an amount of silver.

When Bjorn spoke to Astrid on their wedding night about how she could easily divorce him, that was true. Since marriage was a business transaction between families, it was not that difficult to dissolve the arrangement. The party who wanted the divorce would need to gather witnesses and give his or her cause. If there was property involved, it would be more complicated, but it could still be done.

The Viking Age took place over about two hundred years. It is a small amount of time in world history, but in that time the Vikings made a huge impact on Europe, especially England, Ireland, Scotland, France (Normandy was named from the Norsemen who settled there), Russia, Ukraine, and even down into Turkey and Constantinople where they became the infamous Varangian Guard.

If you are interested in learning about the Viking Age and its people, here are a few sugggestions:

The Age of the Vikings by Anders Winroth.

Viking Age: Everyday Life During the Extraordinary Era of the Norsemen by Kirsten Wolf

The Sagas of Icelanders
Norse Mythology by Neil Gaiman
The Prose Edda by Snorri Sturluson
The Poetic Edda by Snorri Sturluson
Dr. Jackson Crawford's YouTube channel

Acknowledgements

Thank you for reading Warrior and Weaver! It has been a long road writing it. The book started years ago when I had an inkling of an idea that I wanted to write about Viking women who were not shield-maidens. What would it be like to have to stay at home and care for the house and children all while your husband, brother, or son, was out fighting? The book has changed dramatically from what I started with, and I have a lot of people to thank for helping me along the way.

First, I want to thank Mom and Dad for providing me a home in which books and paper to write and draw on were always available. My storytelling began in my room when I wrote and illustrated little one paragraph stories about dogs and cats and friends. You were always supportive of me wanting to write a novel. I know Dad would be proud that I finally did it. I wish he were here to see my novel in print.

My sister Jill: thank you for beta reading and for being such a great sounding board. Your feedback and presence has been wonderful and so helpful. For Steve: thank you for beta reading and proofreading. I appreciate your feedback, and it was great to have a male perspective. The rest of my family: thank you for asking how the book was going. Just knowing that you were rooting for me helped.

Alica McKenna-Johnson, Kilian Metcalf, and Mary Ball: without our group, and the accountability you provided, I'm not sure I ever would have written a novel. I'm sorry you had to put up with all my awful drafts, but if you hadn't done that, I would never have been able to find the story in the mess. Being in our writing group made me a better writer... and I'm still learning.

Alica McKenna-Johnson: thank you for always being there for me, for talking me down when I wanted to quit or when I didn't know what to do. Not only have you helped me as a writer, your advice on how to be an indie author has been invaluable. You were always willing to help me in whatever way I needed. I could not have done this without you.

Stephanie Churchill: thank you for beta reading and being there for me on many fronts. I cherish our morning chats. You are definitely a part of my writer 'tribe!' Thank you for sharing your experiences as an indie author. It's from authors like you, who have forged ahead, that I learn from.

Ellen Fisher and Barry Webb: thank you for inviting me into your critique group when my novel was nothing more than a few notes on a single piece of paper. Your feedback was a big help.

Claire Conway: thank you for talking to me and listening to me 'complain' about how the men in my book were always wanting to take over. Thank you for always checking in on me. It helps more than you can know.

Thank you to all my friends, who are too many to name, and I don't want to forget anyone, who made a point to check in with me and ask the question I needed to hear, 'how is the book coming?' You kept me on track, and on some days it was knowing I would be accountable to you that kept me going!

My biggest thanks have to go to my husband Blake and my son Hunter. You've been my strongest supporters. You've been there every step of the way, witnessed my triumphs and failures, and have stood by me. I love you both very much.

About the Author

K.S. Barton writes historical fiction and fantasy stories of love and adventure set in the Viking age. The author of several novels, she explores themes of family, honor, and strength all within the backdrop of Norse society. When doing research on Norse mythology for a teaching project, she discovered the Norse sagas and immediately knew that she wanted to write fiction about Vikings. She believes there is magic in storytelling. She has an M.A. in Humanities with a focus on literature and history and has always loved to learn about history through stories. She resides in sunny Southern Arizona.

Visit www.ksbartonauthor.com for more details and where you can claim a free prequel of the Norse Family Saga series.

Visit her on social media:
www.facebook.com/ksbartonauthor
www.instagram.com/ksbartonauthor
www.twitter.com/ks_barton

Made in United States
Troutdale, OR
01/11/2024